UMANU

UMANU

ARTHUR DUNOON

REDEMPTION
PRESS

1

Joshua sat by the monitor, watching the universe weave around the ship and wondering how he had gotten here. The relative distance of stars made the ones farthest away stand still as the ship flew past while those closer dashed across the video screen. He had spent much of his time on this journey looking into the vast wonder of the universe and trying to sort out his very consciousness, wondering what change, if any, he had endured.

The change was not so much in his basic personality but in the experiences and knowledge he had endured that tempered his personality, he decided. *Who we are when we know everything is who we were when we didn't. Our identity is less about what we know than it is about the shape of the filter through which information flows.* Even with perfect information and equal information, the individual's perception of what that information means changes how it is used. Biases based on personal proclivities stretch and inflate innocuous facts until they become the fulcrum on which natural laws pivot and decisions are made.

He wanted to believe he was someone else after the Machine. His experience of transforming his conscious and unconscious mind to change the way he thought was an illusion. He had lived billions of years—trillions technically, considering how many times he had witnessed the universe collapse on itself—yet in the linear progression of time, he was a mere sixteen standard years old. All that time only taught him the process of how life came to be and how that life forms the basis of the interaction between a god and its people. To his humans he was a deity, and to him they were the neurons that made up his identity. How that identity was sculpted was merely built upon the raw material already there, not the radical change he imagined.

He hadn't changed, but experience had tempered his pride and showed him the long-term consequences of action or inaction. He was still himself but wiser. He still had that deep longing for adventure. He ached to see what was on the other side of the mountains—even as he knew implicitly how the mountains were shaped and changed. It was the same, but everything was predictable now.

He replayed those first few weeks after emerging from the Machine, trying to discern any difference in himself and to reflect on how he had gotten to this point. How he had ended up on this ship, how he had chosen this path for himself. To leave everything behind and head to the farthest reaches of the empire in search of . . . something. Adventure? Identity? Destiny? These words felt meaningful, but not enough to fill the questioning void inside himself. It all felt like a dreamscape up until now. A hazy memory and a metallic muffled dialogue that he drifted through.

Of the many choices available to him, only one called out and resonated in the void of purpose in his soul.

> Frontier Corporation, a resource extraction company, is looking for an entry-level production manager to serve on the front lines of resource acquisition and development. The successful candidate will be placed in a community of like-minded and adventurous individuals seeking to leverage their knowledge from the Machine to help develop frontier settlements utilizing primitive technology, interacting with indigenous cultures, and aiding in development of those cultures into civilizations with the aim of autonomous production.

It felt as if the description had been written for him. Adventure, wilderness, interaction with foreign and unique species—it was the life on the edge of chaos his heart had been yearning for all this time. So he applied. He was so certain that he was going to get the job that he didn't even have a backup plan when he applied.

He waited for a reply for weeks. Beaten down by the delay, he second-guessed himself, realizing that while the position seemed right for him, maybe he was not quite right for it. The longer it dragged on, the more doubt crept into his mind and the more inadequate he felt. He knew he could thrive in anything, but this was one he *wanted*, and he rarely found himself wanting anything. Then it finally came.

The company had arranged everything and sent him a collection of reading materials to familiarize him with the planet, his role on it, the history, the mission objective. It was all very comprehensive. Though all the data about the planet showed that it was very hospitable and very fertile, he still wondered what it would be like to experience something like this in the flesh rather than just through the mind the way he had in the Machine. *Will it be any different? Is the body merely a collection of biological sensors that supply the mind with experience, or is the flesh a vital part of experience?*

Again his mind drifted.

Joshua continued to watch the vast expanse of dancing colors, each a different star with a different temperature. A magical tapestry of gemstones in the abyss. The universe sprawling before him, unpolluted by the lights of a nearby star or his hometown. With each nebula his thoughts couldn't help but drift back to the formation of the universe he had witnessed over and over again. The slow churning he saw before him here only represented the star systems those nebulae would turn into as the universe aged and the last enclaves of chaos turned to order, and the whole universe began its slow progression back to singularity and death before it's explosive rebirth.

Much like societies tend to do. The thought stirred nothing in him. He had seen it. Thousands of times he had witnessed it. And though he had never seen one in his own universe, it was as common to him as the flickering lights of stars that surrounded him.

He tried to see the face in the heavens as he once saw it in the Machine. He knew it was a futile effort, but the curiosity stirred in him, and he studied the formations of stars and galaxies and tried to imagine the face they would reveal if he could only find the right perspective. If he saw the face of his god in the stars in the Machine, the stars before him now would shape the face of the god of *his* god.

After spending billions of years in the Machine, he was indifferent to the passage of time. Everything moved so much slower out here, yet each imperial standard day passed by without regard for the subjective momentum of the individual. He had lived a trillion days, and one more was as inconsequential in comparison as a grain of sand washed on a beach. He knew he was still sixteen standard years old in body. But his spirit and his mind had lived much longer.

His reverie was broken by the graceful gait of the first officer of the ship. Though it wasn't a glamorous vessel and the crew was small, she carried herself with pride, and the fit and trim of her uniform betrayed her detail-oriented temperament. She had stunning proportions. Her teardrop-shaped head was just slightly narrower than the average woman he had seen. This gave her large feminine black eyes a much larger portion of her face. Those eyes made Joshua nervous with a sensation he didn't remember having before. Her mouth moved as she spoke in that loose and nonemphatic way that made him lose focus and imagine her lips pressed against his. Her gray skin was light and fair compared to his darker, daylight-kissed gray complexion. Her name was Marcella, and her long slender arms and sensual fingers danced hypnotically as she spoke.

"The Captain thought you might like to know where you are relative to your home planet and where we are going," she said in a silky, sober tone.

"I would appreciate that very much." As he spoke these words, he imagined the early civilizations' courtship rituals, and his words felt like a club made of waterlogged driftwood. He hadn't taken the chance to actually talk to her. Intimidated by her femininity, he stole glances from afar and stumbled over his words and thoughts when she engaged him. He was stupefied by her presence and used overly formal language when speaking to her, he supposed to affect the intelligence he felt flee him whenever she was around.

He shook himself from the thought as she turned and called over her shoulder, "Please follow me," her eyebrow raised and a half smile gracing her cheeks.

He obeyed mindlessly as he clambered out of his seat to follow.

As they approached the bridge, Marcella knocked on the bulkhead to announce her entrance. The Captain, Justine, stood looking down at the star chart, then looked up, an expression of concentration slowly leaving her face as her eyes adjusted from the lights of the screen to the dim ambiance of the bridge. She squinted slightly to see the visitor and her first officer.

"Ah, our treasured guest," she said with just a hint of sarcasm. "Please come. Let me show you the landmarks of our journey." Marcella stepped away, and Joshua could feel his senses and sensibilities returning. His thoughts cleared up. Justine did not have the same effect on him.

She no longer had the vigor of youth in her eyes. Too many years of looking at charts and staring into the shimmering abyss, backlit by a dim wash of lights. She was paunchy but not obese, as he had seen others on the space stations. Her forearms rippled with the muscles she used for minor maintenance and equipment calibration. Not the hand-crushing muscles the ship mechanic wielded, but precision tuned to small corrections and adjustments. He imagined the beauty who had brought him there would look this way, too, in a century or two. Life is hard on freighters. But the Captain had a warmth still that belied the social isolation this job demanded.

He approached the charts and could see the red line of their course traced in an arc from his home planet to their destination. "Why is it arced? Why don't we fly straight to it?" he asked, suddenly feeling like the naïve child sitting in the Technician's oversized chair asking dumb questions with obvious answers.

The Captain humored him. Her voice was not nearly as weathered as her body seemed, but it still carried the stern authority her position instilled in people. "We aren't flying to the planet. We are intercepting it. The galaxy is rotating around its central axis at seven-point-five giga-meters per standard hour. If we pointed straight at it, it would fly right past us. So we intercept it by aiming ahead of it and letting it come to us, using known planets and stars around it to do that."

Joshua could see she was excited to talk about this to someone. He imagined her crew had already heard it or didn't care as they made themselves busy with other things, and he could see he was playing a part in the ritual of every ship's captain, allowing them to be the emperor of their tiny domain.

"How then do you set a destination if the galaxy is moving and the star system is moving and the planet is moving—you can't just set a coordinate and go there, right?"

"That's correct," the Captain said with a lilt of anticipation in her voice as she moved to a different console and tapped it to make the display light up. "This"—she gestured—"is our flux gate compass." The image displayed a tetrahedron. "Each planet has a unique signature. The lines of flux in their magnetic field create a planetary Gaussian field in their sector of the galaxy. If we know that signature, which is represented as a binary sequence between positive and negative mag-netic waves resonating at a unique frequency, then we can put that binary sequence into the navigation computer, and it will align the flux gate compass to the celestial object we want to travel to. It's essentially the fingerprint of a planet, unique and mostly unchanging for long periods of time."

She paused and looked up thoughtfully before continuing. "Though the planet moves around the star, the star around the galaxy, and the galaxy through the universe, the flux gate compass measures the rela-tive distance to known points within the galactic body to measure our location in relation to those points. If we want to go near a known star, we can use that star's signature to get us close. Then the orientation of the ship relative to that star tells us if we are headed in the right direc-tion. Though spatially we have no idea where we sit in relation to the rest of the universe, we can approximate that by measuring the number of photons a universal body projects. Since all stars emit photons in all directions simultaneously, the closer you are, the more photons you can observe in a finite window and the more concentrated they are. So if we're here"—she pointed to the display—"we only observe three photons, but here we see six, then the distance between represents the half-distance of an object way over here. And that allows you to calculate the distance to the star. The fewer photons we see, the farther away the object is, and the computer calculates the distance. Wherever the geometric center of gravity of all the visible universal bodies is, that is our reference point, and we know where we are relative to that."

She waved her hand at the screen, and it went to a view of the known universe with the geometric center in the middle of the screen. "Just like planets and stars, galaxies orbit the universal center. And like an irrotational vortex, the older a universe is, the more spherical it is— the younger, the more disk-like, so we know our relative galactic and universal age because of how spread out the universe is. So knowing the relative age, and thus the rate at which it accelerates into singularity, the speed of its revolution, and the relative distance to other celestial bodies or references, we know where the planet is going to be when we expect to get there. We sort of aim ahead of the target to intercept it." She nodded, seemingly approving of her explanation thus far.

Joshua was trying to take in everything to ask meaningful questions, but to his chagrin, he could only grasp the minutiae at the moment. He refocused on that. "If we are traveling ahead of it, though, how do we use the compass to get there?"

The Captain cocked her eyebrow at that and gestured to the rest of the blinking lights around the bridge. "With these," she said matter-of-factly. "Find where it is first, adjust for the galactic rotation speed, adjust for the solar rotation and the planetary distance from the star, and you will land where it's going to be when you are."

Joshua was only slightly embarrassed by the phrasing of the question, as it served the purpose for the role he played in this dynamic. "So how does the flux gate thing—"

"Flux gate compass," Marcella corrected.

"Flux gate compass work though? There are four points of the tetrahedron. Why do you need four?"

"Marcella," the Captain called, raising her voice slightly, "could you explain it to him, please?" She glanced at Joshua. "Marcella received honors in telemetry."

"Certainly, Justine." She walked over to the screen, and Joshua immediately felt his mind get dim.

Marcella's words mesmerized Joshua as the words danced through his mind to the music of her silky voice. "The magnetic field of a planet is in constant flux, but it gives off the same consistent signature unless that magnetic field is disrupted. In order to record that signature, we need to record the signature of the whole planet, mostly from high orbit, but partly on the ground as well. The varying elements have different resistances to magnetism and electron flow, so we can identify the composition of the planet by the magnetic signature it radiates into space. What you may know as static, we recognize as a field of billions of interwoven magnetic signatures, and once one is known, we can decipher its signal from the background noise, and then we can navigate by it. Our galacto-spatial position is based on the distances from these known signatures."

"So couldn't one sensor do all that?" Joshua asked, hoping to goad Marcella into a longer conversation so he could hear her voice and watch her lips move.

"Yes, it could but . . ." She hesitated as she collected her thoughts. "The flux gate compass is a device that tells us where *we* are in relation to the planet . . . essentially." She paused for a moment and then spoke again. "In a two-dimensional plane, you use three reference points to triangulate your position." She flipped to a drawing program and sketched a crude tetrahedron, "All four points are equidistant from each other." She then drew three reference points on the sketch, "Each of these points is a star or planet or whatever we're using to calculate our relative position. In a three-dimensional mesh, you need a fourth reference point to determine that third dimensional position. Each sensor is a known distance from each other, and the distance from each is measured against a known signature to determine our galactic position by using the differences of those distances on the flux gate compass."

Joshua tried to understand, though limited by his attraction and its effect on his cognition. After a few more clumsy questions about how the ship operated and where they were and where they were going, Joshua made his excuses and begged their forgiveness.

Captain Justine smiled at him as her eyes flicked knowingly at Marcella. She mentioned a few preventive maintenance tasks she had to do and graciously accepted Joshua's departure, making him feel like he was doing her a favor.

Marcella followed Joshua out into the corridor and spoke as they walked. "I don't know a whole lot about the mechanics of it, unfortunately. I only know how to gather the telemetry data and how to use it."

Joshua's intrigue suddenly overcame the fog of his seduction, and he was able to stammer out a question. "So how do you find the initial telemetry data? I mean, for a planet we've never been to."

She smiled warmly as she caught his eyes. "The old-fashioned way. You set out for the horizon, and you hope you find somewhere to land."

Joshua paused briefly midstride. "So someone didn't know what they would find when they went to that planet?"

"Well, they had a vague idea. They knew something was there at least. The more of the static you can identify, the less there is left to decipher, and you can start to see patterns and where they originate. But someone had to go there and find the specific sequence that would allow the computers to read the planet's signature anywhere in this sector of the galaxy."

"I wonder what it was like to be that first team to step foot on that planet, where everything was new and nothing was yet discovered . . ." He trailed off in awed reverie.

She grinned. "It was the most exhilarating thing I have ever done."

Joshua stopped. "You were there?"

"Yes." She stepped away into an open hatch leading to her berthing and closed the hatch behind her.

Joshua just stared as she disappeared. His adoration had immediately turned to admiration. He felt like he had met a hero from the history books, yet there she was, just as alive as anyone else.

2

The journey was long, and there was little in the way of activity. The crew stuck to their duties, performing maintenance as needed, cleaning when there was nothing to do otherwise, and exercising themselves in private activities when there was nothing left to clean. There were daily checks of all systems, checking for "leaks, squeaks, shakes, and breaks," as the mechanic had phrased it, but with nothing breaking down, there was nothing to fix, so there was nothing to do but wait.

Joshua occupied his time walking the ship and reading exhaustive operation and maintenance manuals trying to get a sense of how everything worked, how this ship flew, and what the critical systems were. He had no mechanical experience, but his People in the Machine did, so he knew the fundamentals of how these systems operated.

He walked every accessible inch of the ship. It was round like a disk, and though it didn't seem like it, they were flying top-down toward their destination. The whole inner core was a free-floating weighted ball that kept the floor pointed away from the direction of momentum. The momentum of the ship moving this way gave it the sense of gravity they needed to work while underway. Joshua wondered what caused it to do this, but the operation and maintenance manuals didn't offer a complete picture of the operation of the ship, just the individual systems. This meant there were mysteries for him to unravel to keep himself occupied.

Joshua took a break from his reading to visit the mechanic. He was in a homemade hammock tucked into the engine room below the main deck in the inner core, scratching out epochal poems about some thing or another with a writing pad and pen. Joshua tried to press for details, but the mechanic hid the pad and stated flatly, "It's not ready yet."

The mechanic got up from his nest, what appeared to be data cabling draped and fastened in various places to form a loose net. A lot of extra material had been used to make this hammock, but Joshua knew it wasn't his place to question the goings-on of the ship or what excesses might be ignored to keep the crew happy on long trips across the expanse of space.

"You want a tour of the place?" the mechanic asked after a few seconds of Joshua looking around awkwardly, wondering if it would be better to just leave and go back to the monitor, where he spent so much of his time.

"Yeah, absolutely," Joshua said, relieved that he wasn't intruding. *Anything to break up the monotony.*

"Come with me. I'll show you the real flux gate compass. I heard they sort of explained it to you." He led Joshua through a narrow corridor lined with conduit and pipes for various ship systems.

"What are all these?" Joshua asked.

The mechanic glanced at where Joshua was looking and started listing off a number of ship's systems. "Top two are hydronic loops for sub-cooling computers and climate control. The middle two are conduit. Top one is communications, bottom is power. Every system in the ship has sensors and data that are dependent on each other. The controls in the bridge tell every system what to do, and those systems respond accordingly. All those sensors are tied to communications wires that tell the computer it is on or off or will say how much resistance there is or whatever for the computer to calculate when to take an action once a limit is reached. This information feeds into the analytics and diagnostics software that tells me when there is a problem detected. There are also redundant systems in case of failure. The bottom pipes are hot and cold water and a sanitary sewer line."

Joshua traced each one. "So does the sewer water get jettisoned or reused somehow?"

"Yes" was all the mechanic said as he ducked beneath a bulkhead at a hatch. Joshua followed suit, and then as they crossed the threshold, the corridor opened up into a large machine room. The first thing Joshua noticed was the heat. Motors whirred and gauges could be seen all over the place. He had no idea what each thing in there was or did, but the mechanic had moved up next to a large tank and waited to catch Joshua's eye.

"This is domestic water," he said. "This tank is all the fresh water we have on the ship, so it's imperative that we top it off at every opportunity."

"So there is some water loss while underway?" Joshua asked, wondering how water might be lost in a closed system like a ship.

"Yes, there is, unfortunately," the mechanic replied. "Pipes leak, people drink more than they need, and evaporation leaves more than enough moisture in the air to lose water to the environment. Even corrosion is caused by the metal reacting with moisture and absorbing the oxygen from the water, and there is a slight attrition. However, it is mostly a closed system, and that is why I have meters on everything to determine where all the water's at and where it's going. Nothing gets jetted out into space, but there is a certain amount of moisture in the waste tank as well that depletes the supply."

The mechanic showed how the tank supplied hot water to the ship. A coil of copper tubing stretched all around the room, tracing back and forth along the bulkhead with intermediary reservoirs throughout. All this was contained in a carefully planned and monitored system, and at the hot water reservoir, a thermostat read the water was just below body temperature.

"Not an impressive amount of heat gain, but it serves a more practical purpose of absorbing the heat in the room and then sending it out to the sinks and galley services. There are point-of-use water heaters to raise the temp to set points, but it is very energy efficient, as you don't have to put as much energy into the heating of the water. I've seen more impressive systems, but this one serves its purpose." The mechanic admired the dance of the tubing all around the room. "On a ship as old as this one, you can't ask for much more."

"What if something leaks? Won't you ruin a motor that way?" Joshua asked as he, too, traced the tubing around the machine room.

"Only if it gets into the windings of the motor and creates a path to ground. There is a shield over the windings of each motor, and most are made weather resistant at production anyway. But there is always some risk for sure." He continued. "This room is thermally insulated to keep the heat in. Since it could easily overheat the whole ship and make it uncomfortable for everyone, thus using excessive energy in cooling the air, it was better to keep all the heat-producing systems in one place to ensure the heat is contained and used as efficiently as possible."

Joshua listened and then asked, "Do these systems ever turn off? I imagine they never stop, so always produce heat. Doesn't that heat build and build until the system is overwhelmed at some point? How do you get rid of that excess heat?"

The mechanic stopped his busy walk through the mechanical room. The room was loud, but he heard and understood the question. "Every bit of heat that is in this room represents energy used. In a finite and closed system like we have, we reclaim that heat through a heat exchanger full of refrigerant that absorbs the heat from the air and superheats the refrigerant to make it usable in other capacities. We use most of it in climate control." He opened another hatch at the far side of the machine room. "The rest goes through *that*." He gestured at a metallic sphere alone in the middle of the room.

Joshua felt lost in the technical details casually thrown at him as if he could make sense of them. He could feel the cold of the room and the immediate breeze of the hot air from the machine room flowing into the area. He could also see boxes of produce and meats stacked against the bulkhead behind it. "What is it?" he asked.

The mechanic shrugged. "A star drive. It absorbs heat to create energy. I know how it works but not what it's made of." He looked on for another few seconds before closing the hatch. "Heat is expensive out in space." He gestured to the tubing lining the wall and the temperature gauge by the hatch they came through before.

"Well, if you don't know what it's made of, then how can you know what it does?"

"I can tell what it does by what I observe. But I know how it does it by what I know about mechanics and thermodynamics." He gestured widely to the room around him. "Energy always transfers from hot to cold, high pressure to low. The same mass of air in two portions, one hot and one cold—the hot one will have higher pressure, the cold one will have more density. So as it relates to our little mystery in there, I can only say that it takes high pressure air and converts it to a very dense form of itself, stacking it more efficiently than can be found in nature in a molecular sense to a point where it is completely static. It was created in a laboratory by slamming two high-density particles together at very high speeds and creating a vortex that sucked the lighter materials around it in to create a vortex just like the core of every planet, star, galaxy, or black hole, but it is very small scale. Did you notice the smell?" He sniffed as he asked.

"It smelled ionized, but something else there too. Sort of sweet." Joshua recalled the way it tickled his nose and how it felt in his lungs as he inhaled.

"Exactly. That's what the void smells like too. If you ever find yourself without a suit floating through the abyss, take your last gasp for air by sticking out your tongue and tasting it before you die. It tastes like that." The mechanic stuck out his tongue. "The case is as thick as your thumb is wide, and it's really a shell of several tons of metal collapsed into that little orb you saw. What that thing represents is the core of a black hole." He made a fist with one hand and put it in the palm of the other to represent its size and shape. "The mini black hole in there pulls on that shell equally in all directions so it is essentially suspended. All air inside was pulled into that core, and a vacuum exists inside that shell. Of course, the force it generates pulls the air outside the shell inward because it is effectively absolute zero inside, and the shell is so dense, there is no room for even one electron to squeeze through. If that shell were to be broken somehow, the whole ship would be sucked into that tiny black hole, along with a large piece of any planet we happened to be on."

Joshua thought about this. He had observed the black holes in the Machine and knew they functioned the same in his reality outside the Machine. "So how does that generate electricity then?"

Again, the mechanic shrugged, unsure of the veracity of his understanding but wanting to make an effort to explain it. "Well, like a star, planet, galaxy, and everything else, even the black hole has a polarity and a magnetic signature. This interacts with the shell, which has fewer electrons than it normally would because of how tightly formed the atoms are squeezed together." He laced his fingers together to represent the atomic lattice that he was trying to explain. "Essentially there is no room for electrons to orbit around the nucleus of the atom, so many nuclei essentially share electrons, and the rest are squeezed out. Those nuclei still need electrons, though, so electrons are swarming around the outside of the shell trying to find their way in."

He continued. "When we then create a conduit of moving electrons away from the shell, those electrons are able to find somewhere else to go—to another atom that needs electrons."

Joshua interrupted. "But doesn't the shell with so many nuclei needing electrons create a massive magnetic pull toward itself? Wouldn't it be nearly impossible to strip one of those electrons off because the pull was so great?"

The mechanic looked somewhat affronted by the question and was curt with his reply. "Every system exists in equilibrium. There are exactly as many electrons as needed for the system to be satisfied without creating a massive magnetic disturbance. The orb is covered in exactly the number of electrons it needs to satisfy the demands of the protons and neutrons contained within it. This makes an electron field surrounding it able to overcome the huge positive magnetic field with its own negative magnetic field. At the same time, because electrons repel other electrons, the electron shell over top is much larger than the shell it covers, creating a very highly energized shell held in suspension by their mutual repulsion for each other and common attraction for the shell it surrounds. In the end the magnetic field is neutralized, which is why it is safe to go in there and why it doesn't pull everything into it. Because the magnetic force of one proton is reduced by the growing valence shell of the orb itself and the much closer magnetic pull of the wire filament, we can strip off one electron at a time and replace it with another one as the system operates."

"Well, isn't there leakage in electrical systems too? Isn't there a voltage drop as the distance an electron travels increases? Wouldn't this create a bit of an imbalance in the system?"

"Yes, usually. But all vessels in space use gold wire because it doesn't lose conductance over distance. That is also the primary purpose of your mission, in case you didn't know," the mechanic said bluntly.

"My purpose is what? To get *gold*?" he asked in a tone that reflected his skepticism.

"Yeah, that's the purpose of every frontier operator. To shape the dominant species of a planet into a culture so they will mine for resources so we can build more ships," the mechanic said nonchalantly. "Everything else is secondary."

Joshua let his face fall. He could not help feeling like he was part of some fraud to manipulate and extort an unacculturated species. For gold. If the Machine did not really change the people who went through, only protecting the individual from the rest of society, then that made society more adept in the administration of the horrors of history, only directed outward. His thoughts began to follow that trail of logic, wondering what purpose he would serve. He tripped on a wound cable lying on the floor and came out of his thoughts.

Joshua caught the smirk on the mechanic's face and understood it was intended to dismiss him. He was supposed to take his leave to go mull this over, but he was undeterred and still curious about the flux gate compass and how it actually steered the ship, so he asked.

The mechanic sighed, remembering. "Yes, I almost forgot." He moved some boxes and climbed a short ladder to a hatch above the room containing the star drive. There was a long, flat interstitial space above the mechanical rooms but below the main deck where the crew lived and worked. "This," he said pointing to three large black boxes with heavy cabling running to them, "is the *real* flux gate compass." He looked back at Joshua, who had barely poked his head into the tight quarters and didn't seem interested in crawling around anymore than he had to. "You see there's only three of them, right?" Joshua nodded. "The fourth one is centered directly over the center there. Do you see that shaft there?" He pointed at the direct center where a vertical shaft ran straight up. "In there is the engine that pulls us through the void."

"Pulls us?" Joshua asked, unsure he had heard correctly.

"Yeah, *pulls* us. The flux gate compass locks onto a magnetic signature and then dumps that binary signal into a giant magnet that generates a magnetic signature *opposite* of what our target destination is. This creates an attraction to the destination and pulls us right to it. With the lack of resistance in the void, we accelerate to speeds that are unachievable with fossil fuels. On the ground the drive matches the Gaussian signature of the area to repel the planet surface, and then we can just hover there. It's very cool stuff," he said admiringly as he crawled back to the ladder and gestured for Joshua to get out of his way.

"So how do these ships make so little noise when flying then?" Joshua asked.

"Well, I'm not a physicist, but I understand it's got a lot to do with the ionization of the air around the ship. The star drive puts out a massive electrical halo, and when we contact an atmosphere, it immediately converts the air into a layer of ionized particles that forms a sort of nonslip surface on the outside of the ship. It works the same underwater too, which is why we can move so easily in any direction. There is virtually no resistance on the ship. The ship is shaped like a bulged disk so it can create lift and drag in any direction without effort. There is no front, no back, and no left or right side—it's all at once. Simple once you understand how it works."

Joshua still didn't find it simple, and how it worked was only slightly less mysterious than it had been previously. They had climbed back down the ladder into the mechanical room and were making their way back out into the corridor.

Joshua then asked, "So why doesn't the ship light up like a meteor when it enters the atmosphere?"

The mechanic thought for a second and then said, "Well, I don't really know that answer. It's got something to do with the ionization. Light and heat being related to friction, which the ionized surface eliminates, we're able to pass through liquids and gasses and some very loose solids without getting ripped apart. I know it works, but I haven't spent much time figuring out *how*." He shrugged as he showed Joshua the ladder out of the mechanical space in a gesture that said, *Thanks for coming. Now get out.*

3

Joshua spoke to Marcella as often as they had opportunity. She took tea at the same time each day, and Joshua tried to be there when she did. This was the last time he would see her, though, as the ship was within ten light days of arrival and flying at nearly ten times that speed. He read her body language; as this went on, she seemed more open and eager to see him each day. He thought that if there was ever a time to make his move, it would have to be now.

"I want to tell you how much you have—"

She cut him off. "I know. I can read you better than you can me, and I know what you are about to say. All I can say is, it has been nice having you aboard, but there can be nothing between us, as this is where you will be departing, and I will not likely see you for a very long time."

Joshua sat quietly, dejected. He knew it was true, but it seemed harsh to lay it all out so plainly without softening the blow at least a little.

He fidgeted for a moment and then decided to change the subject. "What is it like down there?"

Her eyes flickered as if searching for something far in the past. "It was paradise." She seemed to daydream. "The planet has plants and animals in abundance of every kind and color, the weather is wild and seemingly unpredictable, and the star is warm and soothing. The settlement you're going to is in the heart of the desert, so you won't get much opportunity to see all of it, but it is quite comfortable. There is a very primitive society there that was interacting with the scientists before I left. I'm not sure how that relationship has progressed though."

Joshua remembered the mechanic and his comment. "Do we enslave those people to gather resources for us?" Joshua asked soberly.

"*Enslave?* No. The benefit goes both ways. They learn vital civilizing skills like agriculture, mining, and health care. And we get paid for helping them with resources. It's no different from any market transaction you can think of. There is no service that comes free. Not charity, not commerce. Nothing comes without a price tag."

"Your mechanic said we exploit them for gold," Joshua said.

"That's true in a sense. We do use them to mine the minerals we need, including gold. But in turn we give them civilization and show them how to do many things that elevate them above the aboriginal level and help them grow and expand. The ultimate goal would be for them to achieve our level of civilization." She thought for a second, then continued. "It's not slavery, if that's what you're worried about. Slaves always usurp their masters and always hold a grudge. That would be a terrible practice for any civilization to engage in. It's easier to reward with food and honors and praise and punish with neglect, dishonor, and banishment."

This didn't set Joshua's mind at ease. He knew there would be a lot of interaction with the primitive people but had never thought of it in terms of a give-and-take. But all this sounded a bit more convoluted than that, and it sounded like there was an equal exchange, but that balance was very easy to upset when the disadvantaged were dependent on others to calculate the terms and conditions. It sounded very delicate.

Marcella took her leave to go check equipment, and he stared at the monitor again, hoping to see the planet as they approached it. The ship was slowing ever so slightly as it entered the magnetic field and atmosphere of the star. The radiation confused the onboard systems trying to track the planet's magnetic field just enough that the delay could make them overshoot their mark, so to compensate the ship automatically alternated between opposing and equal magnetic pulses to alternately repel and attract the ship to its destination. The slower the ship wanted to go, the greater the ratio of repelling signature would be in relation to the target. When it wanted to stop completely, that ratio was one to one. For now, though, that ratio slowed to forty-nine to one, then as they got closer, forty-eight to one, then forty-seven, and so on until they reached the planet's atmosphere.

It started as a star that was just a little too bright, and as it continued to grow, he knew it was their destination. He had packed all his belongings the day before and had tucked them away in the cubby next to his cot in his berthing. There was little for him to pack. The three jumpsuits he had been issued were all the clothes he had. His casual clothes were deemed unsuitable for his assignment. His toiletry kit was gutted of all technology, and he was left with the barest essentials for his trip. He had not even been given any instruction on where to go when he arrived; he was simply told where to go right now.

Though the journey was long and he remembered the long days full of idle thoughts, mostly of the Machine and what that experience meant, he still didn't have a complete idea of what he was being assigned to do. He was an associate production manager, yet the way it sounded, he was being asked to be a herdsman or a shepherd. He didn't know if that was something he would be able to manage, especially considering the difficulties he had convincing the People to avoid self-destruction. *Maybe that isn't my purpose though*, he thought.

The features of the planet began to take shape. Even at this distance, he could see a vast blue ocean and land breaking up the azure hue of all that water. The closer they got, the more greens stood out; whole bands of the planet were covered with untamed forests and grasslands. As the planet rotated on its axis, he could see the discoloration of mountains and islands and glaciers and lakes dotting the whole surface of the planet. Similar oases he had once used to isolate and tame his own species during the formation of his ecosystems. This planet was not the one he had sculpted in the Machine, but he couldn't help seeing it that way and all the traumas that came with shaping it.

The ship lurched as it began to enter the atmosphere. Everyone was already in their assigned seats, harnessed in. The flux gate drive reversed its polarity to repel the magnetic force of the planet just enough to slow the entry and keep the ship from careening uncontrollably into the planet.

He could feel the momentum shift as the sense of gravity reduced and the ship slowed. When it reached a tipping point, the inner core flipped, and the sense of gravity reversed as he suddenly felt himself pressed firmly into his seat as the ship decelerated and finally equalized with the planet's gravity after a few jarring moments.

Justine unbuckled her harness and walked unsteadily to the console as her legs tried to adjust to the new balance of effort. "We're hovering at just over two kilometers above the ground. Stay buckled up. I'll program the destination, and we'll be there shortly."

Their target was a metropolis in the desert. A beacon allowed them to locate it by radio, and they slipped silently through the atmosphere to the city below. The desert reflected the blue hue of the moon orbiting above, and they could almost fly by sight but opted to let the instruments do most of the work. The beacon signal finally brought them to a tower standing tall and ominous against the dunes and dirt of the desert around it. It was an obelisk with reflective gold paneling on top to stand as a signal for incoming ships and travelers in the desert. The tip angled so the reflected light would shine toward the horizon for travelers to see and approach. A small gathering of tents dotted the top of a ridgeline, and then the base of the obelisk appeared, surrounded by tents and stone structures. An inner wall ran three hundred meters in all directions, and an outer wall extended a thousand meters from the obelisk in all directions.

Finally a series of flashing lights caught their attention. They glided down to the area where they had been instructed to land, in the courtyard of a building with a high stone wall. A canopy of linen was quickly stretched across the whole roof and courtyard, obscuring the ship and the new arrivals to the city.

The landing gear extended, and once the pads were on the ground, the ship went into standby mode. Once the light indicating the ship had been grounded and all residual static had been discharged, all noncritical systems went to sleep, and the running lights of the corridors lit up a path to a ramp that had extended to the ground.

4

Two men stood at the base of the ramp and waited for the ship's party to greet them.

Joshua gripped the handle of his duffel bag and glanced back, reluctant to leave the security of the ship for this alien environment. He didn't know where to go and was too timid to ask, so he just found an open section of wall and put his stuff down, taking in the whole scene. The mud-and-sand bricks that enclosed the courtyard were stacked high; he could just make out the top of the wall against the backdrop of the canopy that had been pulled over the courtyard to conceal the ship. Torches all around illuminated the area, but their light was still dim, and Joshua found it difficult to absorb the new world he had arrived in.

He saw the Captain hand a folded piece of paper to Marcella. He slowed as he heard the anger in Marcella's voice, the words indistinct but the emotion clear. She gestured with the paper as she sternly asserted her opinions, beliefs, and expectations of the content of that letter in a muted conversation just above a whisper.

Justine cut Marcella off with words that Joshua couldn't quite make out. All he heard was a sharp "These are your orders."

After what seemed like half an hour, Marcella appeared at the top of the ramp with a grim look on her face and a duffel bag in her hand, bulging from possessions she had haphazardly and angrily stuffed in. There was nothing subtle about the fury she carried. She gripped the paper in her hand beneath the strap of her bag so it crinkled and creased. She did not seem to care one bit for its condition. As she walked past Joshua, he opened his mouth to speak, but she cut him off. "I'll be staying here, it seems." Then she stormed through an open breezeway to the inner offices of the rudimentary spaceport.

Joshua stood by, not wanting to be the outlet for her aggression. He watched for a while as the Captain and the mechanic tended to the unloading of the supplies they had brought for the settlement, and a ramp manager checked off the manifest of all items they were expecting. Every now and then, the ramp manager would open a crate and look in, check the manifest, and write a note.

"This one can't stay here. *Undeliverable*," the ramp manager said coolly.

"What the hell, man?" asked the mechanic. Even in the cool desert night, the sweat was starting to glisten on his forehead.

"No technology," the ramp manager stated flatly.

"This doesn't have a computer—it's just a distiller," the mechanic said. "C'mon, man, we get paid by the crate on delivery. You're taking money out of my pocket here. This is what you guys asked for, and this is what was loaded onto our ship."

"We can't have any advanced technology on this planet. The people are primitive. If it falls into their hands, the whole mission is jeopardized. We have protocols. You know it, Frontier Corporation knows it, and this is not approved equipment. It has to go back."

"We just landed a giant piece of technology in this little outpost. What do you suppose the primitives are going to say about that?" He waved his hand toward the ship looming over them, which began a depressurization sequence and let off a burst of air from one of its external ports almost as punctuation to the mechanic's statement.

"That is why we have the obelisk without lights surrounded by a border wall, and why you were only authorized to land at night. That is also why this outpost is in the middle of the desert. Whatever technology we have must be kept far from prying eyes, and if we must abandon this place, we will leave nothing that the ravages of time and weather will not destroy. We have an extremely strict protocol—no manufactured equipment." The ramp manager turned his head away from the mechanic to ostensibly count crates, but it was intended to end the conversation.

"Okay, I get that," the mechanic said, unwilling to let it go. "Just sign for it and send it back with us so I can at least get paid for the effort. It wasn't my decision that caused this."

The ramp manager paused to consider it and seemed to accept these terms. "You're lucky I'm in a generous mood." He signed for the crate, then added it to the roster of outgoing materials.

The mechanic pursed his lips and rolled his eyes as the ramp manager turned his back to him before heaving the crate and carrying it back to the corridors of the ship.

Joshua watched for a few more minutes as the outbound crates were stacked near the ramp. Core Samples, Soil Samples, Genetic Samples, and other generic content labels were painted on the outside of the crates. All were cataloged with their location of collection and any descriptive information deemed useful to the Frontier Corporation or other groups that had access to this region. Joshua had no idea what would be done with them, but it seemed like the whole purpose here was scientific rather than resources.

That notion was shattered a moment later as a skid was pulled out bearing the symbol for gold on the side. Four containers full, and another two were labeled Radioactive.

Joshua turned to follow where Marcella had gone, and his thoughts raced in all directions at once trying to understand this place. It was one thing to read about it and quite another to experience it. How many colonies were there? Where did all those resources come from? If Irka was a hub for off-world transport, how many other cities supplied resources to it?

He felt vulnerable in this experienced and rugged world. He needed to find someone familiar to anchor off, someone who could help ground him a little bit in this foreign land. He needed Marcella.

5

"So you think these orders were issued by mistake then?" The Commandant flattened the wrinkled orders on his desk, making a show of his effort and distaste for their condition.

"Sir, I think they were issued maliciously," Marcella stated bluntly, her hands clenched in fists as she snarled, the flush of her face burning hot. She was doing her best to control her emotions, but being blindsided like this did not give her time to process them adequately.

"Orders don't have motives, malicious or otherwise." The Commandant finished smoothing them and flopped them on the stack of papers beside him on the desk. "What makes you think these were intended to do you harm?"

She pursed her lips and cast an irritated glance at the stack of papers. "Because of my history here, because of where I'm supposed to be assigned, because of *whom* I am being assigned to!"

"You don't think this is because of your skills then? Your importance to the mission here? You think there are others more suited to your role here?" he asked antagonistically with a slight smirk on his lips.

"I think there are thousands of these operations across the empire and hundreds of people capable of doing this job successfully and many who are even more suited to this task than me!" Her fury was abating, but she was not giving up the fight. *This is an injustice!* she thought. *Of course it was malicious!*

The Commandant sighed and leaned back in his chair casually. "Merchant Astronautica doesn't seem to think so. This operation requires *someone* of your talent here, and they seem to think you are the best fit for this operation."

"Sir, I don't know how he pulled it off or why he chose to poison my career again after all this time, but I know *he* is responsible for this." She leaned on the desk threateningly.

He looked at her clenched fists and gestured at the chairs behind her. She took the hint but didn't sit down; her anger wouldn't allow it.

He commiserated. "Well, I don't have the authority to change these orders once they've been issued by your command. I can only put in a request for personnel based on the mission scope and use whoever they send me. Since that seems to be you, you'll have to endure as long as you can while I request to have these reissued." He jabbed his finger into the middle of the paper and continued. "However, it usually requires accompanying disciplinary action to say you are unfit for the role, which has its own repercussions, so I recommend you accept this for now, and I will work on getting you reassigned based on needs elsewhere. Ionia and Scandia territories have already completed the mission you are here to fulfill, but we are investigating another colony that will need the full suite of cultural systems as well. So there's that, if you can hold out that long."

He was bargaining with her, she knew, and the pace at which these colonies were established meant she might have to wait a long time. She knew it was pointless to argue but couldn't help but feel like she wasn't being heard.

He spoke soothingly. "Look, I'll see what you can do at those two colonies. They aren't under my domain, but they are still Frontier Corporation operations, so I may have some influence."

She nodded as she resigned herself to this bargain. Then the anger burned hot again as she remembered who that meant she would have to deal with. "He's *definitely* going to be a problem."

The Commandant's face turned to stone. "You should consider your attitude right *now*, and make sure you don't *make* him one."

She pursed her lips again and understood this to be a direct command. She burned with impotent fury, clenching her fists tight so her gray skin turned white.

The Commandant changed the subject. "Your old pseudonym has been reassigned to you, so no need to try to remember a new name along with keeping your anger in check. You are not to pick any fights out there; I'm already having enough issues there that I don't need your personal disagreements getting in the way. Is that understood, Katesh?" He emphasized the new name.

"Yes, sir, I'll do my best to stick to my work. But I won't tolerate any of his behavior, and if he lays a hand on me again—"

The Commandant raised his hand to stop her. "I told you, I will do what I can to make things right. Just please be patient. You know where to go from here. You are dismissed." He signed the paper and made a note on his calendar.

She saw him write "Request reassignment for Katesh." She guessed that it was more for her benefit, to pacify her, than any real intention.

She felt defeated. Betrayed even. This was her best chance, but she knew it was a long shot. She hesitated briefly before turning to leave.

The door opened, and Marcella stepped out. She was startled to see Joshua standing there, and a look in her eyes asked whether he had heard her private meeting before the look of indifference fell over her face. She hesitated and cast an almost apologetic look at him, and then she turned and walked down the corridor to another door at the end of the hallway with a sign above it that read Processing. The fury still showed in her steps, but the fire had died a little.

The voice of the Commandant came from the office. "If you're waiting to see me, you need to present yourself. I'm very busy."

Joshua jumped to attention and hastily gathered his belongings and dug his orders out of his bag and presented them to the Commandant.

"Have a seat." The Commandant gestured vaguely to the chair in front of his desk. The man wore his authority confidently, his face marked with creases from stresses of years past. There was no hair on his head, no facial hair either. He was well past the conditioning of the Machine, and though his eyes seemed more expressive than others Joshua had seen, they had the tired look of a man constantly shifting from one crisis to the next. "It looks like you are assigned to the field. Have you been told what you're expected to do yet?"

Joshua had only been following a series of pointed fingers and had not spoken to anyone officially about what was expected of him. "No, I haven't been told anything yet." He shifted in his hard wooden seat, his jumpsuit squeaking slightly on the polished wood.

"Well, your primary purpose is to tame the primitives so they can build a society. You'll be training with our top field officer." He reached into a desk drawer and pulled out a book with misaligned pages and a worn leather cover. "This is your field manual." He flipped through the book. "You will use this to guide the primitives toward civilization and give them a set of rites to perform so they will figure out how to live in proximity to one another without reverting to their animal behaviors. It is critically important that you follow these steps. Frontier Corporation has spent centuries perfecting this formula to progress the people as rapidly as possible without advancing too fast. Study it, memorize it, and don't lose it."

The Commandant handed the book across the desk to Joshua. Joshua opened it, making a display of his interest in his assignment. The pages were browned like the cover, and he saw inside a series of diagrams representing various principles and a set of rituals beneath each.

"You can look through that later. Just know that it's important to your job and our mission here that you learn everything contained in that book. Understood?" The Commandant spoke with a crisp authority that told Joshua he was an efficient and productive conversationalist.

Joshua nodded sharply and closed the book. "What happens if they progress too fast?"

The Commandant shrugged indifferently. "They collapse as a civilization, and all progress is basically lost. We have to teach them techniques of civilizing themselves and do it ritualistically so they follow the steps to build a foundation of understanding that we can build upon later. Then they have to learn the purpose of it for themselves. But we *cannot* let them progress too fast technologically, or the genetic imprint of the civilization will not set in. They will simply be animals with tools and will destroy each other more efficiently. Too top heavy and too weak of a foundation. Too much knowledge too quickly, and they will topple catastrophically."

Joshua hesitated before asking his next question, debating whether to even ask it and hoping he wasn't broaching the subject too soon. He shifted in his chair and glanced around uncertainly before asking, "Is it true we are using them to mine resources for us?"

"Yes, it is," the Commandant stated flatly. "Is that going to be a problem?" He cocked his head to the side with a look of deep scrutiny on his face.

"No, sir," Joshua stammered. He hadn't used this title on anyone yet, but the authority this man exuded made it seem appropriate.

The Commandant seemed to approve of the acknowledgment of their hierarchy. "It's a fair trade," he said bluntly. "There's no exploitation. We teach them how to become a civilization, and they bring us gifts they think we will approve of. You will receive many such gifts, or maybe not . . ." The Commandant trailed off, looking at Joshua. "If you're a tyrant, they will cower and withhold their best for themselves. If you're too lenient, they will not give you anything and will learn nothing, and the rituals will not be exercised. This is the same way you teach small children. Authority with expectations and gentle guidance leads to the best outcomes. But the tyrant merely suppresses bad behaviors, and indulgent leaders make production excessively costly. You need to find a balance between punishment and reward and expectation versus indifference. That is how we help them form a civilization, and that is how we are benefited by their production.

"Our purpose," the Commandant continued, "is not to subjugate these people. They are useful to our *wants*, just as we are useful to their *needs*. They don't realize it yet, but they are the best hope for this planet and the god that they represent to find civilization, and we are going to aid in that effort. They tend to view us as gods because we have capabilities well beyond their comprehension, and they will worship you for it. This is similar to the way a pet might interact with an owner, but like any subordinate species, they will worship only long enough to learn your weaknesses, so be cautious and stay in character. You cannot trust them because they don't know what value you bring or why they are forced to endure what they must. The life of a scavenger, which they must leave to become civilized, is a life of freedom—short, tragic freedom. The life of civilization is oppressive, long-lived obligation, so until they have lived under the yoke of civilization for several generations, they will yearn for the freedom of the nomadic life and will harbor hidden resentments for us. Do *not* let your guard down."

Joshua's mind went to his recent memories of cultures being motivated by whips and rewarded with meager rations. He could not shake his reluctance to shape these people through similar means. He remembered, too, how difficult it was for civilization to emerge. How the species was forced into isolation and how many generations it took for them to civilize on their own. How many times they destroyed one another in that effort to reject society and the oppression inherent in it. He empathized with them. It was the same ghost in his genes that called him to the frontier—only to find he was to build the very thing he was running from.

He ran his thumb over the symbol on the cover as he contemplated its meaning.

"I see you are grappling with thoughts of pity and guilt," the Commandant said as he studied Joshua's face. "Don't. They have the option of migrating anywhere they wish. They are not bound to our system with chains or rope. The ones who come to us recognize the benefits of serving our interests. It's up to you to find the right balance that helps them progress into a culture, not just merely a civilization."

"I will do my best, sir." Joshua then asked, "Where will I be staying, and with whom will I be working?"

"You will be working with Shemesh. He is the project lead out there. You would be wise to pay close attention to his teachings . . . just be cautious about what you learn from them." The Commandant scrolled a schedule of names and assignments and stopped when he found Shemesh on the list. The paper showed several groups of names, and Joshua imagined each of those represented a different settlement. "He is in Bashram, at the river delta to the southeast. We will arrange for your caravan. Do not interact with the primitives until you have spoken to Shemesh. He will give you guidance on how to perform your duties as it relates to them. We have a strict code here, and they must always revere us so they seek our knowledge and perform our rituals. You'll understand once you get there." He put the list down and then looked up. "That reminds me, you are now to be called . . ." He trailed off as he dug through his papers for the right one. "Yehoshiva."

Joshua was shocked at this revelation. "Why do we have to change our names?"

"Because you will need to disassociate yourself from your position here. You don't want an actual record of your name imprinted on these people. You are new, so it goes without saying that you will screw up. You do not want the record of your screwups to include the name your mother gave you, believe me. These people will remember your name in their mythology, albeit a bastardized version of it in their tongue. You'll want plausible deniability and all that. But more than that, you need to understand that you are a performer here, a teacher and an actor. You are playing a role, and the easiest way to make a person adopt a persona is to have them step into a character. That character has the name Yehoshiva."

Joshua repeated the name quietly before the Commandant interrupted. "When you're done murmuring, you can make your way down the hall to Processing."

"What goes on there?" Joshua asked, suddenly aware that he was going to have to change his whole persona, and that probably meant costumes and conditioning. He felt disoriented again and felt that sense of ominous dread of facing a transformative experience for only the second time in his life. Now it was real.

"First you will get a haircut, then you'll turn in all your personal belongings, and then you'll get fitted for clothes and personal hygiene equipment that are properly suited to the role you are about to play. If you have any other questions, you can ask the clerk there." The Commandant started working on signing some form and redirected his focus elsewhere. Joshua had not been formally dismissed, but the intent was the same.

Joshua was still processing the complete transformation of his identity. He started to rise and gather his things when he stopped. "Sir, before I leave . . ."

The Commandant glanced up from his paperwork.

"What do we call them?"

"Call who?" He made some notes on one of the papers on his desk.

"The primitives. The indigenous people here," Joshua replied.

"Well, what did you call your people after they became civilized?" The Commandant asked as he leaned back in his chair, his face masked with interest, but his demeanor said, *I have a lot of work to do, so please get to the point.*

"I called them humans."

"Strange, I called mine adamu. I think everyone here has a similar name for theirs. The accepted term for the ones that adopt our culturalization is Umanu. The others you can call primitives." He looked down at his desk again as he began to work. "Will that be all?" he asked without looking at Joshua.

Joshua bowed slightly, not sure of the formality of leaving the office of a superior. Then he walked down the hall to Processing, where he had seen Marcella go a short time before. The hall stretched long before him and seemed to grow as the new knowledge of his purpose there started to sink in. His feet carried him, but he suddenly felt disembodied and lost. What waited for him as he moved through this foreign world? He had no training and no comprehension of what was expected of him, let alone how he would stay in character for these primitives. *What have I gotten myself into?* he wondered as he drifted toward the sign at the end of the hall.

6

Joshua watched his thick black hair fall to the ground one lock at a time. It was normal for his people to bald after they emerged from the Machine, but to his knowledge, no one actively pursued the look. It was just part of the transition. He was young, so he had not even experienced the shrinking hairline both men and women endured until it disappeared completely. Most women had more dignity than to let the few scraggly wisps of hair remain, and eventually it made more sense to shave it all off than to try to shape it. Here, though, he had no choice in the matter.

Frontier Corporation had a strict guideline for hygiene and attire, or so Joshua had heard from everyone so far, if that was a reliable source. His long hair was trimmed short with scissors, and then the barber took out a brush with a lather of soap and spread it on thick over the top of his head. He began the process of carefully shaving Joshua's head clean. "Everyone needs to look the same," the man said cheerfully.

Joshua did not question or wonder why. He assumed it would help remove a piece of his former identity and become part of his costume, his persona. He asked the barber about it.

"Well, some people think they can't tell the difference between two of us. They might not even be able to tell genders apart from a distance." He paused his shaving to think and then spoke. "I don't know if that's true though. They are intelligent enough to know who is mean and who is kind. I've heard they are equivalent to, say . . . a five-year-old. Of course, that's just what I've *heard*. I don't get out and interact with them much."

Joshua thought about this. He didn't really know many children but could remember vaguely how he had behaved and what he thought at that time of his life. How he had viewed adults was the more relevant thought though. "Do they worship us, or what is that relationship?"

"Worship? Hmm . . . not that I've seen. But they fear and respect us and depend on us in many ways. I suspect they don't love us, but some fools say it's better to be feared than loved." The barber chuckled to himself as he shook his head at that notion.

Joshua thought about the livestock back home and how one calf looked the same as another to him and guessed these primitives might view them the same way. Joshua tried to imagine himself viewed as a god or at least as a king. Knowing what he knew about himself, this idea seemed absurd to him. *But that's what the Machine is too*, he reminded himself. For better or worse, he knew that would be his role.

For the first time in his life, he was completely bald. He ran his hand over the smooth skin. The absence of hair made him feel every little draft in the air, and he suddenly felt chilly.

"Don't worry, you'll get used to it. It's up to you to maintain it in the field though," the barber said as he shook the hair off the apron. "Let's get you your uniforms."

Joshua got up from the chair, taking a second glance at the mirror and seeing a completely different person than he had been upon landing. He followed the barber, whom he now realized was the clerk the Commandant had mentioned, to another room full of linens and belts and miscellaneous equipment.

"Take one of each from those bins." The clerk pointed to a row of containers filled with toiletries. Joshua did as he was told, though not sure what anything was. He had only a vague idea of their function. They seemed like simplified versions of what he was used to, but in the rush to collect everything he needed, he wasn't able to identify the use of each item. "Take three of each from those stacks." The clerk pointed at two stacks of white linens. "Take one of these, two of these, and a pair of these and these," the clerk said, pointing at a harness, some belts, some sandals, and some leather bracers. Joshua felt rushed, having barely comprehended his purpose there. The pointing and the neatly sorted bins made him feel like he was on an assembly line. "*One* of those!" the clerk scolded. Joshua just stood there blank faced until the clerk reached out and took the extra harness Joshua had cradled in his arms with the rest of the tangled web of leather accoutrements. Finally, the clerk pulled down a box and handed it to Joshua. "Try this on and tell me how it fits."

Joshua pulled a hat from the box. It was a leather hatband with a length of braided linen. "I'm not sure how it's supposed to fit." He plopped it on his head and flipped the braid to the back.

The clerk came over and turned it around. "It faces forward like this, the sigil on the front, the seam in the back." He took the braid and wrapped it around the top of Joshua's head. "This forms a sort of crown," he said as he used a leather strap to hold the braid in place. "Here, take these. They're extras in case you lose that one." He placed two more thin strips of leather with a loop at each end in Joshua's hand. Then he instructed him, "Put on the rest of your uniform, and I'll show you how to wear it properly. That goes on first, then that one over top of it. That goes around your waist, and that over your shoulders. Put those on last, and I'll come in and cinch everything down when you're done. You should look like this when you are done." He set a picture of a very stern-looking desert warrior in front of Joshua. Then he walked out.

Joshua unraveled one of each of the linens. It was hard to tell the difference between the top and the bottom or the front and the back. He tried to match the picture, but there was so much cloth that he couldn't find the start of it. He tried stepping through a loop of cloth and lost his balance, falling into a stack of boxes in the corner. He tried to stand up, and a tail of the cloth cinched down on his groin, and he fell over again, knocking the rest of his equipment off the bench. He paused for a moment to collect himself and unraveled the now-tangled mess of linen and started over, trying to imitate the image set before him. When he finally got some loose semblance of what was pictured, he told the clerk, "Okay, I think I'm ready."

"Well, you are a fine-looking disaster," the clerk said with a smirk as he walked through the curtain. He carried a ceremonial dagger with him that he put down as part of the uniform and set to removing Joshua's wadded and sagging attire.

Joshua looked in the mirror and was unsure where it had gone wrong. The linens were bunched and tangled, the straps were twisted and too loose on one side, too tight on the other. His leg linens and his chest linens were reversed, and he had no way of knowing how or why or what made one distinguishable from the other. Even the belt, which he was quite familiar with, had a low-tech fastener that he couldn't get to stay tight.

The clerk picked up one of the spare sets of clothing and started dressing Joshua. "Like this. This one first. This is the front, then this one. Start here and wrap it like this. Tuck it here, and then you take this to hold it together." The clerk took the long rectangular piece of linen and folded it until it hung around knee height. Then holding it behind Joshua, he took one tail end and held it against Joshua's belly and pulled the rest around his waist as tight as he could. Then he wrapped it one more full wrap around his body until the other end was at the front. He tucked the top of the tail into Joshua's waistline and took the belt from the nest of leathers and wrapped it around, cinching it tight and threading the end through one loop, over another, and back so it would stay in place. Then he picked up the other linen and folded it in thirds, then folded it in half lengthwise, and tucked the crease into Joshua's back beltline. He draped the tails one over each shoulder. "The harness goes like this. This piece is the front, not the back. I think you know how to wear sandals, and these bracers are worn with the knots outward, but you can strap them like this and then rotate them." The clerk cinched and tugged and pulled on the uniform until it resembled the picture. Joshua put the hat on and tucked the dagger into his belt, and the image was complete.

"What name did they give you?" the clerk asked.

"Yehoshiva," Joshua said flatly.

"Well, now you have been baptized. No longer shall you be called . . . erm, what was your name again?"

"Yehoshi—"

"No, your given name."

"Joshua."

"No longer shall you be called Joshua. You are reborn. Welcome to Irka, Yehoshiva!" As he said this, he picked up the leather book and handed it over, tapping on the cover with his long, weatherworn gray finger. "It's all in here, every ritual. Just study it, do what others do, and you'll be fine."

He picked up Joshua's duffel bag full of all his worldly possessions and handed Yehoshiva a small trunk to store his kit instead. Room enough for only uniforms and essentials, it was the embodiment of all that he had become. *I am Yehoshiva.*

The clerk took out a small jar of some acrid black substance and began painting the name on the trunk lid in an artistic scrawl starting from the S in the middle after a quick letter count. S-H-I-V-A, then to the rest, O-H-E-Y in reverse order to keep the spacing correct. He stepped back and admired his work, then put the lid on the jar. He slapped him on the shoulder and said, "There you go. Now you're official." He then left Yehoshiva there to pack the trunk.

7

Yehoshiva sat on his assigned bunk flipping through a small booklet detailing the many planetary operations occurring simultaneously. It seemed that, spread across the entire globe, similar operations were in active operation by different companies and organizations. Though it didn't go into much detail on each, there was one to the northwest of his current operation that seemed to be doing genetic research.

Zaosh, the commandant of that operation, was combining their genetic structures with that of the primitives to hybridize them. As long as the primitives weren't harmed, they were given a free hand at it. The ostensible purpose was to allow these primitives to integrate easily into the empire once they achieved the level of civilization necessary to produce their version of the Machine, however long that took. It was standard practice to hybridize a primitive species, and then over time, as disease and the inherent benefits of diverse DNA made these hybrid people the majority, the transition into the galactic empire would be easier. With similar genetics, they would be able to interbreed with all parts of the empire eventually, and their unique characteristics would strengthen the galactic gene pool while simultaneously homogenizing their population with the greater empire.

That was the apparent purpose. However, the libertine methods used were not wholly scientific or disciplined as a result of Zaosh's leadership and seemed to reflect his own egotistic desire for legacy rather than the interests of the empire. The consensus opinion around the barracks was that they were barely a legitimate operation, and a change of leadership would be necessary if things continued.

Rumors flew about all the operations, and Yehoshiva listened attentively to all of them. Many made him worry about the true decency of the operations there, but he was trying to keep an open mind. He was eager to learn as much as he could. The worry that he was wholly unprepared and would fail miserably in his duties made him hunger all the more for knowledge about his operation. He read the brief story of Irka and its origins, how it had evolved and why, and was fascinated that when he was just learning to walk, this city was itself being born.

He wandered into the dining hall while he read. He mindlessly grabbed a dish and took a bowl of stew of some sort or another. Without looking up from the reading and the diagrams and the maps, he found a bench nearest the front of the line, where he sat completely absorbed in the material. Without looking up, he took a spoonful of the stew and began to chew the chunks in the broth. He stopped. The flavors were exotic and potent, and the meat had a texture he wasn't used to.

He looked down at the stew for the first time and noticed the bits of meat were not the typical white he remembered from home. This meat was a rich red with a brown sear all around. The broth was brown, but the vegetables were a variety of colors from purple and orange to white and green. He ladled another scoop and examined it, smelled it, and began to sample each piece to decipher how the individual flavors contributed to the whole.

A familiar voice spoke to him as he did so. "Those vegetables are a local product, and the meat is from the dromedaries. It's flavorful, but it gets boring after a while." A dish was set down across from Yehoshiva, and when he looked up, he saw the clerk before him sitting down. "It's Yehoshiva, isn't it?"

Yehoshiva nodded. "I never actually got your name though."

The clerk shrugged. "Few people actually do. They come and go, and it ends up being superfluous information that no one really needs to know. I sort of just progress the story for each individual without serving any real function to their tales. I'm okay with that. I have my own little world, and no one bothers me with excessive demands, so I am content to serve that function. My thinking on it is, if a person is not critical to someone else's story, their name is neither important nor memorable. Few have asked, and even fewer have remembered my name. The former is out of pragmatism, the latter out of courtesy."

Yehoshiva thought about this for a second and how many other people he had passed or interacted with who merely served as exposition in his own story but whose lives were likely equally as rich as his own. "I'd like to know your name anyway."

The clerk smiled. "Clark. Clark Kirk the clerk."

Yehoshiva just stared for a moment. He wasn't sure if it was a joke or if it was sincere. "Is that your real name or your code name or . . ." He trailed off, not sure what else he really wanted to ask about it.

Clark let out a chuckle. "Well, I have little to do outside the compound here, so I don't need a big fancy name, but yes, it's a code name, as you put it. A little joke from the first Commandant when we first got here to establish this place."

Yehoshiva was suddenly intrigued. "You mean you were here from the beginning?"

Clark nodded as he spooned some stew into his mouth and sat back with a look of reverie. "Yeah, about fifteen standard years ago now. Irka was a shadow of what it is now, and back then there was nothing here. We took every care imaginable with the goal of preserving the secrecy of the operation designed to be a hub for incoming travelers. Just a small team of engineers and scientists and people like myself who do a little bit of everything. It turns out people like me are the most universally useful of all of them, so I was kept on the mission as long as I was willing to stay." He shrugged as if to say, *and so I stayed.*

Yehoshiva flipped through the booklet and found the picture of the first mission crew and showed it to Clark. He just nodded and pointed to a person on the left side in the back row. "All the biggest egos of that group insisted on being in the front row and centered. Just that one picture took more coordination and bargaining and calculation to determine who *should* be in the middle based on their contributions than the whole city took to build." He chuckled and shook his head.

He flipped the page to the first picture of the city plans. "It was to be enclosed in two rings of walls. The inner wall enclosed our compound. The outer ring was where the main city would be built. Inside those walls life was easy but expensive and controlled. Outside, life was hard but free. The primitives had a difficult time adapting to city life, but the benefits were self-evident once we got things established."

"Why was this spot chosen? How did you get the resources that were needed? How did you get *water*?" Yehoshiva asked with wonder.

Clark crossed his arms and began to explain the process. "Well, as to the 'where,' this spot was the most isolated from the primitives, so we could work with high assurance that we were not going to be watched for long. It allowed us to use our technology somewhat openly to set the foundation. The resources were largely brought in from other isolated areas around the planet. It's important that nothing be used that can't be explained through convoluted anthropological or economic models." He laughed at his own joke before continuing.

"Water was the most interesting part though. The star drive on the ship was removed in the special gold containment unit. They carried it with two insulated wooden staves. This was to prevent it from contacting the ground and thus arcing and incinerating whoever got too close. Sand, as I'm sure you know, can generate a lot of static electricity, and that electrical differential is enough to move current. And those star drives can move a *lot* of current. So without those protections, a person would be basically killed instantly. When they opened the top, the cold from the star drive absorbed the heat from the desert, and the resulting condensation of even the minuscule amount of water in the air was enough to form a pool, which trickled into a stream and found a natural pattern of flow that ended at a depression not far from the ship. We added sap and some salt, which dissolved in the water and flowed down to the depression. We marked that area, and when we isolated the star drive on the ship again, the water had dried up and soaked into the desert. But because of the hardeners we added, it was easier to remove the material without the sand filling in the holes again. We were able to dig down pretty deep, and with that sand and dirt and clay, we were able to make bricks to build the cistern that supplied the city's water. We are sitting above it right now. It covers most of the area beneath the city within the second wall. You never realized the whole city had a basement, did you?" He winked at Yehoshiva as he flipped to the page with the architectural prints of the cistern's design.

"We stacked bricks all the way around to hold back the soil, and then they dug the overflow channel and bricked it up. We built pillars throughout and then made sloped bricks to create arches across the depression, locked together by a keystone. Then over the arches we laid clay, and then mortared more bricks into place on top of that. We covered it all with another layer of clay, and then they filled it back in with sand and paved over top of it with stones.

"The engineers were sure proud of themselves for this design and for using the primitive materials. We left a couple of vent shafts open for pressure to equalize and made a trough at the surface, which was filled by wicking the water from below into the trough. That was *my* contribution—besides the manual labor," Clark said proudly. He took another spoonful of stew to let the thought settle before he continued. "We built the walls high and thick so they could not be climbed and could not be breached by the curious nomads. It wasn't until we had built all the infrastructure inside the city first that we began the work of constructing the obelisk. We didn't want to intentionally attract attention until it was ready."

Yehoshiva listened intently. Every word was a glimpse into the history of this place. "Is there a reason why it's laid out the way it is?" He referred to another diagram showing the city's footprint and the orientations listed on them.

Clark looked at the image briefly, trying to grasp what Yehoshiva was asking about. "Well, the gate to the inner wall is facing north because if anyone on the outside of it were to look through it, they would be facing the sun and less likely to see something they weren't supposed to. It also has the psychological effect of creating an association with our people and the light, meaning we provide the knowledge that illuminates their world. The inner wall is a sanctuary for us, where we can relax and drop our characters a little bit. Frontier Corporation spells it out in their project plans. I imagine some centuries ago, some high-ranking company official found themselves in a compromising situation in full view of the primitives somewhere and insisted on it thereafter." Clark laughed.

"What about the outer gates though—why four? Doesn't that make the city more vulnerable?" Yehoshiva was curious about the defensibility rather than their function, but Clark answered the first question instead.

"Those four gates serve as the cardinal directions to orient the city. Each industry has a quadrant of the city now, and each gate serves those sectors with materials. As the city grew over time, the most trusted and successful from those quadrants lived there and operated businesses outside the gate. The third wall we have now was built several years ago to enclose the industrial sectors. Each of those areas has two gates out and one gate between the other quadrants." He sketched the city layout on the booklet with his finger.

"That looks like a giant target," Yehoshiva said. "How do we defend against attackers?"

Clark just looked at him for a moment before deciding to answer. "Well, the only attackers there would be are those we would create from mismanagement. That would be really irresponsible." He left it at that before moving on.

"Outside those gates, though, is where the nomads and the poor live and trade. They barter for water and beg for scraps. This is a good opportunity to organically spread our goodwill to the desert people, so we encourage giving out water at those gates. This is also where many of the city inhabitants throw their waste, so the water is contaminated. We had to create a sewage system that was rudimentary enough to function as designed without using advanced technology but would prevent the citizens from contaminating the area outside the gate and keep illness in check for those we need to spread the good rumors of our city and our mission here. So we built an aboveground septic system. The sediment sinks to the bottom, and the gray water gets filtered through varying mediums to remove all contaminants before being given to the poor. We built a building around it so the primitives wouldn't go messing with it and then covered a wall with clay and wrote 'The Ritual of Renewal' on it."

He recited it with mock reverence and smiled as he did.

> It does honor to the Lord God to save every part of yourself for renewal. As your body purifies itself for the Lord, the Lord seeks to redeem the rejection of your body. A servant should hide their bodily functions from their neighbors and shall dispose of it at first light and before last light so they may purify themselves for the Lord inside and out. The Masters shall collect this impurity so the Lord may redeem it. The Masters offer the water of life in exchange, but the Lord gets the first taste of this water. It must be heated until the water dances and the vapor climbs to heaven. And when the Hymn of Offering is spoken twice, the Lord will have received his portion, and the rest shall be for his servants. Do this, and the Lord will bless you with a long life. Share this with the unfortunate and the humble, and you will be blessed with greater fortune for your mercy.

After a brief pause, Clark continued. "It didn't require much coaxing to get the primitives to dump their effluence into the septic system. It took more to convince them to use the bucket. It took even more to get them to cover it and not wait until it was heaping full to deliver but to take it in the morning and in the evening. Most difficult yet was to convince them to not use the same bucket for the two ends of the process! When they saw they could get free water for their deposit, they tried to cheat and bring it multiple times in the day. When the septic filtration ran dry, they were told they had displeased the Lord with their selfishness, and they could take two portions per day, but only with a deposit. Finally, they learned the lesson to boil the water for five minutes at a rolling boil after they would get violently ill from drinking it without 'giving the Lord his portion.' In the end they discovered if they were obedient, they would be rewarded. If not they would be punished, without us ever having to lift a finger." He smiled.

Yehoshiva was awed by the simplicity of this. "It's incredible how organic that teaching is. The mere consequences of nature and sanitation reinforce the ritual. The *religion* is built on the natural consequences of behavior! It's brilliant! Are all the rituals like this?"

Clark winked at him and said, "That's the beauty of it and the elegance of our system. The rituals you have in that book are very different from the ones we give to the primitives. You'll notice that the core idea of the book is retained, but its application is used in different ways and contexts that fit whatever behavior we are trying to condition. The language changes by region too. If you go to Scandia, the same ritual idea will be completely different when you translate it, and linguistic drift makes it lose meaning or take on new meanings over time, diluting and hiding the original intent but creates a whole class of people who study the words intently to extrapolate the core message of these rituals. Long tomes will be written to adapt them to new cultures. They'll get most of it wrong, focusing too much on one aspect over another, but they'll get a lot of it right too. Not that that matters much in the result. Eventually, when we're gone, the Umanu will use the differences in interpretation as justification for war and oppression, but this just helps expose each side to the interpretations of the other, and cooler heads will be able to see a new perspective and have a deeper, more original understanding of the rituals and their applications. Unfortunately, it's all part of the process of civilizing a species. It's the priests themselves that do most of the conditioning though. We just give them the tools to get there. And the way we've written the rituals here will give them a unique and specific interpretation of the core message."

Yehoshiva perked up at this and asked, "What do you think their interpretation will be from here then?"

Clark shrugged. "That's really up to the priests and what they can agree on. It will be largely monotheistic, but they will call us Angels or starpeople or Elohim or helpers of God in some form or another. They will reverently perform their daily duties like basic sewage and sanitation in a ritualistic manner. They will cross rivers and streams and revere basic geology and chemistry as an expression of God. It will be farcical from an objective perspective, but it will be exactly the behaviors they need to learn in order to survive. The priests each have their own understandings too, and while we can give them the tools, they may not learn the lesson the way we would want them to. We don't know exactly what shape *this* religion will take, but we know they will have the core principles, just as they all will at every settlement on this planet and all the others too."

Yehoshiva listened, captivated by the idea of planting the seed of civilization, using priests and religion as the behavioral conditioning force that holds a civilization together. "So how did you select those priests?"

"Well, the secret is in finding people with the right virtues that make priests more tolerant of conditioning. The irony is that these traits aren't valuable to their primitive groups, so they are not sought after and are extremely difficult to fake," Clark said matter-of-factly.

Yehoshiva was captivated. "Like what?"

"Well, things like humility. They won't get many rewards from their kin by being modest, so that's the first one. You can identify them by those who take punishment and abuse without serving it back out. Other things like generosity, discipline, patience, and last, intelligence, tested in that order, let you know you have a genuine and thoughtful Umanu. The seven virtues are always difficult to fake, especially for long and under duress. Suffering tends to weather the brittle veneer of virtue in all but those who truly have it. Which is why suffering exists and why it always will exist, and why we embrace it as part of conditioning the priests."

"The seven virtues being . . ." Yehoshiva goaded. He vaguely remembered the conversation with the Technician, but like all the specifics of that transformation, they faded the further from the Machine he got.

"Moderation, modesty, charity, humility, grace, patience, and industry. These are tough to fake on their own. Though experience can teach them, they are rarely innate qualities. We usually find them in the oppressed—in people who are abused, shunned, starved, and beaten by their peers. They do not hold a social status that anyone else tends to want to emulate, so you know it's genuine when you see it among them. This is the safeguard that prevents the ranks from becoming corrupted by frauds. That is how we select priests here. The path of virtue is a hard one and one that is fraught with suffering, and it's an easier path to stray from than to find. The final test of virtue is to correct those mortal injustices and give the person power, wealth, abundance, and access to others with the same. If they retain their virtues, then they are rare indeed. These are the ones from whom genetic material is used to hybridize and evolve the primitives."

"Genetic material? What are you referring to? Are we harvesting the people *themselves*?" Yehoshiva was suddenly alarmed by the thought of the horrors he was expected to be a part of.

"No, not generally. If a person is martyred by their neighbors, their blood and tissues are taken, yes. Clones are made, females are impregnated, and they are integrated into the genetic bank for analysis to determine which genes are the ones most highly correlated with those virtues. If they prove their virtue without dying, at least to a degree, then they are briefly abducted, and we extract reproductive material from them and use that to impregnate females who have compatible virtues. We try to shape the society we want by rewarding behaviors with opportunities, but since we don't *want* the virtues to be well known, we pretend to ignore the suffering and at times even encourage it, though only indirectly, as it can never be seen to come from us."

Yehoshiva was stunned by this glimpse into the dark recesses of this operation, especially being that it was in the full view and approval of the empire itself. "How is this anything more than colonization then? How do we justify this morally? Isn't this basically how we treat livestock? Isn't this the same as slavery? Why..." He couldn't ask all the questions he had racing though his mind. They all tried to come out at once, and as they tried to force through his mouth all at once, they just got stuck, and his face fell into a horrified and confused expression.

Clark held his hands up in a defensive posture. "We do nothing to hurt the primitives. Our purpose is to serve their god in the best way we know how. The goal is to achieve a virtuous society, so we facilitate that. It's also to develop society. We facilitate that. It's also to ensure that the virtues we enforce are also true and meaningful. Yes, it is a breeding program. These operations always are, by necessity, and that means that those who fail to meet the standard are eliminated over time. Usually, a plague or a systemic collapse is useful for this, and we select the Umanu whom we see value in beforehand and mark them for genetic extraction. The primitives do these things to themselves. We merely pick up the pieces." He held his hands palm up to beg for Yehoshiva's approval.

Yehoshiva thought for a moment, shaking his head. "But *we* build the society around them. We design the institutions, don't we? None of this is organic to these people. We are creating the institutions that they destroy. How can it be that they do these things to themselves?"

Clark shrugged and said, "Because they already do it to themselves without those systems."

Yehoshiva sat silent for a moment thinking. He remembered the Machine; he remembered that these systems *did* arise over time on their own, and they were brutally self-destructive. He remembered that a virtuous society ultimately was the goal, and that was barely achievable without the Machine itself, but Clark seemed to be saying there was another way too. That they were simply doing what the Machine did, accelerating the development of these primitives. It was too much to take in for one night. He was still unsure where he fit in and what he would be required to do.

He made his excuses as he stood up. He didn't feel good about any of this. Coupled with his trepidation at being so far from home and having to learn everything to fit into a completely foreign environment, he now had to weigh the morality of his purpose here. It was logical, and it was true, but it meant that creating virtue inherent in the society he was Master over would require him to facilitate and encourage the sins that allowed those virtues to shine brighter. He had many questions still, but his conscience needed to be settled first.

He wasn't so sure anymore it wouldn't be better to just be a farmer.

8

Morality used to be absolute. Morality was black and white. You did not commit murder, you did not take from your neighbor, you did not lie, you honored God, and you honored your parents through your achievements.

Yehoshiva sat on his bunk wondering how any of this would honor either God or his parents. How could creating a society that embraced sin indemnify him of responsibility for those sins? He could see how that could make a more virtuous society overall. But he knew the ends didn't always justify the means. He didn't know how he could keep his conscience intact while shaping the virtuous society he was obligated to help create.

He flipped through the Book of Rituals. He read each one and thought about how they shaped a society along a path of virtue. How did any of them really ingrain the deep learning they intended to?

He stood and paced his small room, slowly digesting the ideas that had been force-fed to him the week before.

How do I balance the outcome with the methods? Do the rituals indemnify us of our responsibility? He paused at this thought. He picked up the book again and thought about how many times they had been written in plain sight. *If the truth is not hidden, then it is only by sin that a person can fall. Is this* our *escape clause?* He reread the Ritual of Renewal.

It was elegant in its veracity. It was a process that sterilized the water so it could be consumed, but it also was true *every* time. Deviation from the ritual caused illness, which was because of sin. *Which one?* he wondered. Certainly sloth, greed too, gluttony maybe also. It was a dynamic that proved the virtues and punished defiance.

He decided after some contemplation that it was only by presenting the truth and teaching it and giving the primitives a known escape from the consequences of sin that he could be insured against his own guilt. So he had to understand these rituals in order to teach them. He could cleanse his conscience through them. From there, the choices the Umanu made were free of coercion. Anything that violated the rituals and their purpose was by their own volition.

He wondered if this would be enough, or if the rituals were comprehensive enough to provide a script for all of life's decisions. There had to be a catchall. He found himself wandering back to Processing. He needed answers. No one he encountered tried to deceive him, either by sparing his feelings or by mislabeling the reality. Each must have had this conflict in their own heart at some point and all found it easier to understand the purpose by confronting it head-on and rationalizing it however they could. He imagined the Book of Rituals was written with that very purpose in mind—exonerating the exploitation through purpose. Clark felt like a peer. More so than the Commandant, who had also been blunt with him, and even more than Marcella, who had her own battles to fight at this moment.

Acceptance of the logic did not mean he approved of the methods, but he still didn't know what was expected of *him* in all this, so it was merely academic at this point.

Clark was sweeping around the barber chair. Evidently another ship had come in the night and delivered more people for the operations on the planet.

"I was wondering about the priests," Yehoshiva blurted out by way of explaining his awkward entrance to Processing without a true purpose.

"Of course!" Clark put the broom aside and leaned against the counter with all his tools and combs. "What did you want to know?"

"You spoke about the inherent virtues of individuals, that they could be identified easily. I'm wondering how that's done." Yehoshiva had more questions than that, but that was as good a starting point as any.

Clark seemed to read through the apparent question, though, and smiled. "You're asking me how *you* can identify whether your conscience is clear by picking them out. You're wondering how *you* can live with yourself being part of a process like this." He looked down and grabbed a folded towel, unfolded it, then carefully refolded it and set it back down. "I'm not sure I can give you that assurance, to be honest. There are some that are good at that. There are others who don't have to be. I am the latter. I don't know if you will be able to live with everything you will have to do. Only you can make that call. But I can tell you that no society without this process survives itself." He smiled pityingly at Yehoshiva.

Yehoshiva knew this was true. He had no idea what he had signed up for, but now he was committed and had to see it through. He didn't know if there was a way out of his own moral dilemma, but he also knew there was no other way, and *someone* had to do it. He asked hopefully, "So how do I know that my efforts have succeeded? How do I identify the virtuous? How do we select priests? How do I make Umanu?"

Clark smiled warmly at this. "You don't have to create them. They are already there. You just have to know where to look and give them the right conditions to shine." He spun the chair around and gestured to Yehoshiva to sit.

Yehoshiva moved swiftly and sat, and Clark threw a leather smock around his neck and began lathering a soap and spreading it over Yehoshiva's scalp. He took out his stone razor and began to shave Yehoshiva's head again for the second time in a week. While he did so, he spoke.

"You will look in the gutters and in the darkness and find people huddled there. Abused by their neighbors and humbled by their circumstances. You start by finding the humble. From them there will be some who ravenously consume all that is given them. They will try to escape their conditions with drugs or wine, but there will be a few who will share what they have with those others in need. Of these most will be filthy and wear tattered clothes, wearing the aesthetic of their social status, but a vanishing few will repair what they have and present themselves as respectably as they can. They will be as clean and kempt as they can manage. They don't speak out against their neighbors or against their lot in life, but they face it stoically and patiently." Clark stopped shaving and stepped back to look Yehoshiva in the eyes as he spoke. "There's hope and wisdom in these people, and you will see their tenderness toward those around them betraying their closeness to their god."

Yehoshiva took this all in and felt a warm embrace engulf him as the hair follicles stood up on his back. He then looked up at Clark and asked, "How many of those are there truly though?"

Clark thought a moment, shook his head, and shrugged. "I would say one in ten thousand maybe. A city the size of Irka might have three. But we don't just look for those diamonds in the rough. We have to be content with lesser gems as well." He started shaving again. As he was finishing shaving the last of the stubble, he said, "You'll have to content yourself with finding near perfection and working with that. Even the purest heart can be tarnished by a corrupt system." He finished scraping and then toweled off Yehoshiva's head.

Yehoshiva got up from the chair, content that he at least knew a way to preserve his soul against the backdrop of this leviathan he was part of. He asked as he walked toward the door, "Do the rituals help identify the virtuous?"

Clark thought for a moment and nodded. "Yeah, I think they do. The virtuous can see the truth in the rituals. They feel a natural connection to God through them. Most will fake their obeisance to the rituals or do them out of habit, and once in a while they slip up and get away with it, but it always catches up to them. You can always spot fake virtue by the way they tell others how sinful they are or by how showy they are with their virtue. How public they are about it. Once you see the difference, you can't unsee it."

Yehoshiva smiled at Clark, feeling that warmth linger in his heart. He was no longer fearful of destroying the nascent inherent goodness of the people, but he still worried about what role he might have to play in facilitating their growth. He at least knew there was a way to keep his spirit clean.

9

Marcella and Yehoshiva met again in the inner compound. Her demeanor had changed dramatically. No longer vibrant, she was lethargic and downcast. She seemed to be transitioning through the stages of grief and in denial at the moment, unwilling to accept that her career trajectory had taken a hard turn. She had demanded the Commandant issue new orders for her or find her a way off the planet, but she was rebuffed. The Commandant said, "This was not my call, and you don't work for me. You are a borrowed asset."

She knew who had made the request. She just wondered why they had fulfilled it. They knew what had happened the last time, yet they still sent her back. They would realize their mistake soon enough, and they would send new orders for her. She would just have to wait here until they did.

Yehoshiva approached her as she brooded. "I take it you didn't ask for this assignment."

She looked up with disdain in her eyes. Such an obvious question did not warrant a response. She sat quietly for a moment before she added to the silence. "They're working on new orders now, I'm sure. It won't be long, and I'll be off this rock."

Yehoshiva's face betrayed his doubts, but his features eased into a hopeful expression. "Well, would you like to walk the city with me before then? I'm new here, and you're the only person I know."

She stood there for a moment not saying anything. She stared at him, curious about him and how this fresh young man was handling the shock of this wretched place. Her scowl faded briefly as she considered the request.

He started to speak. "Marcella—"

She cut him off curtly as that notion left her and she was reminded that she was now an *actress* in a production she never asked to be part of. "Katesh. Here it's Katesh. In your room at night, you can be whatever your mother called you, but out here you are whatever *they* have named you." She gestured savagely at the Commandant's offices and the other individuals milling around performing various tasks of seemingly little consequence.

He was shocked, and a look of hurt momentarily commanded his face as he turned to leave slowly. He hesitated in deciding which way to go and was starting toward the familiarity of his bunk when she called to him apologetically. "Wait. I'll come." She kicked herself away from the wall she had been leaning against and caught up to Yehoshiva. "What are you called out here now?" she asked, gesturing at the sky and the compound and everything else.

"Yehoshiva," he smiled as the relief and excitement injected life back into his posture.

They walked around the outer city and looked at the public works projects that had enabled the primitive citizens to thrive. It was a school system, a social assembly line, designed to teach the Umanu to teach one another how to do these things and to do them in a ritualistic way to ingrain the learning. Whether they understood the *why* was irrelevant, so long as they understood the who, what, when, where, and how. They could justify the why any way they wanted to, and they did with fantastic and mystical color that belied the predictable and mundane behavioral conditioning that took place.

They barely spoke to each other as they walked, Yehoshiva too nervous in her presence and Katesh too cautious in the presence of the Umanu to say anything out loud. They looked at each other and communicated with body language and flashes of the eyes, Yehoshiva more awkward and transparent in the messages he was sending with overt infatuation, but over time he eased into a natural rhythm. They spoke whole conversations this way in the reaction and contextual emoting only their conditioned minds could translate the subtleties of. The citizens watched them curiously, though with subtlety. Two Masters in their midst seemingly without a purpose was unusual, but it was not unheard of. So the citizens tried to remain casual and deliberately ignored the Masters so they could pretend to be ignorant of the need for sycophancy. The two Masters were content to pretend they didn't notice the people not noticing.

As night began to fall and the Umanu rushed out to put their waste in the septic system, the two Masters stood out of the way and waited for the mayhem to cease. At the least they would avoid getting any of the slopped contamination on them in an accident, regardless of how reverent the people were. It was nearly an hour before they were able to walk freely through the crowd again, as the bustling mob was unrelenting. The ground was covered in filth from the spillage and from leaking buckets, and the stench was overpowering, but the two Masters maintained their dignity and poise through it all.

As they walked back to the inner wall, they immediately stopped inside the foyer and rinsed their feet and footwear off and stripped as much of their outerwear off as decency would allow and went to the showers to scrub their laundry. It was a misadventure, but it was a reason to be out. They performed their ablutions and joined the dinner rush at the compound dining hall.

As they sat, Yehoshiva counted a hundred or so Masters there. The Commandant's staff and the landing pad crews, military personnel of some kind, scientists, and workmen—the mass of people at this city was as numerous as any town back home. Each had a code name, each was performing different tasks and missions each day, and each had a specialization they used for the betterment of the primitives to be rewarded with resources the empire needed.

Katesh just watched him thinking and sat silently contemplating the whole system they had built here and all the people it employed. She felt a tenderness toward this fresh-faced young man. He knew nothing of what all this represented, but the curiosity with which he absorbed it all gave him a sweet innocence that she hadn't seen in a long time.

He has no idea what this will do to him, Katesh thought. Her scowl had turned friendly as they walked, and now as she watched him, she could only pity him. *I'll have to help him where I can.* The protective instinct welled up from deep inside.

As they were parting ways for the night, Clark found them in the halls of the compound and called to them, "Hold up a moment!" He waved at them with a set of papers in his hands. "Your caravan to Bashram leaves tomorrow evening. You'll want to make sure you're packed, but only what's on this list." He looked meaningfully at Yehoshiva. "That means those booklets need to be brought back to me tomorrow, so absorb what you can tonight and sleep in late tomorrow. You'll be traveling in the dark and resting during the day, so you may as well get used to the schedule now."

Yehoshiva looked mournfully at Katesh. Her face reflected the burning anger at the injustice she had been served. This reminder of its inevitability tore away the brief escape she had allowed herself in the city that day.

Clark held out one stack of papers to each of them. Katesh was as wrathful as Yehoshiva was delicate when taking their papers. Katesh did not even look at them as she stormed off into the darkness toward her room.

Yehoshiva stood there for a moment watching her, the ice between them having just melted, only to be replaced by magma. He turned to Clark and said, "I guess this makes it real now."

Clark smiled. "You're going to set the destiny of these people. You're going to be a legend. Just make sure it's a good one." He smiled and patted Yehoshiva on the arm as he turned and walked away.

10

The journey was hot and dry, but it had been traveled by many with much less preparation, so Yehoshiva survived. The dromedaries were chest high on him and the Masters, so they were of no use for riding. They carried the supplies effectively, and the priests drove them on as expertly as the Bedouin herdsmen of their heritage.

Katesh walked ahead, wearing the same garb Yehoshiva had on. No one would be able to tell from a distance that one of them was a man and the other was a woman. She had hardly spoken a word to Yehoshiva the whole journey, but she was well aware that he was there. No new orders had been issued, so she was stuck with the assignment she had been blindsided with. Her demeanor was curt and unfriendly. Losing her highly coveted slot as the first officer of a freighter, even one as ragged as the one they had departed from, and being assigned here made her view everyone around her as a burden and an accomplice to the conspiracy that had defrauded her of her position.

Yehoshiva had tried to speak to her, but she cut him off before he could and made a subtle gesture toward the priests. They were not to speak openly in the presence of these priests. Though there was only so much that could be said with eyes and body language, that was the only allowable communication, and she refused to engage with him or look at him even for that.

The Umanu were primitive, but they were not ignorant, particularly the priests, who endured rigorous training to condition their attention to details in order to serve the Masters. The operation here depended on illusion, and any stray word that broke that belief system could jeopardize everything. Though Yehoshiva had been told all this, it was only through experience that he could truly understand. *He needs to learn the right way to do this so when he makes that inevitable mistake, he'll understand it better,* she thought as they walked in the cool of the evening on the hot sand. *Besides, there's no telling what Bashram has become in my absence, nor how diligently the priesthood there was maintained to the standards of the operational directive. It's better to remain circumspect until we know.*

They walked at night to avoid the heat of the day, when the sand would blister and burn their sandaled feet and the sun would burn their exposed gray skin. The night covered the signs of his distress at the hard journey, and though it was excruciatingly hot during the day, the sleep and the daylight allowed Yehoshiva time to ponder and understand the Book of Rituals. Though he carried the actual book with him, the pamphlet that spelled out the rituals specific to Bashram was more pressing to him, but their comparison was interesting. Even the slight variations from Irka's rituals made him wonder at how different the destination might be.

The Ritual of Silence was on the first page. "The new acolyte should ponder in silence the workings of the world they wander in. For God sculpts the world and listens with every ear and sees with every eye. God is not in the words of the acolyte. God is in the actions." It was an innocuous statement in its form, but the subtlety of the phrasing reminded Yehoshiva that the eyes and ears of this god's people were attentive to his every action and word. This was more than a priestly ritual book. It was a guide to remind them that they were being watched both from the party near at hand and from afar.

Another ritual was the Ritual of Ablution. "The acolyte shall present themselves fresh for new toil in God's name. For God cannot see the acts of a servant whose face bears the complexion of the soil, whose feet carry the manure of yesterday's journey, or whose hands bear the juice of yesterday's burnt offerings. A body wretched from the toil of the day shall not receive visions in the night, for God does not take service from common livestock. An acolyte must be ready at all times to receive the Lord God." It said to bathe regularly before going to bed and wash frequently. The purpose was clear: sanitation in a primitive society was absolutely horrid, and though he had not seen the way they lived in their clustered camps, he could only imagine their lives were brutish and short with or without the guidance of the Masters. His role as a model of behavior meant that he must perform these rituals in the sight of these priests for them to mimic.

The rules went on. The Ritual of Ablution gave specifics for the place of these rituals. All had a purpose clear to those "with eyes to see and ears to hear." Wash in a basin so you don't waste water. Remove your sandals and kneel "before the Lord" to let your body relax and your wet feet, head, and hands air dry before continuing on your journey. Be frugal with the water, but use enough to remove the grime. When you are finished, pour it out in a low point where it can settle, and cast the seed left of your fruit as an oblation to God, "and God will make the path blossom before you." If the path was traveled enough with enough water, a path of vegetation would mark the route, and oases may begin to form. The vegetation also served as a convenient directional marker for ships in the air to follow to the settlement should they become lost. Every ritual worked this way. Every rite was a choreographed perfor-mance of the actions a civilization takes to succeed.

When it came time for a meal, the Ritual of Burnt Offerings pro-vided a delicious and savory dish. The drippings shall be for God. The meat shall be salted and cooked over fire until it is black on the outside. It should be poked often to let the juice run out "as an offering to God"—and to make sure it's fully cooked. The bread should be unleavened, so it doesn't mold or cause bloating as easily. This ritual ensured the priest-hood wouldn't eat undercooked food and die of various forms of food poisoning. No meal shall be eaten in two sittings, as the remainders and the fat and blood belong to the Lord God. There was no refrigeration, and at least this forced the priesthood to cook fresh meals each time. It also conditioned them to cook smaller portions and to serve more con-gregants. *Waste not, want not*, as his mother had admonished him.

It was approaching dawn on the seventeenth day when on the horizon a green strip of land appeared. The heat had yet to start radiating from the dunes and bluffs, so there was no concern that it might be a mirage. It was the river, and even at that distance they were able to see the reflective gold-tipped obelisk shining with the breaking sun. "We will stop here and give praise to the Lord God," Katesh said as the priests scrambled to unload the tents and prepare a place for worship.

The Ritual of the Journey's End: "The Lord's servants shall present thanks and praise to the Lord God when their destination is near at hand, for the journey was long and desolate, but the Lord has delivered them from the wilderness."

The obelisk was still a few kilometers off. They normally would have stopped before the desert turned into the fertile river delta. His face betrayed his confusion at her decision to stop, but he kept quiet. Katesh was senior to him. She knew that the city likely sprawled much farther than it had before, and she wanted to avoid the filth and attention it would have invited had they kept going.

The sun came up fully by the time the tents were spaced out and set. The heat of the day was beginning to radiate from the sand by the time they were fully set up. The water was running low, and food was beginning to run out. Katesh signaled to Yehoshiva to allow the priests liberty to enjoy themselves. A brief look of confusion came over his face followed by understanding. He twisted the Book of Rituals in his hand slightly to indicate he understood the reference to the Ritual of Grace, which told them to use up the rest of their supplies. "At the end of a journey, the servant shall be given their fill of the victuals of the journey. For God's grace has been shed on the Master, and it is proper for the Master to shed grace on his servants. The Master shall present wine and spirits for the servants to celebrate God's mercy on them but shall not join in their mirth. As the toil belonged to their servants so, too, shall the spoils."

Yehoshiva was beginning to see the pattern emerge in these rituals. Sterilize *everything*. Keep your distance from the priestly servants, both physically and emotionally. Always maintain dignity and authority, and always be ready to reward good behavior.

The heat of the day passed. They broke camp after bathing with the last of the water and set off on the last few kilometers of the journey. The desert bore more scrub brush the closer they got to the delta. Even still, they walked for another kilometer before the first sign of green grass appeared, telling them of the proximity of running water. As the sun fully set and the moon began to dominate the sky, they came across a small brook trickling in a shallow wadi.

Katesh recited the Ritual of First Crossings. "And so as the traveler crosses the singing waters, they shall wash their faces and their hands and feet so that God may see their thanks. They shall drink deeply of the singing water as the Lord has sanctified its journey. But do not drink of the standing waters, for those are reserved for the meekest of God's creation. Fill the skins of the singing waters, and when your journey is truly at an end, mix that water with another so they may join in chorus in praise to the Lord."

Yehoshiva listened as she spoke, and a smile nearly escaped his mouth. This rite was to ensure that they only drank clean water. *Running* water makes noise; stagnant water is full of parasites. When you don't need the water anymore, dump it out so it doesn't foul in the water skin. The language of the rituals was designed to reinforce a behavior so that it would be observed religiously *every* time a situation called for it, thereby impressing the learning on the primitive brains.

He yearned to have a free and relaxed conversation with her again though. He watched her finish her rituals as he performed his own, and the priests began their own replicated efforts without understanding the purpose. They obediently followed the rites. Yehoshiva was able to sneak a moment alone with Katesh to talk to her, not openly and candidly like he hoped, but as one executive to another in the silence of the night and the privacy of a distracted entourage.

"Are you going to be okay?" he asked cautiously, nearly soundlessly so the conversation wouldn't carry.

"I'll be fine." She pursed her lips. "I've been here before. Five standard years ago, I left here. That's one hundred planetary years, but this place or the people won't have changed much, so I'll be fine."

"I thought you were only a few years older than me—"

Her hard stare cut him off, and he knew he had made a grave mistake.

"I only emerged from the Machine ten standard years ago. This planet has much shorter cycles, and these primitives die quickly." She glanced over at them starting to mill about, poking fingers in strange holes and examining whatever stuck to them before sticking the finger in their mouth to taste. A look of disgust joined the bitterness and anger already on her face.

Yehoshiva knew what she meant. These people represented the hand she had been dealt, to her chagrin. He tried to distract her from their antics. "What did your orders say you were here for? I thought you were a telemetry specialist."

This didn't improve her mood, and he regretted it intensely as she turned her contempt from the priests to him. "I *am* a telemetry expert," she said through clenched teeth as quietly as her fury would allow, "but my job is navigation. I am here to devise the calendar these primitives will use to separate the sky and the seasons. And the maps they will use for charting their world. So I need to give them weights and measures so they can measure the distance to the horizon so they can figure out how to predict the movements of the stars. Which means I'm here to show them how to build observatories and to teach them how to measure the time of day. Which means I have to teach them writing, all so they can transmit their observations to each other so they can consistently interpret what they are seeing. I have to do all this without using technology. I have to create a ritual for them and give them a reason, so now I have to teach them when to plant and when to harvest, which means I have to teach them farming, in the desert." She began to flush with anger at the colossal burden she had been given.

"I didn't realize you had been given so much responsibility." Yehoshiva tried to appease her and calm her down.

"And what is it you are here to do?" she asked venomously.

"I . . . I don't know. I wasn't—"

She cut him off with a raising of her hand.

"I'll tell you. You are going to watch them perform some tedious trick and learn how to reward them for it. 'Here is your sandal, milord,'" she said mockingly. "'That's a good little primate.' Then you're going to give them a touch on the forehead in a meaningful gesture that makes them feel like you are a powerful and benevolent teacher so they will begin to worship you." She stopped, though she was clearly not finished. She seethed, but a look of guilt replaced the other emotions. "It's not your fault. I just never wanted to come back here."

She turned away as she gestured deferentially. "It's time to leave, milord."

11

Shemesh was seated on a high-backed chair watching the priests perform their Ritual of the Censer. "The servant shall honor their Master and make the tabernacle pleasing to him. For the Master is their conduit to the Lord God, and the Master's mood is the mood God shall hear. Bring therefore incense of fragrant oils and saps and fresh flowers so the Master's mind may be put at ease." Shemesh particularly enjoyed this one because he had argued for its inclusion in the Book of Rituals. "The indigenous peoples stink. They roll around in filth all day. I can't think, let alone guide them toward civilization, if they smell like every foul excretion they and their livestock exude," he remembered saying. He smiled to himself. His reasons were personal, but it was an argument all knew to be true.

There was unanimous agreement, though the concern from the council was that if they treated the indigenous people like servants and made rituals exclusively to ensure the comfort of the field officers, then it was a slippery slope to subjugation and the deep-seated resentment that came with slavery. Consent to this point, too, was unanimous, even by Shemesh, though less enthusiastically, but it was ultimately decided that the ritual would be included because it was a reverent action and forced the priests to be more aware of the odors and smells of the world around them, which contributed to hygienic practices and gave them longer, healthier lives.

The priests would take more care to remove any offensive odor from themselves and to develop concentrations of the pleasant odors of the Tabernacle. This led to a whole industry of indigenous people scouring the landscape to find everything with a pleasant odor. In the beginning, they stripped entire regions of the flowers and trees that produced the pungent saps, barks, and pollens. The land was stripped of everything pleasant, and the animals that depended on that flora for sustenance moved on elsewhere or starved. It wasn't a successful arrangement, so the field officers were asked to endure the odors until the industry to domesticate and cultivate the plants could be established.

Shemesh was obedient but also eager to expedite the process so he wouldn't have to endure for long. He cut corners and made sure the priesthood understood this would be a critical metric on which he judged their obeisance to their position. He was particularly harsh on those who did not wear the particular spice he enjoyed that seemed to complement the primitives' natural odors.

As the supply of the spice dwindled, Shemesh appointed one high priest to serve him directly, to reduce demand for the spice to allow the supply to increase. This also changed the dynamic of the priesthood. The high priests often became too proud of their privileged position and were routinely murdered by other ambitious priests who thought themselves too clever to succumb to the same fate—only to find they were just as easily dispatched by their enemies. Shemesh was annoyed by this but did not discourage it. It meant the priesthood bore the infamy of the orders they followed and kept his name unsullied. He could use it to blame the primitives and their ambitions rather than reveal himself as the architect of their corruption. There were many unsavory things that needed to be done to the people that even he dared not play a direct role in. It was only when he had used them for all their potential that he allowed them to be removed.

These primitives were too clumsy to disguise their guilt, and any true inquiry would have pointed the evidence toward him as the mastermind, so he played a duplicitous game where he would conspire with one to eliminate their predecessor and then "discover" the evidence that led to the new one's execution. It was fortunate the primitives did not have a true social sense of justice or collection of evidence. If the other priests found out about the conspiracy, he punished the conspirator severely, but he only punished them for their foolishness in being discovered. They served at his discretion, and for them to be so careless as to leave evidence of their guilt was irredeemable.

This game became tedious to him over time, so he began the process of developing the competing cultural models that would vie for influence in the society: the economic system, science and industry, and authority. All were competitors to the others and to religion as well. Each could be pitted against one or several others at any given time, and the alliances could easily be redrawn to create a different social ideology.

Shemesh flipped a tetrahedron around in his hand, fingering each point, imagining the system they represented as he looked out on his city. Each of the four faces had a different gem of a different color and character, and each combination represented a different system or philosophy. One point represented the religion the Masters had given these people, another represented government, another science and technology, and the last represented economics. He thumbed the ridge between two of them and thought about the union between those systems and what that created.

A union of science and religion would be a society of philosophers and theorists. Religion and government brought justice. A union of government and economics strengthened logistics. Economics and science brought innovation. Economics and religion brought charity. And the union of government and science brought data analysis. Each one a system that could shape the society and what it would become with incentive. But these were the positive impacts of the union of those systems.

It was only in the combination of three of them that societies became one of four idealized states. Religion, science, and government created equality at the expense of economics, forming an authoritarian state. Religion, science, and economics unified into liberty in opposition to government, forming a libertarian society. Religion, government, and economics formed satisfaction in opposition to science, a socially oriented government, and a culturally conservative population. And science, government, and economics united into militarism opposed to religion—morality suffered, and the state became fascist. Each served a specific purpose at different times. It was his role to decide which was most useful at any given time, and contamination of any one institution was the key to creating the push mechanism to form any one of the four in varying degrees. Contaminate and corrupt religion, if only by propaganda, and you can create a fascist state. Contaminate government, and you create a libertarian isolationist state. There were always distasteful behaviors in every institution that could be highlighted that could help shape the direction of the public reaction and redirect them in a new direction. Repulsion was a powerful force. But it took a generation to make the change take deep enough root to affect the changes desired.

These systems needed to be established first though.

It was amid this process that he welcomed Katesh and Yehoshiva to his domain. "Welcome to Bashram. It's nice to see you again, Katesh." He spoke with a silky tone, his eyes tracing the lines of her body and face.

Katesh clenched her jaw as she replied to his overtly sexual greeting. "Nice to see this place is still standing. No thanks to you, I imagine."

The priests scurried past with their burdens, anxious to be away again, the worry plain on their faces and in their body language as they moved.

Shemesh hid a knowing smile as he began to point out the various features of the town instead of continuing the conversation with her.

He pointed to the obelisk, the outbuildings housing his priests, and the burgeoning cityscape of stacked stones and dried wood with thatch roofs and dirt floors. The fertile river delta was dotted with farms and fields, most of which were dedicated to supplying the priesthood with the fragrances they demanded. Few were for food, too few at least to provide for the burgeoning population that packed into the river delta. "Come," he said, "I'll give you the grand tour."

Bashram started out sparsely populated on the outskirts, but the closer to the obelisk they got, the denser it was. There were farms near the fringes of the city proper. The farms were not true farms in the sense of being cultivated. They were merely groves of trees of several varieties clustered together to make a cultivated forest. All other trees without an explicit use had been culled back and removed until more trees could grow. The "farmer" simply built a hut among the existing grove and began to harvest for sale of the produce. Land rights fell to him by occupation and defense of his territory rather than a deed or title.

The produce went to a buyer at the edge of the city. The buyer then sold the raw materials to an artisan, who would take the sap or the fruit or the nut and process it into a paste or a syrup or a resin and then sell it to a variety of clients who would produce a finished good from it. The same process for stones and gems and metals existed, and the more hands it passed through, the more refined each became.

Because the demand for the spice tree had been specifically addressed by *the* Master, Shemesh, the demand for it created a constant value relative to other goods. So it became the reserve currency of the city in many ways. All other products found a natural price relative to the seeds of that tree, and possessing those seeds ensured the owner was equated to the status of the priests relative to the Masters themselves. There was nothing being cultivated that was intended for anyone's purposes but Shemesh's.

Shemesh encouraged this dynamic. A natural economy formed, and the priesthood accepted more seeds in the process as alms for the Masters and their sacred knowledge. As long as the spice trees continued to produce, the wealth of certain citizens would grow. As long as the priesthood practiced and preached the rituals that ensured the hygiene and health of the people, the population would continue to grow, and the rival tribes in the mountain passes and along the coast would not be able to withstand the military advance of the culture Shemesh was developing. As long as the culture he was developing spread, the rituals, too, would spread, and the civilizing forces would overwhelm the nomadic forces of untethered chaos in the world. This was his charge. Though his methods weren't considered doctrinal, he was effective, and the supply of resources kept flowing, so Frontier Corporation asked few questions.

Shemesh walked ahead, explaining the various layers of the society around them. As they approached the obelisk, the buildings took on a different design. A group of workers were in the process of transforming an old, stacked-stone house into the new smooth-sided square design that seemed to be radiating out from the center of the city. The city was transforming before their eyes.

"This was my initiation," Shemesh said as he caught Yehoshiva watching the workers. "I gave instructions to build my facilities in this design, and the priesthood soon copied. As you can see, it radiates outward until the whole city takes on a similar appearance. You will soon see that every word and expectation you have will be copied and absorbed by these primitives here. Therefore, we must always behave in a manner befitting the results we are seeking to achieve."

Yehoshiva merely listened, his face betraying little comprehension of what Shemesh had left out. This statement was as much a warning as anything, and that he didn't seem to mean the latter part in a way that meant *moral* or *righteous* was lost on Yehoshiva.

"The people here are extremely pliable, and they are integrated into every aspect of our lives. It requires constant vigilance and exhaustive adherence to the rituals you have only just begun to understand."

Shemesh was proud of this living expression of his own personality. The city was his outward expression even as he was stifled in his personal expression. This city reflected his conscious self, and he loved it as he loved himself.

Shemesh showed Katesh and Yehoshiva to their respective quarters within the compound at the base of the obelisk. They were simple, austere quarters, each marked on the inside of the door with the same symbol that was stamped prominently on the cover of the Book of Rituals and their hatbands. It seemed this was the only place they could be anything but absolutely in character. Inside he was free to be Joshua.

Outside he was Yehoshiva. His room had a simple bed, a nightstand with a candleholder, and a desk-and-chair set. The desk held another candleholder for his evening readings and reports, a neat stack of blank paper to the side, a clay inkwell, and a feather pen.

He slid his trunk against the foot of the bed. After taking a look around, he sat for a few moments on the bed, taking in the new limits of his inner self. He had the urge to familiarize himself with the facility, so after putting his things away where they seemed to belong, he opened the door to the corridor adjoining the sleeping quarters of the Masters that led to the showers and the dining area. He stepped out and became Yehoshiva again. Everywhere he looked, rituals were meticulously painted on the walls as a reminder of the tasks they needed to perform—the rituals they were *expected* to perform.

He walked to the shower to bathe and found the Ritual of Ablution prominently painted above a bench. He stood bewildered by the room's plainness and noticed immediately a lack of privacy. He didn't see any gender-specific facilities, so he was trying to absorb what that meant. They were expected to bathe, even here with plentiful water from the river, as if they were in the middle of the trail through the desert—in the open, regardless of gender or decency. First the dry scrub to remove dirt and debris, then a cloth soaked in clean water to soften the caked mud and dirt, then a scrub with a gritty stone, then a rinse. By the end of the bath, he had used five pitchers of water. The scrubbing had abraded the hairs off his head and from his body but had left his skin tender after having never been abused this way before. He knelt there on the reed mat in front of the stone basin where he had bathed and waited for the water to evaporate from his skin before dressing himself.

Another Master walked in and gave him a disapproving look. Joshua wasn't used to being naked in public view and felt vulnerable. Though he had no shame in his own body, there was a certain novelty to the communal shower that he was still not adapted to.

"You missed your back, and your scalp looks horrendous," the man said as he unclad himself to do his own ablutions. He glanced at the floor and the volume of water leading toward the drain trough. "You're using too much water too." The man was not bashful about his own nudity, and Yehoshiva sought to model that attitude though was abashed at the indiscretion this individual had demonstrated.

"I scrubbed what I could reach," Yehoshiva said, looking around him at his tools as he reached his hand back to try to find the spot in the middle of his back that his arm couldn't confidently scrub. He contorted his body away from the man to keep some sense of modesty and averted his eyes.

The man laughed. "No modesty here," he said mockingly. "You have to hide everything about yourself out there, so you'll take whatever freedom you can get, and this is the only place to let God see his whole creation." He smiled and spread his arms and legs and laughed when he saw Yehoshiva get uncomfortable.

"Never been in a communal bathhouse before, huh? Well, you'll get used to it. You can cover up with a towel if modesty suits you better. Just make sure you are thorough with your hygiene. You can 'self-flagellate' with this." The man showed Yehoshiva a rough-baked clay brick with a hole through the side running the length of it. A knot was in the rope on either end of the hole to hold the brick in place and a grip on each end to pull the stone back and forth across the back. "It's the only way to do it thoroughly. You'll need to make it look reverent and ritualistic, so the ritual can be used in the field. When the primitives ask you why you do it, just remember to tell them, 'Because the Lord God has more mercy on me than I deserve, and I must remove all sin from my body, even where I cannot reach.'" The man smiled in that familiar muted way.

Yehoshiva wondered at him. "What is your role here?" he asked directly, curious why there were so many of his people in this city.

"I'm a mechanic. But here, my role is creating an aqueduct network and irrigation systems. I also show the indigenous people how to mill and how to mine. But my primary role is within this compound, building the sacred fortification that allows us to breathe easier without the primitives peeking in at us. This way we don't need to use their laborers in here, and it allows us to speak freely. I'm sort of a jack-of-all-trades. You'll see me a lot. Others probably not as much."

"How many of us are there here?" Yehoshiva asked.

"Twenty or so. We come and go. There is always a field expedition pulling a few at a time out to the fringes of the city or orders issued to individuals to head back to Irka for reassignment, so the actual number is one only Shemesh can really know at any time. It's important to be able to come back to a place and let your guard down a bit after a mission, but even here, we are under orders to observe strict ritualism to ensure we don't make any mistakes." The mechanic was more casual in his tone than the ritualism he spoke of should have allowed. He stood in a stone basin near Yehoshiva's and began a dry scrub-down with the stone on the rope he had shown him.

"What's your name?" Yehoshiva asked as he began to get dressed again. He had forgotten to pull a new garment out of his trunk. He felt the grime from the journey against his skin and stopped dressing, unsure how to proceed.

"Kimdu. What's yours?" The mechanic continued his ablutions with the ritualism they demanded.

"Yehoshiva." He looked around for some indication of what he was to do with himself now.

"I'll call you Shiva for short. Two syllables—that's as much of a name I can remember with everything else going on." Kimdu opened his eyes to the struggle plain on Yehoshiva's face. "You can put your laundry in that basket over there and grab a fresh wrap from that one there. These are universal sizes, so don't worry about not getting yours back. Give it enough time, and you will."

Yehoshiva smiled at this. It was a gesture of friendship he had not received from anyone else yet. Though to be fair, it was his first evening at the compound, and he had yet to meet all the Masters who were evidently in residence here.

Kimdu seemed to be in a mood to give information freely, so Yehoshiva asked another question of him. "Why are we here?"

Kimdu glanced at him, and a whimsical smirk came over his face. "You mean in the cosmic sense? I don't know. We are born, but our purpose is to sort the elements of the universe to a usable form so we can honor the god above us, who can then honor the god above him, and above him, and so on until the one true God emerges from the first

Machine as the first of His kind."

"That's a good synopsis, but what I meant was—"

Kimdu waved at him. "I know what you meant," he said dismissively. "We're here for resources, but we have to pay for them with our knowledge, or we'll anger the god of this place. I'll talk to you later. I'm busy now." He closed his eyes and carefully abraded his whole body while muttering the ritual and its steps over and over again.

Yehoshiva thought this a very practical measure and decided to adopt it in his own rituals. He clothed himself and left Kimdu alone to perform his rites in silence. He turned to the dining hall to see if there was something to be had for supper.

It was quiet in the dining hall, but the smell of alcohol was heavy in the background, with a distinct fragrance of spices and herbs. It assaulted his senses in a way that told him it was unlike anything he had been exposed to before. The walls were the same baked mud color of the rest of the compound, and though there was little decor to speak of, the smoothness of the walls and the polish on the tables spoke of the numerous lives that passed through these halls and shaped the society around them.

The rituals relevant to the dining hall were painted meticulously on the walls. On one was the Ritual of Burnt Offerings as expected, but on another wall was the Ritual of Spirit.

> The servant must prepare the way for the Lord into their hearts. The food they eat shall be on a pure surface. The drink they drink shall be from a pure container. The tables they give offerings from shall be purified. And the place of preparation shall be purified. The spirit of the fermented fruits the Lord God offers to his People shall be extruded and distilled to their purest essence, and the servant shall wet and sanctify all that touches the offerings, giving praise to the Lord through the recitation of the rituals of the day, so the Lord may smell the vapor and be pleased. The servant of offering shall not do the purification, but the honor shall be for those who share in the Lord's blessing.

The remoteness of the frontier and the need for sterility in all things required that alcohol be distilled and all surfaces scrubbed and rinsed and, finally, sterilized with alcohol. All the dishware, all the preparation surfaces, and all the tables were washed with it so that nothing unseen could come in contact with the food. The recitation of the rituals of the day gave the alcohol time to sterilize the surface completely before being wiped off. And finally, the lesson his mother had insisted on teaching him: Whoever cooks watches the rest do the dishes, and everyone shares in the labors of the meal. It was simple in its expectations but deep in its purpose.

Katesh came through the galley doors, revealing the kitchen behind her, looking for whoever was there to help with the preparations. She stopped in front of Yehoshiva. "Ah, good, you're here. I think you know what you are going to be doing while I cook, right?" She was in better spirits after seeing Kimdu's name on a door among others she knew from long ago.

"Yeah, I'll clean up. Where are the supplies?" He looked helpless while busily doing nothing.

"Behind the galley door, there are fresh rags and a carafe of alcohol." She gestured at the door she had come through. "You've cleaned before, haven't you?"

"Yes, my mother used to have me clean before and after each meal, so I have an idea of what to do here." He smirked.

"Well, this isn't your home kitchen, so perform it ritualistically and make sure you are thorough. Is there anyone else in the compound?" She asked, glancing back through the dining hall doors searching for her friend. "How many more do you think we'll need to feed?"

"I saw the mechanic, Kimdu, in the shower. I expect he will be in shortly," Yehoshiva said as he pushed through the kitchen doors and looked around.

She smiled. "Good. At least someone will be able to show you how we do the cleaning around here. I expect Shemesh will be along shortly as well, but I suspect everyone else is either in the field or has already eaten. I'll make four portions." She turned and went back to the kitchen to prepare the meal. "You'll need to start in here anyway, so start over there," she said to his back as she urged him through the doorway.

Yehoshiva obediently moved and set about cleaning at random, uncertain where to begin. The carafe was a glazed pot, fashioned from local clays and silicates made by local artisans, poorly shaped and hideously colored but functional. The kitchen was well stocked and well organized. Vegetables were sorted into bins by like and kind, live animals were in small cages in one corner, and fruits were separated from the vegetables in the opposite corner to prevent contamination and spoilage. Everything was separated and stored neatly. Along the wall after the fruits were the clay cooking pots and serving dishes, and beside that was the butcher table for the animals.

Katesh was annoyed at his illogical approach and started issuing commands as she grabbed a clay pot from the storage. "Start by sterilizing this, then go wash the butcher table." As she pulled the pot out, a clay lid slid off the shelf and crashed on the stone floor. "I suppose clean that up too." She carried the pot to the cistern to add water. "The first thing we need to do is teach the primitives metallurgy so they can forge us some good cooking pots," she continued, half to herself.

Yehoshiva grabbed the broom and swept up the shards of the pot lid and placed them in the bin next to the door. He grabbed the carafe of alcohol as he put the broom down. Behind him the door opened, and Kimdu walked through. "I thought I heard an intruder rummaging around in here."

Katesh smiled at him in a familiar way and laughed as she spoke. "So you're just here to help raid the provisions then?"

Kimdu put his hands up. "Well, if someone was already doing it, I thought I would get away with it and let them take the blame. I guess I'll help out if you promise not to turn me in."

Katesh pointed at Yehoshiva as she laughed. "Help that one with the cleaning. *I'm* doing the cooking."

Kimdu grabbed a rag and turned to help as he replied, "Well, that's good. I have been wondering what death might feel like, so I'm sure your cooking will simulate that nicely. It's fortunate young Shiva here doesn't have to endure this place very long now too." He winked at Yehoshiva as he spoke and dodged a well-aimed bulb root thrown at him in the process. It bounced off the wall next to the door, letting out a spicy fragrance from the juices left where it had impacted. He gestured to the bits of smashed bulb root on the wall. "It looks like your cooking *has* improved," he said, laughing.

With righteous indignation she grabbed a heavy wooden ladle, and wielding it like a cudgel, she stormed over to him. He closed his eyes and spread his arms as he said, "The Lord *is* merciful!" and waited with a smile on his lips for her to bludgeon him.

Instead, she threw her arms around his neck as she hugged him. "If I have to suffer this place, I'm not going to let you get out of it *that* easily."

He wrapped his arms around her warmly. "It's good to see you again, kid. I'm sorry you got sent back here," he said, commiserating, knowing she was here against her own desires.

"Well, it seems *someone* thought I was too valuable to be allowed to live a happy life." She flicked her eyes back out the kitchen doors as she spoke.

"Yeah, well, you know his worship demands only the best, and he gets what he wants," Kimdu said, rolling his eyes knowingly. He let her go from his embrace, and she stepped back and looked sheepishly at the floor.

"I guess I should be flattered then."

"I wouldn't be," he said with an apologetic smile. "Well, what are you standing around for?" He turned his attention to Yehoshiva. "Sterilize that butcher table, and I'll sterilize and set the dinner table."

Dinner was a stew of aromatic tubers, bulbs, and meat of a small burrowing mammal. A stack of flatbread was presented fresh from the oven, and Katesh, Kimdu, and Yehoshiva sat to eat, talking among themselves. Kimdu did most of the talking, recalling the first expedition and how Katesh and he were part of the team then.

"Shemesh was the expedition leader. Most of us were on our first expedition—not me, but most of us," he said winking at Katesh. "Those who failed to adapt were sent back to Irka and reassigned. Shemesh was a taskmaster, demanding everyone work more than our contracts demanded, and it always seemed to be toward something that made

Shemesh's life easier rather than anything else."

"That was a miserable time," Katesh added. "I was lucky I had assigned responsibilities from Merchant Astronautica that *he* couldn't interfere with."

"Yeah, well, keeping your neck out of the wringer was tough considering how intemperate you were back then. Shemesh does *not* like to be questioned in front of others, but this little tinder-spark could never be tamed enough to learn tact." He smiled warmly at her.

Kimdu explained that he had received a permanent assignment to Shemesh's team after establishing the irrigation network that expanded the river delta and attracted the first settlers from the nomadic camps. "My adept use of the people and their rudimentary technology to demonstrate the processes needed to establish a civilization was a highly sought-after skill," he said with false bravado. "My reputation spread to the settlement in Irka, where I was receiving reassignment. Shemesh had stepped in and refused the orders and insisted on my staying to establish the compound and help with the projects necessary to get things in order. Shemesh insisted that I was invaluable to the project and would not be allowed to be removed. And Shemesh knows quality when he sees it!"

Katesh swatted his arm as she rolled her eyes. "Truth is no one else *wanted* you," she teased. She knew it was true though. Kimdu was trapped there but had a reputation that preceded him everywhere.

"The Commandant at Irka relented, and new orders were issued stating I was assigned to Bashram 'indefinitely.'" Kimdu smiled bitterly at this.

Katesh reached over and touched his hand pityingly. She knew he had suffered a worse fate than she at Shemesh's machinations. She told Yehoshiva her story from her own perspective. "I was on the initial crew on a limited assignment for the Merchant Astronautica to figure out the magnetic signature of the planet at the various settlements. I was not part of Frontier Corporation but had proven very clever in disguising my instruments from the primitives. By using tools and techniques they understood, I established a system of celestial observatory monuments at different locations around Irka and other cities nearby to record the constellations most likely to be seen by the primitives in all parts. We set a photochronograph on the tip of the obelisks and tracked the sky the whole time I was here so Fleet could analyze it and come up with the constellations and calendar and everything else that allows the primitives to establish a predictive pattern." She swelled with pride at this memory. "But then, I was assigned to Bashram to do the same. Each settlement has a slightly different orientation to the sky, so we had to establish new references based on where the cities were positioned."

Yehoshiva asked innocently, not understanding, "Wouldn't they be the same though? Don't you base it on the constellations at the equator that are visible in most of both hemispheres?"

Kimdu cut in before Katesh snapped at him. "Yes, but for primitive species, you have to establish numerous competing but equally accurate ways of dividing the calendar. It's like dividing 360 into twenty parts or twelve or even eight. They are all meaningful and all accurate representations of the whole, but the added complexity of conversion isolates one group from another just a little more between two similar genetic groups. They have a hard enough time understanding the system in their own city, so you can keep them from sharing knowledge by changing things like their written language, their spoken language, their calendars, their holy days, and the rituals. The point is to divide them into distinct groups but have enough overlap that they are easily integrated with each other later on if that's what we want to do."

"When would you want to do that? Why wouldn't you always want to do that?" Yehoshiva asked.

Kimdu just looked at him kindly, as a father to his inquisitive child.

Katesh answered him much less patiently, "We are creating societies here that shape these people into a distinct culture with a distinct character. Sometimes you want obedient and docile people, so you create one society that behaves that way, and sometimes you want an intelligent and warlike people and create another society that behaves that way. Sometimes you want a society that's a mix of both, but you want the final result to be obedient and intelligent—you have to have the right levers in a particular order that allow that. Language shapes thinking—sharper language makes aggressive and orderly thinking. Holy days create genetic patterns. If you know how long a baby takes to develop, you set the gift-giving holiday at the beginning of the gestation, and at the end of it, you have a baby born in a specific condition. If you want tough people, babies should be born in winter when food is scarce and health is worse."

Yehoshiva nodded his head in understanding but not acceptance. "I understand all that," he said, "but we are so close to Irka, it doesn't seem like that could happen with as much interaction as these two cities have." He looked at both of them, searching their faces for clues to understanding this problem.

Katesh replied scornfully, "Leadership plays a big part in the shape these cultures take."

Kimdu cut in again. "Katesh was like no one else on that mission though," he said. "Shemesh immediately took a liking to her. Young and energetic, feisty, and intelligent, she was a prize to catch, and Shemesh wanted her for more than calendars and star charts." He looked at her sorrowfully.

Katesh looked down at the table, reliving the bitter memories of his propositions and advances, his threats and his promises—a psychological game that twisted her into a state of confusion and fear and fury that came to a quick boil whenever it came to mind.

Kimdu trod carefully onward, wanting Yehoshiva to know the history but not wanting to push Katesh to her limit. "He heaped praise on her and then tried to leverage his position to make her more than just a colleague." He chuckled as he tried to lighten the mood. "She ended up slapping him in the compound as the rest of the team watched after he tried to press his authority over her. We all wished it had been us to strike him like that, and we all silently cheered for her." He smiled, and Katesh let a smirk break through the anger she was just barely holding at bay. "He became furious, but because there was an audience, he instead recommended her for promotion and sent a letter of praise for her file to ensure she was transferred out of his domain before sending her on some tedious errand to Irka, where she would wait for the promotion to process."

"I was given a commendation for my work on the planet," she exclaimed. "And thanks to Shemesh's praise and recommendation, I was promoted to astronomer first class, which came with a transfer to a position on a ship in the void which I happily accepted and thought that would be the last time I would have to see him, but"—she gestured to the compound—"here we are."

"It must have been a work of cunning that required a lot of string pulling for the Frontier Corporation to convince the Merchant Astronautica to submit to Shemesh's request," Kimdu added.

"There's nothing that can be done about it now," she said dejectedly. "I spent the last five standard years on that ship and was content to never again have to live in such squalid conditions nor abide by the Book of Rituals either. Nor endure *Shemesh* ever again. It is a lifestyle that does not appeal to everyone, and it is especially unappealing to those who haven't chosen it for themselves."

The conversation went back and forth between Kimdu and Katesh for much of the dinner, telling stories from before and talking about what had happened since. Yehoshiva tried to ask questions and talk about the things he knew about, but he could tell his input was tedious to them. He was just a whelp to these two. His only experience was the Machine, and they, too, had endured and survived that but now had experiences as great as anything he had witnessed or performed.

These two had real-world experience that put the Machine's learning into practice. He was once again just a kid in the conversation, though he had lived a billion years and hundreds of trillions of lives. When the simulation ended and his People created the Machine for themselves, he was back in the real world the same person he had been, just more experienced. But he had merely overcome the first obstacle in his trek through life. So he could only listen while these two veterans spoke of what reality was like.

Shemesh came in at the end of the meal. Katesh hung her head and wore a scowl openly as he grabbed a bowl and ladled himself some of the stew. He pulled a piece of flatbread off the stack and began to eat. He said nothing for a moment as he indulged his hunger with a few uninterrupted bites. Katesh and Kimdu continued to talk to each other but quickly decided they were finished with their meal and quickly left to clean up their dishes and take their leave.

As Shemesh swallowed a fourth mouthful, he looked up and smiled at Yehoshiva. "How are you liking things here? Finding everything you need?"

"Yes, everything is well planned out. It is short on comfort, but I expect I won't be seeing much of this place once I get situated," Yehoshiva said, worried by the hasty retreat of the other two and being left alone with the very person he had just been warned about.

"Well, that may be true of most, but you are on a different path. You are to be under my tutelage, and I will show you how to command the indigenous people. The priesthood will serve you, but that will require you to know what the aims of Frontier Corporation are." He took another bite of the stew, which had been lingering in front of him still steaming until he finished speaking.

"What are those aims then?" Yehoshiva asked warily.

"Well, you've probably heard that we are primarily here to develop a civilization out of the indigenous people so we can use them to harvest what resources we need. That is true. But also, we are here to help the god of this star system develop these people into more than that." He blew on the next bite and shoveled it into his mouth.

Yehoshiva waited for him to finish chewing and begin speaking again. "More than that, we need to create a series of competing systems. It's not enough to build one nation that has all the tools and all the power over the whole world. There needs to be many of similar design cultivated across the planet that will grow and spread and run into one another and wage war with one another. Wars of minds, of souls, of economies, of armies even, where they must work to overcome each other and overcome themselves to achieve dominance. The different nations we create will have different notions of the same things. They will call us gods, but they will call us different names than those we give other nations."

"Won't they eventually merge with one another and homogenize their culture until no differences exist?" Yehoshiva asked, remembering the nations in the Machine who stitched themselves together through war and conquest and eventually became one.

"Yes, but our role is to divide them through every means available."

Yehoshiva recoiled a bit. This was the role of a Technician. This was the adversarial role he wasn't eager to jump into.

"I understand your reluctance. You had no idea what you were signing up for when you asked for the position you received. No one ever does. But it is absolutely necessary if we are to aid this nascent civilization to reach its true potential and get it ready for its own trial of the soul."

"I suppose that's true. Competition is what drives most innovation, and it's what strengthens institutions against the failures inherent to their system, which if left unchallenged lead to collapse. . . . I just didn't realize I would be doing that."

Shemesh shrugged. "It's what you're doing regardless, so figure out how to come to terms with it either way. We will tour all the facilities here, and then we will determine what is needed. Once I feel you have reached the point of comprehension, you will go off to another settlement elsewhere on the planet and repeat this process there. Then we will wage war against each other. But the intent is not to destroy each other so much as create a spectacle that drives an eternal wedge between the two cultures so they will always be in competition with each other."

This was the first Yehoshiva had heard of what he was to do here. There was no indoctrination; there was no training. He would be thrown into the fire to lead a people and then face off against his own commander. *And this was expected.* "I don't understand why me though. All the others here have much more experience with the indigenous people than I do, and I am barely out of the Machine. I would think there are a million others who could fill this role much better than I."

Shemesh leaned back in his chair and raised his eyebrows amusedly as he listened to Yehoshiva speak. When he had finished, Shemesh explained. "You are right. Everyone here knows more about these indigenous people than you. Many even have been given much better assessments than you and are much better equipped to handle the nuances of building a civilization. That is why they are specialists. They will build the foundations of the civilizations and teach these primitives how to use them and even how to build them themselves. And then they will step back and be reassigned to other projects. Their jobs are to get these people up to the level we need technologically to extract resources and to keep them self-sufficient.

"I read your profile. You were not so good in the Machine to secure such a role. You were talented enough at watching the drama play out and knowing when to intercede, but you were not deliberate in your construction of the civilization, so the only value to the company you have is as a production manager. You will be here long after the others have all gone, and you will ensure the resources keep flowing and these primates keep producing. Once the fundamentals of civilization have been established and these creatures have developed enough culture to keep the process self-sustaining, then the rest will leave, and you will be here as a watcher.

"Your purpose will be to poke the hive whenever it gets too stagnant and inspire these livestock to destroy their society so they can create once again. To feed them information so they can make great leaps forward and reignite the scientific and cultural arms race. And to feed them misinformation to trip them up and divide them internally. In the end it may be your purpose to push these people toward collapse so the old, flawed society they constructed can be rebuilt. In the wake of every collapse, we can extract the vast stockpiles of resources they withhold, so it inevitably becomes necessary once they get too comfortable with our limited role in their society. For now, though, we are just going to build."

Shemesh watched Yehoshiva's face as he explained this all to him, reading the emotions and gauging the points that made him recoil with disgust. *That is what I will need to expose him to first,* he thought as he watched Yehoshiva recoil at the idea of orchestrating the collapse of the civilization for the sake of removing hoarded resources. *We will start in the mines.*

Yehoshiva excused himself to clean the kitchen before heading to bed for the night. He had that sense of foreboding he'd had before the Machine, and he knew he would face the horrors of his subconscious mind tonight. It would be a difficult night's rest.

12

Joshua stood on a cliff facing a great ocean. The sky was black, but the waves were the vibrant turquoise they would be in the daylight in some tropical island chain. He looked out across the sea and saw wave after wave rippling on the surface, each one greater than the previous. It was a long way off, and Joshua started to count. One, two, three, four, five . . . His mind fell silent, but the counting continued in some deep recess of his mind. When it reached forty-two, the first wave crashed against the rocks below. The second wave crashed shortly after. Then the third wave at a regular interval after that.

Wave after wave came in the same steady rhythm, until Joshua stopped counting. Each one got bigger, and the spray splashed higher. He wanted to run but felt his feet heavy, and the impending doom of the rising and ceaseless tide held him there unable to break free of the hypnotic but calamitous sight. When the waves got to the top of the cliff, Joshua felt the wave spray around him, but he remained dry. Then he looked farther, and the waves had grown larger until he could not look beyond them at how many there were yet to come. The next wave came and rolled over him, and though he remained dry, his feet began to get wet. Then the next wave came, and he was wet to his knees. The next wave came to his waist, the next his chest. With the next, he could feel the cold on his neck. Then the next wave crested, and he knew this one would drown him and carry him away.

But a force held him there and whispered in his mind, *Courage! Wait and see.* As the wave crashed around him, he suddenly found himself standing among a faceless crowd that looked out over the calm waters of the ocean. The crowd stretched to his left and right. Closest to him they looked like him, but slightly off. As he gazed down the line, he saw them slump and sag and sprout hair in peculiar areas until at the edge of his vision he saw what looked like a primitive standing there gazing out over the waves. He felt the power holding him there release, and he was ripped from that vista of the mind and dumped into the world of the body, tortured by the question of what it meant.

He woke suddenly in his room and felt a draft coming from under the door. The blanket had fallen off at the foot and ended up on the floor beside him with his head pinning the tail against his pillow and keeping it from falling off completely. He thought back to the dream and thought he must have kicked the blankets off in his effort to flee from the encroaching waves.

Though the dreams had come quickly when he closed his eyes, he did not feel rested when he woke. Though he had slept, his mind had not rested. He sat on the edge of the bed and thought about the dream. The first wave came at forty-two. *Forty-two what? Years? Generations of indigenous? How many waves had crashed? Too many to count.* There was nothing satisfying about these mysterious messages he often received when he slept. But the final vision of the people there chilled him. That was what he was meant to see in this vision. Though he knew not who the messenger was, he felt it was critical he understand its significance. The thought gnawed at his mind, and he could not go back to sleep. So he got up and went to the shower to perform his morning ablutions and dressed for the day. Dawn was just breaking, but he was not expected to be anywhere until it was well over the horizon.

He cleaned the kitchen, then decided to cook for himself, as he reasoned that no one else would be up this early. He cooked what he knew how with the ingredients available. He had watched many chefs and lived as more than a few in the Machine, and he understood how to cook innately. The flavors and the accents, what went with what and how much was too much. He knew how to create savory, soul-warming meals that made the body accept the tranquility of death only to be revived by a surge of nutrients revitalizing the vessel. He could cook anything—*in the Machine*. Out here, though, food was different. This planet had different foods too. Though they were fundamentally the same as what he had known in the Machine, he was feeding his own soul, and those meals were meals that spoke to his cravings. This rudimentary kitchen, though it was advanced for what the primitives could comprehend, was limited in its capabilities and its stock. He would have to make do with what he could. Though he was certain most of what he saw before him was not processed or selected by the Umanu, he was not shy about trying them out for himself.

He stoked the coals in the stone stove top standing in the middle of the room, all the ingredients and equipment arrayed on the wall behind it. He pulled some fresh eggs from under the caged birds in the corner and put them in a mixing bowl with some fresh milk. He minced some fragrant grasses and diced the spicy bulb root, took a few mushrooms and some sweet peppers, sautéed them all together, and then poured some scrambled eggs on the stone griddle to cook. He began to add the sauté when the egg started to dry out. He added some cheese curd and began to flip the egg into a loose roll before placing it on a dish.

He took some flatbread and warmed it on the cooktop, glazing it with fresh churned butter and sprinkling it with a dusting of a spice from the bark of a bush. Then he added a light drizzle of honey and plated that too. He diced three varieties of choice fruits and combined them in a bowl and then heated some water for tea. It all had an intoxicating aroma that awakened his senses and pushed fatigue to the back of his conscious mind. He removed the fuel from the coals to allow the stove to cool and cleaned up the scraps. Fruit scraps in the fermentation barrel, vegetable scraps in the stock pot to be made into a base for dishes. The mash from both would go to feeding the animals in the cages when it was completed.

He walked through the door to find a place to sit, and Katesh was already there. He paused for a second and decided he could make himself more food. As he turned to head back to the kitchen, she stopped him. "No, please sit. We can share this. It's too much for me alone, and it looks too magnificent for the cook not to enjoy the fruits of his labor." She smiled sweetly at him.

This was a different person than he had traveled with. He looked around nervously, wondering, *Is she talking to me?* He cautiously sat and waited for the contempt she had been showing him to return.

She set a clay plate in front of him, then a carved wooden fork and a wood-handled, chipped stone knife. "I want to say that I'm sorry for the way I've treated you over the past couple of weeks."

Yehoshiva was not certain that she realized just how long her attitude had been abusive toward him. He wilted like a flower in a frost around her now rather than enjoy the nourishment he had originally felt from her light. Which side of her was the anomaly, the guilt or the grimace? He accepted her apology with an obvious reticence. "I understand. Thank you."

"I'm not like that, you know," she said meekly as she arranged the cutlery and plate again in front of her.

"I'm sure you're not. You were very disciplined and generous on the ship, so I would say you have been stressed. I understand that I am new and something of an inconvenience to everyone. I understand that. I suppose losing your spot on the ship was a shock and a betrayal, and you had emotions that needed to be released, and I was a convenient nuisance to absorb it." Yehoshiva spoke cautiously, careful not to let his naïve heart step in any traps.

"Well, it was wrong of me to direct my anger at you. You are proving quite capable, and I never gave you the chance to prove it." Her half apology segued awkwardly into the subject that was really on her mind.

"You are in a very special role here, a dangerously precarious one." She shifted in her seat searching for the right way to express her thoughts. "You should know that you have an opportunity here to guide whole civilizations into the advanced culture we possess, and just because you are new doesn't mean you aren't capable. The rest of us may be specialists, but you are a generalist, and that is really what is needed here—someone who sees the whole picture and can understand what is needed rather than a person who can do a few things very well and neglects the things they don't understand. Every wheel has its hub, and you are to be the axle that guides it. I think you should know that's not a mean feat." Her eyes were downcast as she spoke, and she was fidgety. She obviously wasn't used to giving praise and probably wasn't used to taking it either. She was one who received her acclaim from her work, so she poured more of herself into work than she did relationships.

She continued, still stumbling over her words. "That's all beside the point really," she hedged. "The point is a wheel needs spokes too." She paused at the fragile analogy she was constructing, not sure whether to continue it or abandon the idea. She decided to persist, her hands actively shaping an imaginary idea that took on nothing of the form she was trying to express. "In order to leave a track, you have to work with your spokes. You have to have friends." She paused, and a puzzled look came over her face.

Yehoshiva just sat and listened. It sounded like she was trying to explain to herself why it was important to be nice to people. Like work was not a substitute for alliance building. But he guessed, too, she was trying to tell him she wanted to be friends. He smiled faintly, trying to encourage her to continue.

"I guess what I'm trying to say," she continued after shaking off her previous analogy, "is that you have an opportunity to be a leader here. You can earn loyalty from others by allowing them to fill in the gaps in your knowledge with their skills. Leadership"—she fought for the words—"is not the same as management." She nodded, approving of her own direction.

"Shemesh is a manager," she said bitterly. "He tells us what to do without explaining why or involving us in the decisions and stifles our potential." She sighed softly and then said, "I just don't want you to be like that. You can be something better. Just know you have others here to help you make these people achieve their potential and your own." She paused and looked at him pleadingly. "Do you understand what I'm trying to say?"

As she spoke, the words she used emanated from and betrayed the core of her identity. To Yehoshiva, every word and action, her comforts and discomforts, her attitude and the moments she liberated her underlying character in moments of joy revealed pieces of who she was. He thought about what that meant about her. She was probably very studious in school and serious. In the Machine, she would have strived to perfect the infallible society and would have been frustrated easily by the Technician's calculated destruction, yet she would have relentlessly opposed them at every turn. She had fight in her. Pride, intelligence, and stubbornness that would have made her a handful in her early years now made her very skilled in a few things on which she could shield her ego and build her self-worth. He wondered what her home life was like before the Machine. *Emotionally cold and distant?* But as he thought this, he considered himself too. Before the Machine, the whole world seemed unaffectionate and unemotional. So how was he any different? There was more to it than that. She was this way by her nature and was reinforced in the home environment because of it, which made her much better suited than he was to the world that had been created by it.

He was losing track of her words as she spoke, and his mind wandered. He shook his head vigorously to refocus.

Katesh paused, looking offended. "What do you mean by that? You don't want allies here?" she accused.

His face reflected the fear that welled up from the mistake in body language misinterpreted. "No, no. I want friends. My mind tends to wander. I'm sorry. I was trying to focus."

This did not help his case, and she felt even deeper offense that she was unable to keep his attention. "Well, I'm sorry I'm boring you!" The look of hurt tore at her features as she stood up to leave.

Yehoshiva stood up and seized her by the wrist to keep her from leaving and begged, "No, please, I wasn't bored. I was mesmerized. I'm sorry, please stay. Please talk to me. You're the only one here I know enough to trust. I was thinking about you and who you are. I wasn't bored at all. I was captivated." He blurted all this out, and a look of surprise overcame the offense she felt.

She glanced down at his hand on her wrist, and even as the grip loosened, a spark of something inside her she could not quantify compelled her to stay. She tossed his words around in her mind as she sat back in her chair slowly. *Captivated, mesmerized, trust, thinking about you.* She fell silent and studied him for a moment and couldn't find the words in her muted heart that understood that feeling inside, so she let her mind do the talking, as it usually did. "What are you thinking about as you analyze me? Are you imagining our future together, or are you questioning my motives?"

He was abashed and tried to correct her as the door opened. Shemesh and Kimdu came through the door, eyeing the food they had barely touched. "Must have been quite delicious," Kimdu said with friendly antagonism.

"You'll have to make your own. This is for me and Shiva," Katesh parried as she parted the meal between them, ending the moment she shared with Yehoshiva.

Shiva? Yehoshiva thought. A flicker of hope warmed in his heart, and he realized not all was lost between them.

"Well, if I cook it, you can bet it won't go cold," Shemesh bragged.

Kimdu rolled his eyes at Katesh as he followed Shemesh to the kitchen to clean the surfaces.

"Yehoshiva, meet me in the courtyard in a short while. We will go tour the mines today, and you will get a sense of the purpose of the operations here." He turned to the kitchen to prepare the meal for himself and Kimdu while Katesh and Yehoshiva ate the meal he had already prepared.

Katesh leaned in and spoke in a whisper. "Be careful out there with that one. Not everything he teaches should be learned, and he is going to look out for himself first. I imagine your predecessor learned that the hard way. So be careful."

A predecessor. Yehoshiva had not considered the fact that he was not the first to be in his position, and then he started to wonder what had happened. Though he wanted to remain in that moment with her, the warning brought him back to the reality at hand.

13

Shemesh and Yehoshiva stood at the edge of the open pit mine. The heat of the day drew the sweat from Yehoshiva's unconditioned body and evaporated it before it could show on his skin. Workers tried to cleave boulders with stone hammers that struck stone wedges. Rock chips flew as workers beat against the wall of the pit with little effect, but they stuck with it for hours before resting. Yehoshiva estimated that if this had been the pace set by the miners thus far, it was probably a mine that was at least a decade in production and would take another thousand years to get down to the layer of the crust where metals and minerals could more reliably be found.

"What are they mining for here?" he asked of Shemesh in a low tone without showing the slightest display of a conversation starting.

Shemesh had instructed him in this communication technique as they walked through the city. "This one is just a stone quarry, but even the stones hide valuable crystals. As you can see, there is much work to be done to make it productive. We have a copper and tin mine nearby as well, and we will instruct them how to make bronze from it, but this process cannot be expedited any more than it already has."

"Are we able to create a fire hot enough for that?" Yehoshiva asked.

"We can get close with charcoal, but there is no coal mine here, and oil is a few millennia away for them, so we have to rely on what we have. Unfortunately, we can't get the furnaces hot enough to purify the metals and get clean copper and tin, so there will be some residual metals in there. Once we have something harder than the stone tools they are currently using, we can begin to excavate deeper." Shemesh gestured at an area of the quarry near where they stood. "The core samples from that area came back high in quartz, and the assays came back positive for traces of gold, so we will shift this way and see if we can find a vein."

Shemesh pointed to what looked to be a foreman and gestured for him to come over.

The little man waddled over. He held a bundle of reeds in one hand as a symbol of his authority, and when a worker got in his way, he hauled back and struck the worker with the staff. Yehoshiva was alarmed by this brutality and turned to Shemesh to question it but received a scornful glance before he could speak.

When the foreman got close to the Masters, he knelt down and dropped his eyes, being cautious not to look them square in the face. Sweat glistened off his brow, and his breath heaved from the excessive weight he carried.

"This one is a brute, but he keeps the miners productive. Watch what I do and mimic this with these primitives. This is how we compel them to do what we ask," Shemesh whispered to Yehoshiva.

The man was less than waist high to Shemesh and Yehoshiva and even shorter when he knelt. Shemesh stuck his foot out, and the man leaned forward and kissed it.

Shemesh whispered to Yehoshiva, "If I step forward with the other foot, he will hand me his rod to punish him with it. If I withdraw my foot, he will stand and take our commands."

Shemesh withdrew his foot, and the man stood, eyes dutifully cast down as he did. Shemesh waved his hand slowly, palm down, and the man obediently raised his eyes to Shemesh. Then Shemesh pointed to an area of the quarry and took some seeds from a pouch on his belt and handed them to the foreman. He seemed to know what they were for and seemed happy with the gift. Shemesh then displayed both his hands palms down, and the man bowed at the waist and took three steps back before turning and running back to the quarry to shift labor to the section Shemesh had indicated he wanted them to focus on.

Yehoshiva watched the display and then glanced out at the quarry itself. Many miners were watching the interaction, but one seemed to be paying closer attention than the rest. The man had a red sash on his waist holding his woven reed pants up. Before the foreman had bowed and turned back to the quarry, this man had already warned his comrades, and they began to shift that way before the foreman came with his staff.

Shemesh waited until the exchange had ended and the foreman had left their presence. They watched him rush down the stairs into the quarry, swatting anyone who got in his way. He made his way to the back of the quarry and began pulling labor, kicking and beating other men until they ran from his presence. Shemesh leaned slightly toward Yehoshiva and in a low tone said, "That one is going to meet with an unfortunate end soon. I want you to choose his replacement."

Yehoshiva was startled at this revelation but replied, "I have a replacement in mind."

Shemesh smiled that muted smile that only they two could see and said, "It's the one with the red belt, is it not?"

Yehoshiva indicated it was. "How do you know the current foreman is going to have an accident?"

"Oh, did I say accident? I meant to say he would be executed," Shemesh said casually as he continued to survey the mine. "Tyranny is a tool, but he wields it indiscriminately. His corpulence is disgusting, too, and reflects poorly on our leadership by endorsing him. He takes his commands from us, and thus when he beats his employees at random, we are endorsing that behavior. He has served his purpose, but it has already been arranged."

Yehoshiva clenched his jaw at this and gave a hard stare back at Shemesh. This was not the behavior of teachers and helpers. This was the act of beings who sought to be worshipped as gods.

Shemesh ignored the stare. "We will give the new foreman a percentage share in the profits of the mine. We want to incentivize the economic independence of these primitives to diversify and strengthen the pillars of society." He thumbed the tetrahedron in his hand as he spoke.

Yehoshiva's curiosity overcame him, and he asked Shemesh about it. "Why do you carry that around with you?"

Shemesh smiled faintly as they watched the miners work. "It is a symbol of change and direction and outcomes. It is how I assess what is needed and the character of people and places and how to shape their direction."

Yehoshiva was puzzled. "How does it do all that?"

Shemesh said nothing for a moment and then stated cryptically, "It explains itself once you know what it represents." He was finished with the conversation, and Yehoshiva was only more confused and curious but let it go for the moment.

They stood for a while longer watching the workers pound their blunt stone hammers against the rock face and drive their stone wedges into the gaps in the rock to pry sections off. After they managed to pull a large piece out, the workers gathered the fragments and hauled them up the stairs to pile them nearby, and then one by one they went back down the stairs to go pound on more stones. Shemesh turned and began to walk away, and Yehoshiva followed. There were travois on the road to the quarry that pulled over when they saw the two Masters coming, and the drivers uncovered and bowed their heads in a gesture of submission.

Shemesh was proud of the subservience of these people. It was the high priest who conveyed the signs to the priesthood, who conveyed it to the rest of the population. The people here at least knew what to do to pay deference to the Masters, and a few got to practice in the presence of the Masters on some occasions. The foreman of the quarry was one of the few outside the priesthood who had a direct relationship with the Masters, so this made him a man of power and influence.

Yehoshiva asked Shemesh, "What were those seeds you gave the foreman?"

"Those were seeds of the spice tree that produces the sap I like. The trees are highly coveted, so they are protected by their caretakers, and it is very difficult to get seeds. If I give those seeds out, I am giving wealth that will extend beyond his generation alone, as it will keep producing year after year, and he can sell the sap for the incense or perfume for the priesthood. I have not given those to him before, so this is a proud day for him. Tonight he will die, but his wife and children will not go without. I am training the priesthood to do the same. They will leave seeds with the families of the slain as a sort of insurance. I don't want the family to starve simply because of the sins of the father."

"Why not just fire him then? Why go through this charade?" Yehoshiva still didn't understand the need to kill the man.

"This is a small but highly magnetic society. The technology and the prosperity and health of these people are the envy of all the nomads in the hills around us. They watch and they wait, and over time a few break off to join us here. There is nowhere else for people to go. If I were to fire the man, he would have no chance of getting another job anywhere else. Once a man meets with the disapproval of the Masters, he is shunned. They will lose everything, their families will be ruined, and their children will starve and resent us. And if they survive, they will work to destroy everything we are creating here. They will become bandits and scavengers and will nip at our heels for all time, preying on the frail and the meek. Trust me, this is much more humane. This is the way it must be done."

They came to the outskirts of the city once again, and Shemesh guided them to a grove of spice trees. There was a crude fence surrounding them, but near the road a sturdier stone fence was under construction. "They are very protective of their trees, and today I collect the seeds of the fruit to keep the market supply minimal. I know they are holding some back. Otherwise, there wouldn't be this many trees." He gestured at the dense grove. "We must control the markets, and I have made this tree valuable by my own preferences, so I must keep its value high, or we risk a market collapse and a lot of very unhappy primitive people."

As he approached the home of the landowner, a very wealthy man even by priestly standards, a man similar in size, shape, and color to the foreman of the quarry, came rushing out. He stopped short and nearly threw himself to the ground as he dropped to his knees, catching himself with his hand before he toppled completely over. His eyes downcast, he waited for Shemesh to present his foot to him. When he did, the man kissed it tenderly and then waited for Shemesh to either withdraw it or step forward with the other.

Shemesh held it a moment longer than normal to make the man aware he was deciding. The man waited obediently, but Yehoshiva could see the growing concern on his face as he understood the reason for the hesitation. When Shemesh finally withdrew the foot, the man stood and again waited to take his orders. Shemesh waved his hand again, and the man looked up into his eyes. Tears began to form, and he had a look of guilt on his face. Shemesh made a gesture with both hands cupped palm up and dumped the imaginary contents of the left onto the right hand, making a closed sphere from the two hands.

The man bowed deeply as he backed away and ran back inside the house. He could be heard rustling around, and then the voices of his women could be heard as well. He came back out carrying two sacks, one very large and the other one much smaller, a thick stick gripped in the same hand he gripped the small sack with. As he approached, he bowed again and fell to his knees and presented the sacks in the space between himself and the Masters. Then he raised the stick above his head with both hands for Shemesh to take.

Shemesh smiled at this. He had at least understood the hesitation earlier and the reason for it. Shemesh stepped forward and took the stick and touched the man softly on the top of the head with it. Then he threw it down beside the man and picked up the sacks. He handed them to Yehoshiva and turned around to walk away. The man let out a cry of relief and despair and raised his hands to the sky as the two Masters walked away.

"What was that all about?" Yehoshiva asked.

Shemesh explained. "I left my foot there longer than normal, so he knew I was deciding whether to beat him or let him serve me. His own guilt told him how to make things right, and he knew I knew what he was doing." He gestured at the small bag. "That was his private stash. That was going to make him the richest man in the whole city, but he would have been stealing from me to get it. He brought the stick out to ask for a beating in lieu of execution. Instead, I touched him on the head as a warning. There will not be a next time. His wails are for my benefit. He will begin scheming once I am out of eyesight, but these people are foolish primitives. They don't know that I can still hear them when they cannot see me."

On cue as they rounded the corner, the wails stopped completely, and they could hear the man yelling inside at his women and expressing his anger at the sudden loss of his great fortune.

"Tell me, Yehoshiva. Now that you hear his deception and know his scheme and see his actions, do you think clemency will work on him? Do you believe you can fire him? Tell me what you would do in this situation."

Yehoshiva felt like a tax collector now, extorting the fruits of the labor of these people for the benefit of the ruling Masters. The seeds they used for currency were only valuable because Shemesh made them so, and he used them to pay off the widows of the men he was ordering to die. Before he could speak, Shemesh walked on. He was finished with that conversation.

The sun was starting to set as they arrived at the temple. "Today we collect the offerings of the people. We don't have to actually tax them this way because they are mostly honest about the ritual offerings. For now."

Shemesh allowed Yehoshiva to open the door and pull back the curtain. The temple had a much higher ceiling than the priests required for their uses. And the doors were much taller too. But this allowed the Masters to stand upright as they entered the building and not have to stoop when they got inside. It was customary for all the wealthy and powerful to build their homes this way to accommodate a visit from the Masters. Today was collection day, though, and the room was lined with offerings. Live birds and burrowing mammals. Livestock of all kinds and produce from the gardens. Behind the mountain of produce and livestock were the words of the Ritual of First Fruits. "The servant shall offer their Master the first taste of the garden, the first calf of the year, and the first catch of the day. One of ten shall be the portion set aside for the Masters from all new wares, for their blessings and teachings do not come without sacrifice." It was a little blunter than the others, but the message was clear: one-tenth of all earnings belonged to the Masters. He was a tax collector.

Yehoshiva stood back as Shemesh surveyed the scene. He pointed to a sickly animal, and a priest who was near at hand put his hands together with both palms forward and arced them apart. Shemesh then gestured with his hand, cutting horizontally across the air in an arc where his wrist pivoted, and the priest bowed. Then Shemesh pointed at another animal of the same species and, with extended forefingers, brought his two hands together, then held up four fingers, and the priest bowed deeply. Shemesh then surveyed the remaining offerings and swept his arm over them and held up three fingers. The man bowed deeply again and left. Shemesh indicated it was time to leave, and he and Yehoshiva walked out into the night air.

Without being asked, Shemesh explained, knowing what was on Yehoshiva's mind. "The sickly animal indicates that the owner is having a hard time—that animal will do more for them than it will for us, so I had it sent back. Furthermore, a second animal will help them even more and will allow them to breed, so I had the other one sent along with it. I told the priest to give them four years' reprieve from offerings. It is understood that in four years' time, they will owe double the offerings normal because of my generosity. If they don't pay, we take their farm, and they will be asked to leave the city. We can't have unproductive primitives taking up valuable space. If they can't figure out how to make this work for them, we will take it away and give it to someone who can. As for the rest, I told him to send three in ten to our compound. It will be stacked by the gate before midnight and guarded until we take charge of it."

Yehoshiva was feeling mixed emotions about Shemesh at the moment. The animal was a magnanimous gesture and proved he was no tyrant, though he was not truly sympathetic to the plight of the offeror. It was simply calculated compassion. But the quarry foreman proved he could be. The threat in the grove was exceptional governance. Yehoshiva was still torn as to whether he could make that decision if he needed to. Today was about learning to govern, but the slime he felt on his soul from the way all this was done needed a heavy soap to cleanse away, and that wasn't available here. He remembered what Katesh had said that morning and wondered how she would have done it differently.

14

Katesh sat in the dining hall with papers spread around her, crude drawings and diagrams outlining the critical pieces of her job there. In her denial of the inevitability of her assignment, she had done nothing to prepare for the role she was given. She had some loose direction from the Commandant about the strategy she was going to use for each of the elements she was given responsibility for, but the actual planning and implementation were up to her.

Their language was to be written using cuneiform. They were to use a local weight and measurement standard, meaning she had to invent some metric by which to establish the scientific process. Then she could use this to have them make maps of their region and introduce basic mathematics so they could use that to measure the stars' positions in the sky and relative to the known objects in their environment. Then, since their calendar was solar, they would need to divide the stars into twelve equal parts so they could accurately measure the passage of time and would be able to predict the seasons. Then they would be able to begin farming in a more deliberate way than the seasonal organized forage they practiced currently.

She had a rough idea of the sounds they could make with their mouths, so she could relate a series of slashes to each one, and she would have a crude alphabet. This was simple enough. The more complex the sound, the more complex the symbol. So she could devise a whole sophisticated language in a few hours just by starting on guttural vowel sounds in the simplest marks and then using more complicated marks for consonants. Then she would develop the syntax and phonetic rules that would allow her to combine the letters into simple words and phrases.

Fortunately, she wasn't going to need to use the native language to accomplish this; the people were going to adopt the new language. This "language of the Masters" ensured that, as an open secret language, the priests would disseminate it to the masses, and the masses, seeking to gain an upper hand in society, would learn the language for themselves out of their own best interests. This task was already mostly completed but required a few more tweaks to help the primitives evolve more linguistic complexity.

The second task was also fairly simple. There was a set form for the bricks that built the city. It was twice as long as it was wide to ensure overlap and increase the strength of the structure. The consistency of the bricks, too, was a simple ratio of common environmental components that ensured the weight was the same and the strength was constant. Kimdu and his team had already accomplished the task of teaching the primitives to count so they could accomplish the mass production of construction materials. So using such a ubiquitous material as a standard weight and length made it easy to measure distances and weights.

Kimdu had laughed at this when she ran into him that morning. "You should call the length a foot, and the partial measures a toe."

"Why is that?" she dared to question.

"Because I made the box for the bricks big enough to fit my foot in, of course." He laughed. "I had to leave my mark on this world, and if any part of me is more deserving of such an honor, my dung kneaders should have it. They do more work than my brains ever have."

Katesh guffawed at the image of the excrement from every living creature haphazardly laid on the roads the Masters had to tread over. The idea of a bare foot kneading the fresh piles, partially baked and crusted by the heat of the sun, made her nauseous. She couldn't help but laugh at his sentiment and honored it with a permanent place in this city's history.

The next part would be somewhat trickier. Kimdu would need to help her with surveying the region, and accurate maps would need to be drawn that could be used as a reference for the priests.

The Merchant Astronautica already had full-color topographical maps of the region, so she could use that as the basis of her maps, but that kind of reference could not be given to the priests, and it would need to be adapted to the measures she would use.

Just one more task to get done as the priests developed the fundamentals.

The fourth task was the one she was working on right now. She would need a series of observatories at known distances from each other in order to be able to measure the arc of the horizon so they could estimate the total size of their planet. This would allow them to determine the rotation speed and thus the length of a day. Then they could measure the number of days in a solar year, and from that they could divide it into quarters to give the seasons. Then those seasons could be divided into thirds to give an easy way to gauge the wax and wane of seasonal conditions and optimal activities for each month.

The planning required teaching the priests surveying techniques so they could get the distances and elevations correct. But the mathematics that would be required meant they would need to teach the primitives algebra and geometry and trigonometry; this would require very clever primitives to grasp the concepts. Unfortunately, she had already been aware of Shemesh's penchant for deviating from the norm in terms of priestly recruitment. It would be difficult to find appropriate candidates from the ambitious and power-hungry priests. She thought she might have to take some liberties with establishing a society of her own to get the types of priests she needed.

She couldn't help but smile at how this would gall him. She began to contemplate what sort of cult would be needed to attract the right sort of primitives to facilitate that.

Tammuz walked through the door at that moment carrying an armload of herbs to add to the pantry. "Oh goodness, that looks like quite a project ahead of you," she said without stopping. "I'll go put some water on for tea. I have some lovely herbs and flowers that will help keep your mind stimulated and focused and keep your body relaxed. So much wonderful flora here!" She disappeared into the kitchen.

Katesh could hear some pottery clattering and a fire being stoked from the embers of the stove. A few minutes later, a whistle signified the water had come to a boil and was ready to be poured. Another few minutes, and Tammuz emerged with two cups and a carafe of hot and fragrant tea. The medley of spices and herbs reminded Katesh of the smells of her mother's kitchen and a similar beverage that was very popular on her home planet. "That smells like home," she said gratefully as Tammuz presented a cup to her and filled it.

Tammuz nodded and smiled as she spoke. "The molecules that make up the salts and sugars and proteins that appeal to us are very similar regardless of where we go in this universe. The processes of life are not unique from one planet to the next, and the mysteries of the universe are not isolated. It's very easy to make any place feel like home when you know you can find home all around you in its assorted pieces." She blew at the steam on her cup and took a cautious sip of the concoction. An easy smile crested her weathered face.

"I was never very sentimental about home, but there were some parts that made me happy, and I think this tea touches on a few of them." Katesh smiled back at Tammuz as she gripped the cup in her hands, allowing the warmth of the ceramic to penetrate into her stiff joints. Writing and sketching took practice, and her hands weren't used to the effort.

"I never was either." Tammuz shrugged. "But the forests I grew up in held such mysteries and wonders, I fell in love with life and all the forms it could take."

"You must have had quite the experience in the Machine then," Katesh urged, eager to break from the mental strain of her planning.

"Oh, it was like anyone else's, I suppose. All the traumas and anguishes of learning to develop life and civilization, but I really enjoyed the process of shaping life to suit any environment." Her eyes glistened as they searched that distant memory. She chuckled as she recollected. "My Technician got annoyed at how often I would go back to the drawing board and evolve an organism into a myriad of marvelous creatures and use them to shape environments but then abandon them to start again. I had a wonderful time toying with nature and only grudgingly advanced civilization to the end." She smiled broadly as she bragged. "The Technician couldn't frustrate my efforts there, and everything she tried to do, I simply adapted to. I was 'a natural biological engineer,' they said. And so here I am."

Katesh vaguely remembered this same conversation years ago. But Tammuz was so gentle and kind, she had no heart to dissuade her from retelling it over and over. "I was not at all skilled in that aspect of it myself. I was very good at calculating the rotations and gauging the impacts of asteroids and setting my planets precisely to produce life. I wasn't very enamored by the evolutionary process, so I just got to the civilization as quickly as I could. My Technician kept destroying my civilizations, telling me I couldn't create an enduring one without understanding how life evolved and how evolution and environment shape them. But I wasn't interested. I would just take the most established creature in any environment and force them to become a civilization. Then I used the environment to split the groups. I used economics and technology to drive them as quickly as possible to the point where they were no longer subject to the environment and the Technician couldn't break them down again. I took a shortcut, and his report made it clear that he didn't approve." She smiled proudly.

Tammuz smiled back, her high cheeks squinting her eyes as she did. "You have to be true to who you are. The Machine always reveals that, doesn't it?"

Katesh raised an eyebrow conspiratorially. "We have to resist authority and its corrupting influence wherever it emerges."

Tammuz nodded in silent agreement, her eyes darting to the wall facing the courtyard where the local authority resided. "If you think of any way that I could be helpful to your work here, you be sure to let me know." She stared meaningfully into Katesh's eyes and took another long sip of the aromatic brew.

Katesh nodded slowly, confirming that she would indeed ask for Tammuz's help. "I do have something I would like your help with regarding my current project." She gestured to the papers surrounding her. "I was wondering if you could develop the crops and livestock for agriculture that the primitives will grow once I get their calendar settled and the primitives trained in it."

"Of course. I'd love to help," Tammuz said enthusiastically. "I have so much research going on, but life is leisurely in its evolution, and I have lots of life for leisure as a result." She smiled at her own wording before her brow creased. "What sort of crops do you want?"

Katesh wasn't sure what she meant by this. "What do you mean? High-nutrient crops and plenty of meat to keep the people healthy."

Tammuz shrugged. "Well, if you want a hardworking and stupid culture, you just give them lots of meat and fiber. If you want a smart culture, you need an entirely different diet. There is an epigenetic component, too, that is completely opposite of the expressed components. If you want a society to be strong *now*, you give it lots of protein. If you want the strength to be written into their genes, you deprive them of protein."

Katesh sensed a dive into the evolution she had so pointedly dismissed in the Machine. "I don't quite follow. What do you mean to have it written into the genes by depriving them of protein?"

"Well, dear." Tammuz softened her tone as she explained. "Your genes will code for whatever they need to be the best survivor in an environment. If an environment is lacking in protein and fiber, the genes will prioritize the amino acids it gets from them and increase their absorption efficiency. It strengthens in the genes so that every molecule of those proteins is used. If protein is plentiful, then the genes don't hold on as tightly. This is the epigenetic effect of diet. Whatever a body expresses phenotypically, the genes will reject phylogenetically. And vice versa. You do the opposite to the body what you want for the genes."

Katesh's eyes suddenly wore the weariness of another long process of thinking and planning that would be required to answer Tammuz's question accurately. "I don't know what I want then," she finally said with some consternation.

Tammuz nodded consolingly. "It's all right. We don't need to have answers right now. But you have a project that looks like you will need a lot of intelligence to accomplish. We can start there. You will want high-fat and sugar diets with stimulants in the short term. High protein, fiber, and depressants in the long term. In the short term, they'll be quicker and clearer thinking, and in the long term, their bodies will process the sugars and fats more efficiently, and you'll have more naturally intelligent people. So we'll take this wonderful tea and show the primitives how to gather the right herbs to make it. And I'll start working on high-sugar crops and have the geneticists work on livestock for dairy products."

Katesh let out a soft sigh of relief. "I trust you explicitly, Tammuz. I know you'll know what to do. We are creating a civilization, so we will need all manner of diets and nutrition to achieve that."

Tammuz smiled wryly. "We'll also need lots of different kinds of drugs."

Katesh was stunned but cautiously agreeable. "If you mean stimulants and depressants and such, then yes, I agree."

Tammuz tapped the cup in her hands. "We already have good stimulants, and depressants are easy enough to make. I'll work on finding *and such* as part of my experiments." She winked at Katesh and took her leave to go back to her garden in the courtyard.

Katesh smiled at Tammuz warmly. She was a free spirit and much more interesting than anyone else in the compound, maybe even the whole region. She knew she had a vital ally in this war they would have to wage against Shemesh's malevolence and misogyny. Tammuz was a friend, true to herself and true to her purpose, and Katesh really liked her.

15

Yehoshiva and Shemesh returned to the compound. Already priests were scurrying to and from the sallyport with sacks of produce, neatly piled in an elevated stone bin to keep everything contained. The caged animals were neatly stacked on the platform beside the bin, and the livestock was herded into a pen on the other side of the walkway to prevent them from getting into the produce. It took a little over an hour from the time they had left the temple until all 30 percent was staged outside the gate entrance.

When they opened the gate, Shemesh took a lit candle, which had melted almost down to the nub, from the alcove next to the gate. He plucked it out of the holder and replaced it with a fresh one, which he lit from the old one. Then with the dying flame of the old candle, he lit a standing torch in the courtyard and waited until the sounds of deliveries had ceased. By then a crowd of new faces had gathered nearby, waiting for the order to gather the offerings. It was imperative that it be done quickly and discreetly so the true number of the Masters was never fully known. But there were some things that demanded they expose themselves, and this was one of those inconvenient tasks that did.

"Geez, Shemesh, how much did you ask for this time? We still have a full pantry," someone said in the crowd.

Shemesh could tell who it was and wasn't amused but decided not to do anything about it. "I took 30 percent. We have to show them that our sacrifice carries a high price. Wouldn't you agree?"

The person murmured in reply and kept shuttling goods back and forth to their respective places.

Yehoshiva listened to the exchange and realized that the voice was right. The whole operation was run with the same zero-waste mentality the mechanic on the freighter had explained. Everything had a purpose, and everything had a place. The compound's internal ecosystem thrived with little left to be deciphered by the indigenous population from the refuse.

There was already a full pantry. This seemed like inordinate taxation of the primitives and would lead to so much more waste than necessary. *So Shemesh only did this to assert his authority,* he surmised. This again changed the way Yehoshiva thought about the interactions of the day. *Were they necessary, or were they simply arbitrary imperatives meant to intimidate?*

Yehoshiva began picking up baskets of grains and carrying them through the gate to speed the process and keep the observable movement of their compound to a minimum. The priests were certainly watching from somewhere, but Yehoshiva wasn't familiar enough with the layout of the city to know from where. As he came back into the foyer, Shemesh stopped him and pulled him to the side.

"The primitives are watching. You are to be their leader, so you are not to be seen doing manual labor. That is for the rest of the team." Shemesh's voice was low and stern but instructional.

"I just wanted to make sure everything was done quickly." Yehoshiva tried to defend himself.

"You're not here to labor. You're here to command. The rest of our team is meant to serve your vision. You are not their peer here. You are their manager." Shemesh's voice was not loud, but it was meant to carry. Yehoshiva caught the expression of one of the field team members who had come in that day. It flashed disdain for the comment and for Shemesh, but he kept moving.

"I don't think that is a good leadership mentality," Yehoshiva rebutted.

"You are here to manage this city, not lead it. These"—Shemesh gestured at the other Masters quickly shuttling back and forth—"are not your peers, as I said. You are in charge, and you represent the strategic vision of the mission here. You will need to learn that if you wish to be effective in your role."

Shemesh ignored the obvious signs of disagreement from Yehoshiva's face and turned and walked away. He stopped at the threshold of the inner foyer door. He stopped the Master who had shown the disdainful expression and began gesturing at the foyer and pointing imperiously at the walls and the produce. "I want it done by morning," Yehoshiva heard him say as he turned away. The one he spoke to just stood there with pursed lips and eyes filling with anger as he turned to the task he had been assigned.

Yehoshiva stood there for a moment as Shemesh disappeared into the inner courtyard. He watched the rest of his team moving back and forth for a moment and decided that he would not be that type of manager. He wanted the respect of his subordinates, and that meant he needed to lead, not command. So he picked up some baskets and joined the team in shuttling them into the foyer.

It took less than ten minutes for all the animals to be brought in and separated by species. The livestock would be moved to pasture, where one of the Masters would tend them. The shepherd was a skilled geneticist and a virologist. He was assigned to improve the milk production and taste of these livestock through selective breeding. Parts of the herd would be gifted to nomadic herdsmen as peace offerings and to ensure the selected genes would be passed through the uncontrolled livestock so, over time, the process would ensure that even the offerings were healthy animals with quality produce.

The caged birds were wild, but the staff agriculturalist worked with the geneticist to breed them for egg production and size. The ones that showed the best of the selected traits were released back into the wild. Those that laid fewer eggs and were of smaller size were brought to the kitchen to be eaten.

The burrowing mammals were prized for their fur, a product that was in high demand in the polar regions. The ones with the lightest fur were released; those with the darker fur were retained and eaten. The intent was that the lighter fur would dominate in the wild populations. The primitives knew the Masters wanted the dark-furred ones, and they were highly prized. So if they caught a dark-furred one, they were very proud. But as the years passed by, the dark-furred ones were harder to come by, and only the light-furred ones remained. The Masters intended it this way in order to reduce their numbers through both breeding and targeting.

The produce was sorted by type. The good ones were put into the pantry; anything with mold or rot was put into the stock pot, or if fruit, was used as a mash for fermentation and then distilled into alcohol. This was the responsibility of Kimdu to manage as part of his responsibilities in the compound, but everyone knew what to do, and if they saw something wrong, they owned the responsibility of putting that knowledge to use. Once the fruit and vegetables were stored, fermented, or turned into stock or a meal, the mash and trimmings were dehydrated into feed for the birds and the burrowing mammals, and their waste was collected for fertilizer where Tammuz experimented with her own variants of local plants trying to extract different virtues from them.

The dining hall was busy that night. Two separate field expeditions ended, and the teams returned during the day while Yehoshiva and Shemesh were out collecting taxes. The seeds had been distributed partly to the teams to sow while out in the field. A wild harvest of the spice tree would allow more nomads to bring goods for trade to the market and make the connection to the wider world more concrete and would create enough market inflation to force those specializing in the good to diversify a bit.

Shemesh kept most of the seed for himself but set aside two equal piles, the first for the priesthood to pay a widow's pension. The second pile was for Yehoshiva. "This is so you can adequately reward those who do service for you. This tree takes ten years to mature enough to produce the sap in productive quantities and only produces a few fruits each year that bear these seeds. The people know the seeds belong to us, but they try to hide them if they can get away with it, as you have seen. It is easier for those with only a few trees to hide the seeds because they aren't checked as frequently. So be careful who you give these to. You need to be selective and don't spread them too thin. Use the priesthood to gather the seeds up for you. But don't trust them entirely either. They are only as honest as they have to be. Remember that." Shemesh pushed the pile across the table to Yehoshiva and flopped a pouch similar to the one he carried next to it. "Carry this with you at all times. It is good to have the symbol of reward for the indigenous people to strive for."

Yehoshiva picked up the leather pouch. It had thick straps that folded over the belt and tucked back into the pouch and then back over to prevent it from falling off. "Consider this your wallet or coin purse," Shemesh said as Yehoshiva tried it on. He put the seeds in the pouch and closed the top with a leather pull string, a clever design using primitive technology.

Yehoshiva opened the door to his room and became Joshua once more. A release of anxieties came with the action. Almost a ritual of its own. He sat at the desk, lit the candle, and pulled out a paper and pen. He wanted to write a letter back home to his parents and let them know where he had ended up and what he was doing. But he could not find the words to say what that even was.

Yehoshiva had done those things that were required, and they were not done in malice, the things he knew were going to happen anyway. He knew they were necessary, but he still could not shake the guilt of being part of it. But what could he do? Jeopardize the whole operation by revealing the grand scheme? And then what? These people would take their more advanced technology and use it to bludgeon one another more efficiently than they had before. Was he right to assume they were merely primitive, barely socially conscious beings? They showed enough aptitude to rise to the top of their food chain. But the transparency of their behaviors and the selfish motives they carried did reflect a species still shaking off the chains of the primordial gene pool they crawled out of.

He looked down at the paper and found himself writing already. Nothing literary or coherent, but his hand had already found the words that leaked from his heart.

"Dirty, curious, short, hawkish features . . ." He was describing the primitives. Whatever he intended to sit and write was moot; this was what he *needed* to write. An outpouring of his learning, to put down on paper what he had witnessed so the details of the first impression would not escape him. Though his experiences with the primitives were quickly taking shape, his direct interactions with them were fresh and crying for expression.

"They are a socially adept creature. Perhaps deriving from rodent or primate. Mammal all the same. They are each one distinct and unique in shape and appearance, yet their basic features are similar. Dark hair, browned hairy skin. A pungent and sour odor emanates from all of them, which they don't seem to notice. The hormonal difference between them is evident in that odor. They are bipedal and around half the height of any one of us." He stopped writing and felt he was losing the essence of his heart's motive. He was a stone statue outside. This was the only place he could bare his heart about his experiences. He could think of no one he could write this to. There was no one at home who could fully understand. Though the Machine was their common crucible, there was suddenly a gap between this experience and what others could rationalize or envision. This was somehow more real.

Joshua suddenly felt alone.

The cold of the night began to creep in. His mind began to search inward. It pried apart the memories inside and dissected every element to seek the kernel of the experience. He could only see himself, an effigy of his own ego standing in the midst of the flashing memories. His ego was at one moment laughing hysterically as the faces of the elders around him gazed in disgust, words echoing from their imagined conversations: *What a fool he is. He thinks he's part of the joke, laughing like a jackal.* When it registered, his ego turned cold and melancholy; it began to weep uncontrollably as the images around him continued to torment his thoughts. *You pathetic worm. You think you know sadness? You have no idea what it means to lose everything.* The fury burned inside him suddenly, and he tried to shout back at the voices. *I have lost whole civilizations, heard the suffering of bacteria and the wails of lament from the widows of war. I know sorrow.*

Suddenly the memories and the anger faded, and he heard the voice of his mother. All was black. But her voice was clear and pure.

> You will always have the greatest part of my heart.
> Wherever you go, whatever you do, you will never be alone,
> and you will always have a home.
> No matter how far you travel, how long you're gone,
> or what scarring things you see, you will always be my darling,
> and you will always be my own.

He could still remember the press of her lips on the top of his head as he slept in his schoolbook. He could feel the tears forming and felt the warmth of love, and he knew the rest of his thoughts didn't matter.

A thought drifted through his mind that seemed to be whispered by the wind. *Love my children just as she loves you.* This was not his inner voice. It was one he didn't recognize. But it conveyed greater power than he knew anywhere but in the Machine.

It was the god of this world speaking; he could sense it. Even at that thought, the follicles all over his body stood on end in confirmation. As long as he treated these primitives—these *people*—with love and respect, he would have an ally on this world. At least one.

He began to write the things he admired about them: their industry, their curiosity, their adaptiveness to harsh environments. He sought out the good in them. The voice had spoken possessively of them. Joshua was certain his purpose here was more than mere resources. These people needed help. They needed to become the best version of themselves. It was his duty to make that happen.

He wrote his impressions of the people, what they looked like. And then he thought back to the Machine and thought about how life is shaped in the environment, how each person he saw in the city was a representation of the environment they endured and survived through their evolution. He wondered what the evolutionary conditions that shaped them had been. He found his paper suddenly full on both sides, so he pulled out another and continued writing. Every thought that passed through his mind was dumped onto the page, and he felt his mind relax and unknot itself, and he knew he could rest. There was no order to it, no consistent theme; the ideas bounced from one concept to the next, but it was down on paper, and it no longer needed to sit in his mind echoing and bouncing between his conscious and unconscious thoughts.

He disrobed and put out the candle and lay down. Joshua slept soundly through the night for the first time in weeks.

16

Dawn broke, and Joshua felt well rested. He couldn't remember dreaming, just a deep, radiant warmth engulfing him through the night. He came alert, suddenly believing he had slept through a whole day only to find the sky radiating the warm glow of the sun before it peeked above the horizon. Joshua prepared himself for the day and looked down at the notes on his desk. The scrawl was atrocious, the writing of a madman at the edge of sleep, but it was the formula he needed to put his mind to rest and look at the world with a new perspective. He put the notes on a stack in the corner of the desk and turned to the door to become his other self.

Yehoshiva went through the morning rituals with a newfound sense of calm rather than doing them mechanically as if he were a primitive emulating the Masters. He understood their purpose now and absorbed the rituals, going through them without the halting motions he had before. Something about that rest made everything soak in. His mind was cleared of all the disordered thoughts and encounters he had experienced, reordered, and regurgitated onto the paper. He stood in the courtyard taking in the dawn air. The compound was walled all around, but they kept it very clean, and the air there smelled fresher than the air just outside it. He could feel the moisture in the air and the hint of dew that gave the grasses at the edge of the desert just enough water to scrape out a living.

That thought made him admire their origins and their struggle. A plant forced to efficiency by the scarcity of resources. Of all the seeds that had been cast by the parents of those grasses, some had fallen closer to the river, and some unlucky few had fallen farther from it. Those that required too much water withered and died or never managed to go to seed. But those that managed to eke out a survival at the extremes of what was possible for its species were able to thrive when the seeds it cast got closer to the river. Then its children proved just as if not more capable than the parent. They thrived among grasses that were not used to such extreme scarcity. The next generation was better still. By the time the grasses got to the river, the variant requiring less water had choked out those that required more, though there was more than enough water to sustain both kinds together. The constant fight for dominance in the ecosystem proved that the meekest, who had endured more suffering, would be the inheritors of the world. It was a greater gift to cast the seed farther from the shore to make it struggle and hope the seed was resilient enough to survive and endure.

Yehoshiva stood motionless as he thought about this process. He heard an unfamiliar female voice over his shoulder. "I love the quiet of the mornings here. It lets you see nature for its untouched perfection all at once."

Yehoshiva turned and saw a woman standing there. She was middle-aged according to her face—not smooth like Katesh, but not creased and deeply lined like the Commandant's had been. She wore the same attire Yehoshiva had on except for the subtle difference of the stamp on the hat brim bearing a tree and root symbolizing her specialization as a biologist or similar field.

"I was thinking about the desert grasses," he confessed.

"Ah, I understand. They are magnificent, aren't they? They are hardy and resilient, and when they are transplanted into a place of higher moisture, they tend to dominate if they aren't drowned. I have been researching them to raise as a crop for these people. Come, let me show you." She beckoned Yehoshiva to her corner of the compound, where multiple plant beds were built up containing various species of flora.

"My name is Yehoshiva," he said midstride. He found it odd that everyone here took so long to introduce themselves, as if their names were secondary to their tasks.

"Oh, yes, mine is Tammuz." She spoke over her shoulder. "I wish Shemesh was more formal about introductions, but without the context of some common experience or interest, all the names you learn would be forgotten instantly anyway." The casual dismissal caught Yehoshiva off guard in its gentle bluntness. *There's no wasted energy in obsequious custom.*

As they reached the plant beds, Yehoshiva could see the desert grass growing in one of them. "As you can see here, I have this bed full of the grasses so I can control for confounding variables. I intend for them to grow until they go to seed to see which is the biggest and has the largest seeds. Then I will cull the seeds from the rest and replant those of the one selected. I have a second bed prepared for the seed of the second largest plant. The seeds of the first one I will take to my laboratory at the edge of the desert and plant in the austere conditions it came from. This way I can ensure that we can get the hardiest from there, and then I will repeat the process until I believe we have a grass worthy of developing into a crop. I am close, I think." She gently ran her fingers up the stalk of the grass in the planter. "These seeds are still too small to be used efficiently, but they are good to eat. I make flour from the seeds that don't make the cut. That's where the flatbread comes from." She said this proudly as she admired the seed husks of one of the stalks of grass.

"What are these other plants here?" Yehoshiva asked as she walked around to the other planter boxes.

"This red one is a mountain flower that has interesting medicinal and hallucinogenic properties. It is safe to eat, but it is an interesting experience if you eat too much. I am trying to separate the traits that produce higher doses of the medicinal properties and separate the hallucinogen for . . . other purposes." She smiled coyly. "Then I take them to the wilderness and replant them in the environment they came from and reestablish them for the primitives to discover."

"Why do you need the hallucinogenic ones in nature? Don't we want to discourage recreational intoxication?" Yehoshiva asked, concerned that Tammuz was herself dabbling a bit too much in the flower.

"You have just recently survived the Machine, have you not? So, wasn't it easier for the people to see you through the cloud of hallucination? We are here to honor the god of this system, so we don't come in like pirates and take without leaving a means for his or her people to do just that." Tammuz sounded defensive.

Yehoshiva simply nodded. He disagreed with the methods but agreed with the underlying premise. It had been easier for his People to see him and know him through hallucination, but they seldom retained that knowledge through the cloud of the drug. It was a far more reliable method to find those who understood and meditated on the nature of being. Even without seeing him clearly, they could see his works and understand the system as it was meant to be rather than as it was. It was often a mix of the two that led to the most profound leaps in understanding, but few could ride that razor-thin edge of inebriation and intellectualism without succumbing to the drug. When intellectualism proved empty in the void of renewed physical and intellectual experience, they relied more heavily on the drug to create the revelations they craved and that their reputations were built upon. Their later works became glimpses into the descent into madness, and the incoherence of their writings were no longer works of genius but became examples of the fragile precipice on which genius walks between madness and mastery.

Tammuz was admiring another flower at this point, yellow and short. "This one," she said, ignoring the internal dialogue playing out on Yehoshiva's face. "I just like this one. It's pretty, and it has a sweet aroma."

"There's no other use for it that you've found?" Yehoshiva asked, shocked by this woman using this precious space and resources for aesthetics only.

"No, nothing in particular. It is edible and would make a nice accent to a wine, but it doesn't have the caloric concentration to be cultivated nor does it seem to have any medicinal properties. I just like it. Not everything beautiful has a function. Sometimes things, and people, can simply be beautiful and pleasant and useless." She smiled and shrugged as she walked to the next planter. "This one has high sugar content." She pointed to a reed. "But it demands too much water to be used efficiently, so I need to work with it the same way as the grass there, exposing it to increasingly harsher environmental conditions to make it hardier. I believe that will even allow the sugar concentrations to increase, but for now I am just concerned about being able to at least irrigate it."

She moved to the last planter in the compound. "This one I just discovered up in the hills. It has a citrusy-smelling bark different from Shemesh's little trees, but it will make a nice seasoning for food. I want to cultivate that, but it also has some interesting berries that seem to be edible. I might be able to cultivate this into a couple of different things, maybe split the species and make two different variants for different purposes, one food, the other spice. We'll see. I'm still experimenting with it." She was almost giddy when she finished talking about it. She leaned over and started smelling it, rubbing the short leaves together, releasing a citrus fragrance into the air that she inhaled deeply as she closed her eyes. She seemed to relax a bit more than she already was, and when she turned back to Yehoshiva, she was somewhat dreamy eyed.

Yehoshiva could not help but like her. Then Yehoshiva heard another voice call to him from the courtyard. He turned and saw Shemesh standing there waiting.

"Looks like I am needed elsewhere," Yehoshiva said as he began to walk away.

Tammuz just nodded as she continued to smile with a dazed and relaxed look on her face. *What a strange woman*, he thought as he walked to meet Shemesh.

17

"Today we hold service with the priests. They are all going to be in attendance. This will allow us to review them and ensure they are sufficiently obedient to the rituals they have been given to perform. It's a somber occasion, but it comes with lunch, so it has its perks." Shemesh smiled, but just from the corner of his mouth so as not to appear too cheerful. Most of the priests could not read him, so they would assume he was always stern and severe.

"What should I do during this event?" Yehoshiva asked.

"Simply observe. There will be many of these priests there, and they are not all friendly to our mastery over them."

Shemesh made it sound like there was a growing coup in the priesthood.

"Why not throw out the priests you suspect are plotting?" To Yehoshiva this seemed like an obvious question.

"Patience is the virtue of the hour now. We need them to reveal *all* the priests who are corrupted. There is an attraction to their cause. They are searching for our weaknesses, and they believe they have found one," Shemesh said wryly.

"What do you mean? They believe we are mortal?" Yehoshiva said with some underlying sarcasm.

"They do now," Shemesh said as they neared the temple.

"I'm curious what you have done to plant that notion in their heads," Yehoshiva whispered.

"We shall see what they do. Don't worry. It is all perfectly harmless, I assure you. Just act wounded if they do something unsuspected." Shemesh spoke in a hushed voice as they approached the doors to the temple.

Two priests opened the door for the two Masters, and each took a knee and bowed their heads obediently. Then as Yehoshiva and Shemesh passed by, they pulled the door shut and secured it. Inside the hall Yehoshiva heard chattering. The smell of the sap and spices wafted from the main chamber. The high priest greeted them dutifully, presenting himself on his knees, and waited for Shemesh to present his foot. When he did, the high priest delicately kissed the top of it and waited with his shepherd's crook at the ready for the Master to punish him. Shemesh did not hesitate but withdrew his foot to speed the process along. He spoke simply to the man so he could understand the words. "All is ready?"

"Yes, ready, Master." The high priest's words were halting and not as florid as Yehoshiva had expected. They were just primitives in fancy garb.

"What do you do when I give thanks?" Shemesh asked slowly of the priest.

"Me . . . I make . . . to give hands in the air," the high priest said with a quiver of fear in his voice.

"And then what?" Shemesh leaned in for a closer examination to confirm the high priest was a conspirator as he had suspected. The scent of a yellow desert flower wafted from his robes along with the usual perfumes and body odors.

"I . . . priests are take those flowers to give Master thanks." The high priest seemed increasingly disturbed by the conversation, his voice quivering the more they spoke on the subject.

"Well done. Now let us carry on the ceremony as usual." Shemesh dismissed him as he had done with the foreman the day before. "Where is the foreman's staff?" he asked. The high priest went wide-eyed and ran to a nearby table and retrieved the item. "Good. Keep this handy and make sure to get it to us after the ceremony. We have a new fore-man to promote."

The high priest hesitated, processing the words and translating them in his mind before he bowed.

Shemesh cast a quick confirmatory glance at Yehoshiva as if to say, *I knew this one was corrupted.*

Yehoshiva asked with his own glance, *How do you know, and how many more though?*

The smirk on Shemesh's face said, *We'll see, and you'll know soon enough.*

The two door guards opened the doors to the inner chamber and carried the censers of sap, smoldering and leaving a plume of smoke, in ahead of the high priest. The high priest followed with a bowl of spiced oils. He dipped a stick in the oil and waved it toward the priests in all directions to sanctify them. When Shemesh and Yehoshiva followed, Yehoshiva finally understood the reason for all the incense. Seventy or so priests had packed into that inner chamber, and their bodily aromata began to overpower Yehoshiva's senses. The only thing keeping him from feeling nauseous was the spice and the oil that mixed with the priests' odors and made the smell of the room almost pleasant in an earthy way.

Shemesh sat on the chair at the front of the inner chamber and made a slight gesture to Yehoshiva to stand on his right-hand side. The high priest stood on the cloth runner down the center aisle and knelt before Shemesh. Sweat was beginning to glisten on his forehead as he started a litany that the other priests responded to with their own short, ritualized statement. As this went on, the priests looked more and more anxious. They had all been asked to bring flowers as a means of showing thanks to the Masters. Not all seemed to know why, but all looked eager to get rid of the extra measure.

As the litany ended, Shemesh stood and raised his hands to the air. "Now let us give thanks to the Lord God above us." The high priest stood and raised his hands in the same manner, and all the priests looked at him and slowly raised their hands up as well, visibly confused about what must have been a new ritual.

The high priest then said to the congregation, "Now give Master our thanks." With this, the overt transparency of the primitive priests betrayed roughly a third who could be seen making faces for ill intent, while the remainder looked around nervously and followed those most eager to lead the way to pay the Masters their due thanks.

Yehoshiva would have laughed at the comedy of the display had he known the whole plan. Seeing their faces telegraph their intent and their eagerness to rush to the front made the conspiracy laughably clumsy. He was sure they thought they were being subtle, but his Machine-trained observation skills made the body language of all these primitives, no matter how sophisticated, seem wild and overt.

The mob approached the throne Shemesh sat on, and as they drew the flowers from their garb, Shemesh recoiled in horror. His mouth hung open, and his hands shot up to protect himself from the flowers. His head turned toward Yehoshiva as he tried to flee, and with his eyes, he told Yehoshiva, *Play along.* So Yehoshiva followed suit. He made exaggerated movements of staggering backward and then diving behind the throne to block the flowers. He couldn't help but grin at the humor of it. The little harmless yellow flower Tammuz had shown him that morning was being thrown at them savagely.

Shemesh lay writhing on the platform, yellow petals lining his body. A whole flower lay on his chest. He gasped as he pushed himself back from the edge of the podium and the savage creatures that sought their death.

The chamber doors were bolted locked, and the priests stopped suddenly. Roughly a third of the priests had rushed to the walls when the chaos started, and another third stood aghast at the display and were confused by what was happening. The other third were crowded around the throne, expecting to kill the Masters, when they heard the doors lock shut.

There were the two door guard priests with knives drawn. Those along the wall began to pick up objects to use as weapons as well. They formed a defensive line to block the escape of the conspirators, who took halting steps to rush the defense and then looked back and saw the two Masters standing tall above them, unharmed and unafflicted.

Shemesh asked Yehoshiva with a series of muted gestures, *You saw who all the conspirators were, didn't you?*

Yehoshiva confirmed, *Yes, I know who they all are.*

Shemesh grabbed one of the conspirators by the hair on his head and lifted him off the ground. He looked him in the eyes and smiled a broad, evil-looking grin they had never seen on the faces of the Masters before. Shemesh bared his teeth at the man, who shook with a fear he had never experienced before. Shemesh pulled the ceremonial dagger from his belt and, in a quick motion, buried the blade in the man's chest and ripped down on it until the ribs splintered and the man's hair tore out. Shemesh let the body fall away as the remaining conspirators fled for their lives, crashing into the defensive line of those blocking the doorway. The remaining priests grappled with the conspirators and finally subdued them. They were outnumbered, but they had been so certain of their success that they hadn't thought to prepare for failure.

Shemesh's hand was covered in the blood of the priest-conspirator he had slain. But he found the high priest among the crowd and demanded him be brought forth. "Yehoshiva, execute this man for his crimes against us."

Yehoshiva responded negatively, unwilling to participate in this purge and fighting against the revulsion he felt for the eagerness in Shemesh's voice. "The Master has been betrayed by this man and should have the honor of vengeance."

Shemesh hesitated only slightly as he pulled his dagger and brought it down through the top of the high priest's head. The dagger pierced through his lower jaw, and the life drained from his face as Shemesh withdrew the knife. His ease with the execution said he had killed plenty of these primitives in the past, and he seemed to relish the experience more than he should have, given his position.

Yehoshiva looked on at the display, mortified by the bloodlust his boss displayed but duty bound to hold his tongue and keep his impulses in check. His experiences in the Machine made it easier to contend with the situation emotionally, and there was no denying the guilt of these men in their attempt. But he was not eager to be part of a scheme he had no part in making and was not certain now that their rebellion was unjustified.

Shemesh saw the hesitation and understood. "Who among you shall avenge your Masters in this attempt on our lives?" he bellowed to the remaining priests, his voice a terrifying roar they had never heard before.

One man called from the crowd, already holding a conspirator by the hair. "I avenge. Masters no fear from I." He gritted his teeth as he held the captive.

Shemesh gestured to Yehoshiva to give him his dagger. "Take this dagger and slay these perpetrators." The man took the dagger, which was a full sword to him, and in an ungraceful slash, hacked at the man who knelt before him. He went one by one down the line dispatching the conspirators until they all lay gasping, dying, or dead in a pool of their own blood.

"These men shall not be honored. Their families shall receive no pensions. Their groves and orchards and their homes shall be uprooted and destroyed. Their families shall be cast out and shall never be allowed to return until the tenth generation, for they carry the lust for vengeance and murder in them given by their fathers' seed."

Shemesh caught the disapproving glance of Yehoshiva: *That's a bit harsh, isn't it?*

"Furthermore, their lands shall be salted so that nothing shall grow there, and the stain of their corruption shall be known by all," Shemesh added this point to assert his authority, to Yehoshiva's chagrin.

"The rest of you," he said to the priests, "show me the flowers you came to offer."

The priests obeyed. The man who had slain the conspirators proudly held his aloft. It was the red mountain flower Tammuz had said was medicinal. These people knew it had healing properties. Moreover, it was difficult to find and even tougher to get a fresh specimen such as this one, which meant the man had taken great care to retrieve it and preserve it for this very occasion.

Others presented more common flowers of the river valley. A few others had gone to some extra effort as well, retrieving desert flowers with no known special properties but rare nonetheless. One of the door guards had a river flower that grew only in an area infested with deadly reptiles, another demonstration of devotion. The other guard held a flower in a bowl. He had meticulously dug it up and had taken care to nourish it on the journey from its place of origin far to the east in the high mountains. *Tammuz will love that*, Yehoshiva thought. All these flowers demonstrated the effort the priests put into providing them. They represented the expense and the dangers they faced in order to acquire them, and though Yehoshiva was certain they knew the rumor about the yellow flowers, they had otherwise chosen to present different ones to honor their Masters and their teachings.

Shemesh pointed to the man who had slain the conspirators. "For your service on our behalf, and for the gift of the mountain flower whose healing properties are well known, you shall serve as general of our armies. You shall seek the courage and fortitude you showed today from the men who will serve you. You answer to the Masters only, and you shall have the acquired fortunes of these slain men as your reward. You shall build a fortress to the northwest and shall protect Bashram and the route to Irka. You shall train men to hunt the nomads who harass the trail, and you shall have your pick of these loyal men to serve as your advisers." Shemesh gestured to the handful of priests with more common but harmless gifts. "You as our general shall be called Sword by the Masters, for you shall be the tool of our retribution."

Shemesh turned to one who had guarded the door during the uprising. "To you, for your loyalty in blocking the door and for the great peril you placed yourself in to retrieve that flower, you shall be appointed Commander of the City Guard. You shall maintain order within the city, and you shall seek out justice for all citizens and enforce the laws which your Masters will set forth through you. You shall build an office at the base of the obelisk to be easily found at the heart of the city. You shall seek the most loyal and disciplined of men to serve in your ranks, and you will ensure that the law is enforced equally and without exception. Choose among these men who shall serve as your advisers. You shall be called Shield by the Masters, for you shall be the defender of our society.

"To you who also blocked the door and who bore great expense to bring a flower from a faraway land, you shall be the high priest. The rest of these men shall serve you in these chambers and shall fulfill the rituals as they are written. They shall be given their portion of the offerings, and their families shall grow wealthy for their loyalty. You shall seek only men of humility and obedience and honesty who revere the teachings the Masters have brought to this desolate land and which made it fruitful. You are the vanguard of our teachings and must live as an example to people here so they may see what honoring the Masters as servants of the Lord God shall bestow." Shemesh finished granting his titles and demanded a wash basin for him and Yehoshiva each to cleanse themselves.

There was blood everywhere, and the priests began to drag the bodies away and mop and scrub the floors. Even heavy cleaning would leave that smell of dried blood in the temple, so once Yehoshiva and Shemesh had completed their ablutions, Shemesh stood and called for the new high priest.

When he came in, Shemesh spoke. "From the stones that have built the homes of the conspirators, construct a new temple to the east of the river with the altar in line with the rising sun. I shall give you the specifications when the stone is moved. For now move the stone east of the river and make the ground ready. I shall send a Master to guide the construction."

The high priest bowed low as he accepted his orders. And the two Masters left the temple to head to the quarry. Shemesh grabbed the foreman's staff on the way out as the priests bustled about, still attempting to sanctify the temple.

"I imagine you have some questions or concerns," Shemesh said when they were out of earshot of the temple.

"Well, things were pretty clear to me once they played out. I imagine at some point you let them know that the yellow flowers, which we know are harmless, were somehow deadly to the Masters. Your purpose was clear too—to see who would use that knowledge to try and kill us. What I don't understand is what made you suspect it would happen today and how it would play out." Yehoshiva had many conflicting thoughts at the moment, most of them to do with the high priest who had died by Shemesh's willing hand.

Shemesh smiled, eager to tell the story of how he had devised the strategy. "Months ago, I was in a tent in the field. I have been scouting an area for the new temple for a while, so I was alone and having some tea that I asked Tammuz to prepare for me." He rolled his eyes. "You know how she loves those damn flowers. Before I took a sip, I caught the fragrance of the spice on the evening breeze and knew I was being watched. Not by just anyone, but by a priest."

He let out a muted chuckle. "They assume I use the spice incense in my own quarters as I do in the temple, so I am assuming he doused himself in the perfume as a sort of olfactory camouflage and came to spy on me. He was obviously used to the smell of himself when he arrived, so he didn't notice that he was in my nostrils before he was at my tent. When I took a sip, a flower petal went into my mouth, and I started choking on it. I spit it out, and then for good measure, I smashed the carafe of tea on the floor of my tent where the rest of the flower had been hidden. I feigned an allergic reaction and flopped on my bed for a few moments, making a scene and allowing my possessions to crash about. And when I heard the scented figure shuffle away, I writhed for a few moments longer before I stopped. I waited a while longer, motionless on my bed, barely breathing if I could help it, searching the darkness outside for any more noise. When I thought for certain it was clear, I went out and examined the footprints of the shadowy figure and found the weight shifted suspiciously to the right side." He paused, hoping Yehoshiva would pick up that detail.

He did. "Ah . . . the way the high priest favored his left foot and carried his weight on the right side."

"Exactly," Shemesh declared. "I then had to devise a new ceremony that would allow the perpetrators to exercise their knowledge under the guise of ritual. And the rest is history, as they say."

Yehoshiva wasn't so certain it was over though. "Well, don't you think it's likely some escaped? Don't you think some of them figured this was too obvious of a ploy and played their hand the other way?"

"Absolutely, but those are the people who are clever enough to hide their machinations. I don't want stupid priests. I would like loyal priests, but barring that, I would like clever ones instead." Shemesh was proud of how ingenious his plan was.

Yehoshiva wasn't satisfied with it yet though. "So of those who were left, who do you suspect was also a conspirator?" Yehoshiva asked, wondering if Shemesh even knew.

"Our newly appointed general, of course, the Sword," Shemesh said confidently.

Yehoshiva stopped for a brief moment and then asked, "What makes you believe that?"

Shemesh was prepared with his answer before the question was even asked. "Because he was the most eager to volunteer to slay the conspirators. He did not want them to talk, so he cut them all down before they had the chance to identify him. I imagine he was the organizer of it all too. He was well prepared with a flower that is the exact opposite of what the conspiracy thought they were bringing. It was medicinal, so he wanted to show he loved us and cared for our health. And it is difficult to find, but it is extremely dangerous to track down, as that is nomad land up there. That amounts to stealing, and they are very vigilant in protecting their territories. So it was most likely that he had an arrangement with them. And I suspect if there were any others that were part of the conspiracy, those are the ones he will choose as his advisers."

Yehoshiva was bewildered. "So you've given him wealth and title and told him to go build a fortress to defend us on the road to Irka? Doesn't that strike you as somewhat of a bad idea?"

Shemesh smiled again. "No, not particularly."

When Yehoshiva was not satisfied, he explained. "I have given him orders to build a fortress outside the city to the northeast. This means he will be in control of the only road on the path between the only two real destinations in this region. Yet as a conspirator, he is contemptuous of our rule here, so he will not build there. He will build somewhere else if he builds at all. If it's the latter, we won't have to worry much about the army he assembles, as they will easily be defeated in the field. If it's the former, I have given him the best possible location to build on, so any deviation from that plan will mean he builds on an inferior position and we can destroy him. If he does do what I told him to do and builds a fortress where I told him to, then he will not do a thorough job of it out of spite. He will be expecting that we will merely lob stones at him, and he believes he will be able to withstand that. But we control the provision for that fortress. He will be far from water and far from food, and if faced with a siege, he will not survive. So he will not do that, I can assure you. He will take the families of the conspirators, and he will take the acquired wealth, and he will go to his nomadic allies and will seek shelter with them while he builds up his forces to attack us."

"And you don't see any issue with that?" Yehoshiva still couldn't figure out how that was a good result of what had happened that day.

"No. Our city guard will be fully capable of defending us at that time. You'll make sure of it, and it will give us the chance to test their capabilities as well. Most people get to make their own enemies in life, but you rarely get to shape the conditions that make the enemy an army. We have such a wonderful opportunity to create the conflict that strengthens our people here." Shemesh said this admiringly. He was almost gleeful. "This has been a good day for us so far. Let's go and make it joyful for someone else as well." He raised the foreman's staff as he said this.

Yehoshiva was not joyful, but he was learning more about Shemesh's mind with every act and conversation.

TWO STANDARD YEARS LATER

18

Yehoshiva stood on the hilltop reviewing the defenses of the city. The people were becoming adept at the process of turning the mud into bricks and the bricks into fortifications. Kimdu had trained a small contingent in the techniques of surveying, and peering down the wall, there were few deviations from the engineering prints.

The last bricks were being placed on the gate, and the temporary drawbridge over the defenses was being installed. Sticks and woven reeds were used to make the drawbridge lighter, and tanned leather over both sides fortified it. The nomads with their rebel allies had already made a habit of harassing the workers with stones and spears, and the cost of new labor continued to rise. This gate would at least provide some protection to allow the population to recover and the risk to drop along with the price of the labor.

The Shield presented himself to Yehoshiva in the manner he had been instructed, kneeling and bowing his head. *Much more dignified*, Yehoshiva thought. *No threat of violence from this method.* Shemesh's preference had become even more sadistic, and the priests were now expected to scar themselves to show their obedience, drawing blood and leaving permanent marks. The priests began to use the scars as a mark of seniority in the Shemesh priesthood and would fill the scars with ash to make them stand out. Yehoshiva abhorred the behavior, but Shemesh reveled in the new standard of rank.

"Have your scouts found the encampments yet, Farku?" Yehoshiva asked the Shield. His true name, Yehoshiva had learned, was Farku, and he began addressing him as such. Nothing bred loyalty more than taking a direct concern for the lives of the people he was the Master over.

"Yes, my lord. Few come back but have good report." Farku stood at Yehoshiva's command at attention as Yehoshiva addressed him.

"Good." He surveyed the field before the gates and spotted two suitable locations for the guard to make camp. "I want your best commander to fortify that hill and that one. I want patrols to go out at once, and I want constant reports of enemy movement. This gate will be completed within the month, and then I want you to go on the offensive against the raiders."

Farku hesitated as he searched for the words in the Master's tongue. "Soldier hard to get. Danger very big, money too small. Money not buy as much."

Yehoshiva fondled the pouch of seeds at his belt, disappointed that Shemesh had not deemed fit to increase his portion, even as he looked back at Bashram's arable land covered in the overplanted crop. He had his own supply in production, but the rate at which they bore fruit meant he still had to rely on his allowance from Shemesh. It was difficult to reward the soldiers for their hardship without a constant supply, but the rapid inflation of the seeds made it more expensive to incentivize the people to take such risks. These people could not see the benefit inherent in their task to repel the marauders, and more recruits were needed after every clash. "They will be adequately compensated for their risk. Meanwhile, give these to the families of those lost. Three each." He handed Farku the remainder of what was in his pouch and dismissed him.

Farku bowed deeply while cupping the seeds and took two steps back before turning and heading off toward the gate.

Yehoshiva doubted the scouts that had not returned had all been killed. Many were recruited from the jail and poor areas of the city and found nothing from their past life worth returning to. He wondered what incentive the Sword had to recruit such people, or if his growing mystique was enough on its own.

The Sword stood at the edge of his encampment listening to the cries of a newborn baby behind him. The nomads were sympathetic to his cause and traded food and supplies for the forged weapons and armor the city could provide. The only way he could get those was by killing or recruiting the soldiers that were sent out after him. He couldn't get enough to keep the bellies of his people from growling, but he could keep them from starving. And they were free, so people continued to flock to him. Two or three at a time, they'd slip out of town under the cover of night and bring what they could with them. Some simply traded; others came seeking refuge, which he was too tenderhearted to refuse.

The mountain flowers were in bloom now, so there would be a new supply of the medicine that would keep them healthy and of the newer, darker red ones that gave people visions. The latter was very popular in the city and provided a good resource for trade. He couldn't get enough of it though. They didn't have the expertise of the Masters to show them how to cultivate vast fields, but they had planted it beside every hut wherever they could get it to take root. It was a good supply, but it was never enough, and with more people coming every month, he could not keep up with the needs of his people.

He sighed as he looked around at his rabble. "That child will need to go to the tribesmen if you want any chance of her surviving," he said to his wife, a woman much younger than him who had come to his cause after his rebellion was already in full swing.

She held their daughter in her arms and looked down sorrowfully and rubbed the child's back as she slept on her shoulder. "They will not give her a good life. They will make a slave of her. She will be beaten and raped, and she will never know happiness. You know their ways," she pleaded with her husband.

"The only other option is to send her back to the city." He scowled at his own words. "She will be a puppet of the Monsters." His derision for that outcome made clear his disapproval.

"There are no good choices, but she will at least live to make that choice later," his wife begged him. Her choice was clear. The only thing they both knew was there could be no life for a child in their camps. Sooner or later death would come for them. That much was clear.

The Sword pulled his wife close to him and stroked his daughter's hair affectionately. He refused to name the child so he could avoid the heartache of the hard choices he had to make. No one did anymore, though they did not cease their practice of making more. He thought about the child's future. Both roads led to suffering, but he knew his wife was right. There was no good life for a slave girl in the nomad camps. Again, he sighed and finally acquiesced to his wife's wishes. "I will let you make the decision you feel is right for her."

He paused as he looked at the woman who had been with him through the hardest years of his life. Her skin dark and dirty, the sores of camp life leaving scars where her youth once radiated. He couldn't bear to see such a flower wilt from the water he could not provide. He spoke with the gentle firmness he reserved only for his wife. "Wherever she goes, you must go too. I will not have you share my fate, and I will not let her live without knowing where she came from."

His wife peered up at him, her eyes glistening. Unwilling to go to the nomads and reluctant to go back to the city, she looked to the horizon, and then at the camp, and then toward Bashram. There her eyes lingered longest. When she caught her husband's gaze, she hung her head.

"Don't be ashamed, my love. You carry my hope with you. But you must leave immediately. The gate will be completed soon, and the choice will be made for you if you don't hurry."

She nodded as tears streamed down her cheeks. He took her chin in his hand and raised her mouth to his. As he kissed her, he whispered, "Never forget that you are my dove." He pulled from his belt a carved wooden bird with a rope looped through it—an expensive gift. Wood was warmth, and every scrap counted. Time was survival, and every second delayed was one more missed opportunity. This gift was both.

She held her belly as she walked back to their hut, their home for so many years, to pack what she could for the journey. She showed all the signs once again. He knew his future was in her hands and her womb once again.

19

The great gate to Bashram was completed, and patrols began to venture farther and farther from the city in pursuit of the rebels. Though they were seldom productive in their efforts, Yehoshiva was able to turn his attention back to the city itself to try to bring some order to the chaotic crush of people. As food production increased, the population grew bigger. As their health increased, they lived longer. The simple balance of these two elements ensured that the city continued to grow, and the crush of people pressed at the bounds of the cliffs and walls.

Shemesh decided to lead the construction of the temple himself. Everyone figured he was designing torture chambers and sacrificial altars as part of it since he took such a great interest in its development. The stories trickling back to the compound of the miseries he had inflicted on the priests after the incident at the temple, and even more so on the population, were troubling for everyone in the compound. Whole farms were abandoned overnight, and the families had left to brave the nomad lands rather than stay in the city. Shemesh began to rely more and more on the priests to do his midnight murders of various primitives who dissatisfied him. When the wealthiest in the city, who supplied the goods that the Masters relied on, suddenly turned up dead, the miseries found their way into the compound as well.

When Shemesh told the other Masters that the old compound would be abandoned and moved into the desert near the new temple, it was met with confusion and dismay. This meant the Masters would need to build it and design it, and their other projects would take a back seat to this new ambition Shemesh had dreamed up.

The quarry had become more productive under the leadership of the new foreman, but he was aging. No longer were the beatings random. They were infrequent and justified. The foreman used the labor more efficiently, and rather than them looking over their shoulder, worrying about catching a thrashing from the foreman's rod, they focused more on work, and the stone from their efforts began to pile up. Shemesh used this opportunity to develop great works, including the new compound and the fortifications. Even with an exodus of people leaving the brutal regime he was developing, the projects he created attracted far more, and when the throngs of people began to overwhelm the system they had built there, Shemesh ordered new families to build farms farther upriver, outside the protection of the walls.

Yehoshiva was not oblivious to the gloom falling on the people there. He sympathized with them. Their farms were often raided, and the inefficiencies of their efforts compounded as their livelihoods were stripped. Yehoshiva found Tammuz here frequently as she attempted to coach the primitive people in the techniques that ensured the greatest production. While she was patient with the farmers, her patience was wearing thin with the constant raids and with Shemesh's casual dismissal of their plight.

"Another one of their children died last week," she said as she surveyed their patchy and poorly irrigated field.

"What caused that?" Yehoshiva commiserated.

"The usual. Poor nutrition, bacteria and parasites from lack of sanitation, poor insulation on their shack." She gestured to the thatch and mud hut made from the stalks of the failing crop.

Yehoshiva nodded. He didn't know what he could do about it. It was an issue of drainage, access to the river, stagnant and fetid irrigation ditches, and poor construction. The river was already stretched thin. Irrigation diverted water from the main glade at the seaside, and the environmental changes there were alarming to Tammuz, among others who had scrambled to preserve some vestige of the flora there for study even as the soil eroded from the constant breeze and left the land increasingly barren.

"Is there anything I can do to help out here?" he asked gently.

"No. These people will simply die off over time, and then someone else will come in and struggle a bit less." Her brow furrowed at the thought.

The death toll in taming a wild land was steep, but it was made even steeper by a callous leader who discarded these people so effortlessly by sending them to untamed frontiers. They had little to begin with, and their skills were not suited to such austerity. Though they made a little headway each day, their desperate efforts were quickly swallowed up by the desert, and their lives slipped hopelessly away.

This was only one example of the hundreds of farms left eerily silent as they failed from drought and disease. And nothing could be done to assist them at the moment.

Yehoshiva focused on his projects instead. Since the compound and the temple would be moving, it was important to build the wall for the inner city there too. The walls would be straight rather than the circular ones at Irka. They would form a large square around the compound, and the temple would adjoin it.

Yehoshiva showed Shemesh the plans. Without viewing them, he rejected them with a wave of his hand. "No. The wall will go around the temple as well."

Yehoshiva objected. "That is not allowable under Frontier Corporation regulations. The temple is a building the priests have access to. They aren't allowed inside the compound." He was certain Shemesh was aware of this but pressed the point anyway.

Shemesh got angry and yelled at Yehoshiva so everyone who was inside the compound could hear. "I don't care what Frontier Corporation regulations say. This is where I want the inner city wall." He eyed Yehoshiva carefully and glanced at the open door behind him, looking toward the courtyard where the other Elohim had surely heard them.

Yehoshiva looked at him suspiciously. "What is your reason for that?" he demanded.

Shemesh was not in the mood to entertain this young whelp who more and more frequently found himself at odds with his own directives. "The reason is not for you to know. You are here to follow my orders and run this operation according to my direction. I want the wall to enclose the temple, and I want it open to the priests."

Yehoshiva just stared back at him. The emotionless face of this adversary was difficult to read, even with the subtleties he was conditioned to pick up.

Shemesh leaned back in his chair and examined Yehoshiva.

Neither spoke another word.

Yehoshiva picked up the prints and walked out of the office burning with fury at the attempt to embarrass him. It would be his name on the order to enclose the temple, not Shemesh's. Though Shemesh would sign off on the plan, Yehoshiva would ultimately be responsible for the work and the violation of the policy. This thought incensed him. He was ready to leave the compound to go . . . *somewhere else.* Anywhere. But there was nothing he could do.

As he stormed off, Katesh stopped him. "Hey, Yehoshiva. Stop. Look at me." Her soothing tone penetrated the fire that burned inside, and he calmed down. He didn't forget the embarrassment, but he tucked the fire inside away, spread the fuel out, and let it go to coals.

She touched his arm. "I heard what he said. You'll be fine. We all witnessed that he insisted, and you will be fine. Just don't let him get to you. You have a job to do. Focus on that. Build the inner wall the way he insists, but do it cleverly. You're in charge of fortifying the city, right?"

He nodded. There was nothing that he could see to do about it. The way it was laid out would plainly give the priests access to the inner compound and deprive them of privacy.

"Do you have to start on the inner wall?" she asked helpfully.

He thought about it for a second and then shook his head. "No, no instructions were given specifying when to do what," Yehoshiva said with anger still burning in him.

"Then you decide what your priorities are, and if he doesn't like them, then he will assign you to something else. We all have jobs to do that don't involve construction projects to honor *Shemesh's* glory." She said this with a venomous bite.

He nodded. That was what he would do too. He was an associate production manager, so his priorities were production, and that meant production was the first thing that needed to be protected.

Yehoshiva looked into Katesh's sparkling black eyes and thanked her with a look. She blushed briefly and looked away. She touched Yehoshiva on the arm again and walked off to go to her berthing. She had some planning to do of her own and projects that demanded her attention.

As she walked away, Yehoshiva caught a glimpse of Shemesh standing in the doorway staring at the two of them. Though he was far away, his body showed signs of jealousy. Yehoshiva left the compound without a second glance back. He had work to do.

Kimdu was standing in the foyer leaning against the wall when Yehoshiva walked through the inner compound door. Yehoshiva wore his agitation plainly, and Kimdu stopped him.

"Don't head out there without your game face on," he cautioned Yehoshiva.

Yehoshiva stopped and started plucking at his tunic.

"You look fine, but don't go out there stomping around and angry. You'll give the primitives the impression the Masters aren't so harmonious here."

Yehoshiva didn't know what to say. He pursed his lips and gestured with the prints toward the inner courtyard in Shemesh's direction.

"Yeah, he knows how to get under your skin, for sure. What happened that's got you this worked up?" Kimdu asked, stalling Yehoshiva.

Yehoshiva couldn't find the words to speak but stammered out a few descriptors. "That damn temple. Shemesh . . . the rules say!" He stopped, sighed, and then began again from the beginning. "Shemesh insists on the new compound wall enclosing the temple as well. The rules say the compound is for *our* access only. Now we're going to have priests in our midst. Priests that Shemesh controls. There won't be any privacy, and that increases the threat to all of us exponentially." He began to get more animated as he spoke. The words poured out of him now. "Once the priests are in the compound, there is nothing impeding the spying. We will be under constant observation. We will have to guard every action in every place. We can't let it proceed that way."

Kimdu listened silently as Yehoshiva vented. Finally, after Yehoshiva finished, he commiserated. "That will be a big problem for all of us. Shemesh is designing the temple too, so it's going to be a bit tougher to resolve that issue."

Yehoshiva nodded and then stopped. "But *we're* building the compound." He stroked his chin for a moment as he thought. "Once the temple is built, it can't change. I'll build the wall around the area that will enclose the new compound, and then we'll build the compound to isolate the temple. We will dig it deep to keep our comings and goings secret. Tunnels in and out. A basement for our various projects and a false compound at the surface to comply with Shemesh's directives. *We'll* be isolated though."

Kimdu smiled wryly at this plan. "We can cover the tunnels with roads and landmarks to prevent the primitives from building on top or from being too close to the exits. We can have multiple exit points to prevent them from learning our patterns." His excitement was infectious, and Yehoshiva forgot about the anger he still harbored toward Shemesh's directives.

"I'll talk to Tammuz and Katesh. We can build minarets to help Katesh mark distances, and Tammuz could set up a botanical garden for experimenting with crops and plants. I'll have the miners focus on tunneling. We'll need to justify it all so Shemesh doesn't grow suspicious, but I think we can pull it off." Yehoshiva felt better. They had a plan. He felt empowered by it. Feigning defeat, he could secure victory. He would let Shemesh know he would comply and would ask for the timeline.

20

Yehoshiva stood at the edge of the grass that marked the limit of the river's influence. The temple was excavated, the materials were piled up, and the foundation was set, but there had been little movement on it for some months. Yehoshiva wondered at Shemesh's delay. He must have suspected something, or he must have changed his mind about something, but the temple had been Shemesh's priority up until now.

Yehoshiva had already marked the compound wall to Shemesh's specifications. But his work would need to wait until the temple was too far underway to delay, so around the wall, he was laying the road network for the new city, a grid boxing in the empty desert. The foundation for the defensive wall surrounded it, further enclosing the new temple and compound.

Yehoshiva had already started his security upgrades with a series of guard towers. They were made of mud bricks and had a wooden ladder to climb them. They were positioned to not only view the horizon and any encroaching bandits but also to provide some view of the city to police the area. Each tower was five hundred feet from the next, and each was equipped with a drum and a brazier for signaling. The city wall was two thousand feet square, so besides the twelve that stood at the wall, there were four more in the city that would provide security for the inhabitants. The center of the city would be where the new city guard headquarters would be built, where Farku would be posted. There would be a tunnel directly to it, so Yehoshiva could meet privately with his trustee.

The primitive laborers continued to scurry about looking busy while Yehoshiva viewed the progress of the new city. Little had been accomplished while he watched, but their work was harried and sweaty. Some carried stones from one pile to another, and others talked and pointed at indecipherable landmarks, but each seemed very aware of Yehoshiva's presence, so he began his hike to the quarry to make his rounds and give them the privacy they were clearly hoping for.

The quarry was no longer the unproductive pit it had been years before. The new foreman was every bit the leader they had seen forty planetary years earlier. He was old now but still managed the quarry with the same finesse he had had all those years ago. His family had grown very wealthy from his skills, and two of his sons were managing the copper and tin mines not far away.

Kimdu had taken a special liking to the qualities of this family and had taken them on as trustees for his projects. Each of the Masters had essentially adopted primitives, and even Shemesh did not discourage this practice. The familial lines more and more began to represent the qualities of the Master they served, and this made it easier for them to get more of their work done. The only one who had not thus far adopted a primitive trustee was Katesh. Her work was too sensitive to trust to the primitives just yet. So she carried the full burden herself.

Kimdu was in the process of teaching the primitives to make bronze. They needed harder tools than the stone ones they had, so he requested some copper and tin ore from Irka to begin the process. Rather than simply sending ore, they sent finished tools, produced right in the city by the Umanu who lived there. They were crude by the Masters' standards, but because they were crafted by the Umanu, they could be considered native technology, and the Masters had plausible deniability. This was little more than creative accounting as Yehoshiva saw it, as it was certainly the Masters there that had taught the Umanu the skill. But the tools made all the difference in the productivity of the mines.

Yehoshiva looked up from the edge of the quarry and searched for the silhouettes of the guards manning the four towers. The quarry was critical to the work they were doing, so he prioritized the construction of the guard towers. The foreman had even had the foresight to use scrap stone to build a wall between them and provide increased protection from any raiders that might come near. *Kimdu has quite a specimen there*, he thought.

The foreman presented himself and bowed in the manner he had been taught. It was clear to Yehoshiva now that these primitives had no difficulty differentiating the Masters from one another and presented themselves appropriately for each. The foreman carried scars on his arms counting the number of times Shemesh had been there, but unlike the priests, the scars were not darkened with ashes. *He knows where his loyalty lies,* Yehoshiva appraised.

"We will need double the stone you have been providing. You will need to increase the number of workers and have it delivered to the new city."

The foreman acknowledged the request. "Many willing." He paused, thinking of the words. "Not enough tools—need more." He gestured to the pile of blunted picks, wedges, and hammers. "Strong at start, but not last long. Need many."

Yehoshiva made a placating gesture and said, "I will talk to Master Kimdu, and he will come up with a solution."

The foreman nodded and smiled. Yehoshiva made sure Kimdu got the credit. His trustees would appreciate him more for being the genius behind the simple advance of technology, even if it was simply adjusting the formula to make the bronze harder. It was a lot of theater to make these primitives believe the technology wasn't already invented and perfected across the expanse of the galaxy.

Yehoshiva started to dismiss the foreman when he felt for his purse and pulled out a seed.

The foreman took it and looked disappointed. "Master . . . forgive. Seed not worth much. Money not buy needs."

This was the second time Yehoshiva had heard the seeds were rapidly losing value. They would need to find another currency that would satisfy the people. He reached back in the pouch and pulled out three more and handed them to the foreman. "We'll fix that issue soon too," Yehoshiva said as he dismissed the foreman.

He could hear the old man's body crack and strain as he began to back away. Yehoshiva stopped him. "Make sure you have a replacement trained and ready to take over for you soon. It's getting to be time for you to give up your duties and retire."

A look of terror flashed across the foreman's face, and he looked at the seeds he clutched in his hand. "I not good foreman?" he pleaded, fearing his death was imminent for somehow displeasing the Masters.

"No, you are an excellent foreman," Yehoshiva assured him. "But you are aged and should spend your final days with your family. Find a suitable replacement for yourself, and begin training him to serve the Masters as well as you have served."

The foreman looked humbled. Tears were welling in his eyes, and he bowed deeply to show his gratitude. He backed away again, and Yehoshiva could see a lightness in his step as he walked toward the quarry again. A worker much younger but of similar stature and gait supported him as he walked. The foreman handed him the staff, the symbol of his authority, and hugged him. The young man looked around, confused for a moment, but continued as the foreman directed. The foreman would teach him everything he knew in his final days serving the Masters.

21

Katesh was frustrated by the priests in her charge. They were marginal at best in learning the written language she taught them. They were mostly adequate at remembering the weights and measures they needed to make sense of their world. But their math was inconsistent and didn't make any sense. They could measure one distance, but when it came to adding or subtracting another distance, their answers were infuriatingly inaccurate. Even with the abacuses they had at their disposal (thanks to Kimdu's ingenuity), they still could not comprehend the process.

Few were competent enough to move on to other skills. But Katesh needed them to understand the premise of simple arithmetic before she could begin teaching algebra. They needed algebra so they could then learn geometry, and then they could be of some use as cartographers.

Without the Masters to do the complex math for them, they would have no straight lines in the whole of Bashram. Only the younger, more nimble minds were able to grasp the concepts, but the priests in her charge were those least useful to Shemesh and were frequently unambitious and aging. She needed a younger cohort.

She marched into Shemesh's office without knocking. "I need younger priests. I need smarter priests. I need priests with some comprehension of what we are trying to achieve here."

Shemesh didn't look up from the papers in front of him. "And I need you to request permission to enter my office."

Katesh cocked an eyebrow at that. "I am not yours to command. I am here by order from the Merchant Astronautica. I don't work for you."

Shemesh smiled malevolently at this and spoke gently. "You are here at my compound, eating my food and sleeping in my barracks. You can at least knock on *my* door before you barge in here making demands. I am not compelled to provide you the best of my resources to facilitate your project. I am here to ensure production is maintained and improved. And your mission is not critical to that aim, so I don't feel any compulsion to help you in your efforts. Work with whatever I give you, or find your own solution to your problem."

Katesh reeled back from this but only to realize what he just said: *Find your own solution.* She smiled at Shemesh, and the look caught him off guard. "I'll go find a solution then."

She turned to leave and heard Shemesh call after her, "There's only one priesthood in my city, and they are *mine.* Your solution had better not be more priests! Katesh! Are you listening?"

She was already halfway across the courtyard headed to her room. She had papers in there, fewer distractions, and privacy, and Marcella was a much better planner than she was.

Katesh closed the door behind her and became Marcella again. She stripped the silly hat off and threw it on the chest at the foot of her bed. She loosened her belt and removed her sandals. She needed to be unconstrained to figure out the plan for her new priesthood. *No, not priesthood.* She wanted to annoy Shemesh, not cause trouble for herself. *What then? Clerics? No, too similar.* It struck her immediately. *Kaldees.* They were what the astronomers called themselves in the Machine.

These Kaldees would need to be drawn from the same society as the priests. She couldn't interfere with their fundamental operation here, so she would need to target a different type of recruit. The priests in Irka were recruited for their virtues: moderation, modesty, charity, humility, grace, patience, and work ethic. But the test of those virtues was the critical element. They were given power, wealth, and influence, and those who did not retain their virtues were stripped of their authority and given lowly positions instead. Shemesh had essentially turned this on its head, seeking out those Irka would reject out of hand. He wanted the ambitious, the violent, the greedy, the lazy, those enamored by luxury and opulence. It was easy to find these qualities among any population, so there was little likelihood that her recruits would interfere with Shemesh's aims.

She thought about the qualities that make up a good scientist. Certainly intelligence. But they needed to have an element of suspicion too. Evidence-based reasoning. Logic. They would be unpopular among their peers. They would be prone to rebelliousness. Defiant of authority and frequently seditious. They would be honest or at least devoted to data, not to their own egotistic desires. Perseverance against failure and embarrassment. A sense of objectivity, not subjective. Integrity versus loyalty. Attention to detail, too, would be critical.

Marcella paused and reviewed the notes. She thought immediately of the rebels in the hills, people who rejected the authority of the Masters and their proxies in Shemesh's priesthood. She thought about what would make them leave to join the resistance. It wouldn't be food and hunger and disease. Despite all the suffering within the city, they would have more sustainable health here than scavenging and raiding for it out there. But they had integrity to their own beliefs, regardless of the quality of the information they had at hand. They were willing to endure great hardship to stand against the tyranny that suppressed their individualism and the truth.

What traits would define someone of that character? What outward behaviors define a person who would be more likely to rebel? Independence—they would spend more time alone than in a group. Ingenuity—they would have trinkets and inventions that made their lives easier. Even crude ones would be a sign of their type of thinking. They wouldn't be defined by the trends of the hour. Their houses wouldn't be freshly painted or their gardens full of the spice tree. They would not care about outward appearances, and the mess of their environment would reflect a diverse set of interests.

It would actually be easier to find them now that Shemesh had created a lucrative magnet for those of lower quality. The power, prestige, and wealth that went along with serving him meant that those who eschewed it were much more easily identified. Marcella chuckled at this thought. He had actually helped her weed out the worst applicants.

She tidied up her papers and stacked them for review later. As she tightened up her garb, she thought about the rebels and how she might get out to them to interview. A Master alone would be vulnerable, and the rebels were already hostile toward them. She could see that would be a lost cause. She would have to walk the city and pick out the subtleties of the population to read individuals and make decisions about them. She'd need to have a school and recruitment, and she'd need to enlist the aid of her fellow Masters in identifying the proper candidates. This all had to be done without drawing too much attention, so secrecy would be paramount.

As she opened the door and became Katesh again, she knew she would need to search the slums for the right people, but the danger increased the more desperate the people became. She would need to find a way to improve the image of the Masters and differentiate the rest of them from Shemesh. This would be the challenge, as it meant additional time devoted to projects that would bear fruit only gradually. And she needed people now.

Katesh walked through the hall of the barracks. As she passed, Yehoshiva opened his door. He looked startled to see her but eager at the same time.

"I didn't expect you to be here. I thought you would be out in the field," he said engaging her enthusiastically.

"I need better recruits for my projects, but Shemesh keeps sending me the leftovers of his endeavors. I needed privacy to figure out how to get the sorts of primitives I would need to accomplish my mission," she said as they walked briskly toward the foyer.

"What sort are you looking for?" he asked as they reached the inner door.

She eyed their surroundings cautiously and, in almost a whisper, she replied, "Rebels."

Yehoshiva's eyes went wide. He closed the door behind him, then grabbed her by the arm. "Farku has told me a lot of women and children are sneaking back into the city from the rebel camps. They have been smuggling a particular red mountain flower that is hallucinogenic. Some are staying, others are going, but the rebels are here in the city."

She knew immediately what she needed to look for now. "I need to look for that flower then, and then I will know where to start recruiting."

Yehoshiva cautioned her. "You'll have a harder time finding it now, though, with the gate to the plateau completed. There's little traffic back and forth except by the soldiers, so it will not be easy to find."

"What are the signs of the intoxication then—and the withdrawals?" she asked with increased interest.

"Well, the intoxication part is easy. They will have a glazed look in their eyes, and they will appear to be looking inward, unable to interact with the outside world." He thought for a moment, trying to summarize the withdrawal symptoms. "The withdrawal will be a mental fatigue, a fog, and it will translate into a general fatigue. Some miners were found to have been using it, and their performance was considerably diminished."

"So tired, lazy, and distant." She thought for a moment. "How do they use it?"

Yehoshiva was increasingly animated by their conversation. Though she was looking for information, he was excited by being the one who could help her. "They boil it into a tea and drink it. The tea is red like the flower and stains their teeth for a time." Then his face lit up as he remembered. "Farku has some of the rebels in a holding cell now. They caught them coming into the city just before the gate was completed."

"Have they been there long?" she asked, worrying the information on their contacts within the city would be expired by now.

"Well, the gate's been completed for a few months now, so yes. There's nowhere to put them, and they were caught with the drug. So we can't just let them go." Yehoshiva justified.

Katesh waved her hand to dismiss his apologetic tone. "You have your job to do to keep the city safe, but I would like to interview some of them."

Yehoshiva hesitated for a moment and then acquiesced. "Okay, we can go now. Farku will be at the gate. He has cells there to hold detainees. We can start there."

The sun was still out, though lower in the sky. They guessed they would have a few more hours of daylight to conduct their business before the shadows set in and the city became more electric with the black market alive in every household in the slums. The air was still hot, but the humidity from the river kept the dust down, and the putridity of the fetid water near the growing slums hung heavy in the air.

They approached the slope to the gate. Beside it stood rough shelters with stone walls and doors made of lashed sticks. Though the shelters were spacious, the growing crowds thronging into the city made the meager facilities crowded and unmanageable. Cells had more people than there were beds or pots for their sanitation, and even the food supply was inconsistent.

Katesh did not show her disgust, but Yehoshiva could see the disappointment in the deplorable conditions these rebels were subjected to just to process them. Even outside the gate, a vast encampment stretched that prevented the patrols from effectively pursuing the rebels in the field. All knew this throng of people came from those camps, but there was nowhere to put them, and they couldn't be released into the city. Yehoshiva felt the burden of guilt at their conditions, but his responsibility was to production, so any interference in that also fell to him to manage. Shemesh was not helpful in this capacity and actively undermined his efforts by refusing appropriations for the refugees and by ordering their frequent release into the city, where the squalor and animosity for the Masters would only ferment in the poverty of the slums and the heavy-handed priesthood he employed.

"I'm working on alternatives to the situation. We have many working the fields right now to produce food, but we don't have enough housing for them all," Yehoshiva said apologetically. "It's mostly women and children. The men are staying behind to continue the resistance, and these children will grow up to flee to the wilderness to join them. The gate created a sense of urgency in them, I believe. But these conditions are necessary to be able to vet them. Unfortunately, we don't have enough resources to do it effectively, and there are too many who still have ill intentions against us to be allowed to go free."

Katesh nodded sympathetically. She knew it was the burden of every advanced and prosperous society, but the diseases and malevolence they brought would not be improved by the putrid conditions of their welcoming. She decided her mission would alleviate the burden at the gate somewhat, and that was her priority here. "We'll figure something out to help. The new city will relieve some of the strain, and we can undo some of the animosity by giving them the proper skills to prosper. At least if they flee back to the wilderness later, they can carry some of our teachings with them and it can spread." She commiserated with Yehoshiva.

His tension eased, and a look of gratitude fell on his face. "I will help you in any way I can." He meant it. Their missions were symbiotic, and he was relieved that the burden wouldn't be his alone to bear.

They walked to the guard station and found Farku there. A mound of the red flowers was heaped in the corner, and his agitation was evident as he spoke to a guard whose eyes had a hint of glaze in them. Yehoshiva noticed it right away even as they jumped to attention to greet the two Masters who had come unexpectedly to their facilities.

Farku presented himself with a bow and said nervously, "Master, I not expect come today." He gestured to his guard, who stood dumbfounded, uncertain of what to do. The guard fell to the floor prostrate in the manner Shemesh had commanded, and the darkened scars of his servitude were evident.

Yehoshiva spoke sternly to Farku. "You should always expect me, and you should ensure that your guards are always doing their job, not stealing from the evidence." He pointed at the prostrate guard behind Farku.

Farku looked where he was pointing, confused at the man behind him. He had detected no sign of intoxication. "Him not work hard. I yell make him do job. Prisoners need food, him not feed."

Yehoshiva nodded, understanding the issue. He spoke harshly to the guard. "When did you last use the flower?"

The guard was not used to speaking the language of the Masters and picked his words carefully. "I . . . not . . . flower . . . never."

A liar and a thief, Yehoshiva thought. He looked at Katesh, who said the same with her eyes. Then she added without saying a word, *He must be their contact for smuggling into the city.*

Yehoshiva agreed. He turned back to the guard. "You will begin patrolling outside the gate. You are relieved of your duties here. Farku," he said turning back to his trustee, "make it happen. He will not touch one more prisoner and will never be in charge of the evidence."

Farku responded, "Master's wish my command."

Yehoshiva and Katesh stepped out of the guardhouse and waited. The yelling inside was intense, and a few moments later, the guard hurried out of the door carrying a message on clay rolled in linen with Farku's seal pressed onto it. His fearful expression at seeing the two Masters standing outside stopped him in his rush, and he bowed low as he passed, murmuring something apologetic as he ran toward the gatehouse to report to his new assignment.

Farku came out moments later, his face flush from anger, but he suppressed his rage at seeing the two waiting there. "I not know, Masters. Please forgive I," he pleaded.

Yehoshiva raised his hand to stop Farku from his self-flagellation. "You will need to secure the flowers and the possessions of the refugees better, and you need to screen your guards better. *That* one"—Yehoshiva gestured toward the guard who still scurried toward the gate—"is not the only corrupt one here. I want a full report on the food stores and the confiscated possessions and a list of the guards handling the processing of the refugees. Every action your guards take reflects on the Masters, and corruption will not be tolerated."

Farku's eyes welled up with tears. *He is disappointed in himself—this one is loyal,* Katesh intimated with a brush of her hand on Yehoshiva's. Yehoshiva consoled his trustee. "You are my most loyal and capable servant. You serve me well. Don't think this interaction is a reflection of my loss of faith in you."

Farku's face illuminated with gratitude. "Thank Master. I not deserve praise."

Yehoshiva warmed at this. "We are here to give Master Katesh a chance to interview the refugees. We will use the guardhouse. Please bring them to us one family at a time."

Farku then asked, "Which I bring? What Master Katesh want

know?"

Yehoshiva started to speak, but Katesh spoke instead. "Bring me the leaders first. Anyone the rest pay deference to. Then bring me the ones they avoid."

Farku bowed at this command and, being dismissed, went to the farthest cell, calling his closest guards to control the prisoners while he sorted through them.

Katesh and Yehoshiva sat in the guardhouse interviewing each family as Farku brought them. Most were the wives of rebels. Some were from the nomads; others were slaves who had escaped, looking for a better life than the brutal wilderness they suffered under their nomadic masters. Each group had kept its distance from the others, and there was little interaction between them. The guards did not read the hostility between the three groups, but Katesh and Yehoshiva could immediately see the dynamic at play.

The leaders identified were frequently just the most privileged of the rebel wives, individual encampment leaders, or warriors in their own right. The women were proud and tough, and much of their leadership was built around fear. The nomads were proud and independent and contemptuous of their conditions but were not violent. They were observant but not educated.

The slaves were the opposite. They were avoided by the rebels but seemed to bear the burdens of their imprisonment with a kind of familiarity that proved their conditions were an improvement over the ones they escaped.

Katesh quickly picked up the differences. The nomads would be too proud and stubborn for her purposes. They were a kind of royalty and would not be willing to submit to the Masters. The rebels were tougher. They had more sympathy for the slaves, but they did not fit the mold that Katesh was trying to fill. Some were humble, but the hard life on the run, living off the land or the scraps and dregs of the city, left them bitter and hardened. Only their children would suffice for what she needed. The former slaves held the most immediate promise.

Each told the same story: They had never known their families but were from the rebel camps. Used as interpreters between the rebels and the nomads, they were sold and traded between nomad groups until they escaped. They ate only rejected scraps and slept outside with the dromedaries, their whole lives spent as servants treated lower than the animals they tended.

Their linguistic capabilities intrigued Katesh. They would be much easier to teach the language of the Masters, and they would be humble enough to learn the lessons. Because they were used in negotiations, they had a much better grasp of counting and calculations, and their nomadic lifestyle made them more capable of the cartographic skills Katesh needed. The defensive scars on their backs and arms and the calluses on their hands and feet made them easier to identify.

She addressed Farku. "Farku, gather all the prisoners and their families that bear scars on their backs and calluses on their feet and hands and set them free at once. Let them know they can camp south of the river to the west of the city, and I will come to them there. Bring them food to eat, and I will take charge from there."

He bowed hesitantly as he waited for Yehoshiva to confirm the command. Yehoshiva smiled at Katesh subtly, and she returned it. Yehoshiva confirmed the order. "Make it so immediately, and bring the next family in." Farku bowed deeper and moved swiftly to carry out the command.

Her mother stood before them without balking at the sight of the Monsters before her. She sat in the corner watching the interaction, fidgeting with the wooden bird her mother had given her. She had never seen the Monsters before. Their stature was twice as tall as any of the people from her home, and they exuded power and command. They were terrifying. She had heard the stories of their brutality and how her people were pushed to starvation, and they seemed fully capable of it.

Their gray skin was dark, like they had tanned in the sun, but they bore none of the marks of labor that were all too familiar to her and her people. They were slender but not hungry looking. They had large teardrop eyes, and they showed no emotion. They wore leather and linen garbs that disguised their bodies and gave them a uniformly regal look.

They were terrifying but intriguing. They didn't seem to be violent, though she only knew what she had been told about them.

Her mother spoke in the common tongue to them, and they asked questions of her in the same tongue. When the old man in charge of the prisons spoke to them, they spoke a strange language together that she couldn't understand. It had a poetry about it. It was like a song. Not the way the man spoke, but the way the Monsters did was very graceful. It was beautiful.

She listened while her mother was interviewed. The one she thought was a male was speaking.

"You are from the rebel tribes, are you not?" he asked without the slightest sign of emotion.

"I come from *the* rebel tribe," her mother spoke proudly. The fear in her voice resonated in each word, but she refused to be cowed by the Monsters.

"So you are from the rebel group the Sword leads?"

Her chest swelled from hearing them address her husband's title. "I am."

The female Monster spoke. "You are his wife then," she stated flatly.

Her mother looked shocked. She had not mentioned any details, yet they seemed to read her mind. She looked at her daughter briefly, fear in her eyes, searching for an answer to not betray her family. "I come from his tribe."

The two Monsters looked at each other subtly, then looked at the child. The female spoke. "What is your name, child?"

Her mother looked at her, dread flashing across her eyes as she bounced her new baby nervously in her arms.

"Samara!" she said as she stood, the defiance in her voice overcoming the fear in her heart. She walked to her mother and took her hand. Her mother gripped her hand tightly.

"What do you think of our presence here?" the female asked, her features flat and devoid of emotion.

"My daddy says the Monsters are tyrants. That we have to—" She felt her mother squeeze her hand tighter as she spoke. She must have said something she shouldn't have.

The male spoke now. "And who is your daddy?"

She looked up at her mother, whose eyes were suddenly flush with tears and fear.

"My daddy is the strongest, smartest, and bravest man of all. He was the first rebel!" she said proudly.

The Monsters looked at each other, and Samara could see just a slight flinch in their hands. They seemed to be talking to each other, but she couldn't hear anything.

Finally, the female spoke. "Your family will be released from the cell, and you will follow the slaves to the encampment. I will come to you again there. Do not have fear. You are protected with us. You will say nothing about where you came from or whose family you are from now on. You were a slave. That is who you were. Say nothing more about it to anyone. I have tasks for you."

Samara didn't know what was happening or how the conversation had made such a dramatic leap. They knew they were rebels but now were helping them. She wondered how these Monsters could read their minds and speak their language. She was determined to learn their language and understand all their secrets. She would make Daddy proud.

22

Shemesh was proud of the temple to his eminence. The land had been transformed from a barren desert to a beacon of his exalted status. The windows stood behind him so that in his preaching he could be illuminated in the mornings, signifying his importance as the god of the sun. It rose on his command, and it gave light and warmth to the world and rebuked the shadows where the wretches of the city lurked. In the evening, the bronze facade glistened at sunset, calling his flock back to their worship to pray for the mercy of the sun to rise once more. The high-domed ceiling of his own design reflected in all directions to ensure that travelers in the desert could see from across the horizon and the cargo craft could identify it. The pews were spacious and airy to allow the stench of the priests to be carried out, and the portholes in the dome could ventilate and cool the chamber with less effort. The doors were large and ornately carved wood of the spice tree, taken from the fields of those who fled to the desert. Everything else was bronze—all the hinges, psalters, censers, braziers, and candlesticks. The exterior and interior walls were white as bleached oyster shells. The grandiosity of the building was unequaled in the whole world.

He had his priests carry the crude artifacts of his bronze works back to Irka to trade with artisans. The higher-quality craftsmen there replicated them, and then they were mass-produced. When the quality workmanship was returned to Bashram, his artisans simply copied the design, and he could claim the work was organic to the region. It was a little trick he'd learned early on to expedite his conveniences.

The temple glistened brightly as the priests filed in for the morning prayers. The sun's light was just below the horizon. *Right on time.* He looked at the light reflected on the inner dome, which marked the rising of the sun and signaled his commencement of call to prayer. He hastened to begin the ceremony as the high priest lit the censer and the candles that marked the solemnity of the call to prayer.

As the sliver of light illuminated the dome, he began. He had sixteen minutes to give his opening remarks and begin the prayer that called the sun to the sky at his behest.

Priests were still shuffling in, but he would not wait for them. He raised his arms and began his sermon. "The darkness grows among us. The cold of night has stolen from the hearts of our people the warmth that they once knew. The savage walks among us and invades your lands and corrupts your prosperity in the shadows. And the cries of children are stifled by the stillness in your hearts. It is not the Masters who bring these ill fortunes. It is the greed of the poor that holds them low. It is the lust of the refugee that burdens your glorious city with their multitudinous children. It is the gluttony of the seedless that strips your granaries without compensating your generosity. It is the envy of the rebels that hampers your progress and keeps your wealth from shining like this holy place. It is the pride of the nomad that stops your city from growing. It is the wrath of the elders that poisons the hearts of the people against you. And it is the sloth of the farmer that drains your pantries while they grow fat from their excess. It is your city, and you are the ones who make it shine."

Murmurs of agreement were scattered through the congregation. The high priest had done well to place his agitators. It almost seemed natural. He expected the approval would grow the more they heard his message, despite the absurdity of his liturgy.

"It is for you to grasp the ropes that bind society and guide it toward its glorious destiny. It is your birthright to wield the whip that drives the commoner to strive for the opulence your city deserves. And it is your talent that brought you from the seed of the nomad to the seats of authority you have earned. Your fathers passed their greatness on to you, for you to serve me, and you have shown with every action your obedience to my command."

At this the priests held up their arms with darkened scars and recited the refrain. "It is our honor to serve you, Lord, for you bring the sun that chases away the darkness."

"What shall I do this day?" he asked as the light grew on the dome ahead of him. "Will you chase away the darkness if I refuse? Will you seek out the forces of chaos and despair to bring the light yourselves? What should I do this day?"

On cue a priest called from the back, "Please, Lord, bring us sun. We crush enemy of our city!"

He glanced at the dome. *Not yet—delay a bit longer.* "Why do the rebels still roam the plateaus then? Why do the farms not produce? Why do the city streets overflow with disease and filth and detritus?" *Just a bit longer; almost there.*

"Please, Lord. Tell I what do!" Another agent provocateur.

"I will not command the sun to rise for those who do not seek the glory of their own city. For it does not serve to exert my energy to call it to chase away the devils of the night for those who will not take charge of the city the Masters have given them."

The anxiety of the priests began to grow. The younger ones who had been steeped in the new order were particularly nervous. They began to call out in consternation.

"Please, Lord, save city from dark!"

"Please, Lord, I break beggars for you, raise sun. Please, Lord!"

The cries grew from the priests, and even the unwitting joined in to ask fervently for his mercy.

Shemesh was pleased and raised his hands as the sunlight hit the mark on the dome to signify the beginning of the prayer. "I have pity for you. And I know you do your best. Each day I ask that you only strive a little harder to repair the damage to your great city caused by the decay in plain sight. Your pleas have been heard, and I will call the sun for you."

The relief on the faces of the priests showed him the depth of their belief. Though the tradition began only after the temple became operable, he told them it was his gift to them in silence before, but now they must understand the gifts he had given them and serve him properly.

He began the Prayer to the Sun:

> Oh great light. You banish the darkness and warm the cold of the night. You heal the stiffness and pain of the old and temper the ailment of the sick. You illuminate the shadows and send the vermin of the abyss to their burrows. And you grant color to the world that glorifies your grace. Rise, rise and bring us a new day to increase the glory of all you touch!

Shemesh raised his arms to the sky, and as he did so, the sun crested the horizon, the light shining on the back of his head, transfiguring him instantly into a divine being.

The priests were mesmerized by the display. They never knew the Masters had such power, and Shemesh was the Master of the Masters. He was a god! Their worship of him grew with each ceremony, and their brutality waxed at his urging. But the temple was only the beginning of the new city, and they were well aware their place in it was not assured.

Their scars would grow deeper and darker.

23

The Sword drew a shallow breath and coughed violently. The blood that gurgled with each breath was normal to him now, but he could feel the light fading from his mind. He felt weak and lightheaded, but there was nothing that could be done about it. The ever-present dust in the air scoured his airways, and the constant illness and fatigue and deprivation ensured he could never quite fully recover from his ailment.

He surveyed the camp from the entrance to his shack. The chief that had been appointed by the clan in his stead was plodding toward him, puffs of tan dirt billowing from beneath his sandaled feet as he trod. The men and women of the camp took a wary step back to avoid his path. *How this man became chief after me I have no idea. Some minor heroics in the right company, I suppose.* The man was a brute. He wore a necklace of sun-dried ears of city guards that had crossed his path, presumably. It was rumored that he scavenged the dead of both sides of any engagement and took the trophies as a way of making his achievements look more spectacular than they actually were. Yet his fearsome demeanor and strength ensured that no one questioned his heroics openly.

The Sword sat upright as the man approached. His voice was failing and weak, but he could still speak in an authoritative tone in close quarters, so he waited until the man got closer before speaking. "I have heard you broke our alliance with the nomads. You have poached on their land and butchered their herds. Does this strike you as a wise move?"

The man stared savagely at his dying predecessor and sneered. "We need food. I am in charge of this camp now. I command."

The Sword studied him for a moment, allowing the pause to unsteady his successor, who finally broke the silence. "Your treaty was outdated. They needed to know we have power. They needed to know we are strong, and they are weak."

"Who will be the weakest when they no longer trade with us? Who will be strong when our clans are starving? How will you provide for the people then?"

The agitation was plain on the man's face. Then a smug smile began to form as he spoke, "We are keeping our bellies full. We have found a new source of food." He grabbed the necklace and smiled savagely. "The city sends us plenty of food now."

The Sword's heart fell, and he closed his eyes to the evidence growing around the camp of their new diet. His mind began following a logical sequence to the inevitable conclusion of this collective decision. *The cause is lost. Cannibals eventually eat each other or are eradicated. All is lost.* "How long before conditions change again and your great logistical feat will be exposed as shortsighted and alienating?"

The man reached for the hilt of his weapon as a warning, a trophy of a fallen city guard. "Your tongue is sharper than your blade. You should be careful of your insults."

"If truth and wisdom are an insult, then you have already failed as a leader." The Sword did not reciprocate the provocation but sat still to show his lack of fear of death.

The chief hesitated a moment and let go of his weapon. He ruled by fear and intimidation, but his methods were ineffective against those who did not fear what he threatened. He tried to salvage his authority using logic. "The more they hunt us, the more they send. We won't starve as long as the city stands."

"How long will the city stand while refugees continue to flee? We started this rebellion to throw out the Monsters. You have ensured the people no longer see us as their salvation, but rather another stone to grind them deeper into despair." The Sword could see the consternation on the chief's face. He couldn't hold his weight against a man who didn't fear violence or death, who was chosen by the Monsters for his intellect as a priest and who had proven his courage as a leader of a rebellion against their undeniable talents.

The chief changed the subject abruptly. "Your time will come soon, old man. There's no room here for those who don't earn their keep."

"So you plan to eat me too," the Sword stated matter-of-factly, goading the chief once more as his advice fell like wooden spears against a stone wall.

"There's no meat on you anymore, and your skin is loose and wrinkled. No, we'll give you your rights. You may leave the camp when you choose, but you will only eat what you kill. If you don't kill, you don't eat." The man turned and walked away. His leather cuirass was pieced together and recently tanned, but the dark lines that marked it belied the source of the material.

The Sword sat for a moment longer. *This is hopeless, and I am alone.* He grabbed his walking stick and headed for the open desert to find his final home, as was his final right. *My love, how I wished we could have been together one moment more,* he thought as his slow, labored steps matched his breathing and the dusty air pelted his burned and blotched skin. There was nothing more for him anywhere. There were no allies for him to turn to. As all creatures are at the end, he was alone.

The number of refugees to Irka grew by the day. Few were truly prepared for the journey. Few knew how to prepare. No one knew how many made it to the other side of the desert, but most knew the way and who left. There was simply nothing left for them in Bashram. But reports from the caravans did not mention the droves at the gates of Irka they would have expected given the volume of people leaving, and there was nowhere else for them to go.

Katesh interrogated every caravan that came through for information on the people who left, but none had the news she was hoping to hear.

Few even mentioned seeing anyone along the way. There were raiders from the clans that still harassed them, but the caravans were cautious and well-armed and equipped for the journey. The bandits would have relied on easier prey.

Katesh felt the desperation of the people growing. Refugees did not risk everything including life and limb just for better economic opportunities. They left to find hope, which meant that here, in Bashram, her city, they felt hopeless.

She worked tirelessly to get her Kaldees organized and trained and create *something* that might serve as a beacon of hope within the protection of the city. Progress was slow, though, and the former slaves held on to their inherent distrust of the Masters and the citizens despite the rewards and privilege and comparative comfort they received in their new home.

Yehoshiva found her near the growing suburb of Bashram where the slaves had been given to settle, staring at the people moving in and out of their huts and businesses. "What do you need here? Anything I can help you with?" he asked without introduction.

Her worry was dispelled for a moment, and his voice was warm and comforting to her. "Everything. They need everything," she said with sadness in her voice.

"This isn't what I imagined it would be like out on the frontiers of the empire." He spoke gloomily but assuredly.

"You couldn't have known. No one ever does." She spoke quickly as her eyes darted around. She signed to him. *Ritual!*

He smiled at her and didn't speak. He signed back. *Eyes and ears everywhere, always.*

She glanced at him with feigned disapproval.

He composed himself again and reached into his satchel and pulled out a single yellow flower. "This is a specimen worthy of study." He deliberately spoke to the flower as he approached Katesh. She caught the flirtation immediately, cautious but direct. He spoke to her as he extended his hand. "It might interest you in your pursuits. Perhaps your Kaldees can make use of it."

Katesh took the flower gently by the stem and spun it slowly in her forefinger and thumb, watching it dance hypnotically. "It is a common and useless flower to my knowledge." She assessed it in a clinical tone, but her body and action said, *This is beautiful; thank you.*

Yehoshiva stared toward the suburb with her. A few Kaldees glanced back and then pointedly went about their business at a quicker pace.

"The refugees are not making it to Irka," she stated flatly. She felt the words leave her lips and began to feel a wall of emotions start to collapse inside. She couldn't speak anymore, or she would risk losing the facade of professionalism.

Yehoshiva looked at her and nodded knowingly. After a moment, he gestured to the flower, and in a low voice that quietly consoled her said, "That flower is common and useless. It serves no other purpose that we know of but that it is beautiful. It is by every definition just a weed, collected and thrown away. But weeds are strong and face more adversity than any other plant. This flower is these people. We can't see their virtues other than as the dominant species on this planet, a tool for our aims. But easily interchangeable with any other species on any other planet. Simply a weed that must be tamed.

"We are here to give them purpose, to find their virtues even as they seem to have none. We can dismiss them individually because they are common, but together they begin to form a beautiful mass of potential. We imagine that they will live and die by our conditioning alone. That they will not survive without us. That the suffering they face is entirely our responsibility. Or that they will not figure out how to succeed against the tyranny of Shemesh's order. But like this flower, they have been here long before us. They have suffered long before us. And they will be here long after us, whatever our impact on their development.

"The funny thing about common is that it has endurance. It has strength, and it has perfected itself against the environment it is ubiquitous in. To us, this flower is common. It has no properties that would make it useful, but this flower is growing in an environment where there is very little to spare, and it has earned its place. It has not only succeeded but dominated. That alone is its virtue. It is resilient. This flower will be here whether we make use of it or not. It has struggled to adapt to the environment and the changing of the seasons and the climate but has ultimately proven resilient against it. They scatter their seeds into the desert and hope that their progeny will find a patch of soil that will allow them to endure a little longer. Despite their struggle, they still have hope. Resistance is hope. Rejection is hope. Endurance is hope. And the refugees would not leave here if they did not believe that hope existed somewhere else. Just as this flower would not go to seed if it didn't believe there was hope. Those who remain have found some hope here. The refugees are a symptom of the system they live in, but it is a signal of what the rest of their people feel as well. And yet most remain. They see a glimmer of hope here. Just as this flower has remained." He paused, searching for the words or the courage to say what he was trying to say. "You are giving them hope. We can't save them all from the cruelty of the system they have been given, even though it's us who are responsible for creating it, but you are the only one here who is strong enough to give them a society they deserve so we can see what their potential truly is. You are the reason any one of *us* still remains to do our jobs to give these people the skills and structure they need to prosper. You have given us hope. You have given *me* hope."

Katesh focused on him. Neither stopping him from speaking so freely nor interrupting. For the first time, she was hearing him speak from the heart.

"You have sought to give them something that will truly belong to them. You are the rarest of all flowers. I could search for one across the entire world and never find one of equal beauty or rarity or strength. You have given all of us purpose again here."

Katesh lowered her eyes humbly and then turned back to her suburb. *Ritual.* She signed again as punctuation. She hoped he would continue—she needed the reassurance—but they were too open now to not be spied upon for long.

Yehoshiva looked at her for a moment longer, then finally said, "You are the only one who will find a use for that flower. Not Tammuz, not Kimdu, no one else. Just you. It is the only hope these people have." He reached into his pouch once more and pulled out a full bouquet of the common flower and handed it to Katesh to join the other. "Common can be beautiful too. These are your people. You're what will bring them together. What you are building here will be the culture of this city. Shemesh's order will collapse under its own momentum, but you are building something that resists and rejects that order and will be resilient against the destruction that will certainly come with time. The rest of us can help feed and employ them and teach them skills and keep them safe as best we can, but you're the one who will truly save them." He turned back toward Bashram, hesitating before he took the first step toward that manifestation of anxiety and despair.

Katesh reached her hand out toward him and touched him on the forearm. "Thank you," she said as her eyes began to water.

He smiled warmly at her, pulling gently away and allowing her hand to slide down his arm until their hands touched. Then he signed a playful admonition, *Ritual!* Then walked back to the city, where his unceasing duties awaited.

24

The priests hired thugs and gangs, opportunistic mercenaries who sought the fortunes their lives of poverty could not afford them. They were more savage than even the rebels or priests could be, and they were handsomely rewarded for their brutality. The poor found their lives were unlikely to improve even by the great expanse of the project they labored on. At least in that part of the city.

Each day the divide in society grew wider. Those who served and tried to live as best they could in the system that tormented them found their oppression growing day by day. The priests of Shemesh and the mercenaries they hired found more and more ruthless ways of separating the people and their access to opportunity, and the more savage they were, the more they themselves prospered. Bodies of the unfortunate were being discovered on a daily basis, and the din of sorrow was ever present in the ghettos where the poor resided, having lost loved ones without the closure of ever finding out what happened to them. And as the sorrow grew, the suffering waxed as those capable of earning wages declined and the greater burdens of responsibility fell on fewer and fewer family wage earners.

Yehoshiva continued to build the new city as he was ordered, but his responsibilities left him unable to directly influence the outcomes of the lives of the people. He did what he could, and each road provided new access to opportunities, but those opportunities concentrated only where his work was prioritized, which was where those loyal to Shemesh resided. Shemesh's dictate that the people have access to the Master's sanctuaries provided more opportunities for the rich to be seen with the Masters, and the association with their vile deeds would land on the Masters themselves. Yehoshiva worked to maintain that separation. With each road, he built a tunnel; with each aqueduct, a sewer; and with each tower and garden, an access. It was an essential task for a burgeoning society, but the plan to undermine Shemesh's irresponsible management was also crucial to his own sanity. Though there was little he could affect in the lives of individuals, he could protect the Masters and their reputation at least a little bit, or at least demonstrate that they were not all the same, that there wasn't unanimous consent for the policies enacted.

Roads began to crisscross the new city, and grids of evenly spaced blocks were formed to give some sense of distance when traveling through the various parts. The poor tried to move into the area, but the priests ensured they were humiliated and beaten back to their humble boroughs. All knew that some residents were compensated for the portions of their properties that had been lost to the public works simply by being where the work was directed, but the priests were already well ahead of this scheme and were unwilling to share the fortunes they illicitly acquired, so the poor only watched as the rich got richer and they got poorer.

Yehoshiva was the architect of the network and saw to the construction of the tunnels personally. For every foot of road built during the day, there was a foot of tunnel built in the night, the latter taking the greatest toll on him, as he slept very little. After months of this effort, primitive work crews had been able to dig out the foundation and lay the sand, gravel, and then stone on top of it to create a compact and solid road foundation of fifty feet per day. In the grid, which stretched two thousand feet by two thousand feet, with roads twenty feet wide and blocks of one hundred seventy-eight feet, it would take nearly eight hundred days to complete the project. Two years and then some by the planet's rotation. It went quickly from his view in the galactic standard year, and the city continued to change around him rapidly.

With every block of road that was completed, the priests claimed a piece and began to build their mansions. The merchants and the wealthy who served Shemesh found themselves in good company and were granted land to build on.

Too many nomads had given up the life of desert wanderers. They were unable to establish their own supply lines and were dependent on the produce of Bashram, and the increasing misfortunes that were predictable but unforeseen drove them to the safety of the city. No longer could they move from place to place to pick up resources and raise livestock; they were forced to choose occupations that required learning new skills and giving up their pride as autonomous herdsmen. They were the original people of that land, yet they had been usurped by the technology of the Masters. The long life and high fertility brought to the people who adopted this new way of living left the nomads increasingly isolated and outnumbered. Yet even with the knowledge of what the Masters offered, they found it came with sturdy strings attached. Their pride in their way of life faded, and the burden of their hardship became more apparent. The walls stopped their trade. Their children were lured by the luster of the city growing on the horizon and quickly faded away and deserted their nomadic lifestyle.

With the city population in the thousands, there was no hope for recourse against them. There would be no running them off, especially with the fortifications Yehoshiva had built. They had missed their opportunity to drive off the invaders and were now stuck facing the long slog into bitterness and prideful misery. The world was changing rapidly, and though they were once the masters of this domain, these cities proved far more efficient mastery over the environment, and the old ways had been proven outdated.

The nomads had none of the skills required to succeed in the city, but their pride made them difficult to train or use productively. Their skills as herdsmen were useful for Tammuz's team, and their foraging was a good asset, but they refused to help in any meaningful way and would not lower themselves to do the work that was needed. So they found themselves trapped in the slums, hungry and angry and proud.

Yehoshiva looked out past the northeast gate at a collection of tents far in the distance. This was one of the nomadic tribes that rotated their location based on the seasons and where the most abundant food was for their herds: the hills in the spring, the desert grasses in the winter, and the hills in the fall. In the summer, it used to be along the river where the citizens now collected in little rough houses, but now they camped near the walls and bartered for the water that had once come freely to them.

He saw their meager herd of dromedaries and watched the herdsmen stand staring at the walls of the city for some time. The body language was of a patriarch deciding where to go for sustenance for the herd. Whether to bargain or attack. Twenty planetary years prior, the river had been open to their use, but now as they circled back on their trek, the construction of a gatehouse blocked their way, and they were without the nourishment of the river and the flora and fauna that once flourished there.

Yehoshiva knew what they were after. He wondered how he could arrange it so they could have access to the water on the condition they leave the inhabitants of the city alone. He was in no position to form alliances with the tribesmen. Shemesh had given strict orders to not "contaminate" his city with their kind. Yet this act of preventing them from reaching the waters that nourished their herds was tantamount to a declaration of war against their culture and would result in unnecessary conflict. They might still find a good place to water, but the delta had always been a place for all to share. It belonged to no one. Or so the interpretation of the unwritten rules went before there were any people who sought a static life. The only thing they could do was move on or submit.

The walls helped keep the nomads out. Even the rebels were actively engaged in harassment of the populations. The walls of the city only ensured that the population spread to the artificial limits and densely overpopulated the areas of highest value.

The river became a murky mess in places where the people used the fertile soil to garden and then simply dumped the scraps into the river.

The Masters created a garbage service that would distribute large clay pots around the city for the citizens to throw their scraps into, but the poor would dig through and eat the contaminated waste of the other citizens. Good quality food was thrown away in the wealthier neighborhoods, and the long-term poor found the greatest opportunity for good meals there. The poor fought over territories where more food waste could be found, and the murder rates climbed as they fought with one another.

The priests employed more city guards to keep the poor away from the productive neighborhoods, and the garbage service increased the frequency of pickup to remove all the filth that came with it. A garbage dump was established outside the city in the desert, where the food could rot in the heat and nourish the soil there. It became a collection point for the extremely impoverished, and the raiders from the rebel encampments could find willing recruits. The desperation was palpable and only fueled the problems the Masters faced in improving the lives of the inhabitants.

Every day the encampment beyond the gate continued to grow, but fewer resources were available to aid them, so as the people there traded for food with their meager possessions, they grew more desperate and more violent. Yehoshiva knew they would need to extend the city to encompass that area and find a way to feed those people.

Shemesh's priests reported to him what the citizens were doing. The garbage dump, the river front, the grumblings at the walls, the class envy, the growing crime, the diseases that were increasingly becoming part of everyday life, and the premature deaths of the citizens—all were collected by these spies and reported to Shemesh directly. Yehoshiva was not privy to the content of the reports, but Shemesh ensured he understood the value of each of these social problems.

Elohim should never seemingly foment the conditions that created such misery and squalor. The city was suffering the consequences of its success, but Shemesh used these miseries to ensure that the citizens always looked to the Masters for their salvation. They needed a religion. They needed divisions among the culturally and ethnically homogeneous populations. They needed him to ensure they could carve away from their ancient and barbaric roots as quickly as possible, and his plan ensured they would advance quickly.

Bits of discarded food scraps rotted on the banks as the blackened, fetid sands buzzed with insects feasting on the bacteria and decay. "What do you think the value of all this squalor is?" Shemesh asked Yehoshiva as they walked through the river district.

The river had once been a crystal-clear reflection of the sky above, and reeds and water plants had thrived, but now the river was a place of filth, and it made Yehoshiva disgusted. In a desert where water was so scarce, they had destroyed the sanctity of a river within it. "I don't know. You are surely waiting to tell me." Yehoshiva felt distracted by the odors around him. Only his self-discipline kept his revulsion from making him vomit.

Shemesh chuckled. "I suppose you know me well enough by now." He pointed to the river. "This filth is the first sign of a diseased society. The plagues that come from such waters will thin the population in the weakest part of itself. The poor and unproductive people press to the river. There is no aqueduct near them where they can collect fresh water. They can only drink from the river. All the filth a society creates flows down the path of least resistance, just like the river. It has found the bedrock, and all the tributary waters that flow to it join and follow that lowest path to the sea. The disease that plagues these people can be cured by us. It makes them look to the Masters for their health, and that makes them more appreciative of the benefits of the society they live in here," Shemesh said admiringly of the gray and acrid water flowing nearby.

Yehoshiva wasn't so sure this logic was the right approach for the Masters to take. "I think they lived much cleaner lives before this. Even living in their own filth, they didn't live in other people's filth. I can say that is much worse than where they have come from."

"Do you know what my spies have been saying?" Shemesh seemed to change the subject, but in context, Yehoshiva imagined it was something horrifying. He shook his head and allowed Shemesh to tell him. "They say the people are starting to leave in greater numbers than they are coming. They say the nomadic tribes are rejecting them, and they are flocking to the rebels for aid. They are saying the rebels are taking them in but can't feed them or give them a home. Don't you find that interesting?"

Yehoshiva had a different way of viewing it. "Actually, it sounds horrifying. We could rectify that."

"No, I'd rather not," Shemesh said in his sinister, high-minded way. "You see, when the rebels finally have more people than they can feed, they will press our borders and raid our people here. They may even do worse because of their situation. This will push these people closer to us for protection, and we will be able to control them even more tightly. Fear of an unknown terror is more repulsive than a known one."

Yehoshiva was uncomfortable with the way Shemesh used the terms *we* and *our*. Yehoshiva had sympathy for these people and knowingly defied Shemesh to make their lives better, but in return Shemesh used the good intentions of Yehoshiva's defiance to push these people into even more misery. Boxed in by the walls, they couldn't spread out to find a natural density that suited both their need for privacy and their need for security. Shemesh was making them choose one or the other.

"I don't think control is truly the intention of our mission here," Yehoshiva stated flatly. He was weary of Shemesh's constant scheming.

Shemesh looked at Yehoshiva derisively. "Our mission is to increase productivity. That means we need these people to serve us. I would expect that you would find that easier to understand if you had employed yourself more in that purpose." Shemesh pointed at a dilapidated mud brick tower representing Yehoshiva's efforts at internal security. "Instead of wasting your time with projects like this. What production has this increased, by the way? It seems you have nothing to show for your efforts thus far."

Shemesh was finished with the conversation and sent Yehoshiva to collect the taxes of the wealthiest citizens.

Yehoshiva stood for a moment and turned to walk away. The tower represented security, which helped the people believe their possessions and their persons were protected even if they were away. That allowed the whole family to engage in production. *Shemesh knows this*, he thought. Yehoshiva had taxes to collect; this was not worth his time to argue.

Shemesh watched him walk away. *He's becoming unreliable for what I need from him.* He looked down at the garbage and rot along the riverbank and inhaled deeply. He reminded himself what it had meant all those years ago to go through the Machine. Those who commit to the civilized life always have an easier time of it. Specialization, distribution, leisure, luxury, and love. The acrid aroma of this diseased river was the gulf spreading between two cells. A mitosis that would carry on to create two different organisms of these people, the nomads and the civilized. Not only did he savor the smells that triggered his dormant memories, but he adored what that squalor represented.

Garbage meant he was succeeding. Excess meant he was producing. Suffering meant the poor people who sat on the fence between their old itinerant lives and the new one the Masters promised would soon have to decide what they valued: brutish, short lives of suffering among the plateaus and dunes or the grinding hardship of adapting to a new way of life they could not comprehend. He took one more deep breath to smell that mixture of rot and excretion, a unique but common olfaction that these virgin lands never produced naturally. It was a sign of his happy memories.

His mind wandered back to his home world as he went to meet with his agents at the gate. Yehoshiva was no longer open and free with the information he provided him; he needed to find out for himself what was going on.

25

The sounds and smells of the city were much different now. Even from the compound, they were more desperate. Katesh could hear the coughing from over the high wall every morning, and their proximity muted the free conversations of the Elohim. The sounds of sickness surrounded the walls, and more ears were pressed to the place the Masters took refuge from the din and dinge of the city. They got to the point where they longed for a field operation just to escape the wretchedness that surrounded them, a wretchedness they knew they had participated in creating and that burned at their souls as a symbol of their own misdeeds.

There was no more contempt for these people, at least not among those who were outside the administration of them. The scientists looked at them with a tender curiosity. And those of softer ideologies and training looked at them with sadness and pity.

Katesh was among the former group, not wholly sold on the helplessness of these piteous creatures yet not so callous as to believe they were there by their own designs. She saw Yehoshiva while coming in from the field one day as she was planning what was to become a major scientific leap for these people—the designing and building of observatories they would use to make a calendar and know the seasons. He was on some other management operation collecting taxes or checking the borders or production of this or that. She signaled to him with flicks of her hands; her face revealed no outward expression. *This decay is not in anyone's interest.*

She stopped and turned her attention to a woman and her child covered in filth. The child was barely breathing, and the mother looked up at Katesh with the deep, hopeless eyes of someone who knew the fate of her child and could do nothing but watch it happen.

Katesh spoke in the native tongue to the woman. "What is his name?"

The mother shook her head tearfully as she responded. "We no longer give them names until they are three summers old. This one will not have a name."

Katesh knelt down and picked up the child. She took out a clean rag from a pouch on the dromedary her Kaldees were guiding and water from a skin and cleaned the baby. She disrobed the child to look it over as the mother sat silently and obediently.

The mother spoke cautiously as Katesh examined her baby. "Does the baby meet the Master's approval?"

Katesh was curious about what this meant. "This baby is sickly and filthy. I do not approve of his condition."

The mother's tears flowed freely now as she spoke. "Will . . . will the Master smash the baby then?"

Katesh reeled at the words, taken off guard by the implied expectation. *Who has been smashing the babies?* She hadn't even finished the thought before she knew the truth. *Shemesh.* She glanced at Yehoshiva, who stood nearby, and a look of barely disguised horror painted across his face as he watched and listened to the exchange. Katesh looked at him, and the pain and anger of the reputation Shemesh earned them hardened her resolve. She spoke gently to the woman. "No, there is no issue that we cannot solve. This baby will live a long life. You will name him Moon. For he and his children will walk this planet as long as the moon is in the night sky."

The mother's sobs broke out gratefully as she fell to her knees. "Master, thank you for your mercy and generosity. How shall I repay your kindness?"

Katesh's promise carried a new obligation to these people, which she had just committed to. And now she had to find a way to fulfill it that would protect the baby from harm. She needed a mark of her own that would tell the other Masters the baby was under her protection. But in the meantime, he would need to be cared for. "You will go to the compound of the Kaldees and let them know the baby is to be trained in their teachings. You will let them know Master Katesh has selected him." She looked at the priests, who were blatantly pretending not to be paying attention.

One caught her eye and responded in the native tongue. "Your will, will be done, Master." Then he repeated it in the Master's tongue. "Amen."

Katesh began to examine the child while he was undressed. She was no doctor, but she knew enough. They all did. From their time in the Machine, they could all see the symptoms of illness and what conditions they pointed to. This baby was breathing shallow and wet, his stomach was distended from malnourishment, and he had sores on his body. Upon closer inspection, the sores had parasitic worms in them, worms that were the larvae of the flies that lived in the filth all over the city. The distended stomach was more parasites in the digestive tract, and the shallow breathing was from pneumonia caused by the dust in the air breathed by everyone and the excrement that floated with it.

The baby was clean, but it was not being truly cleaned. The water she used for bathing was the putrid effluence of the riverbank, and the constant dust in the air stuck to it without being wiped off. The mother at least attempted the rituals, but the desperate conditions in the city made this a truly futile effort. The Masters had given them the rituals to follow on the promise that their lives would be made better, yet here was a woman, a sample of all the people of the city, who performed these rites obediently and was not made better for it. The priests dismissed this as the woman living in sin in other ways, but the Masters knew this was not the point of the rituals. Sin could only be corrected if virtues had real rewards. And under these conditions, they did not.

Katesh signaled for the priests to bring the alcohol. She poured it on the baby, who started crying at the burning pain in the sores on his body. She poured more, and before long the parasites had evacuated the sores and could be easily plucked off the baby's body. For the internal parasites, Katesh took some bitter roots she had gathered that had an antiparasitic property. She smashed them up in a stone mortar and pestle, took a pinch, and dropped it into the baby's crying mouth. His lips recoiled with disgust. She took some fresh water and allowed the baby to suckle on the nipple on the skin until it was satisfied. Then she crushed a flower bulb with an anti-inflammatory property and rinsed it into a carafe the woman had for her water. Katesh then signaled for the woman to stand and had her disrobe as well.

The air was warm, but the public display denied the woman the dignity she desired. Katesh was unmoved. This woman's condition was a common one, and this ritual needed to be performed publicly to ensure any onlookers understood they were not alone. Dignity is the chief obstacle to public health and allows issues to fester in the darkness. These people needed to know they were not alone in their maladies, and the best way to break that dispiriting spell was to show they had a treatment.

The woman hesitated at the embarrassment this would cause her but complied when the Master standing before her refused to entertain her modesty. The same sores covered the mother, and Katesh poured alcohol on the woman's shoulders, allowing it to run down her back and front. The woman let out a painful moan as the alcohol burned at the sores. The larvae reacted the same way as before, and Katesh plucked them out. Then Katesh examined the woman's breasts where she nursed the baby; they were filthy. Katesh instructed the woman to wash herself thoroughly every day and to give the baby the water she had poured the blended root and flower mixture into. Then she gently touched the woman on the forehead and handed back the baby, and said, "His name is Moon." As Katesh began to turn away, she stopped and then said, "Wash your clothes every other day and bathe in the fast water of the river. All your water should come from there."

Katesh then moved on. As she walked past, she made eye contact with Yehoshiva, and the flicker of a conversation between the two became the purpose he had been looking for in his work.

These people are dying. We need to help, Katesh expressed with a mournful look in her eyes.

Yehoshiva responded with his own gaze. *I know, and it's my fault, but what can we do?*

Katesh raised her eyebrows and flicked her eyes toward the obelisk. *Your fault only?* She pursed her lips to say, *It doesn't matter.* We *need to do something.*

Yehoshiva committed himself the moment he saw the *we*. They needed a hospital, and they needed Tammuz to prepare medicines for these people. They needed better sanitation and better waste disposal and more alcohol for sanitation, so they needed Kimdu's expertise in distilling to produce it on an industrial scale. They needed sewer lines for the filth to flow and wastewater treatment to remove the debris and filter the water. The citizens needed to be the ones to do it. The Masters had the technology, but the people needed to be responsible for the maintenance.

Yehoshiva watched her pass, and he nodded his acceptance of the mission. He knew Shemesh would object, but there was no refuting that it would increase the productivity of the citizens. Yehoshiva would make him say yes. He was determined to.

It didn't take much to convince several others to participate. They were not there to increase the productivity of the people. They were there to increase the viability of the city through other means, none of which were intended for the purpose of increasing the output of a quarry or a mine.

Katesh and Yehoshiva found quiet moments alone to craft the conspiracy. Katesh's critical eye for the problems and solutions to resolve them was invaluable. Yehoshiva knew the city better than anyone, Shemesh included, and could identify the places where their schemes would have the greatest impact. In their disdain for Shemesh, they were mutually helpful, Katesh knowing how to undermine his schemes most effectively and Yehoshiva knowing how to spin the improvements to make Shemesh see value in them.

"We need to be able to distribute medicine to these people in large daily quantities," Katesh whispered to Yehoshiva as they prepared a meal in the kitchen. They stood close to each other over the stovetop, tossing meat and vegetables into a stir fry and warming tortillas on the range.

"Shemesh will stop it unless it somehow undermines the people's judgment and causes some level of chaos. I think we need to make a wine. The alcohol will help kill any parasites, and the medicines can be part of the blend for flavoring," Yehoshiva blurted out without putting too much thought into the scheme.

Katesh looked at him. Her eyes sparkled, and she gazed softly at him as she admired this insightful comment. She had never seen him in this light—he had grown, he was confident and experienced, and he was a meaningful contributor to the well-being of these people. *Something's changed in him*, she thought.

He stopped flipping the tortillas and looked back at her. When he saw the way she looked at him, he blushed and fumbled awkwardly until he could regain control of his senses. He stammered out a question. "What do, uh, what do you think?"

She chuckled as she nodded in agreement. *Well, that broke the spell,* she thought. "I think we'll need to get Tammuz and Kimdu to lend their support for a few projects. We'll need to show the primi—the *people*—how to make wine for themselves. We'll also need to train them in medical examination. We'll need to get them to reduce their waste and prevent them from contaminating the river to keep the diseases down. Sanitation is critical. That's the first step. How we achieve that depends on what we can get away with." The meat seared, and the vegetables sizzled and steamed as she tossed them.

"If Kimdu can teach them to make wine, I think we can keep most of the food waste out of the river. They'll have an incentive to follow our ways." He gestured with his copper spatula toward the scrap bins they used for the same purpose. "I'll work on a septic system and wells for clean water."

"I'll see if Tammuz can enlist some veterinary help from her team. I'll set up some clinics and get my Kaldees trained as physicians." Katesh let the meat sizzle a bit as she paused. She leaned toward Yehoshiva and nudged him with her shoulder playfully. "Thank you," she said warmly.

He stood there for a second, not sure how to respond. He felt responsible, so why she was thanking him didn't make sense. "I think it's I who should thank you." He deflected. He smiled as he piled the tortillas together and plated them. Katesh scooped up the stir fry and did the same. A small pile of crumbled cheese for garnish and a fragrant sauce of mixed spices were added, and they carried the lunch to their waiting colleagues.

The whispers in the hall of the berthing were enough. Katesh could count on Kimdu and Tammuz for their support in their endeavor, and they were able to get a few more reliable people to come on board to lend support as they were able. Most of the agriculture staff were eager to apply their skills to something useful and began training the herdsmen in their charge to identify the parasites and maladies of the environment and how to treat them, first on the animals. Then when the people of the slums were seen with the same ailments, the herdsmen were able to apply their knowledge to help their fellow denizens. The people were empowered with helping one another meaningfully.

Tammuz had produced a grain crop from the desert grass that enabled the population to be fed cheaply. She had also isolated the different hallucinogenic and medicinal qualities of the mountain flower and developed a variety that produced large quantities of the latter. Since the mountain flower was already ubiquitous in its hallucinogenic form in the slums and wasn't altogether different from the medicinal variant, there would be little difficulty in making it readily available to the people.

Shemesh encouraged intoxication in the people in every form. He explained its value by saying, "We can identify those of sober temperament easier and identify whom we can trust," but everyone knew his priests were corrupted by their dependence on a variety of drugs and that dependence made them easier to keep in line. Katesh guessed correctly that he would not immediately notice the medicinal variant replacing the hallucinogenic one, and the plan could proceed without interference in the short term.

Tammuz identified the antiparasitic qualities of the roots and increased their yields. Every plant she could find with some quality that might increase the health of the primitives was developed and strengthened and then processed into a medicine the Masters could use to improve the health of the population. The issue became getting the medicines in large enough volumes and in a form intoxicating enough to be useful to Shemesh's schemes.

Kimdu worked on plans for a distillery. The reeds Tammuz had been working on were able to survive away from the water's edge with some irrigation, so he used those along with a native yeast to produce an earthy alcoholic brew. He needed to fabricate a hydrometer to determine what the alcohol content was. He closed the end of a reed with a clay plug. In clean distilled water, he marked its water level and then again in pure alcohol, which was produced off-world and transferred into clay carafes for transport, in order to find the high and low limits of the potency. Then changing the ratio of water and alcohol mixed in the container, he was able to mark each line for various percentages so he could estimate the alcohol content.

As the yeast converted the sugars into alcohol mixed into the mash, the lower yield, alcohol-intolerant yeasts were sterilized, and the hardier ones survived up until the point the sugar ran almost completely out. After months of allowing the brew to ferment, he was able to split the brew and add more water and sugar reed, which would allow the yeast to continue to ferment and reproduce. In a short time, he was able to get yields of 15 percent in the mash, which he could begin to distill.

The distillation process was simple, but with the stone and clay tools and equipment available to them, it was inefficient. The crude clay equipment left alcohol content too low to use for sanitation, but it was good enough to mass produce an alcoholic drink. The distillation process would need to be done in a smaller batch form. Copper was smelted to form sheets that were then rolled and coated with clay to form a watertight seal. The primitives were shown how to keep the fire low and hot to get the temperature right for converting the alcohol into vapor and then cooling it into a liquid. The process was not economical, but it increased the alcohol content up to a sterilizing percentage useful for medical purposes. Once the primitives were given the technology, they began to establish stills in every corner they could. Every house saved their scraps and used them to create a mash. The volume of rotting garbage in the river declined, and the people had passive income from the cottage industry. Kimdu began holding festivals each calendar year to judge the quality of the wines produced, and the people competed to win the prize of copper sheeting for stills to produce the more valuable medical-grade alcohol.

To prevent the people from drinking the river water, Kimdu's team used the distilled water to make fruit wine, which they sold as cheaply as it could be produced. The alcohol content was high enough to kill parasites, the flavor was exotic, the fruit contained nutrients that helped with the people's nutrition, and the distilled water base hydrated them. The alcohol also made meals and the people happier, and they began to use it in lieu of water on every occasion. Drinking water became a symbol of desperation.

Tammuz assisted Kimdu with the flavoring. She processed the spices of various saps and pollens and heated them until they were syrups or powders. Dried flowers and grasses, pulverized roots and bulbs—everything with a healing property was blended to make delicious and cost-effective products that were affordable to as many as possible. When the recipe was perfected, they shared it with the people, publicly displayed on the side of the distillery.

Yehoshiva began to hold public ceremonies and used the wine in conjunction with the burnt offerings. He held the ceremonies every week and made sure all the attendees received a full cup, which by the analysis of the off-world chemists contained enough medicine to kill all the parasites the people would pick up through that week. They got food from the festival and grains and breads to nourish them in the days between.

Katesh continued to play nurse to the people, and as the hospital was built up, she took time to see patients. She had no medical training, but all those who survived the Machine knew anatomy intimately, the processes of alchemy and later chemistry were second nature, and observation of symptoms and living conditions common to these people was enough to educate them on what needed to be done. All the Masters who were not otherwise occupied rotated through the hospital on a daily basis. The people began to see rapid improvements in their health.

Yehoshiva found Katesh at the clinic one night tending to the sick. It was not enough that their immediate symptoms be treated but their underlying conditions too.

Yehoshiva stood at the back of the clinic out of sight of the patients waiting for her. He listened as she spoke to each patient. "You need to perform the rituals and do them thoroughly. They will please your god, and in turn your god will give you abundance and health. You must purify your body. You need to purify your water and your food and give God his share. And you must purify your home to give God a peaceful place with you." She touched the woman on the forehead and sent her on her way.

Katesh caught a glimpse of Yehoshiva in the shadows in the next room and signaled for him to come before the next patient arrived. It was not the place for open conversation, so they spoke through their body language and gave context through their spoken conversation, but the look on her face said she was glad to see him.

It's good to see you. Look at all that we've accomplished here, she indicated with her raised eyebrows and a quick gesture at the facility. "Patients have been coming in slowly but are not returning frequently, which is good," she said aloud.

You've been here every night this week, Yehoshiva said with a surprised look in his eyes that shifted to a flick to the memory recall side of his brain. "That's excellent. That means they're getting healthier."

You noticed, huh? She raised one eyebrow as she spoke. "Yes, before long this facility will be obsolete, and we can train the Kaldees to perform these tasks."

I always notice you. He shrugged, somewhat abashed. "That would be great progress for these people."

She looked down briefly, flattered by his attentions. *You notice me, huh?* Her eyebrows raised seductively. "It will take quite a bit of training, but we have time."

Yehoshiva looked down shyly. *I always have.* "Time is on our side, but not theirs. Is there anything I can do to help?"

Her face flushed momentarily at the flattery, then she looked down, signaling her refusal. *We can't make that work out here.* Her head tilted apologetically. "We simply need more of everything. I don't think we have the means to keep this up for long."

He let a flash of anguish flicker through as he looked into her eyes. "Is it too hopeful to think so?"

She wasn't sure if he was referring to their body conversation or the spoken one, so she merely smiled and bowed her head slightly. *As you wish.* "I think it will take time," she said in response to both conversations. A faint smile on her lips made his heart leap, and he promised to both conversations, "Whatever it takes to meet your needs."

A young Kaldean woman came leading a patient through the curtain from the waiting room. She wore a pendant of a bird, and Yehoshiva did not recognize her at first. "Samara," he said in the common tongue.

The young woman was startled at seeing the other Master in the room and bowed low to greet him. She spoke the Masters' tongue fluidly and with more precision than the myriad priests and civil functionaries could muster. "Master Yehoshiva, I was not aware of your presence."

Yehoshiva could tell she was lying; despite her linguistic talents, she was still incapable of disguising her body language from the Masters. "It has been a long time, and you have grown into such a distinguished woman. Your father would be proud of your achievement."

She bowed low as she spoke, trying to disguise the tension in her body. "My father was a mere slave, your grace. He would be proud if I were a shepherd."

Yehoshiva glanced at Katesh, and in a flicker of phrenological conversation expressed his admiration. *You've trained her well to hide her past, and her talent for our language is uncanny.*

"You will achieve great things, Samara. All you learn from us will be useful once we're gone." He watched as that sank in, and the anticipation in her body was palpable.

Katesh flashed a warning at him. *She is not ready to know these things.* "That will be a long time from now, Samara. You have much training to endure before then."

Samara's body deflated slightly as she rose again. "Master Katesh, I should hope I die long before you abandon us."

Katesh smiled kindly for her to see, but the flicker of her eyes told a different message to Yehoshiva. *Don't give her any more ideas; she's as dangerous as her father; more so even.* "Learn everything you can before then, and teach your people everything we teach you. And you will live *long* through them to see us part ways as equals." She let the words sink in, the emphasis on *long* met its target, and Samara feigned appreciation while showing despair.

Samara signaled to the patient confused by the Masters' language and kneeling in submission. Samara then spoke in the common tongue to the woman. "The Masters will see you now." She had almost let her tongue slip as she referred to the Monsters she reviled.

Katesh heard it. Yehoshiva heard it. And they looked at each other hopefully. *She will lead these people when Shemesh's tyranny finally crashes. There may be hope yet.*

Only if we keep her rebelliousness controlled.

Only if she doesn't kill us before then.

26

Shemesh eyed the open trench with disdain. He saw the sewer tunnel and knew the extensive network was intended for more than just wastewater. The height was as tall as he was, and there were notches set into the stone for a floodgate. He traced the road with his eyes and saw no place for the sewage to run into it, and the slope was set to channel fluids to the sides rather than toward the middle. *This is a tunnel*, he surmised. At the end of that road was the new temple. And the compound built up around it led here.

"That young whelp is a schemer, it seems," he said to himself as he surveyed the new city block.

The foreman of the day crew knelt before him, his arm flowing red with blood, waiting for his Master to decide his fate. The blackened scars of his previous meetings stretched up his arms, and the freshness of some of the wounds still seeped black from the ash packed in to stain the marks.

Shemesh spoke to the man before him. "What is this that you apes have been building in the dark of night?" he said with a sneer.

"Forgive I, Master. Night short and not time finish work," he muttered, not understanding the situation.

Shemesh peered down savagely at this wretched beast. "Who has been constructing these tunnels?"

"Night foreman build sewer for drain. Day foreman build road, Master." The man was fearful, and his sweat glistened from his sun-darkened skin as he waited for the fate that had befallen his predecessor and earned him his esteemed role.

"Are you not in charge of this whole operation? Do you not know the plans like the back of your hand?" Shemesh's voice roared as he watched the little man quiver before him.

"Master, I not make plan. I follow only." The stench of his sweat wafted through the arid breeze, heavy with wine and plenty of mountain flower.

Shemesh loomed over him. A dark thought drifted through his mind. He already knew everything he needed to know and was only making a scene for the workers nearby to see it. "I make the plans that you follow, and this is not what I have commanded." He looked around at the workers listening fearfully to the exchange. Barely half could understand a fraction of what was going on, but his gesturing at the open tunnel clearly showed his disapproval at the work.

Shemesh reached down, palmed the man's head, and lifted him up viciously. Urine dripped from the sandals of the terrified foreman as Shemesh stared into his eyes. "This tunnel is not approved." He reeled back and threw the man headfirst into the open cavern below. His shriek ended abruptly as his head impacted on the stone floor, and the dull crack oozed dark red in the darkness.

The workers nearby recoiled with horror and began working faster on their projects. Some just made noise as they worked, idly shoveling dirt onto overfull bags for the shoulder yokes.

Shemesh looked fiercely at the workers, who avoided his gaze. He called out to them in a growl, "Who can understand me?" Most of the workers kept their pace and didn't change. He could see one man who hammered on a stone even faster as his words reached him. *He can,* Shemesh thought.

He walked to the man, and the other workers scurried away. His shadow grew around the man as he approached, and the man slowed and finally stopped his work before prostrating himself before Shemesh.

"You understand me, don't you." Shemesh was not asking; he knew the answer and was waiting for the man to respond in the affirmative.

"Y-yes, I understand." Even his diction was clear, and Shemesh was impressed by his obvious aptitude.

"Then you were avoiding me deliberately." Shemesh's hand rolled the weathered tetrahedron, feeling the gems on each face, finding the one that marked this man's personality.

"I am a simple craftsman. I don't have the mind for planning," the man pleaded.

Shemesh could see from his finished stones that they fit neatly together without gaps or blemishes. This man didn't want to serve him. But who would after witnessing the violence moments ago? Shemesh measured this man's worth, his hand turning the tetrahedron over. Ambitious? No. Intelligent? Yes. Creative? Yes. Disciplined? Yes. He was one who served no one but himself. This man was very likely a rebel, he decided. *This one may prove useful to my purposes.* "You are in charge of this project now. Your first task is to seal those tunnels. *All* of them. At every junction."

The man eyed the hole where the old foreman lay dead at the bottom and calculated his chance of escaping from this alive. He finally spoke. "Yes . . . Master." He lay prostrate but did not cut himself in the servile way others before him had. Though he was well aware of the ritual that others followed, he was defiant.

Shemesh narrowed his eyes and turned away. *This one will serve his purpose another way. By morning he will have left the city.*

Shemesh waited in his office for Yehoshiva. Working on different projects and managing the bustle of an entire city made these meetings infrequent but necessary to ensure his objectives were met. But recently Yehoshiva's actions seemed to be undermining his goals.

Shemesh turned the gold tetrahedron over in his hand. Each face showed its wear, as he frequently used it to determine individual personalities and make decisions. He remembered his time in the Machine; the gods of his people came, and their leader carried a similar bauble. It took a long time to comprehend what it truly meant, but once he understood it, he felt in his soul the value was enormous. Little more than a trinket, it was gold and had different gems on each face and tip. Each characterized a different personality archetype and the overlaps between them. Each tip represented science, economics, government, and religion when used for determining the character of a culture. Each face represented the combined attributes of the three adjoining points and the exclusion of the fourth. It was by this method he could define a person, their use, their opponents, and their basic thought processes. He had become very good at reading everyone and everything very quickly to determine their use to him and his aims.

Shemesh thought about his young apprentice and rolled the bauble in his hand as he did. Yehoshiva was curious. Shemesh thumbed the jewel representing science, an emerald with no occlusions and a pure verdant clarity. Yehoshiva was moralistic too. He thumbed the azure sapphire representing the religious point on the tetrahedron. While Yehoshiva's job was economically focused, he was less concerned about the productive value of a thing than ensuring it was morally extracted and fair. His obvious aversion to authoritarian practices meant he was not useful for subjugating the people he was leading—which the people required. Shemesh had to give them an icon to worship to pull them out of the swirling vortex of animalistic living and stagnation and extinction. Yehoshiva was little more than a philosopher, that junction on the edge between science and religion and the jewels that typified them. *Yet*, he pondered, *if Yehoshiva did happen to adopt a strong economic sense, he would be a force to be reckoned with as his actions brought prosperity to every culture he led.* He thumbed the jade stone at the middle of the face between those points.

Yehoshiva knocked lightly at the open door and came in. "You wanted to see me?" he asked as he stepped in.

Shemesh looked at him, his young face and sun-darkened skin. *What does she see in him anyway?* "Yes, we need to discuss the progress you've been making around the city."

Yehoshiva's eyes darted around at the desk and wondered what specifically he was referring to and how to defend against this next assault on morale. "Is there something wrong with how I've been handling it? Productivity is much higher with the public health initiatives and sanitation."

Shemesh could feel his lip trying to curl into a snarl but consciously fought back the urge to castigate his assistant. "Your efforts have been allowing production at the mines to slip. Look at the numbers." He slid a chart across the desk so Yehoshiva could see the handwritten spreadsheet.

Stone, steady. Copper, up 10 percent; gold, down 5 percent; tin, down 2 percent. "These numbers are basically stable. What's the issue?"

Shemesh glared at him. "That is the monthly data that represents the number of shipments leaving here. This"—he slid another spreadsheet across the table—"represents the shipments arriving at Irka."

Yehoshiva looked at the numbers, and every category was reduced by 10 percent. "So the rebels are attacking every tenth caravan? I can't guard every caravan all the way to Irka to prevent this."

"Security is your responsibility. That's why I allow you the freedom of managing that to your satisfaction. So productivity wouldn't slip. And here, we have productivity being lost by inadequate resources assigned to caravans. This is your responsibility." Shemesh felt a rush of satisfaction as he belittled this arrogant youth. "You need to explain to me how your sewage systems and recycling program make this number any better."

Yehoshiva stared for a moment and clenched his teeth. "I can hire more soldiers, but their currency is worthless. I need something that is actually worth something to pay them with, not these seeds that everyone seems to have growing in their houses." He reached into his pouch and pulled out a small handful and rolled them onto Shemesh's desk. "We need something that is fungible, something rare, something durable, and something with real value."

Shemesh thumbed the tetrahedron and massaged the jade bead as he listened. "You have been using copper pretty liberally for your projects. Feel free to use it as coinage if it suits you. Gold too. If the primitives know we value it, they will value it, and then they will produce more. But you had better make sure these numbers are positive and deliveries are assured." He picked up some more papers on his desk and stared at them silently for a moment.

Yehoshiva seemed uncertain whether this was a dismissal, so he turned to the door to leave.

"One more thing," Shemesh said to him before he left. "You can abandon your efforts to clean up the river. It's not a useful endeavor—no unapproved projects. If the water is cleaned, they will not need to use the hospital. The hospital is the face of our goodwill, and they will forget how much they need us if the cause of illness is removed." Shemesh knew his argument was facile. He was not compassionate by nature, but he knew Yehoshiva was, and this argument would threaten the project he knew he needed to fulfill his sense of decency.

Yehoshiva knew the dynamic and how to appeal to Shemesh's malevolence, so he objected. "Well, it's not the water that created the source of the disease—it was the people. The water won't change their habits, but it might make those properties more valuable if the river looks more attractive."

Shemesh chewed on this idea for a moment. *Clever reversal,* he thought. "This *will* bring us more gold, and we can increase the taxes in those areas. That will be acceptable."

It took Yehoshiva by surprise that the plan had worked. But the increased taxes meant that the current residents would be displaced quickly and their access to the water would be removed. He walked out the door without being dismissed. Shemesh had won in the end. He always seemed to.

As he walked out, he saw Katesh speaking with Tammuz by the raised beds in the courtyard, and his anxiety melted away as he walked toward her.

With one last word, Shemesh drove his victory home. "No speaking in the courtyard—there are ears at the wall."

Everyone turned to look at Shemesh. Every face fell. Their sanctuary was gone.

27

Yehoshiva was in the dining hall seated by himself, looking into the future without seeing any. He was not alone in the hall, but he chose to be by himself. It was the one freedom they still had even with Shemesh's increasingly strict rules.

Whether their purpose was legitimate or not, the outcome was a catastrophic blow to the morale of their team. But with the flow of gold through the city, Shemesh was now crafting new ways to tax and acquire the wealth of the citizens to send back to Irka. This put all their projects and efforts in line with his designs. With the quarry now producing gold, the Masters no longer had to supervise the production there to get the primitives to keep working. They knew the value of the resource to the Masters, so they knew the promise it provided to themselves. Though there was quite a bit of leakage from the mine as miners kept some of the valuable ore, the society created a system that funneled those resources back to the Masters. It was no concern that a few stupid miners got rich illegitimately. They would soon lose everything by their own foolish behaviors, drinking too much and buying luxuries and exotic drugs that funneled resources to the rebels and increased crime and accidents.

They kept working the mines because of the constant flow of illegitimate wealth. Yet as they got wealthier, they wanted less and less to do with the actual mining. Their lives had become too easy to continue to break rocks all day, so the foreman beseeched the Masters to let them bring on more workers.

Yehoshiva could see the deception. But knew he needed to keep the production going. Frankly, he thought, these people would trade in gold and copper and bronze and make it easier to collect for transport back to Irka. It was an acceptable loss. But this greed led down a predictable path, and Shemesh was sure to take advantage of it.

He stared forlornly into the nothingness in his mind. Weary from the constant struggle against his boss to achieve *anything*, he spoke aloud to himself, deep in his own thoughts. "This *has* to end."

"What are you going to do about it though?"

The soft and tender voice came from the ether and startled Yehoshiva back to reality. Katesh sat next to him quietly stirring and spooning her broth, not eating, just being present. His heart lifted, and as his eyes adjusted to the external world, the candlelight illuminated her face like a halo, and she was transfigured into a mythical goddess in his mind. Just her sitting there was enough to lift his spirits, and he knew he wasn't alone. He reached over without thinking of it and gently took her hand and held it for a moment.

Katesh stopped her spoon and looked at him softly, not pulling back, not fighting. She curled her fingers to embrace his.

Yehoshiva looked into her eyes. "Whenever I'm tired and broken, you strengthen me." He squeezed gently and rubbed his thumb on the back of her hand before pulling it away.

She sat quietly, stunned and enamored. She blushed, the dark gray of her sun-darkened face flushing darker in the candlelight. And she said nothing.

"We can't keep going like this, but I don't know what to do," he said after a moment.

Katesh compared the maps. The topography of each had slight variations, and the orientation of the hills and their elongation showed the lack of precision her Kaldees took in their efforts. Their starting references were obvious too. Mistakes in the maps radiated outward on all sides from them. It was a simple task she asked of them: "Survey the hill." But few understood the implication of their flaws.

Only one was predictably accurate. Some flaws, but it showed a greater amount of precision than the rest. "You've done a fine job, Samara," she spoke in the Master's tongue as she always did with her students.

"Thank you, Master Katesh," she said with a bow, her diction as precise as her survey.

"I would like you to lead your class and survey the hill east of the city. We will begin excavating the ground here and begin construction of the observatory. It should take you one month to complete the survey there. Bring me seven prints as accurate as this one." She lifted Samara's print slightly to indicate her approval. "Each one of your team should produce one independently and put their signatures on them."

"It will be done, Master Katesh." Samara bowed, and the wooden bird dangled from her neck. She turned to her class and led them to the small tool shack nearby on the edge of their compound to collect the surveying equipment they had amassed.

The western district Katesh had commissioned was as precise and disciplined as she was. It was orderly and clean, and she saw it as a reflection of herself, the manifestation of her own personality. Because she was not under Shemesh's direct command, other than as a contractor, she had certain liberties the other Masters didn't enjoy, and she took refuge from the rest of the city and its chaos there.

Kimdu helped her with the planning, and she gave him a place there to teach brewing and metalworking and various construction techniques. The district became a magnet for the people of the city oppressed by Shemesh's authoritarian religion. Tammuz showed the people the methods of agriculture, and raised gardens lined every building. The former slaves, many too old now and far removed from their previous life, had been instrumental in their industriousness in establishing the compound, and that legacy was preserved in the children they had borne and the Kaldees who served at Katesh's command.

She felt the pull of leadership in her community, a society growing out of the rejection of the one Shemesh had built. She could feel the tug of a battle between the moral obligation to these people and her fundamental being. She had a need for order and rules, but at the same time, she was unable to force that order on these people who had emerged from the chaos of the wild and lived under the oppression of various masters and leaders, then to find that the life they left was only magnified in the society Shemesh offered them. She had to do something different.

Yehoshiva came up the hill as he often did when making his rounds of the city. The refugees from the wilderness had stopped flooding in, and there was security and relative peace at this edge of their growing metropolis. He looked tired and sad. He was alone in his resistance to Shemesh in his capacity—not alone in the true sense, but only he was in a position to make tangible changes in the lives of the people and influence Shemesh in his motives. He wanted to do right; he had a moral upbringing. But he had an obligation in his position to ensure production always increased, so he had to balance his decisions so he would not lose sight of where he had come from. His intellect and curiosity made him a natural scientist, able to design complex systems and procedures to achieve his goals. This aspect never wavered, and it was this commonality with herself that Katesh found so appealing. Her increasing sense of moral obligation made him someone she found herself gravitating toward. And she knew he needed her to remind him of his compassion.

"Your district is a model for all who see it. You have an incredible gift for organization." This was now his standard greeting for her if there were ears present or nearby. The compliment was his way of expressing love. It was not her way of receiving it, and she found herself holding her own hand at the thought of that moment of vulnerability he had shared with her in the dining hall.

She gave him her standard greeting. "It keeps growing, but it's the people who make it a model. They have taken to our teachings and have hungered for more. They are poor here, but they profit from their serenity more than from their produce." She fidgeted a little and hung her hands in a practiced nonchalance that hid her nervousness from those around them.

Yehoshiva was close now, and his hands began to urgently message Katesh even as he spoke calmly and brightly. "They have true riches then, and the glory of their city belongs to them." *Taxes—that's how he's going to strip these people of their freedom.*

Katesh looked around at her district in alarm. They had little to sell. They provided intellectual services, not material ones. "Their riches are truly of both this world and the next," she muttered as she looked around anxiously. She signed back to him. *Why the sudden change?*

Yehoshiva joined her in looking down at the district in silence while his hands and body twitched the subtle message of his nonverbal response. *He wanted the improvement to stop. I had to tell him something to divert him. Now the river properties are going to be revalued, and those improvements will make it easier to do. I'm sorry.*

She looked at him with pity and sympathy. He was caught in the hardest trap to evade. Both options served Shemesh. She stood in silence for a moment and then reached up and pulled the strap on his harness up farther on his shoulder before letting her hand fall slowly, gently caressing his arm. It was a breach of protocol, but the impact was immediate.

His eyes glistened from his perceived failure, unable to speak.

She spoke instead. "These people have talents that will pay dividends for those who put them to good use. It will enrich their lives to market themselves appropriately." She signed to him a reassurance. *We'll make it work. This won't go on forever.*

Two Standard Years Later

28

Katesh had just completed another observatory and trained a new set of Kaldees to mark the stars they saw through the portals they had set up in a ring. It was a tedious task, as it always was with the Kaldees. They couldn't comprehend what she meant by drawing the sky. So she had to design the observatory with boxes to frame in a portion of the sky and told the priests to draw the *big* stars in that box. Then she set them all back-to-back in the middle of the observatory. They put circles and dots on the paper—at first completely at random; they were drawing representations of the sky.

When she grew furious and threw all their pictures into the water pot, she took the spot of one and drew a quick picture of the sky framed by the pillars on the side and the capstone above. When she showed them that hers looked like what they actually saw, they understood. But they were too slow. By the time they had put a dot or circle where one star was relative to the frame, the stars had already moved, and they were drawing a completely distorted image once again. She made them do it over and over and over again to get them faster at it. Then she told them to only draw the ten biggest or brightest so they would be quicker. This was easier, and over time they charted the largest stars, and they could trace them based on the days in between when they would first appear on the horizon in one priest's pictures until they disappeared from the horizon in another priest's picture.

One planetary year to teach them how to draw ten stars, she thought. It took ten planetary years to construct the first observatory, then five for the second one and three for the third. It got easier as the crews figured out the easiest way to do it. Each of those observatories required attendants both night and day, and it took years to train them to understand the frames, the clock, and the markings on the floors. It was all just to get them to discover the calendar and their planetary cycle.

It took more than two standard years to complete that. But now they had three observatories, each in a different place a horizon apart, so they all drew three different pictures at the same relative time. This way they could triangulate the location of the stars and, from that, figure out the arc of their planet to determine its circumference.

But this required a clock, so she had to show them how, when the sun rises and casts the first shadow, they should mark on the ground of the observatory with a piece of charcoal. When it set at night, they would mark the place of the last shadow with charcoal. Then they would find the center point of the arc, and that would be the midday sun. When the next day came, they would do the same. They would then see that the midday was always the same spot on the ground, and the morning and evening shadows were slightly different each day.

When the morning and evening shadows started moving back the way they were before, the season would be changing soon. When the shadow landed in the middle, it was going to get colder or hotter depending on which direction it was going. Exactly opposite the midday mark, she drew another mark using the center point of the morning and evening shadow lines as a reference. This was the line facing true south. The midday mark was true north.

Once she was able to break the day into different parts and the sky into different parts and show the priests that they would see the same thing every single year, they began to understand what was going on. They were at least able to be left alone to perform their duties without supervision. She still had to collect their sketches every morning and sort them in order by which window the priest had peered out and by what time they were done. The process required an inordinate amount of patience, and she was not of that temperament. She was, however, a Master who had undergone the Machine, and even her lost patience barely registered to these primitive priests.

29

Shemesh's new high priest stood on the guard tower reading a proclamation to the people in the common tongue.

> The heavy price of the rebels' threats to the city and the loss of supplies from Irka and shipments of our great efforts require that a levy be raised to secure the route. A conscription of men is necessary, and a temporary tax is to be implemented to ensure our safety and prosperity. The properties will be taxed proportional to their assessed value, and any family who cannot afford the tax will need to provide a conscript to aid the effort. If a family can do neither, their labor will be required at a rate equal to their tax burden to assist in the establishment of a highway to Irka.

Shemesh had already evaluated the properties whose value he deemed too high for the current occupants, and he had seized a section of the poorest part of the city to establish a conscription center, as he called it, complete with bars and thick stone walls. Farku had died under mysterious circumstances near the gate, and one of his deputies had taken over as the Shield. This man proved very loyal to Shemesh. He wore his darkened scars with pride and showed a particular hatred for Yehoshiva for some slight years before that had pushed him from his secure role out to patrols beyond the walls. This man was eager to be in Shemesh's graces and turned the city guard from a force of good-will to enforcers of the will of the wealthy.

Shemesh gave the command to his high priest to start the assessment immediately. "I want the assessments completed before the month is out. I want the revenues in the temple thirty days later, the number of conscripts for the army, and the number of laborers for the work at the same time. I expect a full report." Shemesh had not instructed his high priest what that report should look like or how to formulate it. It was merely a vague command he knew the priest would fail at. He enjoyed this game; it satisfied some savage part of his psyche, and as difficult as it was to recruit priests now, it was easier to find a replacement than to endure these beasts for too long. He abhorred religion and the limitations of morality, but it was a necessary burden of this job to tolerate it.

The priest had prostrated himself in the middle of the square and cut his wrists to show obedience to his Master, who stood nearby to ensure the speech was properly delivered and the people properly shocked by the implications. The public saw the full display of obedience to *this* Master, and with the weight of the conscription and taxes and the forced labor, they had no delusions about his concerns for their well-being. Shemesh could see the fear in their eyes.

Shemesh reviewed the levy and the number of conscripts. His high priest lay bleeding on the floor of the temple, other priests nearby unwilling and unable to help him as he gurgled and gasped his dying breaths.

Shemesh picked up the staff his priest had carried and took out his ceremonial blade to whittle the end into a point. When he finished he tossed it to the floor next to the dead priest and pointed to another nearby. "You are now the high priest. Go and make as many of these as there are conscripts, and send them out beyond the gate to assault the rebels."

The new high priest looked grimly at his colleague, and the acceptance of his imminent death showed plainly in his demeanor. He prostrated himself before Shemesh and slashed his forearms. The blood dripped off his wrists and mingled with the pool of his predecessor's.

Shemesh looked at him waiting for his death. *This imp*, he thought. "*Go!*" he bellowed. The man jumped to his feet, took the staff, and ran out of the temple to the newly finished courtyard.

Shemesh pointed at the other man. "You will take the laborers to the stone quarry. And they will work there until their debts are paid."

The priest flopped onto his face and with a shaky hand slashed his wrists to follow suit with his new high priest. He cut too deep in his haste and severed a tendon. "Yes, Master. It will be done immediately."

Shemesh saw his middle finger curled. He looked at the priest disdainfully in his handicap and sneered. "You have outlived your use to me here. You will stay at the quarry with them until they are through."

The man didn't ask any questions; his body showed a sense of relief. Without waiting to be dismissed, he shuffled to his feet with one bloody hand and dashed out of the temple to do the Master's bidding.

Savages, Shemesh thought. *The taxes will need to be increased next month as well. They have been hoarding too much gold for themselves.*

Shemesh raised the taxes on the people by half of what they already were. This forced many to sell what they had to come up with the difference. Each subsequent year, the taxes went up by a small percentage, but because they were already too high, even a little bit more made it impossible to climb out of the endless pit of financial insolvency. Eventually, those who weren't making enough to cover their tax debts were forced to sell off everything they could until they had nothing left to sell. The rich had acquired all that the poor had to offer, and Shemesh had collected his taxes to send back to Irka.

The next year, when they couldn't pay at all, their homes were taken in exchange by Shemesh. When these homeless couldn't pay taxes the next year, they were sent to jail. When they couldn't pay the burden of their incarceration, their labor was used to pay their fines—in the quarry.

Each day the prisoners worked producing stone and ore. Each night they returned to the prison and lay huddled in the yard, living off the boiled scraps of society. The next day they would get up and face the day of hard labor, entering the mine with nothing but humble coverings and leaving with the same. They picked up their tools from former laborers who now performed menial, more lucrative tasks while the prisoners labored. The rate they were "paid" was less than the cost of their incarceration, so they never found a way to pay off their debts, and the crime they had committed was not being able to pay their debts.

Shemesh raised or lowered tax rates depending on the demand for such labor and the remaining supply that shambled in at night. It was an easy trap for the citizens to fall into. Those on the verge of falling into that trap saw that the only solution was to leave the city and risk the raids outside the protection of the walls, as they had neither the means nor the health and strength to cross the desert to Irka.

The demand only grew as the wealthy found new ways to employ the labor. When paying the prison system less than half what the non-prison labor would earn in wages, profitability increased. They were able to afford greater assets, and their demand for labor grew. As prison labor was cheaper than market labor, fewer laborers were needed from the market, and more people were unable to pay their debts and were sent to jail as a result.

Shemesh, of course, found that the flow of gold in his shipments increased, and the Frontier Corporation didn't ask questions. Since it was prisoners working off a sentence, and they were technically paid the remainder of what was left after their expenses were deducted, it wasn't considered slavery. None of the people were taken by force; they lived under the laws of the land by choice, as they could have left if they had chosen to but hadn't.

It was clearly slavery to all the Elohim, but it was also clearly a loophole, as law and order were fundamentals that made a society function properly, and prisons were a part of that system.

Yehoshiva contested the matter, in private at first, but when Shemesh refused to listen, he made the issue public. His voice carried through the courtyard, and the echo could be heard outside the walls where some of the Masters were returning from the field. Shemesh dismissed him at that point and relieved him of his duties within the city.

On paper, it was all proper. Even the accounting of the costs was done to show that everything was aboveboard. The costs of food had gone up due to inflation from an excess of gold in the market and a comparatively static supply of food from the fields. The population continued to grow as immigrants from all the surrounding lands— nomadic fathers' second sons, who would inherit nothing by right— sought their fortunes in the city but found only misery.

As the population grew, the demand for food grew. As the fertile lands were covered by the walls and buildings that the Masters built among the hovels and ghettos of the city, farms were pushed out to the edges of the desert, where irrigation was difficult and adequate production was impossible. With the miners in the gold mine stealing gold from the supply, the gold on the market continued to inflate, the supply of currency was too high, the supply of food was too low, and the people were forced to compete with the wages the prison labor system established in the market. The price of food thus consumed all the wages of those who labored.

The public works the Elohim had built only served to increase the value of the land the peasants lived on. When taxes came due, they were assessed on the value of the land, which was based on the surrounding property. When the wealthy were encouraged to buy the riverfront properties, everything next to it increased in assessed value. When those occupants couldn't pay the higher taxes, that land was seized by Shemesh and then sold at a new higher market price to the wealthy landowners of the city, who were eager to find favor with Shemesh. More gold flowed to Shemesh, and more and more of the population was enslaved or escaped.

As the desperation of the people grew, they would revolt, violently retaliating against the city guard sent to seize their meager properties and take them away into captivity and slavery. Whole neighborhoods would erupt into violence, and the violent suppression left many dead and more imprisoned. The destroyed neighborhoods created opportunities for the wealthy to displace and rebuild, and so the pressure increased.

Despair was endemic. That desperation turned the people to any escape they could find. Drugs, alcohol, violence, criminality of every dimension—anything to relieve the oppressive crush of the city and the tyranny of Shemesh. The people were steadily broken down. They ignored more of the increasing decay around them and succumbed to the natural consequences of ignoring the rituals, even as they watched from afar as the wealth of a privileged few expanded and shined mockingly from the gilded districts with paint and brass and the ever-present scent of the spice.

This unending cycle of revolt, suppression, despair, and decay affected only those who refused the cult of Shemesh. So many tattooed themselves to display their desperate loyalty, eager to be recognized and chosen to escape their unearned conditions. But most had no choice, and as the hope faded, they patiently endured the suffering, accepting death as their only eventual escape. Apathetic to the fate of others or themselves and doing everything they could to stay numb and expedite that end.

Yehoshiva sat alone at the table eating slowly. Full of self-loathing, he relived his memory of the last two years of hellish suffering imposed on these people. Even his defiance served the aims of Shemesh in the end. Even his good intentions served Shemesh's aims. Even doing nothing served Shemesh's aims. There was nothing he could do that would eliminate the suffering and misery in the city. He once again felt like the Machine's Technician was unleashing the beasts of hell to ruin something he created. Once again that crushing sense of hopelessness fell over his whole body, and every part of him felt heavy. He was in his twentieth standard year. Nothing in his life made him want to see the twenty-first.

The mood of the whole dining hall was the same. Every plan for kindness and goodwill they employed became the fulcrum where

Shemesh placed a new lever to move society. So they sat somberly eating their own thin broths and sparse vegetables. No one dared empty the pantry, since that meant the demand for the offerings would take from the poor, who were close to having nothing already.

Katesh walked in, in the same dark mood as everyone, and went to the kitchen to prepare a meal of the same thin broth everyone else was preparing.

Shemesh walked close behind her. When he cast his smiling eyes around the room, every head scowled into the bowls as if they were searching for the bottoms. "Why such poor meals? We have plenty of supplies. We have much work to do around here to build the perfect society, and that demands we eat. We wouldn't want the offerings of the primitives to spoil, would we? We'd need to gather twice as much just to make sure the pantry stayed full after all that rot." Shemesh threatened openly.

Kimdu slurped his broth noisily, set the empty bowl back on the table, stood from his chair, and walked out. Shemesh called after him. "Isn't it uncouth to leave dishes for someone else to clean?"

Kimdu yelled up the corridor through the open door. "I'll use it again tomorrow. I don't want to waste the preciously scarce clean water to clean my bowl; leave it where it sits, and I'll use it tomorrow."

Shemesh looked back at the bowl and then looked at the other scowling scientists one by one. Each made eye contact as they, too, slurped loudly, set their bowls down, and got up and left. "I'll use it tomorrow. Don't touch it" was the refrain from all of them as they left.

Shemesh snickered savagely, proud of his emotional command over these ingrates but equally irritated that they didn't see the value of his achievements there. He looked at Yehoshiva, who deliberately ignored him and sat quietly sipping his own bowl of broth. Without saying a word, Shemesh walked into the kitchen, where Katesh had been listening to the whole scene.

Moments later Yehoshiva heard a pot shatter and Katesh yell, "Don't touch me. You can make your own food. Too bad we don't have any prisoners to eat, or you might finally find some satisfaction with their misery at your hand." She tore through the door and stormed off to her own room.

Yehoshiva swallowed the last of his broth as Shemesh opened the door to the kitchen and looked out, hurt and embarrassed and more than a little anguished, from the look on his face. Then seeing Yehoshiva stand, Shemesh's face hardened into a scowl.

Without looking back at Shemesh, Yehoshiva said over his shoulder, "I'll use it tomorrow. Don't touch it." And he walked out the door to the corridor, where the faint sound of crying could be heard in numerous rooms in the normally stoic serenity of the Masters' compound.

30

The days went by more slowly than they had in the past. The people suffered, and though the hospital was still staffed by the Masters, they did their best to make the priests of the new sect understand what they were doing and to replicate the processes. In the end, the best way they found was to homogenize and ritualize the treatment. Every patient received an alcohol wash with a rag to save resources. Every patient was given a sip of the tonic water they had created and taught the priests how to make. And every patient was given food to eat. This was the silent resistance the other Masters could muster against Shemesh.

The brewery, too, was given over to the Kaldees to run. Kimdu would check the potency of the brew once in a while, but he homogenized and ritualized the process for them to create a consistent product, or as close as he could get it.

The septic system, too, was slowly turned over to the citizens, who now were less inclined to trade their slop for a bucket of water that needed to be boiled when they could go to the hospital and get the same and more. They had created a trade system, effort for reward, but now the reward was free elsewhere without the effort, so sanitation suffered. The Kaldees were put in charge of paying willing citizens to clean the septic tanks by hand once every few months, the waste being brought to the garbage heap in the desert where it might leach into the soil and fertilize the ground there for future use.

As well as they could, they turned over the processes to the indigenous people, who tended it as best they could. As the stated missions of each of the Masters expired, they sent word back to Irka that their missions were complete and they would need immediate reassignment.

Tammuz was the latest to complete her work. Katesh begged her to stay with her eyes. It was too much to endure alone. All her allies were leaving, and everyone was demoralized.

"It will be a shame to lose you here, Tam." Katesh pleaded. "I thought there might be some more medicine worth investigating in these yellow flowers you love."

Tammuz looked at her, the weariness on her face only overshadowed by the relief of her reassignment. "I can't squeeze any more value out of these plants here," she said, not giving in.

"Can you at least tell me what you wrote when requesting reassignment? I think we'd all like to know what the magic words are." Katesh prodded, hoping it was a damning report of conditions here.

Tammuz sighed. "I told them there is nothing left of value here, and my work is no longer showing progress in these people's lives."

Katesh smiled tenderly at her friend. "You have no idea how wrong you are about that. But I will miss you dearly."

Tammuz reached into her satchel and pulled a note out. "If you want to read it, I made you a copy." She smiled and pushed her trunk out the compound doors to the waiting priests to load onto dromedaries for the trip back to Irka.

The wording was particular, and the Commandant would certainly be able to read between the lines that there was something not quite right in Bashram. *But*, Katesh thought, *as long as the gold keeps flowing, they can do nothing until some hard evidence crosses their tables.*

Yehoshiva worked obediently to collect the taxes. He was ruthless to those who lived in the gated wealthy district he had built with the belief that he was building something for the Masters and the whole city. Instead he walled in a resort, and those who managed to thrive in the old regime became willing pawns of the horrors Shemesh imposed on their people for the sake of the fabulous wealth he enabled them to obtain. They were loyal to Shemesh. Even if he asked them to boil and eat one of their own children, they would do it and then ask to eat the others as well.

Yehoshiva walked the streets of the new district. He made unexpected visits to the quarter and startled the wealthy citizens in their leisure. The only poor who worked in those areas were in servile roles, gardeners and guards, street sweepers and garbage collectors. Roles degrading enough to be done only by those whose humble lives made this service a privilege but too sensitive to entrust to the slaves, whose motivation was sapped by the inescapable status they endured.

The lords of the manors he went to all had arms covered with blackened scars that marked the number of times they had "talked to" Shemesh. The honor they held in esteem, their only distinguishing qualities being the ruthlessness and deceptiveness that differentiated them from their peers who worked in the gardens and streets and barely earned enough to cover their taxes and feed their families. The taktus, as their pidgin lingo defined the marks, brought them respect and showed their relationship to Shemesh, which meant they could command anything of anyone in the city, and the violence they committed would go unpunished and even encouraged by *the* Master. They were untouchable—except by the other Masters, and Yehoshiva took full advantage of this to squeeze them of all their worth.

The wealthy were resented by the poor. Yet there was no recourse. The poor suffered, and the more they suffered at the hands of the tyranny of the economic conditions Shemesh manipulated, the more they resented the rich. Once they fell on hard times, there was no recovery from the long, slow slide into slavery. The system was designed to benefit the very few at the expense of the many. A clear mitosis of the society was at play.

The only comfort Yehoshiva knew was that the magnet of power would draw the worst characters of the society out, and once the society reached the breaking point, all these savage creatures who held themselves in such high esteem would be destroyed. They self-selected the qualities that would be eradicated, thus purifying the people of the city of their worst qualities. But the suffering they endured over many lifetimes at the hands of these policies ensured the resentment would extend to the Masters themselves. That made the dangers of their position very real and precarious.

He had to do something.

Yehoshiva approached a mansion built by ill-gotten gains and beat on the door.

A hairy little beast opened it, and the snarl on his face indicated he knew immediately what was expected and who it was.

Yehoshiva peered inside as the primitive savage in luxurious accoutrements prostrated himself on the threshold. Yehoshiva's resentment allowed the man to slash his own wrists in obeisance, though it was known that Yehoshiva expected it from none of the people outside this privileged district. The signs of wealth were everywhere. The clues to how the wealth was acquired were everywhere. The red flowers grew in pots in the inner courtyard, and golden tools lay displayed on the superfluous tables and shelves, all made from the spice wood that had once provided the currency of these people. Imports of fine goods stamped with Irka's export stamp decorated every piece of linen, proudly displaying the great expense of the items. And the house was heavily perfumed in the same spices the temple used to disguise the stench of unwashed primitive priests. This household had proven their sins through the symbols of every corrupt enterprise the city could entertain.

Yehoshiva's blood ran cold with bitter hatred as he spoke. "Your taxes are due."

The little beast's blood oozed out onto the threshold and mingled with the dried blood already there. "Master, I's tax were paid six suns before."

Yehoshiva glanced at the dried blood marking each spot where these wealthy leeches had prostrated themselves. They deliberately left it uncleaned to mark their visits from Yehoshiva. This one, though, proved more cunning than his neighbors, but not cunning enough. The blood was all the same dried and darkened color. And the stench of death wafted from behind a row of pots nearby. The foot of some poor primitive worker stuck out. *This monster murdered a servant and used their blood to mark his doorstep to avoid taxes.* Yehoshiva felt a rush of fire in his veins. Shemesh forbade him from harming these wealthy citizens; they were too valuable to the production of the city in terms of meeting quotas to turn them against the Masters. And even this deception would have only made this one's esteem in Shemesh's eyes grow.

"Your taxes have increased to pay for your security." Yehoshiva snarled at the little demon.

"What number owe me?" the little tyrant asked, the timbre of his voice calm and steady.

He has no fear of me or of his expense. He'll recover whatever I take today in a day or two and will be no worse for it. Yehoshiva left the man prostrate on the doorstep and entered the threshold of the mansion to investigate the riches displayed. "I will determine your assessed tax rate on your luxuries. Stay where you are, and I will return with your assessment."

Yehoshiva took a step inside, the high ceiling in the threshold designed to accept the Masters' visitation and the tall doors designed to allow them to enter without stooping. This home was built to flaunt the privileged role they served to the Masters. While the home was clean and fresh, there were subtle hints of the horrors that took place there. Yehoshiva could see well-worn paths through the house and, in particular, one path that led to a drapery on a wall. Where the corridors were open and airy, there was a door hidden behind the drape and colored to loosely match the color of the walls.

Yehoshiva pulled the linen aside and pulled the hidden door open. The stench of unwashed bodies and whimpering drifted out, and as he peered in, he could hear the clanking of chains.

As his eyes adjusted to the darkness within, he saw a dozen young women encircling the wall inside, chained to it and filthy. Three of them appeared pregnant, and one was in a stock in the middle with her hind end exposed and fluid dripping onto the floor from between her legs. The sight was horrifying. Kidnapped women used for pleasure. Yehoshiva stood and let the drapery fall back in front of the open door.

He followed more worn pathways in the mansion and found more secret rooms, each more depraved than the next—corpses, skeletal remains, piled possessions of individuals, a torture chamber, and a vault full of coins, seeds, and other trinkets of perceived value.

Yehoshiva burned inside. He couldn't comprehend the value this could serve to Shemesh's plan. The horrors seen here were indicative of the depravity of this district. He could no longer contain his wrath. He walked back to the threshold where the little beast lay prostrate.

He had been standing until he heard Yehoshiva return. The blood flowing from his wrist dripped off his fingertips, and the pooled blood was in a different spot than where he currently lay. *He doesn't think he has to respect me.* "I want you to gather your entire household and present them here before me." Yehoshiva gestured to the foyer.

The little man scrambled to his feet, feigning relief from lying so long on the ground, and disappeared into the house. Yehoshiva could hear him yelling in the courtyard and the scramble of feet as his household rushed from their hiding places. After a few moments, the household, including the servants, was assembled.

Yehoshiva reviewed the people there. None of the captives were present. "Is this everyone who resides in your house?"

"Yes, Master," the horrid beast lied confidently.

"Which of these are your family?" Yehoshiva asked, seeing the striking resemblance among several and a clear distinction from the rest.

The little man paused to think of his next move. He began separating the servants from those who bore his resemblance, and roughly equal partitions of the people formed, one group across from the other. He was uncertain what to expect next, but his familiarity with Shemesh's brutality was plain in his face. He made an honest separation of the two groups. Hesitating for a moment, he pointed to the group of servants separated from those who were clearly related to him. "This my family," he lied, waiting to see the response of the Master.

Yehoshiva smiled, then drew his dagger. "Which of your servants shall I execute?" he asked, pointing the tip of the dagger at each face as their soft skin flushed and their plush bodies quivered in fear.

The grotesque little villain went wide-eyed. "None, Master. If must kill, take I children." He doubled down on the deception and pointed at the servants assembled across from his family.

Yehoshiva confirmed what he had expected. He pointed to one of the servants who stood glaring at the lying lord of the manor. "You, take this dagger and slay all these *servants*."

The man went wide-eyed, and then his glare focused on the family as he took the dagger from Yehoshiva. The blade was as long as his own arm, but he savagely attacked the master of the household and, leaving him bloody and dying, walked down the line of the terrified family and glared at each in the eyes.

Yehoshiva spoke the common tongue to the rest of the servants. "Make sure none of them escapes." Their eyes narrowed, and they walked over to the terrified family and grasped them firmly while the man with the dagger continued to pace. He chose the son next. Then the eldest daughter. Then the wife. Then the mother. Then the two youngest children and then the rest until they were all gutted and dead.

Yehoshiva felt it was futile either way, but making them feel the pain felt by everyone else in their society even for one brief moment gave him some satisfaction and relieved the burden on his heart to have to bear witness to the great suffering created by Shemesh's policies. When the slaughter was finished, he asked the people again, "Is there any more of his family left here?"

The servants all hesitated, not realizing the Master knew, but when they understood, they all confirmed that there was not. "No, Monster. Only his extended family in the neighborhood remains." The executioner gestured out the door.

Yehoshiva held out his hand for the dagger, and the man placed it in his hand after wiping it on the bloody rags of the bodies at his feet. "You will free the prisoners in the secret rooms, and you will take all the wealth from this household and distribute it in your community. You will tell all your neighbors everything you have witnessed here and everything you find, and you will begin to arm your community. There is nothing in this district that is of value to you or the *Monsters*. You will cleanse your city when the time is right, and you will never again submit to these beasts. Do not act now, but you must hurry to prepare.

When there is only one Master left here," he gestured to the blackened scars on the arms of the patriarch, "then you will destroy everything and everyone that bears those marks and has enslaved your people. We *Elohim* are ending this corruption and sin. Take note of what you see here and their deeds. Never forget that this is what comes of this life, and never submit to these demons."

One by one they bowed deeply to show their gratitude, and then they filed off silently, assembling the wealth of the mansion. Yehoshiva tore the expensive imported linens from the walls and wiped the blood from his feet and legs. Then he stepped over the threshold and closed the door behind him.

The time to end this was at hand, and he made his decision to destroy everything. It was his moral obligation, and whatever consequences came from it, he would bear them happily to cleanse his soul of his guilt.

31

Katesh barely came around anymore. She couldn't stand to. She had completed the most critical part of her assignment there, to develop observatories. With them the primitives could start predicting seasons and know when to plant and harvest, and eventually they would be able to predict the weather based on observations over time. They could start to plan society from there.

Katesh was not happy in the work—no one was anymore—but she was happy for the escape to the fringes of the city for weeks at a time. She never saw the familiar faces of her work companions, one more than others, and this made her lonely, but she was happy in the isolation that this project gave her, and that rejuvenated her soul. At least a little. As long as she wasn't a witness to the wretched conditions that plagued the people of the city, she could still live with herself for not being able to help. So she kept busy training the Kaldees in the sciences.

She gave her Kaldees a star emblem to distinguish them from the rest of the populace, so Shemesh and his thugs would know they were marked and protected. Shemesh was only so happy to oblige. He used it as an implicit agreement to allow his thugs to harass everyone else. Katesh found her district swell with new adherents, and even more problems came with that. But she was content that the magnetic repulsion of Shemesh's cult would drive the most fearful and moral away from Shemesh and into her Kaldees. That would at least ensure their survival long after she and the others left.

Samara hobbled up the hill. Her ancient body was unable to endure this long trek more than once a week anymore, but as Katesh's right hand, she was obliged to try. Her grandson carried the maps from her students and lent her support when her old legs could no longer balance on the steep incline.

Katesh watched this ascent and remembered those many planetary years before when Samara was just a strong little girl defending her father's name in the refugee camp. She still wore that necklace. The thread was knotted in several places and much shorter because of it, but that carved bird was her most precious possession, and she wore it proudly.

"Hello, my dear friend." Katesh smiled gently at Samara as she finished the climb.

Samara smiled back at Katesh. No longer capable of the formalities of obeisance, she simply nodded her head slightly and stood her ground. "Hello, Master Katesh. I hope you are well."

Katesh felt rejuvenated by these conversations, not because of their substance but because of their informality. She no longer put on the facade of imperious authority for Samara, and Samara was all too happy to reciprocate. They were as much equal as any two people from different species could be. Katesh sat with her friend and felt a bond with this Umanu that could not be replicated.

Samara gestured to her grandson as she caught her breath and adjusted her body to find the least painful position to rest. He brought the charts over, and Samara introduced him informally to Katesh. "My grandson Samael is now teaching my classes and is quite capable. He's the best I can offer to replace me when I am gone. I feel that time is near, unfortunately."

Katesh accepted Samael and gestured for him to sit with them. "If you are half the cartographer your grandmother was, you will be an invaluable asset to me."

Samael took this as a signal to talk about himself. "I am well versed in cartography and astronomy, as well as all the processes for construction and the making of products. I am fluent in all three local dialects, as well as the Master's language. I can translate—" Samara raised her hand to stop him from speaking.

She looked at Katesh and smiled meekly. "He's still young and impetuous and conceited. I can't train that out of him; only time will do that."

Katesh could see the resemblance in his face to someone else she had encountered. "Who is his father?"

Samara smirked. "The arrogant chosen one you call Moon." She chuckled at this. "He reminds everyone constantly how his name was given to him by the Master Katesh and that his seed would not fade from this world as long as the moon is in the sky. And now here is his seed. My poor daughter was looking for some way to gain approval for her own achievements, and her suitor was looking to gain my favor and his own authority among your people. A very pragmatic arrangement for them both, but they did produce quite brilliant children."

Katesh just listened as her friend's story went along. The signs of illness were heavy on Samara's body and face. Each breath was labored, and all her hair was white and thin. Her skin was blotched, and it was clear that Samara would not make this trek even once more. Katesh looked down at the beautiful city they had created together. Where cobbled tents and shacks of the slaves and refugees had once stood, now the orderly and glistening city of white brick houses shone brightly and created a beacon of light in a world surrounded by darkness. She looked at her dear friend, now ancient and frail, and reached out and touched her back. Samara leaned into her Master and relaxed. Katesh's large gray hand gently stroked her friend's white hair and dark skin and dust-stained tunic.

As the sun reflected off the rooftops of their great achievement, Samara heaved one last breath and went limp.

Katesh knew her friend was gone, and for the first time she allowed herself to cry.

This Umanu was her greatest achievement. This paragon of all her people was the hope of their world, and Katesh felt a deep, heavy sorrow for her loss. After all they had been through, all Samara had been through, the strength, courage, and integrity of her character were evident in all the people who suffered with her. Katesh drew inspiration from her passing.

Katesh eased her friend's body to the ground and drew her dagger. She gently cut the rope necklace and removed the wooden dove. Samael sat wide-eyed nearby, and as Katesh handed him the trinket, his eyes filled with tears, and he lost his composure in his sadness. Katesh's blade slid delicately across the skin of her friend. The skin and hair and a small amount of blood clung to the blade, and Katesh wiped it on her own clean uniform and then cut the patch of blood off and placed it in her pouch. She resheathed her blade and picked up the frail body of her dear friend and carried her down to the district below.

All who passed by saw the corpse and saw the tears of Katesh, and each in turn fell to their knees and wept openly. Their matriarch was gone, and even their Master could not contain her anguish.

Katesh laid her beloved friend on a table in her own quarters and unwrapped a part of her own tunic and cut it short to use as a covering for the body. No such dignity had ever been afforded to any other of their people, and they knew this moment was a pivotal one.

32

Yehoshiva was numb. He frequently remembered what Shemesh had said to him so early in his career. He was stuck here. Even when the last scientist left and all that remained were the primitives in their hovels, he would be here ensuring the production of the city remained high and the quotas were filled. All their suffering and all their sorrows would be his to witness and to control, and though he felt pity for their plight, he knew he was destined to be the cause of much of it.

He somehow imagined that Shemesh was what Frontier Corporation actually wanted in a production manager. That they wanted Yehoshiva to be like that. He wondered what Kim and Sam might say back home, and he wondered what he would tell his mother when she asked how his little adventure had been. He felt shame for the way things were turning out, and he was convinced that it couldn't have happened without his unwitting assistance. He was a fool. Shemesh was certainly a villain, but so was he. At least he felt he was becoming one. Through ignorance, defiance, compliance, and acceptance, he, too, was the villain who drove these people into chains. That thought rotted away his self-worth and penetrated the protective layer Yehoshiva had built around Joshua deep inside. He couldn't let this go on much longer, or he would not be able to live with himself.

Reports came in frequently about raids on the caravans. The Elohim had so far escaped the fate of the priests who escorted them, but the rebels sought opportunities where they could do real damage to the Masters of the city. Shemesh accepted these losses in stride. The more they raided, the more the people would fear the unknown horizon they lurked on. The more fear they had of the unknown, the more they would turn to the city as the only alternative to that fate, and the more they would endure the savagery and suffering Shemesh's cult offered them.

The raids on the gate and the wall were infrequent now. The rebels had been beaten back, and with the flood of refugees back into the city, the morale of their forces was evidently broken. Though their stone weapons gradually became copper and then bronze, they relied heavily on the black-market trades and raids that kept their camps alive.

They stopped attacking the gate after a great battle had obliterated their forces, and now they stayed on the dusty plateau, only engaging the caravans as they passed by their domain, raiding outlying towns and attacking refugees. Yehoshiva was not privileged with reading or hearing these reports. Shemesh no longer trusted him with operational information— not that he ever had, but now he made it known to the priests that they should give the information to him alone and never to another Master.

Shemesh was happy about the raids because they increased the fear in the hearts of the people. They refused to travel into the desert unprotected, concerned that the bandits would prey on them. They had nothing to offer the bandits but their lives or livelihoods. There was no benefit to picking off individuals with no food, water, weapons, or wealth to acquire. The rumors spread that material goods were not the purpose of the harassment but rather that they were hunted for their flesh, and the people found themselves suffering in the city between the fear of the unknown demons of the desert and the tyranny of the Masters.

The raids increased in frequency, and the caravans were not able to get through to Irka except by chance. This hurt Shemesh's reputation and increased the scrutiny on his operation, so he decided that the raids needed to be stopped. A reward was put out for the rebels and the eradication of their camps. The bounties would be enough to buy land in the new city and pay the taxes and develop them for the next ten years—an enormous sum to the people. This was of course a paltry sum to the Masters and was of no financial consequence given their control over both the monetary supply and the products that could buy, but it was enough to encourage bands of men arming themselves to head into the fray to seek their fortune. Some went in alone, hoping to bring a few stragglers down single-handedly and become rich by their deeds. Most of those died in the process. The wise ones saw the futility in that strategy and brought back intelligence of the raider encampments for a piece of the bounty if a larger team were to succeed.

This led to many competing groups scrambling for the same prize and hurrying plans into action to be the first groups to reach the goal. A small team charging a fortified position on the high ground against trained and hardened warriors was no match, and it became a cursed mission only taken on by the most desperate. Hundreds of the city's bravest men met their deaths at the hands of the rebels in the mountains and plateaus, their corpses littering the trails and their bones scattered by scavengers of the desert.

Yehoshiva walked into Shemesh's office unannounced and asked a pointed question. "Is your goal simply to kill off the brave and desperate of the city, to leave only the timid to survive and breed?" His demeanor toward Shemesh was less formal than it had been before. He had no more respect for this monster than he did for the animals they butchered for their broth.

"This distraction is allowing our caravans to get through. That is the ultimate purpose of our mission here, after all," Shemesh said coolly as he continued to sketch a design on a sheet of paper.

"You've spent the last couple of years devising more and more savage means to dispatch these people, you've emboldened the worst traits in their being, and you've oppressed the weak when they are the key to being loved here and producing something worth preserving."

Shemesh put his pen down and leaned back with a malevolent glare on his face. "Who says we should be loved or that this city is intended to be preserved? Does love convince people to work hard, or do incentives and fear? Is it better to be loved than feared by that measure? Productivity is our mission here. Output is our mission here. We come to this planet and live in *squalor*." He stood up abruptly as his agitation rose. "No technology, none of the mysteries our civilization has scraped out of the muck of existence for eons, all so these *apes* can learn to do it for themselves. All so everything we bring them will erode and rot and fade with time, so there is no trace of our presence once we are gone. We are not asked to be *loved*!"

Yehoshiva stood at attention and seethed with anger. He responded with barely contained fury. "You make plans without telling me what or why or where or *anything*. I spend my time picking up the wreckage of a civilization on the verge of collapse and chaos. A stopgap for the uncontrolled misery you bring to these people. I would expect, as your lieutenant, that you would inform me at least of the purpose of these measures."

Shemesh sneered. "You have no need to know the plans here. You waste your time picking fleas off these mongrels so you can abate the fracturing of your own conscience. You are responsible for these people, and if you weren't so invested in trivialities, you would find your production would rise. If you had one ounce of wrath, these people might fear you enough to produce something worth producing. Instead we have a dying city and half completed, inefficient, ineffective projects everywhere." He gestured toward the new city. "That sewer system you were building went nowhere. The engineering was flawed, and several places caved in. It had to be abandoned, or sinkholes would have appeared right where our most valuable citizens live with their families. Is that the sort of ideal you want to have instilled in the minds of these people? That the Masters from the heavens above arrived here by mysterious means but were incapable of basic sanitation engineering? Your ineptitude is what keeps you here, protected by my goodwill. Protected from the justice of unemployment you deserve."

Yehoshiva was stunned. He had not heard of nor seen any cave-ins, and he didn't know the sewer had been abandoned even though Shemesh had taken control of the project. His youth and inexperience were his only flaws, and he meant well by his efforts.

Shemesh saw Yehoshiva's hesitation and continued. "Those rebel camps you created by fomenting revolt. I know how heavily you tax our most productive and hardworking citizens. Their servants have begun to murder their betters in the full light of day, and now the foremen have demanded higher wages for the risks they have to take. The city guards harass them and seize their medicinal plants, then give them to the poor, who use them to escape their world and drive themselves deeper into poverty until they can't even function on the job. They are lost and turn to crime for their next fix and must be restrained and given manual labor to sweat their addictions out of them. The productive potential of these primitives has been lost due to your supposed *mercy*. You conspire with the others here to undermine my noble goals to turn this city into a beacon of prosperity, and you allow poverty and indolence to run rampant. You have been a thorn in my side since you arrived. Incapable of seeing the true worth of these creatures, you instead divert your attention to high-minded and narrow goals that allow the masses to succumb to their ancestral sloth. Despite my best efforts, you have created this disaster here." As he made this final point, he wondered if Yehoshiva was aware of the truth of these matters. His temper now was only for show as the idea crept into his mind to get rid of this nuisance.

Yehoshiva stood listening, humiliated and feeling the burden on his heart for the accusations Shemesh had leveled at him. One by one, though, as Shemesh's words cut into him, a voice in the back of his mind whispered the truth. He knew he had failed in many respects, but the truth was widely acknowledged by his peers that Shemesh had orchestrated these atrocities. He wondered whether that wasn't the goal to begin with.

Yehoshiva drew in his breath and mustered his strength. "No. You did this. All of it. You take pleasure in the suffering and misery of these people. You slaughter them by the dozens with your own hands, and you devise schemes that undermine their potential. You are responsible, and *you* will be held accountable."

Shemesh was stunned into momentary silence. He recovered quickly but felt the dagger of truth in the words and became defensive. "You have no idea how to create a thriving civilization. These beasts need a villain to oppose and guide their moral compass. This opulence serves as a magnet for their worst character and creates a symbol for these people of the oppression they endure. To create a moral civilization, you must show it the horrors of sin. You must make them feel it all the way to their genes so they resist it with all of their being."

Shemesh continued. "These apes haven't risen far enough to under-stand on their own how dark their nature can get. All civilizations rise out of nature, but nature continues to drag them back down by clinging to their very DNA. Without our help—without *my* help—these vermin would collapse back into the nomadic lives they came from. Without *my* help, they would not know that power and wealth and privilege could exist and that it was the darkness lurking within themselves that kept them oppressed. Without seeing this luxury, they would not know what they could possibly have. Without seeing the true power over life and death granted to them, they would not know how great they could become. Without knowing what magic exists in the world and in themselves to reshape that world, they would never understand what technology they could possibly achieve. You speak of morality, but it is the absolute tyranny that impels these savage beasts to commit to such a quaint notion. It is my achievements here that have ensured this civilization will rise and fall and rise again to reach its true potential on its own! *Me!*"

Shemesh made his best philosophical point to prove how benevo-lent his malevolence truly was. He sat back down and reached for his bauble. It comforted him, and he could feel the bloodstone that repre-sented his own personality, the nexus of authority, science, and wealth. The point that fools identified as fascism and tyranny. He knew it was the only true ideology that made sense.

Yehoshiva saw the soothing effect of the tetrahedron, gilded and jew-eled. He was disgusted by this servant of sin, and he couldn't compre-hend how such a one as this could emerge from the Machine with these ideas intact. "You bring shame to all of us. Prosperity can only come from free people with true morality. Economics and science coexist to make life easier and more efficient, and there's no place for tyrants in that world. Whether you succeed here or not, the suffering you have caused will never be forgiven by these people, and that stain will never wash from the hands of us Elohim. That is your legacy here." Yehoshiva walked out of the office and left Shemesh sitting in his furious, silent self-pity.

33

His sleep was broken by tormenting dreams. He couldn't remember the first one. It had startled him awake, but as he drifted off to sleep again, a new one of the same theme immediately came to him.

He stood at the cliff next to the sea again. The aqua blue reflected a sunny sky, but the sky was black. The stars that formed the constellations glinted brightly, and he knew which one represented his home. As he gazed at them, they began to fall, streaking down to the horizon, each one burning brightly as it crashed into the sea, the fire of its tail burning hot and then a cloud of steam and flame bursting forth. He watched as the universe around him collapsed into the sea. The water began to boil, and he could see the life that hid beneath the soothing waves floating to the top. The color changed, and the waves turned crimson. He could hear the screams of the billions of lives lost in each splash, the tiniest protozoa and the largest marine mammal and amphibian.

He felt nothing. No fear, no pain, no sorrow. But he could hear all around him the cries of anguish and terror. He looked side to side and saw once again the endless row of people standing along the cliff's edge with him. The primitives at the far end fled in terror from the sight, and as the stars fell closer and closer, more and more ran until he stood alone. He turned to see where they had run to, and from behind a wall, fire burned in flickers of red and orange, consuming all that stood in its path. The primitives turned again and ran back to the cliff. Some jumped into the bloody waves, dead before they even hit the water. Others stopped and then tried to turn back to the flames again. There was no escape. They ran to him, and in a tongue he could not understand, pleaded with him, gesturing at the flame and the falling stars and begging for him to help them. But he was numb. Too numb to care. He was indifferent to their plight and could only watch as they were consumed by the flames one by one.

He heard a malicious laugh come from the inferno and turned to look and saw the face of pure evil, horns protruding from his crimson head, blood dripping from his maw. Shemesh's voice echoed through the apocalyptic scene. "Such a quaint notion. *Morality*."

Yehoshiva was not afraid but was powerless to react.

A voice echoed through the stars. "Truth knows neither love nor fear and need not be pure. Just as contaminated water can douse a flame, even a partial truth can douse the lies."

Yehoshiva looked at the bloody water below and felt a power in him to call it to his aid. He raised his hands and pulled them back down. His home star fell and crashed into the sea. A massive wave rose and crested above the cliff. He could feel it pass over him. The latent heat washed over him, and though he could not breathe, he watched it crash into the wall of fire and douse the flame.

The land smoldered as the sky turned blue again. And the people who had gathered before began to rise up again—not all, but some. They came to him, their faces burned and blackened, half charred and melted, but they were half clean. They came to him and clung to him, and as they touched him, the blackness fell away and they were changed. No longer primitive. No longer covered in hair and filth.

The stars lifted out of the horizon again and returned to where they stood before. And the voice called out again. "Umanu."

34

atesh saw Yehoshiva come into the courtyard and Shemesh take his leave. It was her first night back after another couple of weeks. The majority of the Masters had left already, and there was very little activity. The morale in this part of the city and the compound was low, and she had no desire to be here anymore. She had occupied the time since Samara died training her grandson to take charge of the priesthood. She had completely lost interest in the futility of trying to build anything up anymore; it just felt like crumbling sand to her. Nothing mattered because nothing would be permanent if Shemesh's cult remained much longer.

It was fortunate that the people, and particularly her Kaldees, never felt completely hopeless but felt that their achievements were making progress in a world that decayed around them. They attributed all the evils of their world to their own nature and all the glories to Katesh and the Masters, but they were well aware that some Masters were not looking out for their best interests and should be avoided. At the least, they understood that good and evil existed in all beings, that they needed to understand what good and evil actually meant in terms of their social development, and that this idea would allow them to reform and improve their society.

Katesh was relieved that as she let the burden off her shoulders, the Kaldees were more than eager to take it upon their own. It gave her hope. And so she came back to the compound to have a good meal and to see what had become of her peers.

She saw Yehoshiva in the courtyard returning from his daily rounds. Some project or another—she didn't know. The look on his face was one of weariness, suffering, and sadness. Even his smooth, youthful face bore creases, and the lines traced his mood in this place. It had aged him, and she was struck by how that burden and experience made him more attractive.

Five standard years here had changed the boy into a man. In spite of the crush of the city and the anxiety that burdened the Masters when they entered it, she couldn't keep the giddiness from building up in her like an electric shock that she knew would release in the most inconvenient way. There was no avoiding it; she just hoped he wouldn't think she was being odd.

"Shiva," she called to him in an awkward familiarity she hadn't practiced much.

He was surprised to hear her voice. It had been weeks since they had spoken or seen each other more than just in passing. Her work necessitated being out at night, and his was daytime work, so the two barely crossed paths anymore, seemingly by design. Tonight, though, she was here, and there was definitely something different about the way she was calling to him. She still looked as vivacious as he remembered her being on that freighter five standard years ago. Hearing her voice made him hopeful and excited and then self-conscious, especially in the context of the misery that surrounded them. *I hope she doesn't think I'm being odd.*

The two met, and Yehoshiva could see she was anxious for more than just a common greeting. Her body was fidgety, and her eyes were wild with excitement. After a brief pause, she leaned in and hugged him. The awkwardness of it and his being unprepared for it made it bewildering to him. All their interactions before had been discreet and limited by ritual and the ever-looming awareness that they were being watched. Duty and propriety tempered their behaviors even as flirtation slipped through. Katesh seemed somewhat liberated from this inhibition though.

"I didn't think you'd come back here. Is everything all right?" Yehoshiva said uncertainly.

"I have trained the Kaldees in pretty much everything they need, and they have taken on much of the work, so I thought I should come see you . . . all. Here, I mean." She stammered the last bit out. Something in her subconscious was breaking through, and it shocked and confused her. *What is it about him that makes him so appealing?*

"Sounds like your work here is wrapping up then." His voice dropped at the end in disappointment, and he looked down briefly.

"It is." Her own disappointment suddenly became clear to her.

"I think I may have a much longer time here, unfortunately. I don't know when this project will actually end, but there's always more to do, more lessons to teach, and more misery to cure." He glanced back at the door to the foyer and at the city beyond it represented.

"I have lots of other projects too. I may be here a while too. I'm not sure." She didn't know why she was suddenly trying to justify staying in this place. She didn't know where these words were coming from. She realized suddenly that it was *him* and became even more aware of her body, the sense of a dull ache spreading over her sensitive parts.

She was suddenly acting erratic. She stopped making eye contact, nervously brushed the smooth skin of her head where her hair used to be, and clenched her legs together.

All the sudden fidgeting from this normally disciplined and temperamental woman made Yehoshiva uneasy. He wasn't sure what was happening, and he hadn't expected this from her, to say the least. He looked around nervously, incapable of looking at her body squirming like that. The feelings came back from when he remembered first *really* seeing her on the freighter. He wanted to touch her and feel her, and a powerful rush urged him to do it. His focus faded and blurred at the peripherals, and all he saw was her, and every movement and curve called to him. He couldn't hear his own voice, he couldn't see anything around him, and he couldn't think. He said something he remembered sounding like "I have to go somewhere . . . that way." His body went one way as his head and hand tried to lead him another.

Katesh looked at him, bewildered. She couldn't stop moving. She couldn't stop wanting to touch him. She reached up and touched him on the arm. "Please don't" was all she could remember saying.

His eyes went wide and panicked. He tried to walk away but couldn't decide where he needed to be. His mind was shut down, and he reached up and touched her shoulder. His hand slid down her arm and touched her hand. And despite this, he pulled back and walked to the wall, where he stood picking at the bricks. He looked lost and dazed. The long self-conditioning of ritualism and staying in character wrestled with his inner desires, and both his conscious and unconscious mind fought for control.

She couldn't stop her subconscious thoughts from crying out. She stood there for a moment, suddenly self-conscious of what was happening. *I'm such an idiot,* she thought as she turned toward the dining hall. *He probably thinks I'm acting crazy. And I am.* She walked off wondering what was going on with her.

Yehoshiva kept picking at the mortar. *What in the world was that about?* he wondered. The situation was completely uncontrolled, and he felt a strangeness come over him like he was a marionette he was remotely viewing and controlling and only just now aware he didn't know how to make the puppet work. He suddenly became self-conscious. He was not sure he was who she was acting like she thought he was. He was just him, but worse, he was the hapless protégé of Shemesh, and that took its toll on the self-worth of all who claimed that dubious honor. He was a bad student and a hapless survivor of the Machine, a farmer by all measures but here on the frontier because he wanted adventure but didn't have the skill to specialize in anything. He was just an associate production manager.

The self-deprecation and the confusion distracted him from the sound of the approaching footsteps.

"Well, *that* was quite a show," Kimdu said through the fog over Yehoshiva's mind.

"Huh?" was all he could blurt out, not conscious of the fact that the whole display was in a very public setting in front of his colleagues, however few there were.

"That little display over there. Her purring like a feline for you and you a scared little kit not sure where to put your foot. You chose your mouth of all places, and I just want to say I haven't seen a show like that in some time. Good old-fashioned buffoonery." Kimdu smiled with the sad eyes they all wore.

"I've never seen her that way before—not to me anyway. I haven't had anyone be that way toward me before," Yehoshiva said. "I guess I just didn't expect it."

Kimdu smiled, a tender, fatherly smile of a man seeing his boy discover for the first time that someone might be willing to love him. "Well, whatever it is, she has never been that way to anyone that I've seen. So whatever spell you cast on her, it's your problem to deal with now."

"I just don't know what she sees. I'm nothing special." Yehoshiva was suddenly embarrassed that someone could look at him that way, and he did not understand why.

Kimdu cocked his head sideways and looked Yehoshiva up and down. "Yeah, I don't see it either. But no one is special, so if that were the requirement for love, life would be a lonely affair."

He smiled again as Yehoshiva looked at him aghast. "Shiva, whatever it is that makes her behave like that about you, you better just accept it and move forward. You can seize the moment, or you can run away and bury yourself in your work, but you do not have time to figure out what it is that made that happen. If you want her, you need to go in there and be there with her. If not, you should tell her. But the one thing that will never leave your conscience is staying out here all night, picking at the dirt avoiding it. Her body told you how she feels. Whatever that fierce mouth of hers says, her body put you in command of this relationship. So you have to make the decision because she has already decided."

Kimdu patted him on the back and walked off, saying, "Dinner's ready if you're hungry. There's plenty for the both of you, and the chores are already done, so that's all I'm going to say about that."

Yehoshiva stood there like an idiot for a few more moments and then decided he needed to go inside. His spine was straight as a jellyfish, and his steps were certain as a newborn calf. His heart was as rhythmic as windblown rain, and he couldn't think. His palms were sweaty, and his mouth was dry, and though he had the words in his mind to tell her their work was too important, they quickly fell into a jumble, and he didn't have the sense to put them back in order again. He wanted her. He always had. He just didn't know why it was happening this way, now, or ever. It didn't seem to fit with the way things had been going. It was just so sudden.

When he saw her sitting at the table with her head buried in her hands, mumbling to herself, his vision blurred. He could only see her at the end of the tunnel clearly, so he walked the known clear path and sat down across from her. "Hi" was all he could say. He stared at her with a dream clouding every sight and sound around him.

When she looked up, confusion and elation danced across her face, and she smiled that shy smile of a girl whose heart just climbed up the back of her neck. "Hi."

They talked about everything, about nothing. They didn't notice the meals someone graciously slid in front of them. They didn't notice the few people around them smiling at the scene as they faded into the background and left the dining hall. They didn't notice when the candles burned down to the nub and finally flickered and faded out. The moonlight poured in, and the radiant glow of their faces danced as their conversation carried into the early morning. They didn't notice the shock on the faces of a crew leaving for their duties, and when the sun crested the horizon, they didn't notice the look of consternation on Shemesh's face as he came in to see them sitting in the same spot they had been the night before.

Shemesh's interjection was the end of that dream. "I want to see you in my office immediately." He pointed to Yehoshiva.

The mood left them, and Yehoshiva stood to leave. Katesh held him by the hands, and the fury on Shemesh's face burned visibly and violently.

Yehoshiva pulled her up close to him and kissed her deeply and passionately as she melted in his arms.

Shemesh was apoplectic. Tears began to form in his eyes, and he shrieked at Yehoshiva, "*Now!*"

35

"**D**id you hear anything I just said?"

Yehoshiva was shaken from his reverie. Shemesh was looking at him sternly. He had clearly been talking about something, but Yehoshiva had no idea what that was. He didn't care anymore anyway. He glanced around and saw the road plans sketched on large sheets of paper. The cutaway of the road foundation, the sublayer of aggregate, the sand, and then the large stones on top with sand in between seemed like a good enough guess.

"Yes, I like the plan. I think it will work," he said after a few moments of hesitation.

Shemesh looked at him unamused. "Oh, you do? Which part? The part of the plan that involves you needing to focus on your duties? The part where I said relationships should stay out of the workplace? The part where I said, 'Stop this nonsense with Katesh, at once'?" Shemesh stopped and looked at him, asking the questions again with his eyes.

Yehoshiva just looked back at him. He had not heard any of that. He had no idea what time it was or whether he was even at the compound at that moment. He was still in a dream with Katesh. He looked around. The walls were built with bricks in the style of the compound, and the floor was of stone, and Shemesh only had one office—this appeared to be it.

Shemesh just stared for a moment before saying, "I can't tell you not to have a relationship, but I can direct your work. The Commandant wants to establish a new colony to the west of Irka. I will be submitting your name for the job, though I'm not sure you're up to the task. You need to be somewhere without distractions. You are to establish a port city, and then we will connect the trade network to you and send help as soon as it's feasible. For now, you will be scouting the location and collecting samples of the local flora and fauna as well as rock samples to send back for analysis. You will need to build everything by hand to start with. And you will need to build an obelisk so you can be seen by the surrounding population."

Yehoshiva only heard every other word after "You are to establish . . ." He was dumbstruck, numb. He felt betrayed. He wasn't ready; it wasn't right. Katesh was here; this was where he wanted to be—this was where he *needed* to be. With her. "What about my duties? What about the quarry and the defenses? Taxes?" he asked suddenly, cutting off Shemesh midsentence.

"Don't worry about that. Kimdu will be taking charge of all that." Shemesh stopped and looked at Yehoshiva, then said, "You know this is a great honor to be given such an assignment. Not many as young as you are given the chance to start a city from the beginning and nurture it into a thriving metropolis."

"I'm sure it is an honor and a real *opportunity*, especially since I need to clear my head apparently." Yehoshiva had come out of the fog of the dream he had been in.

"You have earned a promotion, you know. You are an assistant production manager now. You have proven proficient in the rituals and can be trusted to set the example for the primitives to the west." Shemesh tried to placate Yehoshiva, who was starting to get annoyed with the conversation. Yehoshiva knew the tripe about ritual proficiency was a lie. It was all just to get him out of there.

"Doesn't an assistant need a leader still? Does a promotion mean anything down here? What does it get me? A title, a pay raise, and what, a personal company transport?" Yehoshiva was getting heated.

"Well, not the last part. And the pay raise is minor. And as far as a leader, yes, normally, but exceptions can be made for exceptional students." Shemesh was becoming snide in his backhanded compliments.

"So where shall I spend this minor pay raise? How many seeds per month am I earning now? Where can I spend all this lavish wealth you've heaped on me for this opportunity?" Yehoshiva was getting more animated, and Shemesh had almost reached the limits of his patience.

"I think you can decide that out west. I'll organize a caravan back to Irka, and you can pack your things. The Commandant will give you your new orders. You are dismissed. You leave at first light tomorrow morning." Shemesh sat down and began to pen a letter of promotion and reassignment.

Yehoshiva walked out and headed to the courtyard to get some fresh air after the heated exchange. Kimdu was tending the planter boxes Tammuz had left behind and turned to him as he came out. "It looks like you just earned a promotion," he said with a lilt of laughter in his voice.

"Did you hear all that?" Yehoshiva asked.

"No, but no one comes out of his office with that look who hasn't. Looks like you'll find a nice peaceful position far from here, I'm sure. You must have taken food off his plate or something. At least you're getting out of here though." Kimdu smiled mournfully. "Well, that's his way. Just do me a favor, would you?" He handed Yehoshiva a sack of seeds from his supplies. "Take these seeds and plant them along your route in fertile ground. It'll make Tammuz happy. I'm sure I'll be out your way—the work never stops."

"Are these the grain Tammuz had been cultivating?" he asked curiously.

"Some of that, and some of the medicinal flower." Kimdu paused and smiled. "Though I'm not sure which of the two varieties is in there. Oh well, I'm sure it will all work out." He shrugged as he turned back to the planter.

Yehoshiva snickered. His anger had diminished quickly and was being replaced by cynicism. "I'll see you another time, Kimdu. Thank you."

"It's nothing. It's all nothing. I'll see you again, I'm sure." Kimdu smiled as he glanced back over his shoulder.

Yehoshiva took a few steps and paused. "He's giving all my chores to you too."

Kimdu shrugged. "Add it to the list, and I'll get around to it. I'm sure it'll be a regrettable decision." He turned back to the garden and chipped at the sunbaked soil to plant a seed.

Yehoshiva smiled sadly at his friend and turned and walked back to the berthing.

He packed everything he owned—even his nightly rantings seemed worth taking. There wasn't much of anything else. Even all his acquisitions didn't amount to much more than he had come with. Despite this fact, this place felt as much like home as his father's old chair. He was being shipped off to the far side of the desert, away from Marcella. Away from the first woman he felt that longing for that told a soul it had found someone it had known since the dawn of time. She was in him now, and it awakened something he couldn't put away to clear his mind. He didn't know if that would even help him.

Joshua felt hollow. He was going to be alone, and he was going to have nothing but time to think about her. It was going to be a prison that would be more agonizing than any he had borne even in the Machine. Left alone with but one thought, one fond memory, and nothing beyond that. Yearning for that moment, reliving it for what might as well have been eternity. He knew how his boyhood friend Sam had felt when he saw Kim that first moment after she emerged from Town Hall. And he could now see why Sam would think it better to die as a wildling than to live in a world where the only thing worth clinging to had been torn from you so violently by forces outside your control.

He felt hungry, but he knew eating would cover the sadness with comfort—a comfort he rejected. He wanted to feel this pain. To let it gnaw at him and to know it better than he knew any other feeling. He wanted to endure the suffering and embrace it. If this was his fate, he wanted to endure it without accepting it. To let it beat him and abuse him, trying to get him to capitulate without giving in to it. His heart knew what it wanted, and fate—no, *Shemesh*—had conspired to tear it away from him. He felt the anger welling up inside again. It burned low and steady. He wouldn't let it rage, where the flame inside would consume all its fuel and die away quickly. He would feed it slowly. He would let that name be a call to battle. He would outwit and outdo his old superior and undo all he had built for himself in his own image.

36

Katesh was not at the compound that night. She was in the field to collect data from the observatories. She had tried to linger as long as she could, but her mission took priority. She knew that. She would try to be back by morning though. She had to see him again. She didn't know why she felt such urgency, other than the hope and meaning her life suddenly had in the touching of their two souls. The feeling would fade, she feared. Too long without that connection, and the memory of that moment would edge toward oblivion, and the world would fill in the void between.

Her work was suddenly dull and meaningless. And though the drawings of the sky were inaccurate and poorly framed, she accepted them anyway without looking at them. She stared down the hills at the obelisk and drifted there in her thoughts. It was so far from where she stood, but she imagined him looking back at her.

Dawn broke, and she rushed the rituals she was to perform to greet the day. The ritual amounted to a series of stretches that limbered up the body, strained the muscles, and aligned the bones so a person could endure whatever burdens the day would bring. She hurried to the compound and then into the dining hall without performing her ablutions.

She saw Kimdu in the courtyard getting ready to collect taxes, and she stopped to ask him, "Where are you going? Your place is here."

"I will be taking over all of Yehoshiva's projects," he said flatly. The genial timbre of his voice had left him, and he was somberly performing his checks on the roster he held.

"All of his projects? Where's Yehoshiva?" The panic was plain on her face as her head darted back and forth searching the empty corners of the courtyard for him.

"He was promoted." Kimdu said this to the woven sack he huddled over, obviously trying to avoid eye contact.

"That bastard Shemesh." The venom in her heart sizzled through her clenched teeth. "Where did he get reassigned to? Is he at least still going to be on this planet?"

Kimdu sighed and looked at her. "I don't know, but he wanted to be here. He wanted to be with you."

The tears started to well up in her eyes, and then the fury took over again. She marched over to the building where Shemesh's office and quarters separated him from the rest of the Masters. She burst into his office without knocking.

He looked up at her sheepishly.

"How dare you send him off that way!" she demanded. "Where did you send him? Is he going back to Irka? Why did you do this? Why now?"

"You could knock and present yourself properly. I am in charge—"

Katesh cut him off before he could finish. "I should knock you on the head for what you've done, you petty little vermin." She leaned into his desk to look him directly in the eyes.

"He's on this planet, yes. I don't have enough pull to cast him out completely," Shemesh said with a regretful sigh.

"You had *me* reassigned off planet," she reminded him.

"That was different. You were Merchant Astronautica—you belong in the void. I gave you a glowing review," he said dismissively.

"Is this what all this is about then? You are jealous of him? I reject you, and you cast me out, then when I find someone that I want to be with, you cast them out too? Is that it?" She caught the look of admission on his face and knew it was true.

A pained look broke through the stern cruelty he normally wore. "What do you want from me? No one has ever looked at me the way you two were that night. I can't have—"

She cut him off before he could make his excuses. "No one ever will look at you that way. It's got nothing to do with your looks or your position or anything else within your control. It's who you are that is ugly. And there's no cosmetic to cover that up." She swept the stack of plans off his desk and onto the floor and walked out, leaving the door open for all to see. Then she went to pack her things. She was going to find Yehoshiva if she had to travel all the way to Irka.

Yehoshiva plodded along over the dry, cracked dirt of the desert. The moisture had baked out of the surface, and it was hard underfoot. But without something binding it together, it was just dirt, not the bricks he would be spending the next few years baking and building with. He was still angry, but his entourage needed the appearance of a Master without emotion. It was dangerous for him to be out there in the desert, especially with the rebels actively trying to kill the Masters at every opportunity. They had failed so far, but no better opportunity presented itself than to find a small caravan of priests headed to Irka in the middle of the desert. Yehoshiva was not about to show weakness that might give his escort pause when it came time to defend him.

He had barely set out that morning, but the pace they were setting put the city far behind the dust and the dunes, and though it was bad practice to walk in the heat of the day, he wanted his distance. He hadn't been able to say goodbye to Katesh, and she had not been at the compound, but his orders were what they were. These priests bore the marks of Shemesh's cult, which meant they had orders from him. Though it wrenched at his heart, he was unable to avoid his duty. So it was better to get as far from Bashram as he could manage before the priests suffered from the heat of the day.

It was halfway between dawn and the midday sun when they finally stopped. "Set up camp here," Yehoshiva said to them as they plodded along. It wasn't an ideal spot, but the green of the river was no longer visible, and they set up camp a distance from the nearby hills. The nomads and bandits would be watching them, and it was better to suffer the heat of the sun than to present an easy target for them along the cliff's edge in the shade.

As the priests set up the tents and provided water for their ablutions, Yehoshiva looked out at the horizon, searching for their destination, searching for signs of observers, and hoping for any sign of someone racing to catch them. He didn't think the latter was likely, but he remembered the old fable about the box. At the beginning of the universe, all of creation was held in a box. God was curious and decided to look inside as he does for all beings, and when he did, the universe burst forth, and all the suffering and chaos that existence could create burst forth with it. He tried to close the box the moment it was opened, but the force contained within was more powerful than even he could control, and when he finally closed it, the only thing left inside was hope. For eons before the Machine, this was seen as a tale of woe, but after the Machine, the fable was truly understood. It wasn't a tale of the miseries of life; it was about hope. The only thing God was able to contain and control was hope, so that was the only thing worth protecting inside the box.

Yehoshiva gazed at the horizon, and he opened that box once more inside his heart. That was the only thing he had control over.

So he hoped.

It was midday, and Yehoshiva tried to sleep. The heat was oppressive, and his normal sleep cycle made it impossible to get rest. He sat up in his tent. The mat he lay on was set on two thin layers of linen, but he could still feel the ground beneath and taste the dirt in the air, and he was miserable. He got up, dressed himself in his full regalia to maintain his appearance, and emerged from his tent to look out at the surroundings again.

He saw movement on the hills. Slow, cautious movement in the depressions that only appeared for a moment and disappeared. He saw the thin plumes of dust get caught in a breeze and carried off. Then he saw one of his priests down at the base of the hills, and he understood. *Betrayal.* At least one of his priests had decided to change sides, but the fact that he got through the camp watch meant that the watchman himself was either in on the betrayal or completely incompetent. Each of those possibilities was as bad as the other and deserved the same punishment.

Yehoshiva left the camp and found a wadi nearby to observe from. If the priests knew he was awake, they had not shown it yet. He needed to know who he was dealing with and how many, and he needed to know who in his camp could be trusted. At this point, he trusted no one.

The priest started back up the hill and spoke to the guard, who then quietly went tent to tent and alerted the other priests. They came out somewhat disheveled but straightened their attire to make themselves look presentable and began to whisper to one another. *So they're all in on it.* Yehoshiva watched as the priest in command approached his own tent cautiously. He waited as the man peeked through the tent flaps, his hand conspicuously gripping something, but the angle he stood relative to Yehoshiva made it difficult to see. The priests were scrambling around the camp now, quietly pulling things off the dromedaries and digging through the packs for food and water. *So they intend to leave me here to die, to give me over to the enemy.* He pulled his ceremonial dagger from its sheath and stood up tall. He was going to end these clothed animals for their sins.

As he stood, the priest peering through his tent flap looked alarmed. He rushed toward Yehoshiva still clutching the item in his hand, and as Yehoshiva drew back his dagger to strike, the priest flopped to the ground in his submissive posture and held the thing he carried aloft. It was a rolled piece of paper.

"I sorry, Master—other Master coming. We not have tent for both."

Yehoshiva eyed the man suspiciously, then took the parchment and read the message.

> I have abandoned my post to come with you. I will be charged with desertion, but I don't care. I can't stay there and pretend it's okay. I have been followed, so be alert— there are eyes all around us now.
> Katesh

As Yehoshiva read the letter, he let out a sigh. He had assumed he was going to be attacked and would stand alone to face the enemy as his own priests betrayed or abandoned him. Instead, his anxieties were overcome by relief and then elation to know that she had come for him.

"The Master can share my tent with me," he said without displaying the joy he had inside to see her.

She walked up the hill, maintaining her composure and poise despite the heat of the day. When she got to the top of the hill, she was greeted with a cup of water, which Yehoshiva ritualistically put his lips to and then handed to her in a gesture of trust the priests understood to be the practice when greeting strangers in the desert. She took a long sip from the cup and then handed it back. Yehoshiva repeated the process, tipping the cup until the water touched his lips and then handed it back until Katesh had drunk all the contents of the cup and was able to speak again. Her composure was dignified as a Master's should be, but Yehoshiva could see the distress in her eyes.

"Bring food and a waterskin for our guest," he said. "We will take it in my tent. Prepare a wash basin and a sleeping mat for the Master."

The priests obeyed immediately and rushed around gathering the requisite materials. Two presented their own mats to use, as there was no spare for a Master who was not expected on this journey. In a few moments, the tent was prepared for two Masters to sleep in, and the priests hurried out and stood by waiting for orders.

"Double the watch and make the animals ready for rapid departure if necessary," Yehoshiva said as he led Katesh into his tent.

The priest bowed low and started to assign tasks for the others in order to fulfill this new assignment.

Katesh knelt and washed her feet, hands, and face and pressed the damp cloth to her armpits and inner thighs beneath her clothes to cool the magma that pounded through her veins.

"It's not wise to do what you did," Yehoshiva said with a thankful and hungry look in his eyes.

She responded similarly with the same look on her face. "We must do what must be done. The journey was hard, but there is no time for wasting. We are being watched, and there is danger nearby." She signed that the priest had not been expecting to see her when he saw her at the bottom of the hill.

Yehoshiva nodded. "There is always danger for those who bear the knowledge of life."

It was a ritual without a script, but they knew that speaking candidly with the priests within earshot would present enormous dangers, as they were not to be trusted. Everywhere a Master went, they were watched. Everywhere a Master went, they were hunted. The predator was a short, stupid creature half their height and barely capable of thoughts beyond their immediate needs or wants, but they were a predator nonetheless. Any weakness would be uncovered and exploited.

Every servant who finds themselves subject to another tries to balance the scales. Some fight, some flee and observe, others fornicate or join forces to learn the skills of their oppressors. Each is an opportunity to test an enemy in different ways to learn their weaknesses, be it a vice, an injury, or even a romantic entanglement creating an emotional blind spot. The enemy pokes and prods and creeps in close to know you intimately, and ultimately, they learn how to defeat you. Servants always usurp their masters.

Yehoshiva eyed the tent flap and looked around to see if there were any shadows cast on the tent walls and smelled the air to see if their acrid aroma hung in the air longer than the breeze would allow. He was certain they were alone for the moment, so he reached out his hand and took hers and then pulled her close and kissed her deeply, his lips firm but gently pressed against hers. After a moment lingering in that timeless oasis in each other's embrace, they separated and whispered together.

"We can't stay here long. The hills have eyes, and soon they will have knives," Katesh said in an almost soundless breath.

"We'll move before long. Take a short rest, and we'll move. I'll keep watch." Yehoshiva was awake anyway, and the heat of the day radiated off the desert floor and seemed to reflect directly into their tent. When he looked over at Katesh again, she was sound asleep. Her solo escape through the desert and the night shift she normally worked made this her normal routine.

Yehoshiva searched around for another weapon they might use but found nothing of merit. The tent poles could be used as staffs and the stakes could serve as daggers, but there was little else they could use to arm themselves in desperation. He of course had his ceremonial dagger, but Katesh was defenseless.

When the heat of the sun passed and the air began to cool once more, Katesh woke without a sound and dressed just as noiselessly. She emerged to find Yehoshiva standing nearby, guarding the tent entrance and keeping an eye on the hills. Faint movements could be seen by the trained eye, and he was able to count a dozen or so individuals waiting for something. It seemed there was a signal of some kind that was to come from his camp. He heard Katesh open the flap softly, and he whispered so only her attuned ears could hear. "I count a dozen, maybe more, waiting on some signal. Arm yourself, and let's break camp."

She reached for the tent pole supporting the entry flaps and held it like a walking stick. It was just slightly taller than her, but it would outreach any weapon these primitives brought to the fight. Yehoshiva called to the priest in command, "It's time to break camp."

The priest bowed and began to issue commands to the others. They broke the camp down as Yehoshiva and Katesh watched both the hills and the priests, wondering what the signal would be that would move their observers to assault.

A breeze stirred up the dust in the encampment, and Yehoshiva watched the priests shaking the sand out of the mats as they stacked and bound them together to drape on the dromedary. Then the tents themselves were folded and draped and the floor linens the same. Still, the observers didn't move.

When the priests had finished packing the animals and were ready to move out, they stopped and began to perform the Ritual of Altars. What stones there were on the site were piled up, and the spot was consecrated with oil so dust would cling to it and begin to form a mound of windblown dust behind it to serve as a trail marker in the future.

It was at that moment the observers began to move. The priests saw the movement and dawdled just a little bit too long before mounting the dromedaries, trying to buy time without drawing suspicion.

Yehoshiva and Katesh saw the stalling action for what it was and the overt effort at subtlety on the priests' part and were not amused. He started walking in the direction they were headed, pretending not to notice the active betrayal, and Katesh walked behind him using the tent pole as her walking stick. As they passed by, the priest in command hopped down and begged them to lighten their burden. "Sun too hot, must carry light self." He played innocent, blatantly attempting to unburden the Masters of their weaponry.

"You may carry these for us," Yehoshiva said, placating the priest. He pulled off his hat, and Katesh did the same, and they gave them to the priest, one in each hand. As the priest looked at the hats, unsure what to do with them, Yehoshiva drew his dagger, stabbed the man through the center of his chest, and withdrew the blade.

The look of surprise didn't fade as he slumped, and Yehoshiva plucked Katesh's hat from his hand before he fell to the ground. He retrieved his own with only a little bloodstaining it in the process. The other priests saw that their plot was uncovered, spurred the dromedaries, and drove on as fast as they could, leaving the two Masters standing in the desert waiting for their observers to close with them. The dromedary the priest in command had been mounted on was lazing around waiting for someone to tell it what to do. When the observers had reached the bottom of the hill and had amassed their ranks, they all yelled in unison to build their spirit and charged at the two Masters. The dromedary ran away at the sound of the growing cacophony and walked on across the high, flat desert plateau they were on.

Yehoshiva and Katesh just watched this display. It was comical in their eyes to see thirteen primitives dressed in their most frightening and binding and certainly least breathable armor rush at them from the bottom of a hill in the still, hot afternoon sun. As they scrambled up the hill, they held clubs, hand-carved spears, and stone hammers to bash the Masters with.

Yehoshiva said what was on both of their minds. "This hardly seems like a fair fight, does it? Perhaps we should have given the priests our weapons after all." They both smiled and stood motionless, Katesh leaning on her staff, Yehoshiva relaxing with his hand resting on the hilt of his dagger as they watched.

The fighters started to thin at the front as the weaker runners or the more heavily burdened fell behind. Some lost their footing on the sudden steep incline of the last rise of the hilltop, and what had been at the bottom a unified force was at the top a thin gasping line of overdressed children.

"May I?" Katesh asked, gesturing to the first one to approach.

"Yes, milady." Yehoshiva smiled, recalling that day they first arrived at Bashram together.

She remembered, too, and rolled her eyes at him as she readied her staff. As the little man rushed forward with his wooden spear, she jabbed him in the face with the tent pole, which was half as wide as his head, breaking his nose and splitting his brow, and then spun around and smashed the other end into the side of his face. The impact crushed his cheekbone, and he fell limply to the side face down in the dirt, where the blood spilled around him. He lay limp as the next fighter charged at them with her own spear.

Katesh easily parried the first assault, and the fighter stumbled past her into Yehoshiva's dagger, which he ran through her belly and tore out the side, ripping through the leather cladding, which proved little more than cumbersome decoration.

The next fighter came, and Katesh swung the heel of the staff up in an uppercut that shattered the lower jaw and flung the fighter to her back. As her feet carried forward, Katesh brought the tent pole down on her throat to finish her off.

One by one the fighters scrambled to the top of the hill, and each was similarly dispatched. Yehoshiva allowed Katesh to finish off the last one. "I took the priest out first—I think this makes the count even between us."

She smiled. "Well, it would be, if I weren't so compassionate." At that she swept the staff low at the last fighter's legs and connected with his knee. It buckled and snapped, and the man fell screaming as he dropped his heavy club and crumbled to the ground. He lay there writhing in pain as his leg was folded out ninety degrees from its normal position. The snapped tendons and shattered bones made the leg flap around as the man writhed, unable to equate his own flailing as the source of his anguish.

Katesh said to him, "Make sure you tell your chief the Masters still stand."

The man cried out in agony. "Please, take I with. Chief no keep hurt men. No food. Chief eat dead. All do. Help I."

Katesh spoke to Yehoshiva with her eyebrows. *Interesting.*

Yehoshiva shrugged in a way that said, *It makes sense that they would.*

Katesh looked down at the man and said, "You are my enemy, but my mercy is this. You may choose to live and drag yourself that way to Bashram." She gestured with the staff in the direction they had come. "You may die on the way. It will certainly be agonizing, but you may make it if you are strong enough. Or I can give you mercy and kill you where you lie."

The man looked at the desert. He tried to roll over, but the excruciating pain of the lower half of his leg moving ended that modest ambition. He lay there for a moment and looked at his comrades and then sighed before saying, "Kill I. Please. Thank Monster."

Katesh nodded as the man closed his eyes. "You were foolish to try, but you were brave enough to face death when you saw your fellow fighters die fruitlessly. You have earned a good death." She raised the staff above her head and brought it down hard on the man's head. Without any resistance, it smashed clean through, and what was once a face now was a compressed puddle of blood, bone, and brain soaking into the thirsty soil beneath.

Yehoshiva looked at the bodies for a moment and picked up the nearest one to lay near the consecrated rock pile. He lay them in a circle wide enough for all to lie flat shoulder to shoulder. He picked up their weapons. Crude hammers with twine wrapped around them tied to a stick, crude axes of the same design, the wooden spears, and the wooden clubs, among them only one sword that was badly notched and dulled. He heaped them all together around the stones and then examined his handiwork.

"It should have been obvious that they would turn to cannibalism. The only food or water they can get is either from the nomads or the blood of their victims. The only food given to them is seized or torn from the flesh of the dead." Yehoshiva stared at their corpses. "The leather can be only one thing then, since they have no livestock." He lifted a crudely stitched bracer and examined it. "There…" He showed Katesh. "This is someone's tattoo. That confirms it."

Katesh looked at the bodies and then said, "Well, we should take that as evidence for the Commandant at least. This was a problem of Shemesh's creation. Whatever his talents are, he is letting this little sideshow get out of hand."

Yehoshiva looked at her and then at the bracer. He pulled it off and stood. "We need to end this. It doesn't honor the god of this land."

Katesh nodded. "What do you want to do?"

Yehoshiva replied, "I think we find our priests and thank them for their loyalty, then we will continue to Irka. We will present our findings to the Commandant, and then we ask for resources to wipe out this stain from the land. If Shemesh thinks he needs an enemy of his own design, then he has created that in me. This problem was partly of my making as well, and I must wash myself clean of the guilt of their existence." He said this somberly as he turned the bracer over in his hand.

Katesh nodded in agreement and then started walking in the direction of the priests' escape.

It was a little after midnight when the Masters found their lost flock. They were drinking the alcohol and eating the food they deemed their fair keep. The priest in command was dead, and now they were rudderless and wandering, so they were taking advantage of the opportunity and the cool of the night to enjoy themselves in their newfound liberty. They had no plan for tomorrow, but tonight they were going to live like Masters.

Katesh and Yehoshiva stood at a distance listening to them carrying on. Each was a caricature of their favorite vice. One, surrounded by food scraps, leaned against a pack. Two were wrestling, one clearly angrier than the other, who had his genitals out, laughing at the one grappling with him. Another was picking through the equipment and examining it to see if it hid anything of value. Yehoshiva's trunk was open, and his rantings were scattered all around. When the one digging through the trunk found the sack of seeds Kimdu had given Yehoshiva to spread in the new land, another one too drunk to walk straight charged at him to take what he had rightfully stolen from the Master's possessions. The seventh lay passed out next to the glutton, sleeping soundly with a skin of alcohol resting on his belly. Two were still missing, and they wondered where they had gone and what they had taken.

Yehoshiva whispered to Katesh, "We'll wait until they pass out, and then we'll strike."

She nodded in agreement and raised her eyebrows at him to communicate. *You have a plan?*

Sort of. He shrugged back at her. They moved carefully to a shallow wadi nearby and waited. The drunks would be no problem, but the glutton had difficulty sleeping with a full belly of high-fiber travel foods. That would be the first that needed to go—the sloth next to him might as well be dispatched at the same time. Then the greedy one, who seemed more sober than the rest. Then the envious drunk, then the pervert with his genitals hanging out, then the angry one. Finally, the last one, grooming himself by the dromedaries, could be taken out. Yehoshiva signaled the plan to Katesh, who raised her eyebrows at him saying, *I hope it works out exactly like you plan.*

She smiled. Yehoshiva smiled affectionately at her.

It was another hour before they all found their places to settle down and enjoy their vices. The missing two never returned. Yehoshiva and Katesh crept close to the glutton and the sloth. Yehoshiva drove his dagger into the throat of the glutton, muffling the sound of surprise escaping his mouth, and then did the same to the sloth. Katesh had crept over to the greedy one and bludgeoned him with a rock. Then she moved for the prideful one, who stood at the commotion. She struck him with the rock as well, crushing his forehead and sending him staggering backward into the midst of the dromedaries, who started grunting and scattering. The lustful one lay naked on a mat nearby and didn't even move with the commotion.

Katesh looked around for the other two. Yehoshiva had already cut the throat of the envious priest, and then the wrathful one stood up staggering, eyes wide with realization of this apparition before him. Yehoshiva drove the dagger into his chest and dragged him until his body finally fell off the blade and lay motionless on the ground.

Katesh looked at the lustful one and kicked him to wake him up. When he didn't respond, she kicked him again. She leaned over and felt for a pulse but found nothing to indicate life. He was already cold to the touch, so she shrugged. "It seems he died of alcohol poisoning. Well, that's one for the god of this world then." She stood up.

They rinsed off and performed their ablutions and packed up what they could for the journey ahead. Yehoshiva inventoried his trunk and found many of his writings and his Book of Rituals missing. They left the corpses of the betrayers where they had died and did not even mark the site for a memorial. These men were to be forgotten.

They pressed on, making better time than they had with the priests in tow. Even with the stops to fight the bandits and to kill the priests, they made it to Irka in twelve days' time because they pressed on into the heat of the day and rested fewer hours. They also were freer without the ritualistic performances in front of the priests, making it possible for them to get things done faster. Even at that pace, they made time to secure their relationship with their god.

Katesh told Yehoshiva the last night before they made it to the outskirts of Irka, "When I go in there, I will have deserted my post." She was unsure if he knew the implications of that charge.

Yehoshiva thought for a moment. "Then I think the best thing will be to consecrate our bond and enter a covenant together. Right here, right now." He said this with a certainty that made her blush with pride.

"I think that can work. Wherever you go, I will need to be reassigned nearby. Those are the rules." Katesh smiled at his plan. She would have led him to that conclusion, but she was glad he jumped there before she had to.

He took a strip of cloth from a priest's robe and draped it over his wrist. Then he took his dagger and gently sliced their hands, which were pressed together fingers to palm with thumbs raised. The blood from both of their hands oozed and pooled into the crease between their pressed hands. He took the strip of the cloth and wrapped it tightly around their hands, Katesh taking over when it got too far out of his reach. Then he said the words of covenant to her. "As my blood mixes with your blood, so shall my future mix with yours. My genes shall merge with yours, and we shall build a dynasty from this covenant. Today I give myself to you, from now until the end of my days."

Katesh repeated the words.

Then Yehoshiva poured water on their clasped hands. "Let the water be the reminder of our covenant. Wherever it stands or flows, it shall purify our vows."

Katesh picked up a handful of dirt and sprinkled it on their hands and said, "Let the soil be the symbol of our covenant. Wherever it settles or blows shall be a foundation for our promises."

Then they leaned into each other, gently blew into each other's ears, and said together, "Let the air be the life of our covenant. Wherever it flows, it shall carry the whispers of our bond until we breathe no more."

At the end of their vows, they leaned close and kissed. They each found a strip of leather cut from the bindings on the dromedaries and expertly wove two rings that they placed on each other's thumbs. It was not a purely traditional ceremony, but the words were the same, and though their marks were only leather and not the traditional gold, they were still bound by their covenant together and would be assigned together wherever they went hereafter.

37

Yehoshiva was standing outside the Commandant's office waiting to be called in. Katesh was inside. As the more senior officer, it was her responsibility to explain the mess that had become of Bashram and their covenant and their assignments. After about half an hour, the door opened, and the Commandant's voice bellowed through the door. "Get in here. I want to hear it from you too."

Yehoshiva entered the office and spotted the Commandant behind his desk with a look of consternation on his face. His furrowed brow reflected a man who now had to unravel a looming disaster and salvage what he could of the operation before it came crashing down around him. "What is your perspective on this ordeal?"

Yehoshiva started at the end, not sure which part the Commandant was referring to. "Well, Katesh and I entered into a covenant, and—"

The Commandant raised his hand to stop Yehoshiva from continuing. "I don't care about that part—we'll work it out. Congratulations and all that. Tell me about this *Sword* and how all that came to be. Why do we now have a band of primitives that are allowed to live when they are growing to hate us? Why do we have priests betraying our people to this enemy? Why are these primitive bandits willing to starve to death and cannibalize each other just to get away from the society we are creating here? This is absolutely not the purpose of this mission, and it interferes with everything we have achieved. Tell me what you know about what's going on."

Yehoshiva paused for a moment, looked nervously at Katesh, and then started to tell the Commandant about the various schemes Shemesh had designed. His justifications and his intentions. His cruelties and malicious governing, pitting rich and poor against each other, exacerbating the plight of the poor. The slavery. It had only been five standard years on this planet, one hundred planetary years, but Shemesh had managed to create a growing empire of hatred and evil that still failed to produce the result he was aiming at and caused undue suffering and delays in the process.

The Commandant sat quietly for a moment, then sighed as he leaned back in his chair, furrowing his brow as he analyzed the information he had just heard. "This letter you gave me about your recommendation for reassignment by him—is this your request?"

"No, sir, that was his idea," Yehoshiva answered as his body sprang to attention.

The Commandant eyed him. "Why do you suppose he thought promoting you so soon in your training would be a good idea? Do you feel like you are up to the task that you are being recommended for?"

Yehoshiva did not know how to respond. He wasn't sure what the next role would entail, but he did know he hadn't learned everything necessary for the civilization that would grow out of it. "To be honest, sir, I don't know if I'm up for it. I would love the opportunity to learn, but I don't believe that I am the one to lead such a mission just yet. I have limited construction experience. I have very little experience running a priesthood—the scheming and rituals that seem to be necessary are not my forte. I am a decent administrator, but I am not certain I am capable of the task for which I am being recommended. Not as the lead anyway."

Yehoshiva paused for a moment as the Commandant nodded slowly. Yehoshiva continued. "As to the justification for Shemesh promoting and thus reassigning me, I'm not certain. He said my relationship with Katesh was a distraction, and it would be better if we were separated."

The Commandant looked at Katesh.

She added, "Shemesh made a pass at me when this mission was still in its infancy, and I rejected him. He then promoted and reassigned me back to the Merchant Astronautica. I think Shemesh promoted Yehoshiva because he was jealous of our relationship."

The Commandant sighed and looked down at the recommendation in his hand before flipping it onto the desk. "I remember that ordeal, sorting through that administrative nightmare, though I don't remember anyone saying why all that came to be. I do know that he specifically requested you back, and now this covenant between you two"—he gestured at the fresh scabs and rings on their hands—"and this reassignment and promotion request for you in particular is very convenient. So I am inclined to believe your stories."

The Commandant looked thoughtful for a moment and then continued. "But Shemesh knows the rules. Two people in a covenant cannot be separated by reassignment—both are reassigned together if there is any reassignment at all. So do you have a similar recommendation?" the Commandant asked Katesh.

Katesh fidgeted and stammered before sighing and finally admitting, "No, I don't, sir. I am here without orders, and my assignment is still active."

The Commandant nodded his head slowly, then responded, "Well that makes you absent without leave, which carries a sentence that must be carried out. As chief adjudicator, I am obligated to ensure that the punishment fits the offense. You understand that, don't you?"

Katesh looked down at her hands and rubbed the ring with her thumb. She nodded in acknowledgment.

"And judging by the freshness of the scabbing on your hands, I would say this covenant was not premeditated but more of an afterthought. Did you enter this arrangement on the outskirts of the city here before you came to me?"

She nodded. So did Yehoshiva.

"So my justice needs to be served based on the information that was true at the time of your offense. You were not bonded at that time, but you were known to be affectionate toward each other. You were reassigned." He pointed at Yehoshiva. Then he pointed to Katesh. "And as you told me earlier, you had a field operation that would keep you away from the compound. So you left the field and then came across the desert to find him. You encountered the betrayal of the priests and then a conflict with bandit cannibals. You executed the betrayers and then entered a covenant before arriving here. Is that an accurate overview of the last couple of weeks?"

Yehoshiva and Katesh looked at each other and then back to the Commandant. Both nodded in agreement that the synopsis did accurately reflect the overview of the events that had recently played out.

"Okay," the Commandant said, "then based on that information, my ruling for you is this: One month suspension without pay to be served here at Irka. Six months half pay to be served at your reassignment. Then one standard year 'not recommended for promotion.'"

Yehoshiva furrowed his brow, confused. He looked over at Katesh, who was fighting back a smile. The relief in her eyes told him this was a particularly light sentence and, moreover, a reward. The Commandant dug through his mail and found a letter that he handed to Katesh. It was still sealed. "I think if you look at the date on that, you will note it predates your offense, and since you are not technically a member of the Frontier Corps, I have no control over this."

Katesh broke the wax seal and unfolded the letter. At the top it was addressed from the Merchant Astronautica.

> To First Officer Marcella, Astronomer First Class:
> Your successful establishment of numerous observatories and the foundations of astronomical study in the indigenous population of your current assignment has been noticed by the Merchant Astronautica. Your skill and talent for all things regarding navigation are far superior to that of your peers and demands that you continue that service for the betterment of our people and to advance the mission to which you are currently assigned. It is our honor to promote you to the rank of Navigator Third Class, assigned to the Irka Operation until your services become necessary at an assignment of your choosing.
> Thank you for your service and continued devotion to the operation to which you have been assigned. We look forward to your continued success in the future.

The letter concluded, and Katesh looked up at the Commandant. He smiled at her and said, "Congratulations, Navigator. Come back to me when your suspension has been completed, and I'll issue new orders. I believe you read the part about assignment to the *Irka* Operation, not the *Bashram* Operation. So I commend you on your prescient return to your post commander. As you were assigned to my post and your orders have promoted you and thus require reassignment, I think you would agree that you were simply following orders to come here. Your clairvoyance is most impressive," he mocked as he took the note he had written with her punishment.

"Due to this new information in the case of your absence without leave, I have no choice but to throw out the charges, as you have your leave right there in your hand, and it predates your offense by some time, it seems."

He tore up the paper and placed the pieces on a stone tray to burn in the brazier later. He looked back up at her. "I'll write up a new set of orders for both of you. For now, take a transient room in the barracks, and we will talk about your new orders and responsibilities later. You are dismissed." He nodded toward Katesh.

She popped to attention, and as she turned to leave, Yehoshiva caught a glimpse of the relief and joy in her eyes and the straining of her neck saying she was holding back an enthusiastic smile. She walked through the door, uncertain of where to go but eager to have been dismissed. The sound of her walking back and forth in the hall faded as the door drifted shut behind her.

Then the Commandant turned his attention to Yehoshiva. "This news of the bandit cannibals is troubling. I was not aware they had grown to such strength and were becoming so reckless. This needs to be dealt with. I am putting you on temporary assignment with our strike team. They will need to know everything you know, and then you will join them in eliminating this encampment. I believe it will serve you well to understand combat operations and strategy. Just remember you are not in charge there. You are there to learn and to share the intel that you have available."

The Commandant wrote a brief note and signed it. "Give this to the Captain and tell him to speak to me if he has any questions. Once you are done with that little mess, I'll have your new orders ready."

He leaned back in his chair again and thought for a moment. "You mentioned two priests had escaped. Did they take anything?"

Yehoshiva let out a guilty sigh and nodded in the affirmative. "Yes, sir. They took the Book of Rituals and many of my writings. Most of it was worthless, but there's no telling what information they can glean from that, if any."

The Commandant looked up at the ceiling with disappointment and then leaned forward in his chair against his desk and steepled his hands, thinking. After a moment he finally said, "I think we'll be okay on that one. I'm not sure it's the first that has been lost, and the rituals they see painted around their cities are similar but different from the ones in the book. They may not fully appreciate it, and it should decay with time and poor preservation. Do your writings have any secret information in them?"

Yehoshiva tried to remember what his rantings contained. "Personal complaints about Shemesh. Some interpretations of the rituals, some poems, some dreams and visions I've had. Rantings, really. It was an emotional and psychological outlet for me. I can't really remember anything specific."

The Commandant just stared at him, sizing up the information he just heard. Finally, he shrugged. "I think we can make it work. But I'll need to notify the company of this. I'll need their approval to take measures to mitigate these issues." The Commandant looked down at his desk and took a fresh paper off the stack and began to write, then stopped and looked up. "You're dismissed."

Yehoshiva hesitated, deciding whether to say the thought that had crept into the back of his mind. "Sir?" He waited for the Commandant to look up at him before proceeding. "I think Shemesh intended for me to be killed. I think he may have planned it. They were his priests, and they seemed to be expecting the bandits and the stealing of my property like they were searching for something."

The Commandant's face relaxed into a look of sympathy. "Yeah, that's what I believe as well. All evidence suggests that, but without hard proof it's not going to be an easy case, and technicality will exonerate him. Don't worry, though, it will all be taken care of."

"Thank you, sir," Yehoshiva said before turning to the door and walking out.

The Commandant just waved his hand in an accepting gesture as his sad gaze followed him to the door. He called after Yehoshiva as he stepped through the transom. "One final thing." Yehoshiva stopped and leaned back to look the Commandant in the eyes. "You can leave your code name at the door here. You are no longer assigned to the Bashram operation. Welcome back . . ." He glanced at the dossier next to him and said, "Joshua."

Joshua smiled, popped to attention, and said, "Thank you, sir!"

38

The Captain was in his office in the barracks, which doubled as his berthing. He was doodling on a scrap of paper when Joshua checked in with him. The man looked up at Joshua's face and then at the paper he had presented and reached out and took it. "Hmm. Okay. Guess you're with me for a bit then," the Captain said. He wrote another note out and handed it back to Joshua. "Take this to the supply sergeant and come back to me in some PT gear."

Joshua looked at the note. It just said, "Basic Kit-temp. –D"

Joshua dropped his hand with the note and walked out to go find the supply sergeant. "Other way," the Captain called out from behind him as he turned to the right. He glanced back at the Captain, who had once again returned to his doodle.

Joshua found the supply sergeant not far from the Captain's office. She was doing calisthenics and body-weight exercises by her bunk. As Joshua approached, she slowly got to her feet with a look of irritation at the intrusion. She took the note and nodded. "I guess you'll be with us for a bit then." She caught her breath. "Not a lot of missions to go on, so we spend a lot of time exercising and training." She motioned to the floor behind her by way of explanation. "I guess you should follow me."

She grabbed a bag at the entrance of the supply closet and threw it at Joshua. Then, before he had it open, she started tossing PT uniforms, towels, a tan jumpsuit, a pair of boots, a harness, and equipment at him. She dug around and found a small day pack and flung it in his general direction as well. Joshua tried to catch it all and stuff it into the sack at the same time, but items just kept coming. Soon there was a pile of equipment lying loose on the floor around him. Still more came out. Canteens and a knife. Then she stopped throwing items at him and grabbed a repeating crossbow off the last shelf with three bundles of bolts. "Okay, this is your kit. Stuff it all in there. I'll show you how to pack it for the field. We'll go practice with the crossbow so you can get the feel of it in a bit. This is the primary weapon we use against primitives on any planet."

Joshua looked around at all the gear. None of it was technology the primitives would have available to them, so it was all considered high risk. "How is all this stuff approved for use in the field?" He turned the knife over in his hand.

"You Frontier Corps geeks are the primary mission and have your set of rules. We are here to clean up when you screw up, so we live by different rules. We are soldiers, so we do not play fair. And we are out of FC's jurisdiction, but we have to make some compromises." She looked around at the mess on the floor and then up at Joshua. "Well, pick this up, and let me know when the Captain is done with you." She stepped over the mess and left Joshua to pick it up.

Joshua returned to the Captain with his PT shorts and shirt on. Both were desert brown.

The Captain looked him up and down. "Put your boots on. We're going to go break them in." He was still drawing the same doodle as before—a naked woman with an overly feminine face and an extra-small head to accentuate the attractive characteristics for their people. Joshua glanced at the Captain and then stepped aside and pulled the boots out of the sack and slipped them on over the socks he'd been issued.

He laced them up and tied the laces together and tucked the laces inside the boot top. He had lived as a soldier hundreds of times in the Machine, so he knew the tricks of the trade. But this body was not hardened for this kind of work, so he knew it wouldn't be pleasant for him to break in these boots.

He stood up and presented himself to the Captain. "I'm all ready."

"You can put the rest of your gear away in your rack." The Captain pointed to the room that Joshua and Marcella had been assigned at the end of the squad bay.

Joshua looked where he was pointing and gathered his gear. He took the opportunity to see Marcella, if only briefly.

Marcella was sitting on one of the cots in the room when he arrived.

"Hey, I'm going to be training for a bit, and then at some point, we're going to go take care of the bandits. So I'm going to be busy for a while."

She smiled up at him. "Don't worry about me. I'll stay busy. Just come back to me when you can."

He shoved the rest of his gear under the other cot and kissed her good-bye. Even being married, their physical relationship was still new, and there was an awkwardness to it. Now she would be left behind to pine for him as he went and played soldier. The honeymoon would have to wait, but he needed to find time to be with her even with new and unfamiliar duties to perform. He examined her face as she turned to the pamphlet about Irka's history, and then he walked out to go train with the Captain.

Joshua and the Captain ran in circles around the empty landing pad for two full hours. Around and around and around. Each lap was less than a quarter kilometer, and Joshua estimated they had run around one hundred times. He felt sick with fatigue. Sweat soaked his PT uniform as his body purged what little moisture it held.

The Captain finally stopped and looked at Joshua. He took a moment to catch his breath and recovered after a minute or so. He had been doing this for a long time, and his body was used to such abuse. Joshua, on the other hand, was not.

Joshua hunched over, breathing heavily. His body ached, and his heart was pounding hard. Though he was used to the deprivations of life on this planet, strenuous exercise in the heat of the day was not something he had forced himself to endure.

The Captain spoke to him with an even tone, not the slightest sign of distress in his voice. "How do those boots feel?"

"They . . . feel . . . wet. And heavy." Joshua forced his words out between breaths, his chest heaving.

The Captain just smiled and laughed at his poor fitness. "They get heavier the more you sweat, but the sweat will stretch the leather and make them fit like a second layer of skin. I won't torture you anymore today. You can go back inside and go get familiarized with your equipment. The supply sergeant is waiting for you."

The Captain walked through the corridor to the adjoining barracks and went back to his office. Joshua stayed there heaving, but he was catching his breath now. So he followed the Captain to the barracks.

Joshua found the sergeant on her rack reading some newspaper from her hometown on whichever planet she called home. She barely looked up from the page as she asked, "Ready to go play with your new toys?"

He nodded.

"Okay." She flopped the paper down and turned to climb out of bed. "Go change into your jumpsuit and bring all your gear. I'll go over it with you here. We'll shoot your crossbow after you have an idea what everything else is for."

Joshua walked back to his room and found Marcella napping lightly. She woke when he started pulling his boots off. His socks were wet from sweat, and he had hot spots on his feet from the boots. He drew water from the cistern at the back of his room and performed his ablutions. The water felt good on his sore feet. When he peeled off his PT gear, it clung to his body with so much sweat that he struggled to pull it off. Marcella stood and helped him out of it, her hands touching him and feeling the heat of his skin as the blood pounded and burned in his veins. She soaked a rag and held it to the back of his neck and then his back. She put it under his armpit for a few minutes while she helped him dig out a jumpsuit and socks.

"I'm exhausted," he said as his muscles unknotted themselves with the dull ache of muscle beginning to repair itself.

"I'll massage you later. Make sure you stretch so you don't hurt yourself." She sat on the bunk next to him and continued to apply the cool wet rag and wipe him down. His arms were the dark gray of a life spent in the elements, but where his old uniform had shielded his skin, it was pale and unblemished.

"I've got just a few minutes before I have to go." He paused, uncertain how to proceed.

Marcella smiled warmly at him. "Then I guess we better get to know each other better." She leaned in for a kiss and then, holding him by the arm, leaned back on the bed and pulled him close.

He didn't need the full few minutes. He got to know her very quickly for the first time.

She smiled at him, laughing at his haste and his uncertainty and eagerness. She stroked his arm and said, "We'll have more time later. You've got work to do."

He stood up slowly, slightly embarrassed, and retrieved his clothes from the bag. He put on the fresh socks and then the jumpsuit. He placed his PT gear in his washbasin to soak and took his bag and equipment to the supply sergeant's rack.

"Dump everything out, and I'll go down the list and have you pack each item into your day pack," the sergeant ordered.

Joshua dumped everything and spread it out so he could see what he had.

She started reading down the list. When Joshua didn't know what a thing was called or what it was used for, she pointed at it and told him. Infrequently used items were put at the bottom, spare clothes and hygiene were in the middle, and frequently used and combat necessities were at the top. She then had him put on the belt and harness and adjusted them to fit him properly. Then he picked up the canteen pouch and clipped it to the harness.

She stopped him. "Don't ever let your canteen be empty before a mission or half full during one. If you drink from it, you finish all of it. If you can't drink all that yourself, you share it with the team until it's empty. The sloshing will give away our position, and you will put everyone in jeopardy." Then she let him put the canteen away. She took the bolts for his repeating crossbow and slid the quick clip point down into a pouch on his harness straps. Then she fastened his knife to his other strap, handle down.

Item by item she went through his gear and made sure he knew how to use it. She made him jump up and down to make sure everything was secure and no clanking or squeaks could be heard and then led him back to the courtyard for weapons training.

The sergeant showed him how to load the magazine of bolts into the repeating crossbow, then she showed him how to fire it and gave him a few practice shots at a wooden crate to get the aiming down. "You can feel free to come out here and practice your aim as long as there's no ship here. It's free to use, and you don't have to worry about the primitives seeing. You can relax a bit and just have fun. Remember the safety rules though: Treat every weapon as if it were loaded. Keep your finger straight and off the trigger until you are ready to fire. Never point a weapon at anything you do not intend to shoot. Keep your weapon on safe until you are ready to fire. And know your target and what is behind it. Got it?"

"Yes, sergeant. Thanks." He continued practicing with the crossbow until he got the action down right. He would need to practice cocking it to get the motion down for combat, when he might not be able to learn a fine motor skill in the moment.

Joshua and Marcella walked through the city of Irka examining the changes that had occurred in the last few years. The city was thriving—a sharp contrast to what was happening to the southeast in Bashram. The taxes were low, and the system wasn't punitive or designed to squeeze and bankrupt the people to drive them into poverty. There was an income tax because it was useful to know what the economic generation of the city was, a flat percentage for everyone, from which the administration could extrapolate the gross domestic product of the city. The movement of money and the Masters' control over valuable industries ensured revenues for those goods were sufficient to finance any operation they deemed a public necessity, so the income tax was minimal for economic tabulation purposes.

At the city gates, people paid a nominal head tax of a single minted coin in order to have an accurate count of how many entered the city on a daily basis.

An annual head tax of a flat fee per person was expected as a means of keeping an accurate census but again was a modest amount. If a person couldn't afford the head tax, the city provided it. It was a useful tool to know how large the population of the poor actually was, so paying their annual head tax meant the city accountant could subtract the "loss" from the total count, and the absolute value was the number of impoverished in the city's domain. Every effort was made to increase the available labor demand to lift those people out of poverty, and the city thrived. There was no excess demand on the citizens, as almost everything came through revenues. It was a sensible system that provided population data that was useful for the Masters to know.

When the city became too crowded, the Commandant added walled expansions around the four gate communities where the middle class and poor were starting to gather. Then, when that was completed, those walls were connected, and the third ring of the city was formed. This made the inner compound, the outer commercial and wealthy district, four middle-class districts, and four intermediate industrial districts separated by category.

All food processing was done in the northwest industrial district. In the southwest industrial district, the distilleries were in full production, and vegetable bases were turned into stock and the mash turned into feed for livestock. Spice production found a home here as well. In the northeast corner were the stockyards. Dairy and eggs and meat for food production, feathers for beds and pillows, bone meal for dietary supplements, and fats for soap manufacturing—every part of the animal was used to make some product, and those products were produced in the southeast industrial district.

Each sector attracted the people that each job appealed to. They lived in the residential sectors nearby and mingled and reproduced with one another to make children of even greater concentrations of those personalities most amenable to the work. From there, the strength of those traits and interests and creative diversity and economic efficiency continued to expand and made Irka a beacon of prosperity in the world.

Though it was desert, agriculture still thrived. The work of Masters like Tammuz had produced drought-resistant crops that were grown in vast fields of brick planters, where fertilizer was used. The city was impressive and organic, and the adoration of the Masters was evident in the people all around.

Everything had its place and its use, there was no waste, and the system was self-sustaining.

The Masters similarly trained the primitives, the Umanu, who demonstrated all the capability of maintaining this civilization on their own. The Masters here created the engine of invention and shaped the society intelligently in order to improve the primitives' lives and their capabilities. As a result, the productivity of the city far surpassed that of almost any other on the planet despite the scarcity of resources or water in the area.

It was this contrast with Bashram that made it so remarkable, and Marcella and Joshua admired it as they walked through the city for what felt like the first time. It was a truly extraordinary creation, all built in the interest of improving the indigenous people.

Irka felt like home to them. The sense of ease they carried just from one day here was greater than all the days in the last year combined. Here there was no anxiety about the next project; no one felt like they were being used or manipulated to perform some task that would be leveraged for ill intent. Everything that was done here was done with the expectation that it would serve to improve the lives of the Umanu, and they would become more productive and happier participants in the operation that the Masters would benefit from. The role of production management here was taken to mean improving the lives of the people so they would improve the efficiency and output of their system.

Marcella and Joshua looked around the dining hall that night after their excursion through town. They didn't spend long walking the city, and they never felt the crush of desperate people. Now as they sat in the dining hall searching the faces of the Masters around them, they found no one who carried the emotional weight they had endured for so long.

When the meal had ended, they scrubbed their portion of the dining hall, did their own dishes, and helped scrub the kitchen down. It only took a few minutes because of the extensive labor pool, but they were glad to help. This wasn't their city per se, but it was the same wherever they went now. Their People and their rituals kept the culture bound together and gave them an identity distinct from those elsewhere in the universe, living dull lives in quiet farming towns, waiting on the next harvest and town hall meeting.

Joshua thought back to his life before and remembered yearning for more. And here he was, on the fringes of his own empire, living that dream his heart searched for years ago. He was happy here, and nothing could have spoiled that feeling for him—in Irka. Marcella held his arm as they walked back to their berthing. There was a look in her eyes now that told him sleep would still be some time away. He leaned in and kissed her, and they disappeared into their room.

39

The days went by in a flurry of exercise, training, battle simulations, hand-to-hand combat, knife fighting, timed dummy kill practice, and extensive map reading to devise the battle plan. Joshua told them all the info he had on the bandit encampment and Bashram. The borders of Bashram extended along the river valley to the hillside, so they knew at least the limits of the camp. He told them where Shemesh had initially instructed the Sword to build a fortification and where they had been attacked on the first day of their journey to Irka. This allowed them to extrapolate the rough location of the enemy encampment. Four of the hills they requested imagery on had an encampment. This meant that not only would it be impossible to wipe out the enemy in one shot, but the likelihood of some of them escaping to create new encampments was likely. They needed to assault multiple locations in rapid succession to eliminate the threat. Any survivors would spread their ideological disease to other populations, and the movement would only be strengthened.

It took another month of planning to get an approved strategy through the chain of command. The Commandant was insistent they should strike all at once, but the logistics of that required more man-power than they had available, and the delay in getting them there would mean the disease would spread even further uncontained. They discussed aerial bombardment, but again the resources for that were too far out of range to be practical. And the use of the technology required for such an endeavor would create a spectacle that would ensure the movement would grow and the tale would travel far and wide and would not paint the Masters in a good light.

The battle plan and the date had been set. In two nights' time, they would engage the enemy.

The Captain addressed his platoon. "All right, guys and gals, listen up. When we hit the first target, we sweep and clear everything. Orders are that they are to be completely exterminated. That means for you, *civilian*"—he looked at Joshua—"that men, women, and children will need to be removed. They are cannibals. The disease they carry is not curable, and they can't be trusted in the society. They can't be allowed to be left alone either. This is the only way."

The soldiers murmured and nodded. Yehoshiva looked around, concerned that he was the only one who didn't know if he'd be able to handle that.

The Captain continued. "If a man goes down, leave him there and continue. Clear the entire camp and move to the next objective. My team will recover any casualties. We'll provide medical treatment on scene and move in once the all-clear is given." He pointed to the map. "The distance tops out at just under ten kilometers between these two encampments, so we will have a long night to complete all the objectives before daylight. Polar Command will provide us a lift to the insertion point here." He pointed to a spot about a kilometer away from the first objective. "They will provide extraction here." He pointed to the final objective. "These primitives don't seem to be using projectile weaponry, so we are at a very steep advantage. Just don't let them in close, and this should be a quick and clean operation. Any questions?"

A question came from the back. "What time is our insertion?"

"We will arrive on scene two hours after sunset, which puts us waiting for pickup here at one hour after sunset. So stand by to stand by. Polar Command has assured me they will have the bird here on time. But we all know what that means."

Joshua heard a chorus of grunts, scoffs, and grumbles.

"If we end up getting caught in the daylight, we complete the objectives and go firm for the day to avoid technology assets from being detected. So I know it's extra weight, but bring something to eat. From the sounds of it, you won't want what the targets are cooking."

Yehoshiva looked around at the soldiers nodding in agreement.

A female soldier in the front raised her hand. "Sir, worst-case scenario, we get runners and have to chase, then the next objective perimeter is not secure in time. What is the plan?"

"The standing order is to eliminate *all* inhabitants. No one escapes. Give chase, and we'll regroup before assaulting the next objective. Stragglers can join my command team, and we'll push one of our team to take your spot. *This is a priority one mission, people.* No survivors, and full recovery of all technology. So everyone better triple-check your gear before you step off the bird and make sure everything that goes in with you comes back out. That means assault teams are going to be pulling bolts from the bodies, so bring your extraction tools. *Not one bolt* left behind. Understood?"

"Yes, sir," everyone said in unison.

"Good to go. Everyone rack out for a few hours. We'll be drilling tonight. Dismissed." As the Captain said this, everyone popped to attention and then began to scatter.

As Joshua started to leave, the Captain approached him. "I hope you're up for what 'no survivors and full recovery' means. We have a lot at risk on these ops, and anything left behind endangers future missions, both targets and technology."

Joshua hesitated before admitting the truth. "I'm hoping I'm not put in that position. I know it's necessary, but I'm not sure if I can do that part of it."

The Captain nodded. "Honesty is a good quality. You will be with my team the whole way in, but if we need to replace someone in a squad, you're going to need to step up. It's not normal protocol for a civilian to join us on ops, but I was given specific instructions to get you tactical experience. Apparently, you're going to need it. My hope is you will have the boring task of chasing me around all night. But if not, you will have a teammate to keep you in line. Just do what they say and leave the heroics and the hard stuff to them. Pull your weight, and everyone will be happy."

He patted Joshua on the shoulder and started walking away but then stopped. "By the way, I know you've had some experience with combat already and came out alive, but if things ever start to eat at you, find someone to talk to. Don't bottle it up, and don't let them tell you to be ashamed of your feelings. We've all seen things in the Machine that have inoculated us to most violence of life, but real-life decisions don't pass so easily. Each of us is a teapot full of all our emotions, and whatever you don't pour out hardens into a crust. If you're always happy, you withhold your sadness. If you're always angry, you withhold your joy. When that crust finally fills the pot, nothing will come out of it anymore—you can't *feel* anything but what was left to calcify, and it becomes who you are. Negative emotions destroy you from the inside, so let them out. That's the code we live by here."

Joshua grinned. "I like to dance in fields of flowers."

The Captain laughed. "Not that though. Keep that stuff bottled up."

Marcella sat waiting for him. She had overheard the speech the Captain gave, and a sense of dread came over her. Joshua was a capable fighter, and he was intelligent and strong. But he was good hearted. He felt sympathy for these people that the soldiers had never acquired. *Will he be able to handle it emotionally?*

He came in and sighed heavily. "Extermination," he said sadly. "These lives are my responsibility. I created them." He sat heavily beside her and began to cry. "I did this."

She soothed him as she stroked his head and neck gently. "No, *we* did this. But you're going to clean it up."

40

They were assembled at the landing pad waiting for the transport to arrive. The Captain found Joshua and knelt beside him. "We've got new orders," he said bluntly.

Joshua sat upright from leaning on his pack. His full attention was on the Captain.

"Gather 'round, everyone," the Captain yelled to his platoon.

They assembled, leaving their packs where they were, and gathered around the Captain.

When it looked like everyone was there and paying attention, he began to speak. "So we've had a slight change in the mission." He looked around. "Three squads will conduct the eradication mission. Use standard mission practice for that. One squad will set a perimeter, one will flank, and one will conduct the assault. Assault team sets the pace. One hundred percent tech extraction, do you copy?" he asked, looking around.

No one was surprised, but they all nodded and said, "Copy that."

"That part stays the same. However, you'll need to break out a two-man team from each squad to fill in for any casualties and to gather intel, etcetera. My squad will be conducting a side mission once you are safely on the ground." He looked at Joshua. "I'll need you to identify this Shemesh and his cult. We're heading into the city to arrest him."

Joshua's face lit up with excitement and worry all at once. The change was unexpected. The target was even more so. "What about all the people there? How are we getting into the city without them seeing all these weapons? How are we going to get him out of there without attracting attention?"

The Captain shook his head. "I've been given permission to take out any and all hostiles, and it doesn't matter what they see at this point. The city is being abandoned, and the society there is expected to collapse. We have the go-ahead to use all necessary measures to get all Elohim out."

Joshua looked around at the rest of the soldiers. They were unmoved by the news; this was situation normal for them, and they had already adapted in their minds. "Okay, then, what is the plan?"

The ship landed and the teams boarded. The Captain spoke to the pilot and updated the mission plan. He objected, raising his arms and voice in disgust, but finally relented. The troops began to file on board, and as Joshua began to pick up his pack, he heard Marcella call to him from the landing pad entrance.

Joshua ran up to her and gave her a kiss. "We're going to arrest Shemesh. We're going to pull everyone out and abandon his project there."

Marcella still had the glaze of sleep and fatigue in her eyes, but a look of deep worry overcame the sleepiness in her face, showing her tension in her shoulders and back. She leaned in and hugged Joshua tightly, knowing this meant he was going to be heading there instead of the open desert to eliminate these Amalekite rebel bands. She whispered, "Be careful. He's a cornered animal, and he's ruthless." She peered into his eyes, and the glint of the moon that illuminated the pad radiated from them. Her gray skin was shaded blue in the light, and her smooth, radiant beauty was enough to make him forget what he was doing at that moment. A perfect memory of his beloved. He pulled her in close and kissed her deeply and passionately and held her as if for the last time.

The voice of the Captain called from the ramp. "All right, soldier, you've said your goodbyes. Let's go, or the memory will have time to tarnish."

Joshua looked back and saw that he was the last one to board. He gave Marcella another quick but passionate kiss and then picked up his gear and walked to the ramp and into the ship. Her taste lingered on his lips, and he wanted to savor it as much as he could to preserve every fragment of that parting memory. He was entering battle, and though his mind should be focused on the task ahead, he wanted to hold on to the person who had brought all this to fruition.

As the ship lurched upward, he leaned against the bulkhead with his squad and thought about Marcella. He realized she was an agent of change. At every moment he had known her, she knew what she wanted, knew what was right, and stood up for all of it. She was bold and strong and was every bit the leader he imagined he wanted to be. She was the one who brought the tectonic shifts in his life all along. She was the true leader of the Elohim at Bashram, and she was the one who created the most stable and enduring element of the Umanu there. Bashram would be her legacy, and he was there to make sure that legacy would endure.

The Captain sat by him, and in the dark of the corridor echoed the thoughts in Joshua's own mind. "You have a great woman there. Few of us are worthy of something that good, and most of us never get the chance to find out what that is like. She must see something equally great in you. You're very lucky."

Joshua was somewhat abashed by the statement. "Thank you." He turned the conversation back to the Captain as the ship flew through the night toward the first rally point. "I never asked if you have someone waiting for you somewhere."

The Captain smiled. "No, you didn't, but no, I don't. This life is too hard to maintain the balance necessary for that. I was married once, but it became clear that I was limiting her potential, and the duty stations I could serve in were less than ideal for me too. So we ended it amicably and went our own ways to follow our own ambitions. She was a top choice after the Machine, and I was always just destined to be a soldier." He pulled out his dog tags and revealed the gold ring that still hung from the chain. He spun it between his thumb and index finger, recalling the memory. "Sometimes loving someone means setting them free to achieve their greatest potential. Nothing like the pragmatism of enduring the Machine to make you realize your own limitations and the potential of others."

Joshua saw the sadness the man carried and probed further. "Where is she now? How did she feel about it?"

The Captain smiled. "As a twist of irony, she's here. Not here, here. But at the base on the moon. A researcher. I haven't seen her in a long time and am too afraid to find out if she is still . . . alone. But I know she's there and safe—and, I hope, happy."

When Joshua tried to speak, the Captain cut him off, "Hold on to what you have—we don't get to decide where fate guides us. Even more powerful than our knowledge and realism are the shifting currents of the unknowable chaos of fate and destiny. We parted because we were both pragmatic people, but we were brought close by something else. You don't have control over everything. Sometimes things were just meant to be even if they don't make sense."

The Captain changed the subject abruptly. "Put all that out of your mind for now though. We are approaching the first drop-off and will need to be ready. We're going in hot, and I need you to guide us through to the objective."

Joshua nodded in the dim light of the corridor, and the Captain tapped his knee in a friendly gesture affirming the order and then got up and walked to each squad leader to confirm everyone else was ready to go.

The ship landed some distance away from the first objective, and the four teams filed out silently at the bottom of the ramp. The Captain spoke softly to the platoon sergeant, who was taking command of the cleanup mission. After the man ran down the ramp to assemble the squads, the ramp was raised and the ship lurched upward to head to the second waypoint near the outskirts of the city. The Captain approached Joshua and gestured for him to follow him to the cockpit. "I need you to show the pilot a safe place to land close enough to get us into the city without alerting too many guards."

Joshua followed and at the projection screen found a place within the walls of the unfinished city where it should be safe to land. The month that had passed was not enough time to make much progress there, so it should be lightly guarded and open enough for a quick insertion. "There. I think that's our best bet. Shemesh spends a lot of time at the temple here, and this will put us close enough to clear that area. Everyone in that quarter is part of Shemesh's cult and can be eliminated. The ones with black marks on their arms are his adherents."

The Captain confirmed the spot with the pilot, who moved in a wide trajectory to avoid the encampments and loop around the city to land at that spot. The trip was short, as the ship flew at inconceivable speeds, and minutes later they were in position. The ship touched down softly, and the team assembled in the corridor near the ramp. Once the Captain pressed the button, they filed out with weapons drawn and began eliminating the guards and workmen, who stood awed by the sudden appearance of the ship.

Joshua knelt on the ground at the bottom of the ramp and waited for the Captain to signal that the area was secure. After the Captain touched a button on the ramp that made it retract and signaled to the pilot to take off, they knelt in a silent circle waiting for the signal to move.

The Captain whispered to Joshua, "Okay, this is your show. Let's go."

Joshua was nervous but nodded and started to move toward the temple. One by one the soldiers peeled into a wedge formation to move toward the temple. Everyone who appeared was eliminated. The bolts were not recovered, but they were not concerned with that at this time. They had one objective, and the totality of the collapse after this mission would ensure most of their efforts were hidden.

The temple complex loomed larger as they approached the gates. The streets were silent save for a few guards they silenced along the way. Joshua opened the door, and the soldiers filed in and began clearing the courtyard, one team sweeping left, another right, and another straight up the center in textbook fashion. They encircled the temple, preventing any escape from side doors or secret passages, and then Joshua and the Captain moved to the door.

The Captain gave a three, two, one countdown with his fingers.

Joshua opened the temple door and moved in behind the Captain with crossbow drawn. There were a couple of priests, taken out immediately, but at the altar, a passage revealed itself where the linens had been pulled back and the altar shifted out of place.

The Captain peered down into the shaft and then said to Joshua, "We can chase him, or we can move on to the next objective. Do you know where this passage goes?"

Joshua shook his head. "Shemesh was in charge of the construction of this temple. I didn't know this existed until now."

"Where would he go from here?" the Captain asked, pointing his crossbow down the shaft.

"There were a series of tunnels I had dug to provide access for us to this area without interacting with the people here, but Shemesh had them blocked up. I'm not sure if any were left open for his use. It is something he would probably have done, though, given his deceptive nature and his need for religious mystery." Joshua pointed to the marks on the dome above indicating his use of signs and signals to mark the sunrise and magnify the faith of the people in his power over the sun.

The Captain let out a sigh and fired a bolt down the shaft. It clanked and clattered off the stone walls and then fell silent at the bottom. "Okay, let's go to the compound then and get the rest of your team out of here."

Joshua nodded and then caught the glint of something from the altar. He reached into the lectern and pulled out the small gold bauble Shemesh carried everywhere with him. "He was definitely here," he said with disappointment. He tucked the tetrahedron into his pouch and followed the Captain out of the temple to the reassembly outside in the courtyard.

A few more priests lay near the gate, and the four teams went to the rally point to move out into the city once more.

With the moon high in the sky, they reached the compound gate and moved in silently. There were few other citizens around, and Joshua cautioned the soldiers not to fire on anyone in this sector, as they were not adherents of Shemesh. They moved into the courtyard and closed the door behind them.

"Okay, that's Shemesh's office," Joshua indicated. "You can clear that and get whatever intel you need from there. I'll go to the berthing and see if anyone else is here. I think only Kimdu was left, but I'll make sure."

The Captain signaled to a team and sent them to Shemesh's office. Then to another to stay put and guard the entrance. Another he sent to clear the rest of the courtyard, and the last team he signaled to follow them. "Okay, let's go get your friend."

Joshua knocked on Kimdu's door. After a moment, the door opened, and the bleary-eyed Kimdu answered. "Yehoshiva! I didn't think I'd see you so soon. And so late. What's up?"

The Captain appeared in the dark, answering the question with his presence.

"So they're finally doing it, huh? About time," Kimdu said, quickly sizing up the situation.

The Captain asked quickly, "Is there anyone else here? We need to evacuate quickly. Grab what you need and assemble in the courtyard."

Kimdu peered down the hall and answered in the negative. "No, no one but me and Shemesh, and Shemesh has been spending his time at the temple lately."

Joshua nodded. "Yeah, we just came from there. He's escaped."

Kimdu shook his head. "Yeah, he's a sly one. I figured he had an escape plan, though I'm not sure how he knew you were coming."

The Captain interjected, "That doesn't matter right now. We need you to get ready and get out of here. We're burning everything that isn't coming with us, so pack light and pack quick."

Kimdu nodded and closed the door.

Minutes later they all assembled in the courtyard. The team that searched the office came back with bags of prints and plans and documents showing evidence of the schemes. Two teams grabbed torches and moved through the berthing and the office and other outbuildings, setting fire to furniture and documents left behind. Then they assembled in the courtyard again.

Kimdu carried his trunk on his broad shoulders and was dressed as smartly as he would be if given the full opportunity to go through the morning rituals. Two of the squad tried to take the burden from him, but he refused. "You've got your jobs to do. I'm just cargo. You've already got enough hanging off you that you don't need to burden yourselves with mine as well. I've got this."

The Captain obliged him. As the flames and smoke began to rise from the buildings, the squad moved out into the silence of the old city. They moved quickly to the new one, avoiding any new encounters that might reveal their presence even more than had already been done.

They waited a few moments, and the Captain activated a wrist-mounted beacon to signal the ship for pickup. In a few moments, the ship appeared and landed, and they all filed up the ramp in the darkness and took off.

They landed again far outside the city and waited for the second beacon.

The Captain sat with Joshua, who was chatting warmly with Kimdu. "Great work out there."

Joshua parried the compliment. "Well, Shemesh escaped, so it wasn't a complete success."

The Captain shrugged. "We'll get him sooner or later. If he's on the lam long enough, they'll probably just isolate the planet to keep him from escaping. There's not enough technology here to give him that opportunity yet, so we've got time to track him down."

Joshua was doubtful. "He's clever, and that means he may find his way to other operations and regions. He'll give the primitives technology they aren't ready for and sow chaos everywhere before we do."

Kimdu offered a meaningful dissent. "Well, he's not that clever. He's cruel, and cruelty shows very telltale signs. We will find him by the societies that are created around him. He can't go anywhere now. He's on the run and out of options. He's a prisoner here, and we have nothing but time."

The Captain swatted Joshua's leg and said jovially, "Your buddy's right. He can't go anywhere. And we have all the means to hunt him wherever he is. Don't worry. He's a fugitive, and they will already have let all the other operations know that by now."

Joshua nodded, still uncertain this was completely over. "We'll see." He thought for a moment and then spoke again. "When you fired that bolt down the escape hatch, did it sound strange to you?"

The Captain knelt again and thought for a second. "Yeah, it did. The echo wasn't right. Like it was a dead end."

Joshua nodded in agreement. "And I didn't hear it strike the ground. Only the ricochet off the walls and then silence. Like it got stuck in something."

The Captain let out a sigh. "Yeah, you're right. We should have gone down to see what was there."

Joshua felt a growing disappointment in their decision. Kimdu, on the other hand, looked at both and said, "I'm sure he had some kind of door down there leading to the rest of the tunnels. You won't hear a long echo if there's something like that deadening it, and if there is an escape hatch, there are probably supplies down there too. So who knows, you could have spent all night chasing shadows down there and never got anywhere. He'll pop up, and you can get him then."

The Captain looked at Kimdu gratefully, and Joshua smiled warmly. Kimdu was wise as always, and his positivity was what kept him sane even in the face of such adversity. He was impossible not to like.

The second beacon came in at that moment, and the rest of the operators were ready for extraction. The Captain went to the pilot and made space ready for them.

41

Joshua looked at the Commandant as he finished his postoperative debrief. The mission was a solid success. There were no casualties, and though Shemesh escaped, all the Elohim were evacuated successfully. He was still disappointed in the outcome though. Joshua fumbled with the bauble in his hand, the gold tetrahedron Shemesh carried everywhere. "Sir, I'm not sure we did the right thing in not following the tunnels. Shemesh could have been down there waiting. He would have had to be close by. I should have—"

The Commandant cut him off, waving his hand in the air. "You can't run around in the dark chasing shadows. The mission was those rebels. Shemesh was a bonus, and unfortunately, we didn't get him, but it's no concern. He's here on this planet. There's nowhere to go, and every mission on this world is now getting the brief on him and a direct order not to give him quarter or to give him transport. If we have to quarantine the whole planet just to keep him here, we will."

"Isn't Shemesh his code name? Can't he just change it? It's not like we can put up wanted posters with a bounty. How will anyone know who he is?" Joshua asked somewhat flippantly.

The Commandant smiled a knowing smile and chuckled. "We have ways of finding him, we have ways of tracking him, and we have ways of identifying him. No other operation is going to welcome some random Master wandering in from the desert in foreign clothes with the harried look of the hunted in his eyes. Shemesh will lie low and regroup. He'll pop up somewhere, and we'll be ready. Actually . . ." He reached over to a fresh stack of papers and thumbed through them until he found the one for Joshua. "*You'll* be ready."

He handed the orders to Joshua and leaned back, allowing him time to read. "All ports and cities are aware that he is a fugitive from the law at this point and have been warned not to accept him into their cities for any reason. He is not to leave this planet unless it is in chains." The Commandant jabbed his finger into the desktop as he said this. "All the returning Elohim have corroborated your stories from down there, and he has been deemed an enemy of the operation. We'll find him eventually. He'll go into hiding, and no doubt he will sow more chaos, but we will need to be vigilant."

Joshua perused the first portion, the boilerplate form letter these seemed to come in. Then he read the next section with the actual assignment. "I don't understand. You're sending me back to Bashram?" he asked incredulously.

The Commandant steepled his hands and leaned toward his desk. "You know the city. You know the people. You know the resources. You need to set it up the right way. Right now, they're rudderless. Very soon, once they figure out there's no one there, they will descend into chaos and destroy themselves. The remnants will still be there, and that is your opportunity to fix what Shemesh destroyed. We are working on a story to tell the Umanu there so they know what happened and who is at fault and that the rest of us do not stand by his actions. It's imperative that we make those messages clear so they can comprehend it and the message doesn't get muddled with time."

Joshua furrowed his brow. "How are we going to do that?"

The Commandant seemed pleased by this question. "We create a mythology. We have sculptors even now creating stelae that will be sent to Bashram to tell the story. Basic pictographic stuff, but it'll be easy to interpret for the Umanu there. Did you happen to check the date when those orders are effective?"

Joshua looked at it again and shrugged. "I'll be honest. I don't even know what the date today is."

The Commandant let out a hearty laugh and stood up to walk around the desk. He clapped Joshua on the back and ushered him to the door. "You have one standard year to do some training. You'll be assigned all over the planet here as an observer in the various organizations, and you'll go to Polar Command, where you will have access to the Machine." Joshua had a horrified expression on his face, but the Commandant saw it and reassured him. "We have modules that will show you the basics of strategy, investigative work, management, city planning, and the like. You are going to need it. You're being promoted."

Joshua was suddenly unsure of himself. He was searching for an ulterior motive or some sort of ploy. Years of working with Shemesh had conditioned him this way. He couldn't find a way to blunt his disapproval. "Sir, the Machine was a grueling ordeal. I don't see how I can go through that again, or why. Did I do so poorly here that I need to be lobotomized?"

The Commandant stopped short of the door and reassured him. "You're still clinging to that old notion. The Machine experience you went through is to figure out what your interests are, what your aptitude is, and tell us where you need to grow. It's traumatizing because it's so broadly focused. This training is to give you opportunities to do this job a million times within the span of a single day. Then we'll send you to other operations to see how they are running their show in real time. You'll need to understand the cultures, the religions, the technologies, and the people so that when Shemesh does pop up you'll know him by the change in the culture he contaminates. You did great work out there for being so green. Now it's time to sharpen your skills."

Joshua thought about Marcella. "What about my wife though? She's supposed to be assigned with me, isn't she?"

The Commandant smiled again, warmly this time. "She'll be with you. We don't send anyone into the Machine without someone they trust to keep an eye on them and protect their psyche. It's not just for you though. She has orders too. She'll be touring as well. She'll get training herself very similar to yours. We have a contract with Merchant Astronautica to use her skills to develop these Kaldees everywhere. To set up observatories and plan astrological cults around the world the same way she did in Bashram. She is very impressive, and her efforts got a lot of positive feedback from your peers there."

The Commandant opened the door. "We'll make sure everything is arranged for you both. Have a happy honeymoon."

Joshua stepped through the door and stopped again. "Sir, what about the rebels? What happens if some *did* escape? How can we be certain there weren't more out there?"

The Commandant just shrugged. "At this point it is probably impossible to contain the spread of their ideology. The nomads are still alive, and it has been reported that they are flush with slaves from the bandit camps. I can only imagine that we will be fighting this same nuisance, these *Amalekites*, for the rest of our time on this planet. Rest assured, though, any life that commits to such self-destructive behavior as cannibalism invariably sows the seeds of its own destruction."

Joshua was not as blasé about the possibility as the Commandant was. "Sir, they will only get stronger, particularly with Shemesh out there goading them to that end."

"You will need to make sure they never have the chance then. You will need to hunt them in every crag and gully they hide in. But you will find that wherever their numbers swell, you can be sure that Shemesh is nearby as well. So you'll need to be prepared for the long war."

Joshua nodded. He understood the necessity, and the logic was unassailable. He took a step toward the barracks and stopped again, the Commandant patiently waiting for the question that lingered unanswered the whole conversation. "Sir, what is Shemesh's real name? Why was this allowed to go on this long? Why was he put in charge and allowed to brutalize these people?"

The Commandant stared for a moment and finally relented. "His name is Lucifer. He is a Satan. His role is to corrupt and attract the evil inherent in new civilizations. He creates wealth and power and unaccountable sin to expose all those of poor character and highlight those qualities for others to see and revile. His people become emboldened by their power and then are destroyed by their own people. This is his purpose—quality assurance, testing the product to failure so it can be built better. The people are our product—we create

Umanu. He was doing what he was expected to do. But Elohim should never take pleasure in that work nor should their hand *ever* be the one that bears the knife. And certainly should never conspire to assassinate their fellow Elohim." He pointed to Joshua. "He went too far."

Joshua thought of all the horrors Shemesh—*no, Lucifer*—had committed. He was disappointed by this revelation. But at the same time, he understood. There was a necessity to it. He saw it.

As the emotions played out on Joshua's face, the Commandant added a personal revelation. "You will be working for me out there. You can call on me for any support you need. And"—he took a step back and grabbed the door to shut it—"you can call me Gabriel."

42

Lucifer limped along the beach under the light of the moon and the stars above. The wound was a week old, and though he had cleaned it, it throbbed and was deep enough to need serious medical attention. The bolt from the crossbow had ricocheted off the walls and stuck in his leg. It was a lucky shot, and though it missed the arteries, it was still excruciating. There was no escape from that hole. The tunnel had not been completed to connect to the main sewer, and he was trapped in that hole and barely had time to get in there before the assault on the temple.

He murmured to himself as he walked, the waves crashing on the beach with the incoming tide. "That insolent whelp. Gabriel too. This was all planned, and now they are certain to have the planet locked down. No matter. I'll need to start another city and insulate myself. I'll build tunnels and an army that will raze their cities to the ground. I've been at this for a long time, and I know as well as any of them how to build civilizations and how to break them." He felt the sharp ridge of an exposed shell jab into the side of his foot, and the anger and the pain cemented his hatred for those who had put him in this position.

He headed west. He had to travel only at night to avoid being seen and to cover as much distance as possible. He knew there was an operation along the sea where a great river flowed from the south to the north, but he had no way of knowing how far it was or how long it would take him to get there. He wouldn't be able to leave from there anyway. They didn't have a port, and the operations would be on high alert for him.

"I'll need to set up a base of operations somewhere in the middle. I'll need to control the nexus of the two continents, and from there I can get the people I need." One labored step after another, as he plotted his next moves.

"I can give them technology freely now at least. No more restraint. I'll need it to make my escape anyway. But whether these apes can comprehend it and use it effectively is the real question. How can I have come to this? I was the great Apophis! I was Shemesh!" he roared into the wind blowing from the ocean that muffled his voice and gave him cover as he walked. The water crashed and then glided across the sand to wet his sandaled feet, erasing his footprints as he walked on.

"If it takes me five hundred years to escape, I will do it. I'll break their sacred codes and give them technology, and these *vermin* will make me a ship to get me off this rock. They can't keep me here forever."

He saw a flicker of light on the horizon. A flame was burning in the distance. A camp.

As he drew nearer, he saw the telltale signs of a rebel band: makeshift tents, mixed equipment of city guards and peasants, and bound slaves waiting to be traded to some nomadic tribe or another.

He kept his knife sheathed as he got closer. There were no sentries at the perimeter. The camp were all sitting around the fire roasting some beast they had killed. The scent was foul, as the animal was not cleaned nor gutted, but he knew he couldn't slip past without alerting them. "No trouble though," he said out loud. "This may be my best opportunity anyway."

The camp was startled to see him appear from the darkness. They all scrambled to pick up their armaments and form a rough defensive line.

Lucifer looked at each of them and counted them and then their placements for the meal. All were accounted for.

He took a cautious step closer to the fire as the primitives began to yell at him, commanding him to stop.

They were yelling in their common tongue. "Don't come any closer. We'll kill you!"

Lucifer spoke calmly even as the rebels began to fan out to encircle him. "You have done well for yourselves here. I believe you *are* strong enough to kill the likes of me. But perhaps you would listen to reason. Perhaps you would like to kill *all* the Masters."

A few had violence in their eyes and continued to move to flank him. A few paused to think.

There you are—there's the hook. He continued to speak in the common tongue. "Perhaps you would like to rule rather than rebel. Perhaps you would prefer to be the Masters yourselves."

The rebels were not speaking, not responding with words, but some were listening, and some were thinking. About half continued to encircle and seek an advantage, and though he was ready to react, he made no aggressive moves to give them justification yet. He continued calmly. "Perhaps you enjoy living off the scraps of a decayed society. Perhaps you enjoy fighting for every meal and eating your dead. Perhaps you are comfortable with this way of life while your peers in the city lavish in luxury."

A few now had fully stopped their advance and simply listened. The others continued to creep in, hefting their weapons, planning their first strike, and looking for their opportunity. Lucifer continued in a steady tone. "Perhaps you enjoy being on the run and hunted. Perhaps you see no benefit to the technology and wisdom of the Masters."

More and more began to look around and stall their advance and start to listen. Five of them were behind him. He could hear the creak and twist of their armor and their feet digging softly into the sand even over the din of the waves behind him. He continued casually. "Perhaps you wonder about the wisdom the Masters have acquired and where we came from. Perhaps you wonder how we control nature while you continue to live subject to it."

He continued to listen and count the aggressive rebels. Two more had stalled. "Perhaps you would like to have all that for yourselves. Perhaps you would like to know the answers to the questions you have asked yourselves and would like to be certain of the outcome of the destruction of my kind."

One more stalled. Each word and phrase revealed the motives of those who began to listen. He took another cautious step toward the fire to reveal his towering form and to put distance between the remaining two aggressors. The light flickered and reflected off his gray skin in a red hue that unnerved the rebels. "Perhaps you are shortsighted in thinking that killing just one of us will unburden your planet of these gods from the sky. Perhaps you believe that more will not come to find you just as I have found you."

Another stalled and listened. *One left.*

"Perhaps you will believe the tragedy that has befallen you will be rectified by killing just one of the gods. That your hardship will be redeemed by it. But remember where you came from. Before the gods came, you were nomads and slaves. It was the gods who brought the food and the tools that allowed you to grow powerful."

The last aggressor stopped and listened. "Perhaps the vengeance you seek is toward your own kind. Perhaps it was their corruption that led to your fate. The gods brought gifts, and your own people abused them. Used them to dominate and oppress their own people." He mustered all the pity he could project to commiserate with them.

"Perhaps it's not the gods you are angry at. Is it not those select few of that corrupt religion that wielded all the wealth and power and enslaved and used your brethren for their ends? Perhaps it is they whom you seek to destroy. Perhaps it is those who bear the marks of the beastly cult that are to blame. Perhaps you have mistaken your hatred for your own kind for your wrath against the gods. My kind did not create the corruption of your people. That was inherent to you. We brought gifts of civilization, and it was your kind who betrayed the benevolence and turned it toward violence and destruction."

They began to crouch again, and one even laid down her sword as she listened.

Good, he thought. *This is the beginning.*

One called from the shadows boldly, "What do you come here for?"

Lucifer smiled broadly as he answered, "I'm here to offer you the power of the gods."

Again the voice called from the shadows. "But what do *you* come here for? What do you ask for in exchange for this gift?"

He thought for a moment. "Small sacrifices, ones you will not notice nor care about."

Another spoke up nearer, one of the more aggressive ones. "What do we call you then?"

Lucifer thought for a moment before answering. "You may call me Moloch."

.

Order Information

To order additional copies of this book,
please visit www.redemption-press.com.
Also available at Christian bookstores
and BarnesandNoble.com
or by calling toll-free 1-844-2REDEEM.

Ingram Content Group UK Ltd.
Milton Keynes UK
UKHW010728070623
423023UK00004B/408